Ribbon In The Sky

G·K
Hall
&Co.

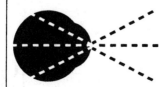 This Large Print Book carries the
Seal of Approval of N.A.V.H.

Ribbon In The Sky

Dorothy Garlock

G.K. Hall & Co.
Thorndike, Maine

Published in Large Print by arrangement with Warner Books.

G.K. Hall Large Print Book Series.

Printed on acid free paper in the United States of America.

Set in 16 pt. Plantin.

Library of Congress Cataloging-in-Publication Data

Garlock, Dorothy.
    Ribbon in the sky / Dorothy Garlock.
      p. cm. — (G.K. Hall large print book series)
    ISBN 0-8161-5468-6 (alk. paper)
    ISBN 0-8161-5469-4 (pbk.)
    1. Large type books. I. Title.
  [PS3557.A71645R5 1993]
  813'.54—dc20   92-32528

This novel is dedicated
with love to
my daughter,
LINDY,
For her unswerving faith,
and because . . .
and because . . .
and because . . .

CHAPTER
———1———

It was almost time.

The boy's eyes, wild and dark, glanced at the sun dying in the west, then anxiously scanned the dirt road that curved around the schoolhouse. The south wind blew softly, stirring the willows where he waited beside the stream. When a limb brushed the black curls that tumbled on his forehead, the hand he lifted to hold it away from his face held a scrap of blue ribbon that fluttered in the breeze.

This morning the ribbon had been tied to the lilac bush.

Mike's eighteen-year-old heart pounded with dread at the thought of the risk his sweetheart was taking. Her father would beat her—in the name of God, of course—for meeting any boy. Mike hated to think of what he would do to her if he found out she was secretly meeting one of those *wicked, idol-worshipping Catholics.* Reverend Pringle considered Catholics to be heathens. He was as sure that they were bound for hell as he was that darkness would come at the end of the day.

Mike's thoughts reached back seven years to the day Reverend Pringle and his family had come to town. Mr. Colson at the dairy had told him to take a complimentary pail of fresh milk to the new preacher. Mike was excited. It was his first day on the job. He ran up the walk to the house and, like a puppy who was all paws, stubbed his toe on the top step and sprawled on the porch at the man's feet. As the pail flew out of his hand, milk splashed on the Reverend Pringle's trousers and shiny black shoes. Mike remembered lying there for only a second or two before jumping to his feet. He forgot about his badly bitten tongue and the blood filling his mouth when he looked at the preacher's stormy countenance. More than anything he wanted to run, but it was impossible because the heavy hand that fell on his shoulder held him in a firm grip.

"What's your name, boy?" The voice rolled like thunder.

"Mike . . . Dolan, sir. I'm sorry—"

"Who sent you?"

"Mr. Colson . . . at the dairy. He said to welcome you and—"

"Is your pa a member of my church?"

"No, sir. We're Catholic."

"One of *those!* I should have known!" The preacher pushed him so hard he staggered back against the porch rail. "Ah . . . yes. I heard about the wild Dolans as soon as I hit town. Wild and sinful! Drinking, playing cards, and dancing their way to hell." He gave the milk bucket a kick and it rolled down the steps. "Brother Colson will hear of this. Now get off my porch and stay off."

"He didn't mean to spill the milk, Papa."

For the first time Mike noticed the small girl sitting in the porch swing. She was dressed in white from head to toe. The skirt of her dress was spread out and as she spoke she absently ran her hands along it, smoothing out nonexistent wrinkles. Her white-clad legs were crossed at the ankles, and white-buttoned shoes dangled above the porch. Fat curls the color of his brother's sorrel horse bounced around her shoulders. A large, flat bow lay across the top of her head and freckles spread a path over her nose. What Mike noticed the most were her eyes: round with fear, looking at her father as if she expected a slap for what she had said.

"Get in the house. I'll deal with you later."

The curt words sent the child scurrying off the swing. She slipped around the corner of the wraparound porch. But before she disappeared she paused and looked at Mike.

"I know you didn't mean to," she said with tears in her voice and in her eyes.

Mike was unaware of it at the time, but years later when he thought of how much courage it took for Letty to speak up for him, he was certain it was at that moment he had lost his heart to her.

The screen door was flung open wide. An older, taller girl came out onto the porch to stand beside the preacher. She was also dressed in white. The curls that framed her small pinched face hung to her waist, but they were skinny and mousy brown. Mike glanced at her before he bolted down the steps. She stuck out a pointed tongue and wiggled it. That nastiness could not go unanswered! Mike stopped short at the bottom of the steps, spread his mouth with his thumbs, poked out his tongue, and crossed his eyes.

"Did ya see that. Papa?" the girl screeched and pointed a finger. "He made a face at me!"

Mike picked up the bucket and ran, sure that he would be fired and never earn enough money to buy his own horse; but Mr. Colson didn't fire him and since that time he'd worked after school and during the summer at the dairy. When he finished school last spring, Mike was given a full-time job, but it didn't pay enough for him to support a wife. Good-paying jobs were scarce in central Nebraska. Two of his brothers had gone west to find work in the logging camps and had urged him to go with them, but the thought of being away from the girl who meant the world to him was too painful for him to even consider it.

With a little groan of anguish, he wished that he could marry Letty and take her away from that crazy old Holy-Roller preacher and her equally fanatic sister. Cora was three years older than Letty and claimed that she had been "called" to preach the Gospel to sinners and save their souls from hell. She and Letty had been trained from childhood to sing duets to inspire the worshipers. When the crowd was sufficiently worked up, Brother Pringle would preach a hellfire and brimstone sermon, haranguing his flock for their sins, moving a chorus of voices to shout, "Amen! Glory hallelujah!" Since Mike had been raised as a Catholic and was used to quiet chants and tinkling bells, this frenzied religious display seemed bizarre to him.

Now, as he sat resting his back against a tree, he mulled over the problems the style of worship had made in his life. Suddenly he saw a flutter of something white. *She was coming.* His sweetheart was graceful and slender, gentle and soft. His heart leaped at the sight of her. He watched her come along the path as if she were on the way to the privy behind the empty schoolhouse. The hem of her skirt swished about the tops of her high-laced shoes. She had told him that her father thought the newer skirt length of three inches above the ankle to be *worldly* and immoral. He had even made such immodesty the topic for one of his Wednesday-night sermons and urged his flock to be aware of the sins of the *flesh.*

Rich auburn hair tied at the nape of Letty's neck framed a face that was not exceedingly beautiful, but Mike adored every feature and every freckle that dotted her nose. She was his love, his life, and he loved her with every beat of his young heart.

Letty stepped behind the screen of hollyhocks that grew beside the privy. Out of sight of the road she began to run toward him, her feet making no sound on the path.

"Mike! Mike!" She jumped lightly over a fallen log that lay between them and threw herself into his arms. Mike lifted her off her feet, swinging her around.

"Ah . . . sweetheart! I love it when you run to me!" His voice was husky and tender, his lips nuzzled her ear.

The feel of her soft body against his and the sweet-soap scent of her filled his head. It was both wonderful and painful to be in love. Letty filled every corner of his heart.

"Fifteen, almost sixteen and never been kissed by anyone but me," he teased and kissed her long and hard.

"I'm scared, Mike!" she said when she could get her breath.

"Scared?" He held her away from him and looked down into her worried face. "What is it, honey? What's scaring you?"

"Papa's talking about pulling up and going out on a soul-saving revival crusade. He says we'll be in the war soon. He says President Wilson will drag us into it, and he needs to save as many souls as he can before the troops are sent to fight the Kaiser."

"Why doesn't he ask God to keep us out of the war? He claims to be able to talk directly to him."

Mike's angry dark eyes met her brown ones without flinching. She knew his opinion of her father. Mike usually managed to keep it to himself but sometimes he just exploded when she talked about her fathers beliefs and his domination of her.

"Your pa says it'll be his plea to God that'll get prohibition voted in to make it against the law to buy and sell whiskey in Nebraska." Mikes voice was husky with sarcasm.

"Are your folks for prohibition?" she asked after a pause.

"No. My pa and brothers don't like it at all."

"And you? Will you be a slave to demon rum like your pa and brother?"

"They take a drink now and then, but they're not slaves to it." He said crossly. Then to take the bite out of his words, he shook her gently then hugged her to him. "Demon rum! That sounds like something your pa would say."

"I know. I'm sorry." Her lips moved against his neck when she spoke. "The Bible says to honor thy father and thy mother. It's wicked of me to go against them and sneak out to meet you. But, oh, I love you so!"

"And I love you, darlin' girl." He kissed her mouth softly, lovingly, again and again. "I was outside the church last night and heard you and Cora sing."

"I wish I'd known you were there."

"And I wish I could take you away from here and take care of you." He held her tightly, his hands stroking her back with long, slow caresses until she was molded so closely against him that she could scarcely catch her breath for the excitement that beat through her.

"Cora is urging Papa to go on the crusade."

"I'm not surprised. What does your mother want to do?"

"Oh, Mama will do whatever Papa wants. I think she likes the revival meetings under a brush arbor, sleeping in strangers' houses, and having

7

them wait on her almost as much as she likes listening to everyone praise Papa."

"When is he planning to go?" Mike asked, dreading her answer.

"He's looking for a preacher to take his church. If he can't find one in the next couple of weeks, he'll wait and go early in the spring. Oh, Mike, I don't want to leave you."

Mike pulled her down on the soft grass beneath the willow.

"I don't want you to go. We'll think of something. Right now I just want to be with you and hold you."

"I could hardly wait for the day to go by. You're my sweetheart, but you're also . . . my dearest friend."

"How were you able to get away this time of day?"

"Papa went out to the Hendersons. I think old Grandpa Henderson is dying. Mama and Cora went to read scriptures to Granny Wilder. She can't see to read anymore."

"Granny Wilder's kids are pretty upset about her plans to leave her house to the preacher. Is that why Cora is being nice to her?" Mike instantly regretted his cynical remark when he saw the flicker of a frown cross Letty's face.

"I told Mama I was sick so I wouldn't have to go. I had to stick my finger down my throat and throw up to prove it."

"It's been a week since I held you, kissed you." Mike's words came out in a sort of trembling sigh.

Letty unbuttoned his shirt and slid her hand inside along muscles that quivered at her touch, "I know. I know."

"Sweetheart, I love you and . . . want you!" Muttered words tumbled from his lips as he pressed fevered kisses along the soft skin of her throat and the beginning swell of her breast.

She heard his harsh breathing and the hoarsely whispered words. Not daring to open her eyes, she unbuttoned the bodice of her dress. She wanted to lie under his searching lips and forget everything but him. It was wicked how much she loved him. At times she thought she loved him more than God. More than Jesus. He was the only person she had ever been close to, close enough to share her thoughts, her dreams. His lips moved slowly along the side of her neck, then she felt his mouth on her breast, warm and wet, tongue caressing, sucking at her nipple. He groaned a muted, strangled, incoherent sound and began to tremble.

"Tell me to stop!"

Letty's eyes were soft with love. "I don't want you to stop. I want to give back to you as much as you've given to me."

"Oh, sweet girl! I don't want you to *give* to me. I want you to want me as much as I want you."

"I do! Oh, I do!"

"But . . . what if you get . . . caught?"

"I didn't the last time."

Her arms held him closer, her body strained against his. He covered her face with kisses, releasing his pent-up desire with each touch of his lips. His hand moved under her skirt and between her thighs, stroking the soft inner skin, then moved upward. She gave a muffled, instinctive cry as his fingers found the slit in her drawers and probed gently.

Letty knew perfectly well that what she was doing was a sin. But when she was with Mike, the reality of everything seemed to slip away from her, leaving her in a wonderfully happy world. Her mouth answered his hungrily. Feeling the familiar longing in that hidden place between her legs, pressing against him, her breasts tingling as they accepted his caresses. Her excitement mounted. She forgot who she was, where she was, and opened her legs, letting him have his way. Her body writhed and strained upward, aching for what she knew would come with their union.

When Mike entered and filled her, Letty flew off somewhere high and exquisite. She floated along with her feelings, wanting to scream out with the joy of it. How could this be wicked when it felt so good?

"Letty . . ." Her name was a caress on his lips.

She murmured his name as her lips glided over his straight dark brows, short thick eyelashes, cheeks rough with new whiskers, and to his waiting mouth. All of her unspent adoration was lavished upon him now.

When it was over, the tears came because it had been so beautiful.

"My precious girl—" He kissed away the tears,

understanding why she cried. He pulled her skirt down over her thighs and legs and cuddled her to him. "Don't ever forget that I love you," he said in an urgent, husky whisper.

"Thank you for loving me."

"We're going to spend our lives together," he promised.

"What are we going to do?"

He edged up to lean against the trunk of the willow and pulled her onto his lap.

"Sweetheart, maybe I should go up to Montana and work in the logging camp this winter. By spring I'd have enough money to come get you and take you back with me. Somehow, someway or another, we'll make it."

"Oh . . . I don't think I could bear not to see you all winter. What if Papa finds a preacher to take his church and we leave? How will you find me?"

"I won't go until I know there's no chance of that. Honey, I can't marry you and take you to my folks. Your pa would raise such a stink about you marrying a Catholic that my pa wouldn't be able to sell a single load of coal to anyone but Catholics, and there's not very many of them left in town."

"I know."

"Our day is coming, sweetheart. We've got to be patient a little longer."

"I've loved you for such a long time," she said in a soft trembling voice. "Do you remember the first time we saw each other? You spilled the milk you were bringing to Papa."

"How could I forget that? I remember the first time we talked for any length of time. It was the close of the school year. I was fifteen. The upper grades had gone to the river for an all-day picnic. Thank goodness Cora was sick and didn't go. You were different out from under her watchful eyes. I bribed Roy Carroll to exchange places with me so I could sit by you in the wagon. I remember that we played volleyball." He laughed and raked his knuckles down the side of her face. "When we played blindman's bluff, I cheated so I could catch you. I thought you were the prettiest, sweetest girl I'd ever seen." He kissed the end of her nose and whispered, "I still do."

"There's plenty of pretty girls in town you could meet without having to sneak around about it. They could go to dances and ballgames with you. I don't know why you bother with me." She snuggled her nose into his cheek and kissed the line of his jaw.

" 'Cause I love you, that's why. Someday we'll go to dances and ballgames, and you'll see they're not as wicked as your pa says they are. When can you meet me again?"

She slid off his lap. "I don't know."

"It would be pure hell to be away from you all winter, sweetheart." They were standing close, dreading to part. His dark eyes devoured her face. She brushed the black curls from his forehead with trembling fingertips.

"It would be awful," she whispered. "I wish you didn't have to go."

12

"Working in a logging camp may be the answer, sweetheart. I don't make enough money at the dairy to support us. Besides, when we marry, we'll have to leave here. Your pa would make life miserable for us and for my folks if we stayed."

"You're right. Kiss me again before I go."

Tenderly, he threaded his fingers in the hair on each side of her face. He bent his head and reverently kissed her forehead, then her lips. He was filled with indescribable love for her.

"Turn around. I want to be sure there are no leaves or grass on your dress or in your hair. Here's the ribbon." He pressed the scrap into her hand. "Tie it on the bush if you can meet me."

"I love you." Her back was to him. "Don't . . . forget me . . . ever!"

"How can you think *that?*" he whispered in her hair. "Every thought I have is of you. Every plan I make, every dream. I love you."

Feeling bereft as he always did when she left him, Mike watched her until she was out of sight. Far off down the creek bed a crow sounded its lonely, mocking call as if laughing at human problems. A wagon bumped along the road in front of the schoolhouse. A skinny, forlorn-looking old dog trailed behind it with his head hanging low, his tail between his legs. Mike had seen that dog a hundred times, but today he looked older, more friendless, as if he had been cast out to fend for himself.

An emotion as strong as fear gripped Mike as

13

he watched the dog. It was as though he had a sudden glimpse of a long, solitary future.

Much to Cora's disappointment, Reverend Pringle put off his soul-saving crusade until spring rather than leave his flock without a "shepherd."

The last week in September Mike left for the logging camps in Montana to look for work. Letty's world fell apart. She went into such a deep depression that her father was sure the devil was trying to possess her soul. Her mother passed her lack of energy off as "fall complaint" and made her take a double dose of Black Draught and drink sassafras tea until she was running to the outhouse every half-hour or so.

Time passed with terrible slowness. At the end of the second month Letty's greatest fear was realized. The day beneath the willow she had "caught." *Mike's baby was growing in her body.* Sick with worry and weak because she was plagued with constant nausea, she lost weight and was almost continually in tears. Her mind was in a constant turmoil. She had no one to confide in. Days and nights of worry had frayed her nerves until she thought she couldn't bear it. She lived in dread of what her father would do when he found out. As far as her parents were concerned, she had committed the ultimate sin.

Guilt played no part in her anxiety. What she had shared with Mike had seemed so right. She prayed constantly that she would hear from him even though she knew he wouldn't write to her for fear that her father would intercept the letter.

One day she met Mike's little sister at the store and casually asked if they had heard from Mike.

"No, but Mama got a letter from Duncan. He said Mike didn't get no job in Montana. Mama thinks maybe Mike went on to Id-d-ho or some-place like that. Ya know what? My goat ate Mrs. McGregor's hat." The little girl put her hand over her mouth and giggled. Her dark eyes, shining with mischief, looked so much like Mike's that Letty quickly turned away before she disgraced herself with tears.

On Sunday morning, while listening to her father's sermon Letty considered whether she should go to Mike's mother, explain her condi-tion, and ask for help in finding a place to stay until Mike came back. Almost as soon as the idea formed in her mind, she discarded it. If her father found out, he would see to it that not one member of his church bought coal from Mr. Dolan. Mike had said that with five children still left at home they were having a rough time making ends meet. She couldn't add to their burden.

Her father's booming voice brought her back to the present. He was preaching on sin, guilt, and forgiveness.

"Forgiveness is mine, saith the lord! There is no sin too big for God to forgive, my friends."

A heavy frown settled on Letty's face. God would forgive her, but her father wouldn't. He was the most unforgiving person she had ever known. He still hadn't forgiven Grandpa Fletcher for not wanting him to marry his only daughter. Grandpa had said the only reason Albert Pringle wanted Mable was because she didn't have the sense of a nanny goat and she could play the piano. Her mother had told her daughters the story. She had met Albert Pringle when he came to hold a brush-arbor revival meeting in Piedmont, a small town in northwest Nebraska. The Lord had told her to go help the preacher spread the message. She had gone despite her father's objection. At the time she had been only a year older than Letty and twenty years younger than the man she married. Mable Pringle was very satisfied being the wife of the preacher. She loved being looked up to and envied by the women of the congregation.

"Come home, O sinner, come home!" Reverend Pringle's voice was rich and full and sweetly pleading. "I say to you, brethren, the last days are come upon us. The Lord cometh, and no man knoweth the hour. Repent and be saved!"

Song books and Bibles were laid aside and the people around Letty began to stir.

"It is written that the wages of sin are death."

Two women went forward to drop on their kneel at the long bench in front of the platform. One cried, one buried her face in her hands.

"Come all ye who are weary and heavy laden and *He* will give you rest. Jesus died on the cross for your sins. *He* will pardon and cleanse."

16

A man from the back of the church went down the middle aisle to the altar. A chorus of voices followed him.

"Amen! Hallelujah!"

Reverend Pringle never ceased his entreating pleas. Tears streamed from his eyes. His lips quivered.

"Have Thine own way, lord. Thou art the potter; I am the clay." In an angelic pose, with his profile to the congregation, he lifted his face to the ribbon of sunlight that came from the upper window.

Letty twisted her handkerchief and wondered why she was embarrassed by her father's tearful display. She had seen and heard the act many, many times. Today, however, it seemed almost obscene.

"Ye who have lived in darkness in this weary world of sin, come home. Come home. Come home. You are doomed, my friends, unless you seek the light. Turn your feet from the paths of sin and set them on the path of righteousness. Ye are but poor pilgrims wandering in a sinful world of woe. Take their hands, dear Lord, and lead them home."

A shrill scream pierced the air.

"Hallelujah!" the preacher shouted. "Praise the Lord! Sister Bonander has got the old-time religion in her heart!" He raised his arms above his head. "A soul has been saved. Thank you, Jesus."

Cora nudged Letty and motioned toward the piano where their mother was playing "Softly and Tenderly Jesus is Calling." It was time for them to sing. Letty turned stiffly to look at her sister. She had the same pious look on her face their father had. The realization came to Letty that it was their *church* face. She had a strange desire to giggle. Slowly she shook her head.

Cora seemed to be pleased to have the stage to herself. Her mouth tilted in a half-smile. She gave her sister an "I know something you don't know look" before she stood and moved to the piano, her hands clasped to her breast, her head bowed.

Feeling as if she were somewhere on high looking down, Letty waited until her father was bending over one of the *sinners* at the altar, then rose and walked quickly out of the church.

"Explain yourself, sister," Reverend Pringle roared as soon as he entered the house.

Letty came from the kitchen, her legs trembly, her stomach fluttering like a flag in the wind. She had changed into an everyday dress and had tied an apron about her waist.

"I came home to get dinner on the table, Papa."

"You left your sister to carry on alone."

"Cora sang exceptionally well this morning." Mable removed the hatpin that anchored her hat to her high-piled hair.

"At least I have one daughter that I can depend upon. I want an explanation, missy." The Reverend's unblinking eyes fastened on Letty's pale face.

"Ah . . . my throat is sore."

"Liar," Cora said under her breath as she passed Letty to go upstairs.

"You walk out of church again before the service is over, young lady, and you'll not be sitting down for a week. You're not too big for, the strop. Do you hear?"

"Yes, Papa."

"Did you gargle with hot salt water?" Mable asked.

"Not yet."

"Well, do it. I swan to goodness. I don't know what's got into you lately."

Letty followed her mother to the kitchen. Silently, she began to dish up the food. She tipped up the iron skillet to pour gravy into a bowl and some of it slopped down the side, making a puddle on the stove.

"For crying out loud!" Mable exclaimed.

"It's heavy, Mama."

"It's no wonder you're weak. You haven't eaten enough lately to keep a bird alive."

"Maybe she's having trouble keeping anything on her stomach." Cora had come into the kitchen. She snickered softly and picked up the meat platter to take to the dining table.

Letty kept her head turned so that Cora didn't see the panic that seized her. She honestly believed that her sister hated her. Cora had always been sly about tormenting her. When they were small, she would pinch Letty and yank her hair to make her cry during prayer meetings, then

19

stand back and watch as she was scolded or spanked. Letty and Mike had talked about her sister. Mike said it boiled down to the fact that Cora was jealous because Letty was the prettier of the two. He also said that Cora wanted all of their father's attention.

Glory! If Cora only knew! She was welcome to all of it . . . forever.

"Come girls, The Reverend is waiting."

CHAPTER
2

Letty followed her mother to the dining room, wondering why she never called her husband by his given name, Albert. She always referred to him as The Reverend in the same hushed tones she used when she spoke of God. Her mother, Letty thought, was exactly the kind of wife her father wanted. She was totally subservient to his wishes.

After a prayer which was both lengthy and loud. the meat platter was passed to the head of the table. Reverend Pringle took a generous helping and passed the platter on. Letty helped herself to a small serving from each dish passed to her. Although each bite faced a battle in descending her tight throat, she persisted in nibbling at the food. Her stomach felt as if it would jump out of control at any moment.

"We got a good collection plate today." Reverend Pringle tucked the corner of his napkin into his shirt collar. "Almost eight dollars."

"That's a dollar more than last Sunday," Mable said happily. "Sister Treloar told me this morning that they'll butcher a hog for us as soon as the weather turns cold." She looked at her husband as if she expected praise for imparting such good news. He only nodded and forked another potato onto his plate. "The Cashes will give us honey as part of their tithe. We'll get potatoes and turnips from the Hendricks."

"Turnips? Ugh!" The corners of Cora's mouth sagged. "James Hendricks can afford to give us chickens, Papa. They've got the largest flock of white leghorns in the county."

The Reverend nodded his head in agreement. "It'd not hurt them to share with us. Mable, the next time you're with Sister Hendricks, you might mention how fond I am of chicken."

"The Bible says it's more blessed to give than to receive," Cora said, smiling sweetly at her father.

"Yes, sister, it says that." Reverend Pringle smiled fondly back at his eldest daughter, then frowned at the younger one. "Eat your dinner, Letty. Many a poor orphan would be glad to have what you're pushing around on your plate."

"I'm not very hungry."

"Are you sick?" Cora asked sweetly.

Letty looked across the table at her sister and saw the high color on her cheeks and the smirk on her face. Cora's eyes met hers and held them.

21

She knows! Oh, dear God!

After a silence broken only by the thump of her heart pounding in her ears, Letty drew in a sharp, hurtful breath and wished that she could just drop dead and escape the scene that was coming.

"Are you bilious again?" A note of impatience tinged her mother's voice.

"Maybe."

"You're not. You know you're not *bilious.*" Cora took a long drink of buttermilk, leaving a white ring on her upper lip. With deliberate slowness she licked it off. The eyes she fastened on her sister's face was as watchful as those of a snake ready to strike.

"Maybe I am."

"You know you're *not!*" Cora set the empty glass down with a thump, and Letty knew her sister was going to drag out her torment as long as possible.

"Bilious or not. Eat your dinner. Waste not, want not, I always say." The Reverend spooned gravy over the potatoes on his plate.

"She's sick all right," Cora exclaimed.

"Hush your prattle. She's not sick."

The rebuke from her beloved father stung Cora, causing her to stop her game of cat-and-mouse with Letty and get right to the point.

"Tell Papa how long it's been since you washed your monthly rags, Letty, dear!"

"Sister!" Reverend Pringle looked up, startled, then pounded the end of his knife handle on the table. "Such talk should be only among women-folk. It's not decent."

22

"This affects all of us, Papa. Letty hasn't had her flow for two months. It's my guess, she's been fornicating and a bastard is growing in her belly."

Reverend Pringle's fork fell to his plate as the import of Cora's words reached into his mind. Silence, broken only by his strangled breathing fell on the room.

"Oh, dear! Oh, my!" Mable looked as if she were about to swoon.

"Bulb . . . bulb . . . ugh . . . er—" The choking sounds came from Reverend Pringle.

"Cora! How can you say such a thing about your sister?"

"Because it's true, Mama! Ask her!"

"Say . . . she's wrong—" Mable gasped. Her face had turned as white as the tablecloth; her double chin trembled.

"Well, *sister,* say I'm wrong." Cora's eyes, bright with excitement, rested on Letty's anguished face.

"Oh, lord! Oh, sweet Jesus! I feel . . . faint—" Mable dipped her napkin in a glass of water and held the wet cloth to her forehead.

The Reverend was still making unrecognizable sounds.

"Was it Hadley Wells?" Cora rested her elbows on the table and leaned forward to ask in a conspiratorial whisper, "Did you catch him between fits? Or was it one of the wild Dolan boys?" The questions hung in the air for a long silent moment. "See there, Papa. She can't deny it."

Letty looked at the three accusing faces. She

23

didn't know them. They were strangers. They wouldn't understand no matter what she told them. Refusing to answer Cora's accusations, she jumped up from the table and ran up the stairs.

"Letty!" her father roared.

"Oh, Lord, help us!" her mother wailed.

"I was right," Cora chortled happily. "One of those horny Catholics got in her drawers!"

Letty reached the top of the stairs, stumbled into the room, and slammed the door.

"Mike! Oh, Mike!"

A long time later, when she had no more tears to cry, Letty lay on the bed with her fist pressed to her mouth. She had expected her father to come to the room with the buggy whip. The family had been shocked beyond measure. Letty, meek and obedient, had disgraced them. The house was quiet. No doubt the three of them were discussing a face-saving plan.

Oh, Mike, what will become of me without you? The words battered against Letty's brain. Let Mike know, God, she prayed. Let him know and he'll come back. Letty knew that divine intervention wouldn't come soon enough to save her from her father's wrath. It had been wrong to lie with Mike when they had not stood before the preacher and said their vows. They had said them to each other as they lay pressed tightly together beneath the willow. She thought of him as her husband. They had shared their innermost thoughts and dreams. Their bodies had come together so naturally, so sweetly. And, oh, she loved him so much.

Suddenly, without warning, the door of her room was flung open. From between the spread fingers covering her face, Letty saw her father standing in the doorway. His tie was askew, his usually well-combed hair looked as if he had been in a violent windstorm. His face was beet-red except for the white around his mouth. The hatred that blazed in his eyes struck her like a lash.

"Bitch! Slut! Whore!" he spat. His head jutted forward and the cords on his neck stood out. "You'll not make me the laughingstock of this town with your bastard! You'll not ruin me!"

"Papa . . . don't—"

"Hush up!" He bellowed. "Hush your lying mouth or I'll put my fist in it. You're a bitch in heat is what you are!" His voice rose until it was a strangled screech.

"Where's . . . Mama?" Leny shrank back across the bed until she was huddled against the wall.

"Go from this house. You'll never set eyes on her or your sister again! Hear me." He kicked a ladder-backed chair out of his way and swept his arm over the top of the bureau, sending the lace doily and dresser set crashing to the floor. He stopped at the side of the bed, his face frozen in a mask of hate. Spittle ran from the corner of his mouth.

Letty cringed and held up her hand in an attempt to ward off the blow she knew was coming.

Watching his hand come toward her face was the longest second she ever lived. The slap sent her head flying back against the wall.

"Whore! You're ruined all I've worked for. Besmirched my name! Damn you to hell and damn your bastard!" His voice rose to a deafening roar.

"Please, Papa—"

"Don't *papa* me, you bitch! I'm not the papa of a fornicater, a forsaker of God, a harlot, a . . . scarlet woman! From this day on you are *dead* to this family. Do you hear me? Dead!" As he paced the floor in long strides, the words poured from his mouth. "You are no longer a member of my family. You will take your hot little twat and leave my house. But first you'll tell me who it was that crawled between your legs and planted a bastard in your belly. Who is it that's laughing at me? Was it one of those damn Catholics who's been trying to drag me down?" He stormed across the room, pounded the opposite wall with a balled fist, turned, and came back to tower over her. "Well, was it?"

Letty was so frightened she feared she would throw up. Her father looked so frenzied, so ugly and maddened. She was paralyzed with shock and fear. He grabbed her shoulder with one hand and slapped her with the other. Somehow it calmed her, released her from shock. At that moment she made up her mind she would not tell him if he killed her. When she didn't answer, he struck her again with such force her ears rang.

"Tell me, damn you!"

26

"I'll not tell you anything!"

The blows came repeatedly first on one side of her face and then the other. "Whose bastard are you carrying?"

"I'll die before I tell you." she shouted. Her eyes looked so defiantly into his that he released her shoulder and backed away from the bed. "And my baby is not a bastard in the eyes of God. He was conceived with love, something *you* know nothing about."

"You're possessed of the devil!" he gasped. "I can't bear to . . . look on your face."

"It's the same face I wore when I passed the collection plate this morning." The courage to defy him became stronger.

"Damn you to hell and back. Don't leave this room. Tonight I'll take you to Huxley. You'll take the train and never come back."

"Where will I go? What will I do?"

"It matters not a whit to me where you go, what you do, or whether you live or die."

The coldly spoken words killed something in Letty as surely as if it had been cut out with a knife. She slid off the bed and looked him in the eye. When she spoke. It was as if she had suddenly become another person.

"I'll leave here gladly. I'll not die and neither will my baby. It would give you too much pleasure."

His mouth closed like a trap; his eyes turned glassy. He stood there as if suspended while his face became expressionless and his eyes looked through her.

"Ye who have sinned shall be cast into the fiery furnace."

"This morning you said that there was no *sin* too great for God to forgive."

"God may forgive you. I won't!"

"I don't want *your* forgiveness."

He turned his back on her and walked from the room. Letty sprang to the door and slammed it so hard the house shook. Anger, an emotion she seldom exhibited, bubbled up out of her misery. The anger turned into a red rage. She pounded on the closed door with her fists and kicked it until her toes were sore.

"Hypocrite!" she shouted. "I've sinned, but so have you!

"Double-tongued charlatan!

"Faker!

"I'm ashamed that I'm the daughter of a sanctimonious hypocrite! I'm glad I'll never again have to see you cry your crocodile tears and pry money from poor dirt-farmers. I'm ashamed of you! Ashamed!"

As if her legs were melting, she staggered to the bed, sank down, and rested her forehead against the cool brass bedpost.

Gradually her head cleared. Every word her father had uttered came back into her mind. Tonight after the service he would take her to Huxley to catch the train. Trying to keep at bay the pain in her heart, Letty began to plan. Where could she go? She hadn't the slightest idea how to find Mike in the vast land to the west. Could she stay in Huxley, find a job and wait for him? No. Her father was well-known there and would be sure to find out.

Letty searched her memory for a relative or a friend who might take her in. The only relatives were Grandma and Grandpa Fletcher who lived on the farm northwest of Boley. Papa didn't like Grandpa Fletcher and refused to go there.

Mama seldom mentioned them, although she got a letter from them about once a year. One time the family had stopped there on their way to a new church. Letty had sat on Grandma's lap and watched her make lace. Grandpa, she remembered, had a white beard. He argued a lot with her father, smoked his pipe, and drank corn liquor from a jug. If she went there, would they be as outraged about her condition as her parents had been? Perhaps she could tell them she was married and her husband was away working. What would she do if they refused to take her in? She pushed it from her mind. She would have plenty of time to think of that later.

The next few hours were spent in selecting what she would take with her. First, she dressed in a striped cotton shirtwaist and a serviceable brown gabardine skirt. She laid out the jacket and brown hat that went with the suit. Then she made new piles of dresses, nightgowns, underwear, and stockings on the bed. To these she added her heavy coat, a scarf, and mittens. She took from a bottom drawer soft cotton material that she had planned to use to make underskirts and teddies.

Someday she would make a dress for the baby—her precious baby and Mike's. She wondered what Mike would think when she told him. Oh, he would be so proud!

As for keepsakes, she had only two. From beneath the paper lining in one of the bureau drawers, she took a valentine Mike had given to her. Inside the heart-shaped card was a picture of a couple sitting on a park bench. The man was whispering in the woman's ear. Above them was written, "Heart of my heart, will you be mine?" Letty blinked away tears, pressed the card to her lips, then tucked it into the pocket of one of the dresses on the bed. From between the pages of the Bible on the bedside table she took a sprig of dried violets. She and Mike had picked them the first time they had met secretly over a year ago. Placing them carefully between the sheets of a pad of paper, she added it to the pile on the bed.

Letty heard the clock strike seven. Soon her father would be leaving for the evening service. She stood beside the window and waited for a glimpse of him going down the walk. She was leaving this house, her parents, and Cora forever, and she was glad. Each side of her face was bruised from her father's blows; her heart was sore from her mother's betrayal. Letty couldn't remember ever feeling affection for her sister. Cora had always treated her as the *enemy* and had pecked away at her self-esteem for years. That was over now. Whatever the future held for her, it couldn't be worse than living here.

When Letty was younger, she had accepted her father's duplicity. She had become used to the fact that the conduct he exhibited at church was different from his conduct at home. She was aware that he uttered contrary sentiments at different times in relation to the same subject. Lately, she could no longer justify his actions. It was clear to her now. Her father was just what she had said he was—a hypocrite.

Dry-eyed now, Letty could even think of her mother without the terrible pain knifing her heart. Her mother had not shown her one ounce of compassion. But then, she told herself, she should not have expected any. Her mother was merely an extension of her father and rarely expressed an independent thought. There was no room in her life for anyone but him. Cora had made her own place in their lives by becoming as much like him as possible. Letty realized now that she had always been the outsider.

The front door closed. The sound resounded throughout the quiet house. Letty saw her father's erect figure—his black hat set straight on his head, his Bible under his arm—going down the walk.

"Goodbye, Papa. I'm not one bit sorry that I'm seeing you for the last time. You never loved me. You never loved anyone . . . but yourself."

Letty turned from the window and hurried to the attic to get a suitcase. After it was packed, she carried it downstairs and set it beside the back door. Without the slightest hesitation, she went to her parent's room and from the bottom drawer of the bureau, lifted the small cedar chest where her father kept the cash collections. The key was under the dresser scarf. She found it and opened the chest. It contained more than two hundred dollars in bills. Letty counted out half of it and put it in the purse that hung on her arm.

"Papa will call it stealing," she murmured to herself. "Let him call it what he wants. It isn't stealing. You said I was dead, Papa, no longer a member of this family. You are dead to me, too. All of you. I'm taking my inheritance."

She wanted to leave as quickly as possible. While she waited for darkness to come so that she could go to the carriage house and hitch Isaac to the buggy, she ate a plate of food from the leftover noon meal and drank two glasses of milk. Her jaws were sore and it hurt to chew, but common sense demanded that she eat. After she finished, she made up a packet of food to take with her. Had she had time to think about it, she would have been surprised to realize how calm she was and that she no longer had the nervous nausea in her stomach.

She wrote a letter to Mike telling him where she was going. The Dolans lived on a small piece of land outside of town. On her way to Huxley she would stop and ask Mike's mother to forward her letter. She had never met Mrs. Dolan, but because Mike thought the world of her, she had to be nice.

When darkness finally came, Letty carried her suitcase to the carriage house, put it in the buggy, and called to Isaac. The horse trotted to her when she held out an ear of corn. Fifteen minutes later she was on her way.

Dreading to pass the church, but knowing she must, Letty felt her heart beat harder and faster, Her thoughts raced. Would latecomers recognize the preacher's horse, and buggy? Would they think she was a thief and try to stop her? Letty slowed the horse when she saw a man and woman walking toward the door. The church would be full judging by the number of wagons and buggies parked at the side and along the road.

The building was well-lighted and music floated out into, the night. Her mother was playing the piano with extra zeal, adding in the extra flourishes that made her style of playing distinctive. As Letty passed the church, the congregation stood and began to sing:

"I am bound for the promised land,
I am bound for the promised land.
O who will come and go with me?
I am bound for the promised land."

"So am I," Letty said aloud. "So am I." She slapped the reins against Isaac's back and fixed her eyes on the road ahead.

A mile out of town she turned up the long lane that led to the Dolan house. It was not yet pitch-dark. She could see the outline of the house. No light shone from the windows. She calmed herself by thinking that perhaps the Dolans were sitting on the porch. But, she reasoned, it was a little too cold for that. The gate leading into the yard was closed when she reached it. She wrapped the reins around the brake handle and started to step down. Two huge dogs came from beneath the porch and flung themselves at the sturdy wooden gate. The snarls and barking frightened Isaac. He whinnied nervously, fidgeted, and sidestepped. Letty grabbed the reins to hold him. She glanced toward the porch, waiting for someone to come and call off the dogs. No one did.

Deeply disappointed that no one was at home, Letty turned the horse back down the lane. If her heart had been pounding any harder, she was certain it would burst. She reached the end of the lane and turned toward Huxley. Isaac moved along easily in the darkness. She was grateful that his eyesight was better than hers. Letty had never been afraid of the dark. but she was completely alone, and it was a good ten miles to the next town.

Now that she had time to think, it occurred to her that she wasn't alone and that she never would be alone again. For the first time since she had become aware that she was pregnant, she felt a deep joy. Growing within her was living proof of the love she and Mike shared. The babe was a part of her and a part of him. *She would be a mother and he would be a father.*

"The ties between me and my child will be strong." She whispered the vow aloud, then to the child, "You will have the love of your parents. I swear it."

Lamplight shone from the windows of a farmhouse set back from the road. A horse whinnied a greeting to Isaac and ran alongside the fence until it could follow them no longer. The wind came up, swept dry leaves along the road. Stripped to their bare limbs, the trees looked sullen and unfriendly. Letty's breath curled on the cold air. Winter was on its way. She shivered and wished for the wool shawl she had packed in the suitcase.

Mike was never far from Letty's mind. She thought now of his jet-black curls and laughing dark eyes. He had been shaving for a year and his whiskers were as black as coal. He had been so careful not to leave telltale scratches on her face. It wouldn't matter now. She was free! Free to love him. Free to be with him. As soon as he heard where she was, he would come. She hadn't told him in the letter that she was pregnant. The news was too precious to have eyes other than his read it.

Letty bridled her thoughts and refused to plan any farther ahead than reaching the train station and buying a ticket to Boley. In an hour her father would arrive home. She had no doubt he would be relieved that she was gone. She would leave the rig at the livery if it was open. If not, she would water the horse and leave him tied to the hitching rail.

It wasn't until Letty could see the lights of Huxley ahead that she met anyone on the road. A horseman came toward her out of the darkness.

Her heart leaped with fright as she watched him approach.

"Howdy." The man spoke and lifted his hat when he came even with the buggy.

Letty returned the greeting in a low voice, hoping it was too dark for him to see that she was a woman alone. After he passed, Letty peered around the side of the buggy. He had stopped, turned the horse so he could look back at the buggy. She held her breath, then let it out slowly when the rider put the horse in motion again and went on down the road.

Later she was to wonder where she had gotten the courage to make the trip. She had never been this far away from home alone even in the daytime.

A clock chimed loudly from a church tower as she drove into town. Nine-thirty. She had made the trip in an hour and a half. Isaac was sweating. She went directly to the livery, reaching it just as the proprietor was shutting the big double doors.

"Wait, sir!" she called. "I wish to leave my horse."

The man ambled toward her as she was getting down. "I seen that rig before."

"Yes, sir. I'm sure you have. It belongs to the preacher over at Dunlap. He lent it to me and I said I'd leave it here. He'll pick it up tomonow."
Letty tried to lift her suitcase up out of the boot.

"Where ya headed, miss?"

"The train station." She continued to pull the heavy case upward, but couldn't lift it high enough to clear the footboard.

"Well, leave it be. I'll drive ya. I'm thinkin' it's too far for ya to be haulin' that suitcase."

"I would certainly appreciate it. Do you know what time the train comes in?"

"Where to?"

Letty thought a minute, then said, "Chicago."

"Ya gotta go north to Lincoln to go east or west." The liveryman climbed into the buggy and took up the reins. "Giddy-up. Ain't it late fer ya to be roamin' round all by yore ownself?"

"Maybe. But . . . I just heard disturbing news about . . . my aunt in Chicago."

They turned into the street leading to the station. "Lights still on. The agent'll tell ya' 'bout connections in Lincoln."

CHAPTER
3

The station was deserted except for a bald-headed agent in the barred ticket cage and another man sweeping the floor. The man from the livery set Letty's suitcase inside the door, gave her a rather disapproving look, and left. Letty was glad he hadn't asked him to mail the letter to Mike's mother. He might have told her father when he came for the horse and buggy, and it would have meant trouble for the Dolans.

Letty crosed the room to the ticket window, her heels making a hollow sound on the board floor.

"Where to?" The agent got up from the desk and came to the window.

"Ah . . . Lincoln."

"One dollar and twenty-five cents." Letty gave him a five-dollar bill. He gave her the change and slapped a ticket down on the counter . . . Jasper!" he yelled.

"Yessir."

"Put this red tag on the lady's suitcase. Make sure it's on good now. We don't want it to fall off."

"Yessir."

"Train'll be through at eleven-twenty. I leave at eleven, but I'll put out the signal for it to stop."

"Thank you."

Letty sat down on the end of the bench that stretched across the room. It would be an hour and a half before she could get on the train. It seemed an eternity. She thought of how easy it had been to lie to the liveryman. She was sure he would mention her destination to her father when he came for the horse and buggy. Let him think she was going to Chicago. He would be glad she was going so far away. When she reached Lincoln, she would buy her ticket to Boley.

At eleven o'clock the agent turned off the light that hung over his desk, locked the barred ticket cage, and left the station without a look in Letty's direction. Time passed slowly. The porter moved in and out of the station, carrying out stinking spittoons and returning with clean ones. He dipped up cigar and cigarette butts from sand-filled stone urns and wiped off the benches with a wet cloth.

"Mister?" Letty called hesitantly.

"Yes'm."

"Will you mail a letter for me in the morning?"

"Ah . . . yes'm."

Letty stood and pulled the letter from her pocket. She reached into her bag for a coin and held it out to him.

"Here's a fifty-cent piece. Buy a two-cent stamp and place it right here." She pointed to the upper corner of the envelope. "You keep the rest for your trouble."

"Yes'm. I will."

Letty placed the coin in his palm along with the letter. Jasper's eyes were riveted to the coin. Four bits! For that much he could stay the whole night with Tulla Sue and she'd let him do everything he wanted to do to her. He raised his eyes to the ceiling and murmured: "Thanky, Jesus, fer bringin' that little lady here tonight."

The train pulled into the station a full thirty seconds before eleven-twenty. After it came to a grinding, lurching stop, the conductor climbed down carrying a small wooden box and placed it in front of the steps to the passenger car.

"All aboard!"

Letty went forward with her ticket in her outstretched hand.

"Step aboard, miss. I'll pick up your ticket later. Hey there, boy. Get that suitcase on down to the baggage car. The conductor pulled a thick railroad watch from his pocket and flipped open the lid. "We're pulling out in one minute."

A dim light lit the almost empty coach. Letty took the first vacant seat she came to and slid in next to the window. Fear of the unknown swept over her. She was on a train for the second time in her life that she remembered. This time she was alone. Seven years ago, when her father took the church at Dunlap, they had ridden the train to Huxley from a small town fifty miles south. It had seemed like a great adventure at the time. A shiver of fear ran through her and set her body to quivering. She stared at her reflection in the train window as if looking at a stranger.

How long? Oh, how long until Mike would come for her?

Jasper shoved Letty's suitcase in the baggage compartment. The sliding door slammed shut and the conductor waved his lantern to signal the engineer to start the train. With steam hissing and black smoke rolling from the smokestack, the iron wheels grated against the rails, and the huge locomotive strained to pull the cars from the station.

Letty continued to look at her reflection in the window. The day's events had put such a strain on her that she felt faintly ill. It seemed unreal to her that she was alone on a train in the middle of the night. She tried to keep her thoughts away from the hateful things her father had said. A lump, difficult to swallow, rose up in her throat. She would not think of it, she told herself sternly. She would think of the years ahead—with Mike, and she would think about the baby and the love they would lavish upon it.

But the hurt was too deep to brush away at will.

Before she knew it, her thoughts were back in the room upstairs, and her father was shouting obscenities at her. A chill formed around her heart. She vowed she would never, as long as she lived, forgive her family for what they had done to her.

Jasper waited until the train had been swallowed up by the night and all that was left was the click-clack of wheels against rails. He took from his pocket the letter the woman had given him. A wide smile covered his face as he tore it into small pieces and scattered the bits of paper along the cinders between the rails. When the last piece was gone, he dipped into his pocket for the half dollar. His fingers caressed the coin, loving the weight of it in his hand, thinking about the pleasure it would buy him.

Jasper quickly scanned the platform to make sure he had done everything the boss man had told him to do, then took off running down the wooden cross-ties toward the shack along the tracks where Tulla Sue would make him feel like a king.

Exhausted and emotionally spent from the sleepless night and the long wait in Lincoln, Letty arrived in Boley twenty-four hours after she left Huxley. She stood on the dimly lit platform and waited with several other passengers while the luggage was taken from the baggage car. A billboard attached to the station wall advertised the Hewitt Hotel as having "lodgings in good style." It also said "reasonably priced."

"Someone meeting you, dear?" An older woman, stylishly dressed and with a buxom figure spoke to Letty.

"Ah . . . no. I'll stay in a hotel tonight. Tomorrow I'll go out to my grandparents' farm."

"Are you going to the Hewitt by any chance?"

"Yes, ma'am."

"Good. I own the Hewitt. My man will be along shortly. You can ride to the hotel with me."

"Thank you."

Letty climbed into the middle seat of the three-seat conveyance when it arrived. The owner sat behind the driver and plied him with questions about the happenings in town while she was away. Letty was glad she didn't have to make conversation. She was tired but keyed up too. She had never stayed at a hotel. Her father had said it wasn't proper for a lady to go to one of *those* places. Well, proper or not, she couldn't sit in the railway station all night, and she sure couldn't find anyone to take her out to the Fletcher farm until morning. The price of the room was what worried her. She had already spent seven dollars of her precious money. The Lord only knew how long she had to make it last. If her grandparents didn't take her in. she'd have to come back to town. Oh, Lord! She didn't dare think of that.

The business places of Boley ringed the town square. All were dark except for a billiard parlor and the lobby of the hotel on the corner. The rubber-tired vehicle, pulled by a single horse, turned off the square and stopped on the side street. The driver first helped his employer down, then Letty. She followed the woman into the lobby and stood hesitantly beside the door. Sparkling chandeliers hung from the ceiling. Deep leather chairs occupied by men in dark business suits sat in groups on thick carpet. Cigar smoke filled the air.

"Register at the desk, dear," the woman said gently when she turned and saw the bewildered look on Letty's face. "Herman will take your suitcase up to your room."

Checking into the hotel had not been as terrifying an experience as she imagined it to be. It was going to cost her seventy-five cents to stay here tonight, but it was worth it. After Letty washed, she used the water closet down the hall, put on her nightdress, and crawled into the bed.

Mike. I'm so scared! A picture of him standing among the willows danced before her eyes. He was smiling and holding his arms out to her. *Don't be scared, sweetheart. I'll take care of you.* Her last thoughts were of him before she fell into a deep sleep.

Later, Letty was to be grateful she had met Mrs. Hewitt. She asked at the general store and at several other places in town, but no one had heard of Jacob Fletcher. Discouraged and on the verge of tears, she entered the hotel lobby and sank down in one of the deep chairs.

"Did you find someone to take you to your grandpa's, dear?" Mrs. Hewitt came and stood beside her chair.

"No, ma'am. No one seems to know him. May I sit here a little while?"

"Of course. Did you ask Mr. Caffery at the livery?"

Letty nodded. "He doesn't know where Grandpa Fletcher lives."

"Well, he hasn't been here but a couple of years. How long has it been since you've seen your grandparents?"

"Ten years or more. But I know they live near Boley. Their letters come from here."

"That doesn't mean a lot. People in the country send their mail to town, by anyone who happens along. Who else have you asked?"

"The man at the feed store, the drugstore, and the bank."

"Ask Doc Whittier. He's been here a long time and knows everyone within fifty miles. His office is above the drugstore."

With hope alive once more, Letty hurried down the street and up the stairway that clung to the side of the brick building. The printing on the frosted glass in the door read: DOCTOR SAMUEL WHITTIER, GENERAL MEDICINE. COME IN.

Letty went in. The man closing a glass-doored cabinet was short and stooped. He had thin gray hair and a gray handlebar mustache. Sharp blue eyes scrutinized her through round wire spectacles.

"You sick?"

"No, sir. I'm looking for my grandpa, Jacob Fletcher. Mrs. Hewitt at the hotel said you might be able to help me."

"What about him? What's that old buzzard up to now?"

"You know him?"

"For nigh on forty years."

"Thank goodness. I'm his granddaughter—"

"His granddaughter, huh? I remember when that scatter-brained Mable Fletcher ran off with a crazy preacher that came through here stirring up folks. Leaving like she did almost broke Leona's heart."

"You know where they live. Oh, that's a relief. Now I've got to find a way to get out there."

"Where you from, girl?"

"I came in on the train from Lincoln."

"The Fletcher place is up near Piedmont."

"Oh. I was real little when I was here last. I thought they lived near Boley."

"Boley's the hub for a lot of places."

"Oh, shoot. Do you know when the next train comes through?"

"I'm going up to Claypool." The doctor reached for a battered old hat and slammed it down on his head. "You can ride that far with me. I'll find someone to give you a ride on up to the farm." He eyed her closely. "Are you going to stay a while?"

"I plan to."

"Good. Although the stubborn old coot swears he doesn't, Jacob could use a hand with Leona."

"Is Grandma sick?"

"Has been for years. I never understood why that daughter of theirs never came back to see about her. Well. there's no understanding some folks. Go fetch your suitcase and put it in that touring car parked out front."

Once out of town, Doc Whittier drove the touring car as if he were trying to escape the hangman. Letty sat in the front seat beside him, holding onto her hat with one hand and the door with the other. She could count on one hand the number of times she had ridden in an automobile. The wind assaulted her, burning her eyes and stinging her cheeks. The trees seemed to whiz by as the car bounced over the rutted road. They splashed across a small rock-bottomed stream. Doc Whittier laughed with glee when they were sprayed with water. He shoved on the lever to give the automobile more gas, and the car roared up the bank on the other side. Wearing driving glasses to protect his eyes from the dust, he sat hunched over the wheel clearly enjoying himself.

Abruptly, they turned off the road and onto what was no more than a cow path. Fresh cow manure squished beneath the rubber tires. At one time it was so thick that the back of the car fishtailed, causing Letty to gasp. The doctor let out a whoop of laughter. The homestead at the end of the track consisted of a log house with a

46

sod roof and a barn that leaned to one side. Within an enclosure made by a single strand of barbed wire going from tree to tree, a small herd of thin cows munched on dry grass.

The doctor drove into the yard. Chickens squawked and scattered, hogs squealed and ran toward the trees on short stubby legs. A woman with a young but tired-looking face herded children out the door and gestured for them to wait beneath an oak tree.

The doctor got out and took his bag from behind the seat. "This'll take a minute or two."

The woman followed the doctor into the house. The children stared with open-mouthed fascination at the automobile. After a while a small boy disappeared around the corner of the house, then appeared leading a piglet on a rope. He came up close to show Letty his pet. She smiled at him. Encouraged, he began to run in circles to show her how the piglet would follow. A little girl suddenly upended herself and stood on her hands, her dress falling down around her head. One of the boys swatted her on the bottom. She squealed, then began turning cartwheels. Letty clapped her hands in appreciation of the show. The child beamed.

Doc Whittier came out followed by the woman. He spoke a few words to her, then put his bag behind the seat. The woman herded the children back out of the way, and they watched as he adjusted levers and cranked until the motor roared to life. Letty waved to the children as the car circled the yard, and they headed back down the track.

"Was one of the children sick?" Letty shouted.

"Naw," the doctor shouted back. "The damn fool cut off his big toe with an ax. The woman did a good job on it, but he'll be laid up for a while." He yelled a few more phrases that Letty couldn't understand over the roar of the motor. She was glad when he gave all of his attention to his driving. The speed at which they were traveling was frightening and she held onto the sides of the seat when they hit bends in the road.

Claypool, when they reached it, was no more than six weather-beaten buildings stretched out along the road. The touring car roared into town in a cloud of dust. Horses hitched to buggies and farm wagons along the street shied and tugged at the reins holding them to the hitching rails. Men in overalls and women holding tightly to the hands of young children came out onto the board porches of the business places to see the automobile and its occupants.

According to the smile on the doctor's face, driving was clearly one of his pleasures in life. When the car rolled to a stop in front of the general store and the roar of the motor died away, men came off the porches and gathered around. They gave Letty furtive glances, but none spoke to her.

"Howdy, Doc."

"How long'd it take ya this time, Doc?"

"Didn't make good time. Had to stop off at the Ramsey's."

"Heard that Lyle cut off his toe. Haw! Haw! Haw!"

"You'd not be laughing if it was your toe." the doctor growled.

"The radiator's boilin', Doc. Ya want me to fetch a bucket a water?"

"Yeah. I'd be obliged."

A skinny short-haired dog came out from under the porch, walked slowly up to the front wheel on the car. hoisted his leg, and sprayed it well.

"Hey there!" Doc shouted, hitting the dog on the back with his hat. "Get the hell away from there. You do that every damn time I come to town. I just had those wheels varnished."

The men laughed. "Ole Sport thinks them tires needs coolin' off, Doc."

"Ole Sport's piss is eating the varnish off the spokes!"

"He likes ya, Doc."

The doctor snorted. "Any a you fellers want to take this young lady out to Jacob Fletcher's place?"

There was sudden silence while all eyes turned on Letty. The doctor had given the cue that it was all right to look openly at his passenger. It was an introduction—of sorts. The women on the porches stared. The faces closer to Letty were male, mostly hard. They reflected the times as they reflected the place. Here in Nebraska times were hard. The men worked day after day, year after year, to eke a living out of the soil for them-

49

selves and their families. The hands that lifted to touch the brims of hats were large, worn and calloused.

"She Jacob's kin?"

"Granddaughter," Doc said.

"Looks like a city girl."

"Reckon she is."

"Won't be stayin' long is my guess."

"It'd be all right with me if'n she does." The young man who spoke had straw-colored hair springing thickly from the scalp. It was parted in the middle and combed over a receding hairline. Letty's eyes flew to his, then quickly away. He was staring with admiration.

"She's going to see her grandma and it's nobody's business how long she stays." Doc Whittier stood with his feet spread, his hands on his sides, and looked at each of the men.

Letty's face reddened. She felt as if she were on display. The men and Doc Whittier were talking as if she wasn't there.

"It's a fer piece out to Jacob's." The man who spoke leaned behind another man to spit tobacco juice on the ground.

"I know how far it is," Doc Whittier growled impatiently. "Every single one of you fellers owes me a bill. I'll knock two dollars off on the one that takes her out to Jacob's."

"Hell. I reckon I can take her, Doc." A man edged toward the side of the car where Letty sat, leaned against it, and eyed her boldly. His grin showed tobacco-stained teeth. His eyes wandered over Letty until the doctor's sharp voice brought them back to him.

"Your wife's expecting, Phillips. You'd better get on back to Piedmont, tend to your younguns, and keep an eye on her."

The grin stayed on the man's face, but it was different. Letty knew instantly that he didn't like being called down in front of her and the other men. He continued as though the doctor hadn't spoken.

"Name's Oscar Phillips, ma'am. Ya'll have to come callin' on Clara if you're stayin' long. It's bound to be lonesome out at Fletcher's for a girl like you."

"I'm not sure how long I'll be staying. My . . . husband will be coming for me."

Oscar Phillips looked down at her ringless fingers then back up to her face. Something about the way he looked at her caused a trickle of fear to run up her spine.

"I live at Piedmont. Anybody can tell you where Oscar Phillips lives. Be glad to come fetch ya and . . . Mrs. Fletcher."

"Thank you. I'll tell grandma."

"I'll take her, Doc. And without no pay. I ain't forgettin' that you spent two days with us when the kids come down with scarlet fever." Letty's eyes moved past the man standing close to the automobile and sought the one who spoke. He was older, his hair iron-gray. His bib overalls were worn but clean and patched.

"I'll be obliged to you." The doctor turned to

51

Letty. "Get out, missy. You'll be in good hands with Mr. Pierce. He's got daughters about your age."

Letty waited until Oscar Phillips moved back before she opened the door and stepped out on the running board.

"Ya ain't goin' to be ridin' in no fancy automobile, missy," Mr. Pierce said. "I'll fetch the team and wagon. I'd as soon get started so's I can get home afore dark."

"It's a long way out there," the doctor said to Letty. "You want a bite to eat before you go?"

"No, thank you. I'm not hungry."

"Fetch a couple of those apples out of the barrel there on the porch, Lester," Doc called. He went to the edge of the porch, took the apples, and wiped them on his coat sleeve. "Stubborn as old Jacob, ain't you?" he muttered and dropped the apples into Letty's handbag.

Letty was anxious to leave. She held out her hand to the doctor.

"Thank you, Doctor Whittier."

"Don't mention it." He gripped her hand firmly. "Tell Jacob there's a young doctor setting up practice in Piedmont. It's a hell of a lot closer than Boley. But I'll come if he gets word to me."

"I'll tell him."

Doctor Whittier took her elbow to help her into the wagon when he saw Oscar Phillips step forward to assist her. Letty sat down beside Mr. Pierce, turned, waved, and sighed with relief that she was finally on the last leg of her journey.

CHAPTER
4

Letty watched the vanishing hills pick up colors of sun and sky and the prairie of bleached grass stretch into nothingness. The sky had split into layer upon layer of floating white clouds. An eagle appeared and spiralled upward, climbing higher toward the sun until it was only a speck in the vast emptiness.

Oh, to be an eagle to fly high and free. She would fly and fly until she found her beloved. Together they would make a world of their own, a family, out of their love for each other.

A sudden chill set her flesh trembling. Letty clamped her jaws tight to keep her teeth from chattering. It seemed to her that everything familiar was dropping away into the distance behind her, and the more it receded, the more frightened she became. Would she be turned away from her grandfather's house? If that happened, she would be left with nothing but her own strength and wits to aid her. In all her fifteen years she had never been allowed to think for herself. Decisions were made for her—all except for one. She had chosen to sneak out and meet Mike, and she didn't regret a single minute of the time she spent with him. *Mike, Mike, where are you?*

The air was getting cooler. Letty hugged the shawl around her shoulders. Neither she nor Mr.

Pierce had said a word since they left Claypool. In the hills now, the trail was overgrown and full of holes and jagged stones which Mr. Pierce skillfully avoided when possible. The team plodded on. A dead possum lay beside the road, its body grotesquely bloated. A jack rabbit bound out of a thick growth of sumac and raced ahead of them to disappear in the brush. The only sounds to disturb the silence were the caw of a crow, the jingle of harnesses, and the thump of horses' hooves. Then from a distance, Letty heard the whistle of a train.

"Is my grandpa's place near the railroad tracks, Mr. Pierce?"

"About a half mile, I reckon."

"If I'd known, I could have got off the train there and walked."

"Train don't stop till it gets to Piedmont."

"How far is that?"

"Five miles, as the crow flies."

Letty was conscious of the curious glances the man gave her. She forced herself to look straight ahead; her face remained calm, her feelings well bottled up inside her though she had never felt more like crying in her life.

They traveled a long way in silence, covering mile after mile of prairie before the track led them through country sprinkled with groves of oak and elm trees and scattered with little flat-topped hills that rose above the rolling terrain.

"How much farther, Mr. Pierce?"

"Jist a hoot 'n' a holler now. That's the Fletcher

place yonder." He pointed toward a clump of trees.

Letty's heart raced until she thought it would gallop out of her chest. She held her cupped hand to her brow to shade her eyes as she stared toward the farm. After a while she could make out the buildings. The house hunched low by the side of the road, a barn and a windmill behind it. Tension knotted her stomach. Nothing about the place seemed familiar. Why should it? She had been only four years old when she was here. All she remembered of the visit was sitting on Grandma Fletcher's lap and that Grandpa Fletcher had a white beard.

As they neared she could see that the house was built of rough lumber that had long since weathered to a soft, mellow gray. A narrow porch with a railing around it stretched across the front of the house, hemming in two front doors. The yard, thickly blanketed with large yellow leaves from a maple tree that loomed naked over the house, was enclosed with a paling fence, weathered like the house. A gate hung between two cedar posts. Above and behind the white-oak shingle boards of the roof, the wheel of the windmill turned lazily. The yard sunounding the farm building and house was tidy, the barn and sheds mended. It was not merely a farm; it was a *home*. The thought charged through the confusion in Letty's mind.

"Here we are." The wagon had stopped beside the gate.

Letty climbed down and stood holding onto the

wagon. The front door opened. Letty felt an anguished moment of fear and a desire to run. The man who came out onto the porch had a head of thick white hair and a white beard.

"Howdy. Mr. Pierce," he called.

"Howdy, Mr. Fletcher. Brung ya a visitor."

"Won't ya step down and sit a spell?"

"Thanky, but I'd better get on back. Been to the blacksmith in Claypool. How's the missus?"

"Fair to middlin'. Yours?"

"Mrs. Pierce's tolerable, thanky. One of the younguns stepped on a nail a while back."

"Sorry to hear it."

A flush started at Letty's throat and worked up onto her face when she realized she was being ignored for the second time that day while men made small talk.

"Give a howdy to Mrs. Fletcher from me and Mrs. Pierce."

"I'll do that."

Mr. Pierce looked over his shoulder to see if Letty had pulled her suitcase off the tailgate of the wagon. Old man Fletcher wasn't pleased to see the girl: that was sure. Well, it wasn't his affair. He slapped the reins against the backs of the horses.

"Good day to ya, Mr. Fletcher."

"Mr. Pierce," Letty called. "Wait. I want to thank you."

"Ain't no need. I done it for Doc."

"Well, thanks anyway," she said lamely. "Goodbye."

The wagon pulled away. Letty licked dry lips and waited. Her grandfather stood there, making no move to welcome her. She tried to swallow, but her throat was closed with fear. His steady look was so unnerving that she was afraid she would burst into tears. Finally he spoke.

"Well, come on in, girl."

Letty picked up her suitcase and went through the gate. The old man's face was well-creased, weather-seasoned. Sharp eyes bored into hers as if he were trying to see into her mind.

"Hello, Grandpa. Do you remember m-me? Letty?"

"Letty who?"

"Letty Pringle. Mable's youngest daughter."

"I figured ya was one of Mable's. Hellfire! Last time I saw ya, ya was ass-high to a duck. Mable's girl. Well, I'll be switched. What ya doin' here, girl?"

The harsh tone of his voice sliced through the last bit of Letty's control. Unwanted, embarrassing tears flooded her eyes; her lips quivered.

"I . . . I came to v-visit."

"Yore Pa know you're here?"

Letty shook her head.

"Ya run off from home?"

She shook her head again. "Papa th-threw me out. I had no place to go," she blurted. "I'll not be a bother. I p-promise."

The old man growled an unrecognizable word. With his head cocked to the side, he looked steadily into her pleading eyes.

"Warn't ya prayin' loud enough to suit the bastard?"

"It wasn't that exactly —"

"Never mind." He cut off her words with an impatient wave of his hand. "I've had a craw full of that self-righteous, mouthly jackass. Dry up before yore grandma sees ya. Hear? Gimme that." He took the suitcase from her hand and went into the house. Clutching her handbag to her breast, Letty followed.

The minute she stepped through the door, the feeling of home closed around her. The small house had the smell, the feel, and the look of a place loved by the people who lived in it. Dominating the small room was a huge piano draped with a fringed scarf. A round stool covered with faded blue velvet was pushed up under the keyboard. Two straight-backed chairs, also velvet-covered, and a library table were the only other pieces of furniture in the room.

Jacob set Letty's suitcase down and went through the door into what appeared to be the heart of the house. It was a long room that spread across the back with a fireplace at one end. A black iron cookstove with pots, pans, skillets, and sundry utensils hanging around it took up the other end. On a line stretched diagonally across the range, dish towels were drying.

These details came only vaguely to Letty's notice as her grandfather moved past a round oak table to where her grandmother sat in a huge padded chair.

"Looky here who comed to see us, Leony. It's Letty," he said with a gentleness that seemed strange coming from such a big gruff man. "Mable's youngest girl has come a visitin'."

"Hello, Grandma."

Grandma Fletcher looked like a child sitting in the big chair with a quilt over her lap. She was a tiny, doll-like woman with snow-white hair twisted in a knot on the top of her head. The skin on her face was as soft and pink as a baby's. Eyes as blue as the sky sparkled with pleasure. Her lips curved with the welcoming smile Letty had hungered for.

"Well, now. Don't this just beat all? Bend down, child, and let me get a look at you." Letty knelt down. Her grandmother reached up, took the hat from her head, and held it in her lap. "My, my, my. Ain't you just as pretty as a picture."

Tears began to roll down Letty's cheeks. She glanced quickly at the big, silent man standing beside the chair. He was scowling down at her. Oh, Lordy! He had told her to dry up. She couldn't bawl! She just couldn't. Her reasoning did nothing to stop the tears that flowed. She turned her face away and tried to wipe her eyes with her sleeve.

"The child's plumb wore out, Jacob." A gentle hand came up to Letty's head and smoothed the hair back from her forehead. Letty buried her face in her grandmother's lap and let the tears flow.

Here was the loving acceptance she had been searching for all her life.

During the days that followed Letty proved to be a great help to her grandfather. She took over the household chores. The only outside work she was permitted to do was feed the chickens and gather the eggs. After a while Letty began to wonder how Grandpa had managed to take care of his wife, the house chores, and the farm. Letty liked to cook. Although she had cooked at home, she had not learned to make biscuits and pies. Under her grandmother's supervision she made both and they were surprisingly good. There was an abundance of foodstuff; milk, eggs, potatoes, pumpkins, hams. bacon, deer meat, and also huge tins of flour, sugar, and crocks of lard.

While she worked, she and her grandmother chatted companionably. Leona asked if Mable and Cora were well. Beyond that, the family or the reason her father made her leave home was never mentioned.

Letty had never known a sweeter, gentler person than Grandma Fletcher. Leona had a weakness in her legs that prevented her from standing on them. She told Letty that it was caused by a high fever during an illness about five years ago. Her legs were useless but not her hands. They were always busy. With Letty to fetch for her, she was able to do a number of household chores. She churned, shelled beans, peeled apples for pies, pieced quilts, and crocheted.

As the days passed. Letty would have been almost happy if not for worrying about what her grandparents would say when they found out she was unwed and expecting a child.

Fascinated by the love that existed between the two old people, Letty was certain it would be the same between her and Mike. Never a cross word was spoken. Grandpa's face would soften when he was with his Leona. He lifted her as carefully as if she were a baby when he moved her from the deep padded chair to the one he had mounted on rollers to take her to the other parts of the house. The look of peace and happiness on Leona's face amazed Letty. It was no wonder Jacob loved her to distraction and was always trying to figure out ways to make things easier for her.

To this home Jacob had brought his bride forty years ago. It bore no mark but theirs. In Letty's upstairs room was the iron bedstead and the dresser with the cracked mirror they had brought with them. Covering the bed was a patchwork quilt Leona had made from pieces of her dresses and Jacob's shirts. It was called a crazy quilt because the pieces were put together without a pattern. Each piece of material held a memory, Leona said.

One day during the noon meal. Leona asked Letty if she played the piano.

"I play some but not as well as Mama."

"We bought the piano for Mable. I taught her what little I knew. She had natural talent and learned the rest by herself."

"The blasted thin' was the ruination of her," Jacob grumbled.

"She played it beautifully." Leona reached across the table and gave Jacob's hand a squeeze.

"She taught Cora and me to play," Letty said. "But she always played for the church service."

"Damn brayin' jackass wouldn't a give her a second look if not for the playin'."

"We don't know that, Jacob. You're a good cook, Letty." Leona said, trying to change the subject, but Jacob refused to let it die.

"Never could abide a religion made up of don'ts, cryin', and speakin' in tongues. Jist all a big show if ya was to ask me."

"You'll make some man a good wife someday, Letty." Leona was just as determined to change the subject.

"If'n a clabberheaded, flimflam of a preacher don't glom onto her first and fill her head with tommyrot notions."

"There's no danger of that!" Letty blurted. "I'll never, never marry a preacher!"

"Then ya got more brains than yore ma had. She thought he was somethin' grand standin' up there cryin', preachin' 'n' havin' folks put their hard-earned money in the hat when he passed it." Jacob speared a biscuit with his fork.

"Now, Jacob," Leona chided gently.

"She still thinks he's grand," Letty said, feeling the weight of her mother's rejection once again.

"Mable chose the kind of life she wanted. We had no hold on her." Leona reached for Jacob's hand again.

"Ungrateful twit is what she is."

Letty looked up to see her grandma slowly shaking her head at Jacob. After that an uneasy silence fell on the room and it lasted until the meal was over.

As the days passed, the guilt that lay like a stone on Letty's heart grew heavier. Already her dresses were getting too tight at the waist, her breasts were sore and swollen. More than anything, she dreaded telling her grandparents her secret. Jacob planned to go to town on Saturday. Now that Letty was here, he no longer had to fetch one of the neighhors to stay with Leona while he was away from the farm. Did she dare ask him to mail the letter to Mike's mother that lay on the dresser in her attic room?

By Friday night Letty's nerves were at the breaking point. She logically reasoned that if they wanted her to leave after she told them her secret, she could ride to Piedmont with Grandpa the following morning, that is if he could get one of the Watkins girls to stay with Grandma. The Watkins' were their closest neighbors, and the girls had been hired from time to time to help in the house.

After the supper dishes were washed and put away. Letty wiped her hands on the towel and hung it over the stove to dry. The lamp in the middle of the table cast a soft, cozy light. Grandma was braiding carpet rags; Grandpa sat at the table making a list of what he had to get when he went to town. Fearing her grandparents would turn on her as her parents had done Letty was nevertheless

63

determined not to spend another sleepless night thinking about what she would do if they asked her to leave.

Her throat felt as if it were clogged with a cotton ball. She cleared it and went to stand behind one of the highbacked chairs. A wave of sweat moved across her back and sprang through the pores of her hands and face. She gripped the knobs on the chair as if they were a lifeline and she was being washed away in a flood.

"I've got something to tell you and—" Her voice started out strong, then weakened and fell away.

Grandma looked up and saw the worried look on Letty's face. Her hands stilled, then fell into her lap. A little scowl appeared on Jacob's forehead. He slowly placed his lead pencil beside the scrap of paper he had been writing on.

"I . . . ah . . . I thought I could just c-come here, stay a while, and I-leave. But you've been so good to take me in that . . . that I feel bad about not telling you the reason Papa threw me out."

"You don't have to tell us about the trouble you had with your father," Grandma said gently. "We're just grateful you came and that we got to know you."

"You might not want me to stay after I tell you!"

"Say what you've got to say, girl," Grandpa said gruffly.

"I'm . . . going to have a baby and I'm . . . not m-married!"

Silence. Both of her grandparents gaped at her in shock.

"Jehoshaphat!" The word finally burst from Jacob's lips."

"Oh, dear me. Oh, goodness gracious."

"I'm not a bad girl!" Letty exclaimed when she saw the stunned looks on their faces. "Oh . . . please—"

"You poor child."

"Mike will come for me as soon as he finds out where I am. He went to the logging camps to earn money so we could get married. Papa wouldn't've let us, 'cause . . . cause Mike's a Catholic."

Leona held out her hand. "Come sit down and tell us aboui it."

Letty grabbed her grandmother's hand and sank down on her knees beside her chair. The story poured out of her.

"I'm not the bad girl Papa said I was. Mike and I love each other. If Papa knew it was Mike, he'd see to it that the members of his congregation didn't buy coal from Mike's father. All Mama and Papa and Cora live for is the church. He said he said I was never to come back and that as far as he and Mama and Cora were concerned I was . . . dead."

"Mable let that Bible-spouting bastard throw you out!" Jacob exclaimed. "Now ain't that a ring-tailed tooter considerin' what she is."

"Mama never disagrees with Papa. If . . . if he told her to jump in the fire, she would. She didn't come near . . . not even to say goodbye."

"Mable doted on him right from the start." Grandmas hand stroked Letty's hair.

"Harumph! She was hoodwinked by that clap-trap. It's clear as the nose on my face. With her not having the sense of a goose, it was easy fer him."

"Well, we can't look back. We got something new to look forvard to. Put some yarn on that list, Jacob. I've got to start making booties for my great-grandbaby."

"Then I can stay until Mike comes for me?" Letty searched the faces of her grandparents for a sign of disapproval. There was none.

"Of course you can stay—as long as you want."

"Grandpa?"

"I ain't a mule's ass like yore pa is. He's a bull-headed, low-minded scallywag if he thinks all Catholics are bound for hell. Harumpt! They'll have to stand in line behind some Holy Rollers I know of," he snorted. "The first time I set eyes on that bounder and heard him caterwauling 'bout how he could heal the sick 'n' save souls, it made my rear end crave a dip a snuff. I'll tell ya straight off, girl, God ain't working through no jackass such as Albert Pringle."

Grandma Leona laughed softly. "I guess you can tell that Jacob doesn't think too highly of your father."

"I'll never forgive Papa for the things he said. I shouldn't have done what I did out of wedlock, but . . . but I'm not . . . I'm not what he said."

"My word. Of course you're not." Leona clicked her tongue against her teeth in a gesture of sympathy.

"You . . . don't feel that I've . . . disgraced you?"

"Pshaw. When you love so desperately, the flesh is weak. You and the boy were wed in your hearts. We'll just introduce you as—let's see—Letty Graham. Graham was my maiden name. When your young man comes, you can suddenly become a widow and the two of you can be married. It's going to be all right. You'll see."

Jacob snorted again and painstakingly added yarn to his list.

Leona Fletcher didn't live to see her great-grandchild. One morning in late March while sitting in her huge padded chair looking out the window at the change spring was bringing to the land, she quietly slipped away. Jacob was devastated. He went through the days that followed in a grief-induced stupor. After the burial he rode home in the wagon with Letty only to get out and, in a cold spring rain, walk more than three miles back to the Lutheran cemetery.

When he didn't return, Letty became worried and urged one of the Watkins boys who was helping with the chores to go look for him. He found Jacob sitting on the ground beside Leona's grave and brought him home. Racked with chills and fever, Jacob took to his bed and would have died if not for the young doctor who came out from Piedmont and stayed for two days and two nights.

"Mrs. Graham, your grandfather is very sick." Doctor Hakes, a slender young man with a serious-looking face, stood at the door with his hat in one hand, his medical bag in the other. The mustache he wore to make him look older was blond and thin.

"Will he . . . die?"

"Not if we can make him take care of himself. He's sound as a dollar for a man his age. What about you? Will your husband be here in time for the baby?"

"I don't know." Letty's face turned as red as a beet pickle. "He's working up north." *Why was he looking at her like that? Didn't he believe her?*

"Yes, I heard he was off working in the logging camps."

"He'll come as soon as he can."

"Will you be staying on here after your husband joins you? Jacob will be lost without Mrs. Fletcher."

"We'll not leave him if he wants us to stay. Right now he doesn't seem to care about anything," Letty said.

"Well, life goes on." The young doctor said tiredly. "You'll have to make arrangements for someone to come stay a while after you give birth."

"Grandma said Mrs. Watkins would come or send one of her girls."

"From the position of that baby it appears it won't be long until he'll be clamoring to get out. From now on carry only half a bucket of water at a time."

"It won't be for another month."

"First one can come any time. I'll be back day after tomorrow to see Jacob. I'll examine you too."

"Will you come when I . . . when I have the baby?"

"Of course. Send one of the Watkins boys for me." He chuckled. "That horn Jacob rigged up to let the Watkins know when he needs help is pretty doggone clever." He took the doorknob in his hand, turned, and regarded her with fine deep-set eyes, saying nothing but looking thoughtful, waiting for her to speak.

"Thank you. Grandpa will pay when he is better."

He nodded, slammed his hat down on his head, and went out.

Letty pressed her face to the window and watched the doctor's buggy head back toward town. He had scoffed at Doc Whittier's toy automobile, saying that when he was ready to go home, his horse knew the way and he could catch up on his sleep.

Letty looked across the road to where Harry Watkins was plowing the field. It was spring. The days had gone by, slipping carelessly into the past. She had stored the image of Mike's face and his promise to come back for her into the voiceless regions of her mind. At night in her lonely bed, she took them out, playing them over, savoring every tender word, remembering the sweetness of his kisses, and praying he would come to her soon.

So much time had gone by. In another month her baby would be born.

Mike, please hurry—

That night Letty wrote a letter to her mother telling her about Grandma Leona's death. It didn't matter to her now if they knew where she was. She doubted that it mattered to them either. She wrote the bare facts, omitting any mention of herself. When she finished, she simply signed it Letty and sealed it in an envelope. Then, with her lead pencil, she carefully edged the envelope in black to prepare her mother for the sad news within.

CHAPTER
5

Mike Dolan lay on his back looking up at blue sky. He shifted, gathered his strength to sit up but at first movement, pain exploded in his side. He fell back and silently swore. The pain pinned him to the ground and pounded him fiercely, relentlessly, clawing at his insides, ripping him. defeating him. The goddamn pain was going to kill him! He tried to control it by breathing deeply, but the air he drew into his lungs set his chest on fire.

Was he dying?

Letty's image, clear and beautiful, appeared before him, and his desire to fight the pain ebbed. Why was he trying to hold onto this worthless, useless life? He tried to speak, to call her name, but nothing came out. Her features began to waver. He lifted his hand to push aside whatever it was that was pressing down on his face.

"Don't take off the mask!" The stern voice reached into his consciousness.

The gas mask. He remembered. He had been shot too. Nothing worked; his limbs, his mouth, not even his brain. *Let it go, Dolan, give it up.* He was not afraid of dying—it would be a relief. He was tired of being alone. The excruciating pain that carried him into a black void eased as darkness and warmth enveloped him.

He had no fear as he gave up the struggle to live. Behind closed eyes, the calm, beautiful face that had haunted his dreams for the past five years appeared once again.

"I'm scared, Mike."

"Letty, sweetheart, don't be scared. I'll be with you always—"

The war was over.

It was strange to be lying in a hospital bed and to hear men cheering. For the past three weeks it had been as quiet as a tomb. Mike had come through the Belleau Wood offensive only to be struck down by a bullet in the side during the Meuse-Argonne battle shortly before phosgene, a gas the Germans used in projectiles fired by their artillery, cloaked their position. He had been lucky. A friend had told him to throw his coat over his face and breathe through the heavy cloth. He had done that until the corpsman arrived with a gas mask. It saved his life. Unprepared for gas warfare, men had dropped like flies. If it had not been for his quick thinking, Mike, too, would be sleeping forever in Flanders alongside a countless number of other American soldiers.

The war was over. Now there would be no more wallowing in muddy trenches, no more charging over the next hill, bayonet ready, and no more nights spent wondering if he would see the dawn. During the last year and a half, he had lost friend after friend and had seen enough of blood and death to last a lifetime.

The men in the ward had first cheered at the news of the armistice; then they cried tears of joy. They were going home—home to wives, mothers, and sweethearts. Mike never felt so lonely as when one of them talked to him about his sweetheart or showed him pictures of his wife and child.

He'd had a sweetheart . . . once. A slim, brown-eyed, auburn-haired girl with sweet, soft lips and a beautiful smile. Now all he had were memories and six inches of frayed blue ribbon that he kept in his pocket. It had been five years since he'd said goodbye to his sweetheart and headed for the logging camps. In his foolish young heart he had believed that he and Letty would live out the days of their lives together.

Mike tried not to think about the last time he had been home. He felt a hundred years older now than he had that spring. With money from his winter's work in his pocket, he had gone home to Dunlap to fetch Letty and take her away so they could be together. He closed his eyes against the painful memory.

72

Letty was dead! Lost to him forever.

His mother had told him the news as gently as she could. A week before his return, a letter edged in black had arrived at the Dunlap post office for Mrs. Pringle. Everyone in town knew that the preacher and his wife had received bad news and waited to express their condolences. Finally, the family announced that their daughter, Letty, who had been sent to take care of her bedridden grandmother, had sickened and died. A memorial service was held at the church and a collection plate passed to pay for the burial expense. Shortly after that the Pringles, racked with grief, packed up and left on a tour of revival meetings.

Later his mother had shown him the letter she had received from Letty months earlier asking her to tell him that she was with her grandparents. Take the train to Piedmont, Nebraska, the letter said, then ask directions to Jacob Fletcher's farm.

Even after Mike had drunk himself into a stupor, he had no peace. He thought of going to where Letty had spent her last days. But his mother convinced him that it would be too painful.

"You should let the past go and look to the future." she said. "Someday you'll find a nice Catholic girl and settle down. Your Letty will be only a pleasant memory."

Mike took the train to Pennsylvania. For two long years he labored in the coal mines, drank, fought, and caroused. During this time he grew two inches in height, put on thirty pounds, and acquired the reputation of a man who would fight at the drop of a hat.

When the United States entered the war, he was one of the first to enlist. His daring and commitment to duty earned him the rank of sergeant. His brawling and hell raising took the promotion away. Every soldier in his platoon wanted to be by his side in the time of heavy fighting. He was also the man they avoided during the infrequent lulls.

One night in a cold, dark trench, while the German shells were falling all around him and his chances of living until dawn were slim, he promised himself that if he lived through the war, he would go to Piedmont, Nebraska, and talk to Letty's grandparents if they were still alive. He would visit her final resting place and tell her that he had not broken his promise to come back for her. If he could do that, maybe he would be able to let go of the memory of the young, sweet, vulnerable girl who had clung to him and whispered, "Mike. Mike, I'm so scared."

The hospital bed felt like a prison. Mike sat up. The men who were able to get out of bed had gathered together in one corner of the long room. They had sung every war song they could remember. Now they were repeating everyone's favorite:

"The American soldiers crossed the Rhine,
   parlez-vous,
"The American soldiers crossed the Rhine,
   parlez-vous,
The American soldiers crossed the Rhine,
   parlez-vous,
The American soldiers crossed the Rhine,
   to kiss the women and drink the wine.
Hinky dinky *parlez-vous.*"

Soon they were making up their own risqué verses. Laughter and merrymaking rang throughout the hospital ward, but Mike Dolan's mind was far from the scene.

Through the months and years Mike had kept a clear picture of Letty before him, remembering the dark richness of her hair, the depth of her eyes, and the trusting way she had given herself to him. He never failed to think of her when he saw a rainbow—a ribbon in the sky.

Mike reached fior his pack of personal belongings and took the frayed ribbon from the envelope. He hadn't looked at it for a long time. Now he pulled it between his thumb and forefinger, feeling its satin softness. Even though it was faded and tattered, to Mike it was as bright and new as the day he had plucked it from the lilac bush. He closed his eyes. Once again he saw it attached to the bush, fluttering in the breeze. This little scrap of blue was the tie that bound him to the memory of that wonderful summer when he and Letty—young, so in love, and so very innocent—

had been one in spirit as well as in flesh. For an instant he felt her fragrant hair on his face and her slender, warm body pressed against his.

Wearily. Mike lay back on the bed, fell into a deep sleep, and dreamed he was getting off the train at the station in Huxley. The band was playing, the platform was crowded with a cheering throng, but he saw only one person. *Letty.* She ran to him and flung herself into his arms as she had done when they met beneath the willows. Her soft arms encircled his neck, her lips searched for his. The scent of lilac was in her hair.

Mike, Mike, I love you so much!

He woke with a start. The hospital ward was dark and quiet except for an occasional groan or whimper from a seriously injured soldier. Mike stared up at the whitewashed ceiling. The heavy hand of loneliness gripped him, wrapping its icy fingers around his heart.

He sat up on the side of the bed, the tears sliding silently down his gaunt, whiskered cheeks.

"Letty . . . Letty—" A strangled sob escaped him. "Oh, sweet Mother of God, take away the pain."

A freezing mist blew into northwestern Nebraska the last week in March, coating everything with a thin layer of ice before it turned into heavy snow. Letty was grateful it was happening now instead of a few weeks hence. She had seen the effects of a late spring blizzard when one blew in the year Patrick was born. Early leaves and blossoms were killed. For three weeks longer, spring pasture was denied horses and cattle that were already gaunt from a meager winter diet.

At the Fletcher farm the fall harvest of pumpkins, potatoes, yams, turnips, and cabbage was almost gone, and the live-stock had been put on short rations to stretch the hay and corn. What had seemed an ample supply of firewood had dwindled faster than expected because the winter had been so severe. Letty had taken the team to the woods and dragged in all the deadfalls she could find. With a two-man saw, she and Jacob had sawed the logs into usable lengths for the fireplace and cookstove.

Now, along with Harry Watkins and twelve-year-old Irene Watkins, she was picking up coal along the railroad tracks. Last night, when the coal train came through, it had scattered chunks of coal along the right-of-way as it crawled up Colfax Hill.

Letty picked up a chunk of coal in each hand and tossed them into the wagon. Then she lifted her head to the wind and sniffed.

"I smell smoke. I bet there's a hobo camp over there in the woods." She glanced at flaxen-haired Irene. "Keep your cap pulled down. We don't want those men to realize we're women."

"They could be runners bringin' a load of whiskey down from Canada," Harry said. "Pa thinks it's a meetin' place."

"I'd rather it be hoboes than whiskey runners."

"Pa heard that Oscar Phillips was haulin' whiskey in and sellin' it to bootleggers."

"No! What'll become of his kids if he's caught?"

"Ma figures he's thinkin' you'll take care of them, Letty," Harry teased.

"He'd better think again," Letty said staunchly, straightening her aching back, and glaring at him.

"As soon as Clara was put in the ground he come courtin', didn't he? We heard he brought ya a couple cottontails the other day."

"How did you know? Oh, forget it. Everybody knows everything around here. I told him to take the rabbits home to his kids." Letty cast a glance down the tracks. "I can see the siding. We'll get almost a half a wagonload."

This was the third time they had picked up coal spilled from the freight train. Now that the war was over, the country was in a transitional period: Nebraska had been hit hard by the influenza epidemic. Men had come home from the war to find their mothers and fathers gone, their families scattered. Letty didn't know whether things were as bad all over the country, but here the epidemic had taken a heavy toll. Almost every family had been hit. She was thankful that Grandpa and Patrick had been spared. Financially they were better off than most of their neighbors even though they had very little cash.

Jacob loved to barter and usually came out ahead. He traded two of his hogs to the grocer for flour, their monthly allotment of two pounds of sugar each, and coffee and tea. He and Letty butchered two hogs, smoked the meat, and rendered the lard. Two more were traded to the Watkins' for promised field work in the spring.

Two years ago when the eldest Pierce girl married and moved away and the school board couldn't find anyone else, Letty had taken the job of teaching the ten pupils at the rural school. This year the board had run out of money and couldn't pay her for the remaining months. She had continued to teach the remainder of the term because she felt an obligation to her students. She worried constantly about what the school board would do if they found out that she was an unwed mother.

Jacob had fussed about her before-dawn trips to the track. But they needed the coal to supplement their woodpile. He had slowed down considerably of late, and his weather-beaten face showed every one of his more than sixty years. After Grandma died, Letty hadn't been sure that Grandpa would ever come out of his depression. *Then Patrick was born.* Two days after she had given birth, a Watkins boy had come down with the measles and Mrs. Watkins, who had been taking care of Letty; returned home to her brood. Grandpa had to take over tending Letty and the baby which he did with surprising skill according to Doctor Hakes.

Grandpa had taken to Patrick like a duck takes to water. Now the two were thicker than thieves. Letty smiled thinking about it although her face was so cold she thought it would crack. In six weeks her son would be five years old. This last summer he had asked her if he had a papa like Jimmy Watkins. She had told Patrick his papa was dead and, as far as she was concerned, he was.

It was on her son's first birthday that hope for Mike's return had died in Letty's heart. She had waited and grieved long enough. It was time to put the past behind her. What had meant so much to her had evidently meant so little to Mike that he had not even written to tell her he had changed his mind. Therefore she never had the opportunity to tell him that he had a son. Patrick was hers and hers alone. She prayed to God he'd never have to know that he had been conceived out of wedlock or that his father had been nothing but a irresponsible *boy*.

Something else in Letty died that spring—her youth, her dreams of a love such as the one shared by her grandparents. Twice she had been deserted; first by her family, then by the man she loved. She vowed that never again would she lay her heart down to be trampled upon. She had Grandpa and her son. That Patrick resembled his father had become an unwanted reminder for Letty. The child had the same dark hair, the same inky black eyes, and at times the impish grin on his little face was amazingly like Mike's. Except for those fleeting moments when the resemblance startled her, all thoughts of Mike were banished from her mind. She had cut him out of her life completely.

As Letty carried a large chunk of coal to the

wagon, she saw the flicker of a large bonfire through the trees.

"Let's go. Harry. We don't know how many men are up there."

"I've got the old double barrel under the wagon seat. I'll take care of you and Irene."

"I know you will, but it's foolish to flirt with trouble."

Harry had not gone to war as had the two older Watkins boys because one of his forearms was noticeably shorter than the other. The handicap didn't seem to bother him in the least as far as work was concerned. Letty was sure, however, that he was sensitive about it. One of his brothers had been killed in the battle of Argonne; the other had stayed in the Navy when the war was over. During the last few years Letty and Harry had become good friends. He was a year younger than she was and desperately in love with sixteen-year-old Oleta Pierce, but unless he was lucky enough to find a job, there was no hope of his marrying her any time soon. He told Letty it wouldn't be fair to Oleta to marry her and take her home to a house already crowded with a family of eight.

When Harry climbed upon the wagon seat and turned the team toward home, Letty and Irene perched on the tailgate with their back to the wind Letty squinted up at the gray sky. The clouds were thickening, lowering. It could snow again by nightfall.

By the time half the coal was unloaded at the Fletcher farm, it was almost noon.

"Keep an eye peeled, Letty," Harry cautioned. "Pa's seen some rowdies round here lately. I don't think you'd be bothered in broad daylight, but ya can never tell."

"Does he think they're bootleggers?"

"Yeah. He thinks someone's got a still hidden around here and is supplyin' 'em. Anythin' to make a quick dollar."

"Grandpa heard in town that the boozers are drinking whatever they can get their hands on, even Bay Rum hair tonic and cooking extract."

"Pa says some folks make home-brew. The guzzlers drink denatured alcohol and get jake-leg 'n' pickled brains. Glad I ain't a drinking man. Well, we got to get goin'."

After Harry and Irene left for home, Letty headed for the house, then paused to wait as a big gander squeezed out from under the porch and came toward her.

"Hello, John Pershing. You'd better get back under the porch and take care of your ladies. We're in for some bad weather. If they stray off and get lost, you'll not have anyone to boss. Brigham Young'll not put up with you messing around his hens. That rooster will be all over you like a swarm of bees."

The gander honked, stretched out his long thick neck, and flapped his wings. With his head held high, his tail feathers pointing up, he eyed her arrogantly and marched on by.

"You're a silly goose, John Pershing," she called. "Did you know that?"

Patrick threw open the kitchen door the minute Letty stepped up onto the back porch. He gave her an assessing look, a concern on his serious little face.

"Are you awful cold, Mama?"

"Not really. What have you and Grandpa been doing?"

Letty came into the warm kitchen and closed the door. She looked pale and weary; her dark-brown hair was pulled back from her face and twisted in a knot on the back of her head. Some of it had come loose from the pins when she jerked off the knit cap. Lord, she was tired, but it wouldn't do to let Patrick know. He had become overprotective of late. Letty was sure it was due to the many stories he had heard about people dying of influenza. She wished she could do something to lift the worry from the child's mind.

After shrugging off her old sheepskin coat and hanging it on the peg beside the back door, she went up to her room to take off Grandpa's overalls and put on a heavy wool skirt.

"What in the world are you two doing?" she asked when she returned to the kitchen. Her button box was upended and buttons were scattered all over the table.

"Me and Grandpa's been makin' a snooterbuzz."

"A what?"

"Snooterbuzz. Show 'er, Grandpa."

"You show 'er," Jacob said from the padded

chair beside the fireplace. "You know how to do it. C'mere, I'll loop the string on your fingers."

The child stood between Jacob's spread legs and held up his hands while the string that ran through the eyes on a big black button was tied to make a loop, then hooked over his middle fingers.

"Whirl the button till it's twisted good, then pull back 'n' forth. The button'll spin."

Patrick tried several times but he didn't get the results he wanted.

"Damn thing!"

"Patrick! You know better than to swear." Letty shot a glance at her grandpa before he turned and hid his grin while pretending to kick at a log on the grate.

"Grandpa does," the child said stubbornly.

"Grandpa is not a little boy."

"You said damn once when you burned your finger on the flat-iron."

Letty threw up her hands. "So I did, but I shouldn't have."

"Looky, Mama. It's workin'." The button whirled as Patrick's hands went in and out. "Grandpa's goin' to make me one that'll sing."

"That's just dandy. You can play your snooterbuzz and I'll play the piano. Think you could keep time to 'Skip To M'Lou'?' "

"Yeah." Patrick shouted. "And 'John Henry' 'n' 'Little Brown Jug' 'n' 'Crawdad Hole.' "

"We'll give them all a try later on."

The clock on the mantel struck the noon hour.

Letty glanced at it, then looked about the familiar room. It was much the same as the first time she had seen it except that a cowhide lay on the floor in front of the fireplace instead of Grandma's braided rag rug. Grandpa had dropped a bucket of coals and burned a hole in the center. Letty loved this room and everything in it. She felt safe here.

"We need to get dinner over with. Doctor Hakes is coming this afternoon."

"He's bringin' *her*, ain't he?" Patrick stopped his hand and jerked the string off his fingers.

"Yes, he is. I told you last week that he was bringing her on Saturday so that she can go to school on Monday."

"I ain't goin' to like 'er. I won't play with her." Patrick's face was set in mule-stubborn lines.

"Well, now. Isn't that a highhanded attitude for you to take." Letty pushed the hair off her forehead with the back of her hand. "Maybe she won't like you. Ten-year-old girls don't often want to play with spoiled little boys."

"I am not little. I'm not spoiled. I'm almost five and Grandpa says I'm smart. So there!"

"Grandpa is going to get in a heap of trouble one of these days," Letty mumbled under her breath.

"Grandpa won't like her either. He likes me."

"Well, I should hope so. You're his great-grand-son. But that doesn't mean he can't like a poor little girl who doesn't have a mama. Now clear off the table so I can set it for dinner."

"I'm not poor even if I ain't got no papa. I got a mama and I got a grandpa." Patrick stood stiff as a poker, his expression mutinous.

Letty hurt because Patrick was hurting, but she didn't know what to do about it. Lately, he had become possessive and jealous of her and his grandpa. For his own good he needed to have to share their attention with another child.

When Doctor Hakes first told them that the county would pay them five dollars a month cash money if they would take in an orphan girl, Jacob had been dead set against it. Letty argued that it would be good for Patrick. He spent too much time with adults, especially in the winter. Doctor Hakes promised that if they would keep her until school was out, he would find another home for her or send her to an orphanage. The girl's mother and two smaller children had died of the influenza; her father was in jail for bootlegging. Jacob relented not because of the child, but because having her here would be good for Patrick.

Letty understood her grandfather's concern. Shortly after she had given birth to Patrick, he had told her that her mother was not his natural daughter, but one he and her grandma had taken in. Mable's unmarried mother had given birth to her and left her in Boley. After spending the first six years of her life in an orphanage, she had been brought by Doctor Whittier to the Fletchers. To them she had become as much a daughter as if she had been born to them. They lavished her with love and with all they could afford. She repaid

86

them by running away with Albert Pringle, an itinerant preacher, and ignoring them for the next twenty-five years except for one visit and three letters. Mable had not even replied to the letter telling of her foster mother's death.

At first Letty was terribly disappointed to learn that Grandma and Grandpa were not her *real* grandparents. She wanted so desperately to belong to them and have them belong to her. She had opened her heart to them as they had opened their home and their hearts to her. Gradually, she had come to realize that being blood kin was not all that important. Her own family had turned their backs on her when she needed them most. Now Grandpa needed her and Patrick as much as they needed him. They would stay with him for as long as he lived and try to make up for her mother's neglect.

Woodrow began to bark as they sat down at the table. The shaggy mongrel, who Letty had said could be meaner than a stepped-on snake when he wanted to be, or gentle as a lamb when it suited him, was named for President Wilson by Jacob who thought the man had about as much sense as a pup or he'd have kept the country out of the war.

"It's Doctor Hakes," Letty said, peering out the window.

"Hope Woodrow bites 'er," Patrick mumbled.

"What did, you say, young man?"

"Nothin'."

"Harumpt," Jacob snorted.

87

"Grandpa! You promised."

"A man's got to clear his throat, ain't he?" Jacob winked at Patrick.

"Yeah, Mama. A man's got to clear his throat."

"Hush up, you two, and behave." Letty opened the door. "Hello, Doctor. You're in time for dinner. Come in. It'll take me just a minute to set two more places at the table."

Doctor Hakes pushed a little girl into the kitchen ahead of him, closed the door, and took off his steam-fogged eye-glasses.

"I'll not take the time, Mrs. Graham. I've got a call to make and there's a storm brewing in the northwest. This is Helen Weaver."

"Hello, Helen," Letty said to the top of the child's head because her chin rested on the top button of her worn coat.

"Ma'am."

The doctor knelt beside the child. "Helen, I told you that Mrs. Graham was a nice lady and that you'd like it here. She's the school teacher too." Helen continued to look at the floor. Doctor Hakes looked helplessly up at Letty then back at the child. "Mrs. Graham plays the piano," he said hopefully, tilting Helen's face up so she had to look at him.

"She won't like it here." Patrick's voice boomed in the quiet room. Letty gave him a quelling look and he hung his head.

"It'll take a little while for us to get acquainted, Helen. Let me take your coat and cap."

The child's hair was so dirty that Letty immediately thought of lice. The dress under the coat was several sizes too small for her thin, small-boned body. Black stockings sagged over the tops of ankle-high shoes laced with broken string knotted in several places.

"I have to leave now, Helen." The child looked quickly up at the doctor. "I don't want to get caught out in a blizzard."

Helen's blue eyes quickly filled with tears and her lips trembled. Letty put her arms around the child. The poor little homeless waif was all alone and scared.

"You know, Helen. I've always wanted a little girl to teach to cook and sew. I know how to crochet a doll—"

"I don't want to know how to sew," Patrick shouted. "I don't want no old doll, either! I can plow 'n' fix the wagon 'n' hunt rabbits." He jumped up from the table and ran into the parlor.

Letty's eyes followed her son, then glanced back to find the young doctor staring at her. He raised his brows in question. Letty lifted her chin and shook her head.

"Don't worry, Doctor. Helen and I will get along just fine. Did you bring her things?"

"They're on the porch." Doctor Hakes went out. Letty followed and spoke as soon as the door was closed.

"Why is she so scared? Is it because this is a strange place?"

"The child has been in a number of strange places the last few months and some of them were not pleasant. That's why I brought her to you."

"What about her father? How long will he be in jail'?"

"Not long enough to suit me. He'll probably be out in a month. The County Health Board was all for sending her straight to the orphan's home. I talked Mrs. Knight and the sheriff into letting her spend some time with you. If anyone can help a troubled little girl, you can."

"Thank you. I'll do my best, but right now I've got my hands full with Patrick."

"He's jealous, isn't he? He's never had to share you with anyone."

"Patrick has just realized that he doesn't have a father. It's made him cling to me and his grandpa. He'll get over his jealousy after Helen has been here for awhile. You'd better get back to town, Doctor. I'm afraid we're in for a spring blizzard."

"I've known you for five years, Letty. Can't you bring yourself to call me Wallace?"

Letty looked into the thin, serious face of the dedicated doctor who had aged ten years since she first met him. He had been a true friend, one of the few she had made during the time she had been here.

"Why . . . well, I hadn't even thought about it." She reached for the small cardboard box that contained Helen's possessions.

"That's what I thought. Goodbye, Letty." He stepped off the porch and headed for his buggy.

"Goodbye . . . Wallace."

"Oh . . . ah, Letty—" The doctor turned back. "Sheriff Ledbetter thinks someone in the area is supplying whiskey to the bootleggers. A lot of strangers have come through town lately. Be careful. Leave school so you'll be home before dark."

"That's the second warning I've had today. Harry Watkins said the same thing. I'll be careful. And don't worry about Helen."

CHAPTER
6

A long olive-drab, double-breasted overcoat, the kind issued to soldiers during the war, flapped against the man's legs as he stepped off the train. The collar of his coat was turned up to meet the wide brim of the hat that sat low on his forehead. A growth of black whiskers emphasized his gaunt cheeks, burning black eyes, and grim mouth. Responding to his "keep your distance" attitude, Mike Dolan's fellow passengers shied away from him.

He swung a canvas bag over his shoulder, turned his back to the cold, damp wind, and headed for the row of buildings that made up the town. By the time he reached them, he was shivering in the wind and his long legs needed stiffening. Irritated that he was still weak, he plodded on, realizing that gulping cold air into his lungs was not doing them any good. Four months had pased since his release from the hospital in France and six months since he'd been wounded during the battle of the Argonne.

Although buffeted by the wind, he managed to climb the three steps to the boardwalk that fronted the stores. Piedmont wasn't much of a town: but since the train stopped here, there had to be a hotel or a rooming house where he could get in out of the cold. Damn! He'd forgotten how cold and damp spring could be on the Nebraska plains. He peered into the glass windows of the general store, pushed open the door, and went inside. The huge round Acme Giant heater stood in the middle of the room radiating heat. The stovepipe went straight up before making a sharp curve to run along the ceiling and out through the side of the building. Dropping the canvas bag on the floor, he held his stiff fingers out to the warmth of the stove. When his eyes became accustomed to the dimness, he scanned the room. Four men were staring at him.

"Howdy. Pretty damn cold out there." Mike pushed his hat back, showing the glint of a couple of gray strands among the blue-black clipped hairs at his temple.

One of the men spat tobacco juice in a can near his feet and grunted a reply. Another sat spraddle-legged on a bench, his stomach hanging between his thighs. Two more lolled on straight-backed chairs, feet stretched out to the stove, hands hidden in the bibs of overalls. One of them had a bottle of lemon extract stuck in his front pocket.

This must be dry territory, Mike thought, if all the alcohol they can get is cooking extract.

"Get off the train, did ya?" The fat man leaned sideways to pick up the can so that he could spit in it.

"Yeah. Is there a hotel or rooming house nearby?"

"Larson Hotel. Other side of the street."

A few long minutes of silence followed during which Mike noticed the man with the cooking extract in his pocket eyeing his boots and canvas bag. He waited for the question that was sure to come. When it did, it was straight to the point.

"In the war, was ya?"

"Yeah."

"Had a cousin what fought. He's got a coat like that. What division you in?"

"Seventy-seventh." Mike's mouth settled into a grim line after he said the word.

"His is the 45th. Name's Hugo Phillips. Know 'im?"

"No."

"Heard the 45th did most the fightin'. Did ya get in on any?"

"Some."

Mike opened his overcoat to allow the heat to warm his chest, hoping his short answers would discourage more questions. His eyes wandered over the usual array of store goods. There was everything here from dried apples to push plows.

"Hugo said you boys had ya a high old time over there with them Frenchy gals. Said they was hotter'n a firecracker. Ain't that what he said, Arlo?"

"Yeah 'n' said he got hisself a god-awful dose of clap off one of 'em." The fat man clasped his hands beneath his belly and laughed. "Haw! Haw! Haw! Said it warn't polite-like ta keep it all to hisself, so he passed it 'round ta all the gals. Haw! Haw! Haw!"

Fat bastard! Mike wondered when the man had last seen his pecker without looking at it in a mirror.

"Hugo said them French women was wild for a piece a doughboy ass."

"I heard that all a feller had to do was crook his finger 'n' one of 'em would lay down 'n' spread her legs. Goddamn! I ort ta a joined up 'n' got me some a that!"

An eerie quiet followed. A look of pure rage hardened Mike's mouth and turned his dark eyes as cold as the bottom of a well, but when he spoke, his voice was low-pitched and smooth.

"I agree wholeheartedly. You could have screwed the Germans to death, and the boys in Flanders' fields would be coming home."

Silence.

Four pairs of eyes stared at him. He stared back with a sneer of contempt twisting his mouth. Slowly, while looking each man in the eye, he pulled his overcoat together and buttoned it. He stood by the stove for another long, silent minute before he picked up his canvas bag and crossed the room to the counter. The clerk was scooping sugar from a barrel into paper sacks, weighing each one and marking the weight on the sack.

"I'll have some lemon drops."

The clerk looked at him, glanced at the men beside the stove, then removed the wooden lid from the big glass jar on the counter.

"Five cents a scoop is 'bout what it weighs out to be."

"Couple of scoops."

"Soldier boys get extra in my store," the clerk said, adding another scoop.

"Obliged to you."

Mike had developed a fondness for the candy since he'd had to stop smoking and was seldom without it. While the clerk sacked the lemon drops, he thought about asking the location of the Fletcher farm but changed his mind when he realized that four pairs of ears were straining to hear every word he said. *Bastards.* He'd like to plant his fist in that fat man's face and his foot in the rear of the cocky bumpkin.

"Ten cents."

Mike placed a dime on the counter, stuffed the sack in his pocket, and left the store.

"Touchy bastard, warn't he?" Oscar Phillips curled his lips in a sneer, took the cooking extract out of his pocket, and uncorked the bottle. He glanced at the clerk, saw him shake his head, and slammed the cork back in the bottle.

"Betcha he was one of them officers Hugo told about what sat on his ass behind the lines and let the foot soldiers do all the fightin'."

"That was one mean son-of-a-bitch." The fat man reached for the can and spit.

"His eyes was colder'n a well digger's ass."

"I never did trust a cold-eyed man that stared right at ya."

It was hard to believe that two days could make such a difference in the weather. The sun shone warm, a light wind blew out of the south, and the sky was blue above white fluffy clouds.

Spring had arrived.

Mike sat on the porch of the hotel with a good breakfast of eggs, sausage, and hot biscuits in his belly and read the Boley newspaper the boy had brought from the train station this morning. One particular headline caught his attention:

SISTER CORA PRINGLE TO HOLD REVIVAL MEETING

The highly successful evangelist known as "Sister Cora" will bring her special brand of gospel to Boley June 6 through June 30. The grandstand at the fairgrounds is being readied for the services that are expected to draw hundreds of her faithful followers from all over the state of Nebraska.

Sister Cora turned to full-time evangelism and healing four years ago. Since that time she has held meetings in such cities as Omaha, Denver and Kansas City and has become famous for conducting her revival service in a theatrical style.

The evangelist comes to Boley after four weeks in Oklahoma City where she claims to have "laid hands" on the lame and they walked and on the blind and they could see.

Frankly this reporter is skeptical about that but admits to the fact that the lady puts on a good show.

Mike muttered a curse word. *Sister Cora!* The bitch had made Letty's life miserable with her spying and tattling. Now she was "laying hands" on the sick and filling her pockets with money from poor stupid fools. Old man Pringle and Letty's weak-minded mother were in Oklahoma doing the same thing according to what he'd heard in Dunlap. It was a puzzle to him how his sweet Letty could have come from such a family of frauds. At times, Mike thought, the stupity of the masses was unbelievable.

Mike rolled up the newspaper and stuck it in his hip pocket. He had spent the last two days in the hotel room resting and reading, going out only for meals, while he waited for the rain to stop. Before going to breakfast, he had asked the desk clerk for the directions to the Fletcher farm and where he might rent a horse. There were a few automobiles in town, and he was sure he could hire one, but he wanted to be alone when he visited Letty's grave.

This morning he felt a sudden sense of urgency that he didn't understand. He had lived with his loss for five years, and this pilgrimage to the grave of his lost love wouldn't change anything. What he did hope to find out from Jacob Fletcher was why Letty had come out here in the first place. It was hard for him to believe that her father had sent her because her grandma was sick. It was more likely that Cora had found out Letty had been meeting him and that she had been removed from the "evil clutches" of a Catholic.

The horse Mike rented was a big buckskin with a long stride. He folded his overcoat, tied it behind the saddle, and mounted. He had learned to ride almost as soon as he had learned to walk. The buckskin reminded him of the horse he had bought with the money he earned at the dairy the year the Pringles moved to town. When he was young, his dream had been to live someplace where he could raise horses, a few cows, and farm a little. Now he had no dreams.

It was a hell of a note when a man had no dreams.

A mile out of town Mike came to the fork in the road and turned to the left as he had been instructed. He had passed several farms, some well-kept and prosperous, others run-down and dirt poor. Had soft, sweet Letty spent her last days in one of those places where the chickens wandered in and out of the house and the hogs lay panting under the porch?

On a long stretch of road that ran parallel to a narrow creek, his horse shied when a wild turkey flew out of the bushes.

"Whoa, boy. We scared that gobbler more than he scared us."

Mike spoke reassuringly to the horse, and when the animal calmed, turned him toward the creek and splashed into it. The buckskin thrust his nose into the clear running water. Minnows darted away from them; a carp rose from a muddy hole along the bank and slid beneath a rock. Below the ripples a bass shot like an arrow into the deep water. Beside the stream, beech, poplar, and water maple grew. The banks were thick with wild berry and honeysuckle bushes. In such a beautiful place it was hard for Mike to remember that not many miles away there was a town, and closer yet railroad tracks snaked through the land.

There was no place in the world like America. No place like Nebraska in the spring. For the first time since he had disembarked from the boat in New York Harbor, Mike felt as if he had come home.

When he was on the road once again, his mind went back to the directions he had received from the clerk.

"It's easy to find. The Fletcher farm is the third farm past the Lutheran church."

Mike rounded a bend in the road and saw the church ahead, its spire rising above the treetops. As he drew nearer, he could see an acre of gravestones to the side of the white building. An ornamental iron gate stood open between the cemetery and the churchyard.

Letty might be buried here.

It was the logical place, close to her grandparents' farm. An emotion like panic swept over him. Did he really want to find the place where his beloved, beautiful, trusting Letty lay sleeping in a cold, lonely grave?

Ashes to ashes, dust to dust—*Oh, God!*

He ached with emptiness.

With jaws clenched, he dismounted, tied the horse to the rail outside the churchyard, and went into the cemetery. At first glance his mind recorded a dozen or more new graves, the bare soil banked over them.

The quiet here was absolute. He stood for a moment, hat in hand, the slight breeze stirring his hair. After drawing a few shallow breaths, he reached into his pocket for the ribbon he planned to tie over Letty's grave. He looked at it, blinked the tears from his eyes, and moved slowly down through the rows of gravestones, searching for his sweetheart's name. McDermon, Herrick, Parker, then . . . Fletcher. He stopped and read the words on the gray granite marker:

LEONA GRAHAM FLETCHER
beloved wife of
Jacob Fletcher
Born June 10, 1850
Died March 4, 1914

This must be Letty's grandmother who had died a few weeks before Letty. Mike stood there for a long while. Mrs. Fletcher's grave was the only one in the plot. There was space, so why hadn't Letty been buried here? Had her father refused to allow her body be placed in a Lutheran cemetery? He ground his teeth in frustration as he did each time he thought of the man.

Mike walked the lanes in the cemetery and read the names on every gravestone. He was headed for the church to ask to see the church records when he saw the door open and a man come out. He came slowly across the yard toward the cemetery. Mike went to meet him. He was an old man with a kindly wrinkled face and a mane of thick white hair. His gnarled hand clutched the curved head of a cane as he walked carefully over the uneven ground.

"You seem to be searching for someone. I wonder if I may help you."

"I'd be obliged. I'm looking for the . . . grave of Letty Pringle." Mike had to battle with himself to get out the words. Aloud they seemed so . . . final.

"Pringle." The old man spread his legs and balanced himself by leaning with both hands on the cane. "I don't believe there's a Pringle in the cemetery. I've been through the church records many times and I don't recall the name."

"She died five years ago."

The old man shook his head. "The Reverend that was here at that time has passed on. So many have gone to their reward including the men of

God. I came here a year ago to hold the church together until a younger man could be found."

"She was Jacob Fletcher's granddaughter," Mike persisted. "Her grandmother is buried here."

"I know Jacob. His farm is down the road. He and his great-grandson come to church every Sunday. The boy's mother, Mrs. Graham, never comes with them. I asked Jacob about it, but he got huffy and told me it was none of my business." The old man laughed. "Jacob Fletcher is a good man, but cantankerous at times."

"Is this the only cemetery in the area?"

"The Methodists and the Catholics both have burial places. Piedmont has a public cemetery."

Mike looked back at the small neat burial plot. "I was sure she'd be here. Thank you for your trouble."

"I hope you find her."

Mike's jaws were clenched so tightly they hurt. Sweet Holy Mother of God. Why was he putting himself through this torture? It was worse than what he'd suffered in the trenches in France. He mounted his horse and turned down the road toward Jacob Fletcher's farm.

You fool, he told the voice in his head, once you stand beside her grave and the ribbon is tied to a bush again, you'll have nothing to hold onto. That's the reason for putting himself through this torture, the voice of logic shouted back. *I've got to find her, so I can let go, or I'll go out of my mind.*

Deep in thought, Mike let the horse meander on at its own speed. He passed a farm with a thick grove on the north side. A dog ran out, followed along behind, and barked. When he reached the end of the grove, the dog turned back.

Ahead and to the right, set back from the road, was a one room, unpainted schoolhouse with two privies behind it. A horse and light topless buggy stood in front. Two children sat in the buggy and a woman, after locking the schoolhouse door, climbed in beside them. Mike paid scant attention until he noticed that the buggy was coming down the lane and would reach the road at about the same time he was passing. Mike pulled up on the reins, stopped, politely tipped his hat, and waited for the buggy to pass.

In the few seconds it took for the woman to turn the horse onto the road ahead of him, his eyes flicked across her face. Then it was turned and he saw only a smooth cheek and a rope of thick auburn hair hanging down her back. She stung the horse's rump with the end of the reins and the animal took off in a fast trot.

Mike sat his horse, feeling as if he had been kicked in the stomach with a lead boot. The beginnings of panic fluttered in his chest and his skin felt as if it were being pricked by a thousand needles. Good God! Was he losing his mind? That woman had looked amazingly like Letty! Could she be a cousin, the other granddaughter the preacher back at the church spoke of? Mike kicked the horse into a run to catch up with the buggy before it turned into the next farm

He had to see her again.

The woman glanced over her shoulder. Mike saw only a blur of white face before she turned and lashed the horse with the whip, sending the light buggy careening down the narrow road.

What the hell! Why was she trying to outrun him? Why was she afraid?

Mike pulled up on the reins and slowed his horse to a walk. Before the buggy reached the lane leading to the next farmhouse, the woman looked back again. He had fallen farther and farther behind. Surely she didn't feel threatened now. Mike's heart was pumping in his chest.

Somehow he wasn't surprised when she turned in at the Fletcher farm. He debated with himself as to what to do and decided that he would go on by and wait until she had turned the horse over to her menfolk and gone into the house. Did these people see strangers as someone to fear? The preacher hadn't been afraid of him. Then it occurred to him that her man could be running a still, that she thought he was a lawman, or that they'd had trouble with whiskey runners.

After dawdling for a few minutes on the road, he turned back and headed for the neat homestead. Hell! He'd come this far to see Jacob Fletcher and he wasn't going to let a nervous little twit keep him from it even if she did look amazingly like Letty.

CHAPTER

7

Letty had had only a glimpse of the man on the horse. Her first impression was that he was big, very big, had dark whiskers on his cheeks and that he looked mean. Doctor Hakes and Harry had both told her to shy away from strangers and to get home before dark. Heck! It was still daylight. She had let school out early because she'd had only Helen and Patrick, and Patrick wasn't supposed to be in school until fall. Her four older students would be working in the fields from now on, and the other four were down with sore throats. Since the epidemic, parents kept their children home if they as much as sneezed.

She had been startled when the stranger seemed to be trying to catch up with them. Cautioning Patrick and Helen to hold on, she raced to reach the Watkins' lane. After the stranger slowed his horse to a walk, she knew she could reach home before he could overtake them. By golly-damn she was glad she'd decided to bring the buggy today, or she and the children would have been walking.

Jacob sat at the grindstone beside the open barn door sharpening a plow. Letty stopped the horse at the watering tank and jumped down. Patrick and Helen scrambled out on the other side.

"Whatcha doin', Grandpa?" Patrick ran to Jacob and leaned on his thigh.

'Suckin' eggs."

"Ah . . . you ain't. You're sharpenin' the plow."

"If'n yore so smart, why'd ya ask?"

" 'Cause."

"Good reason."

"Can I help?"

"Guess so. Pick up that can and dribble a little oil on the grindstone."

"What does that do?"

"Makes boys like you ask questions."

"Aw . . . Grandpa—"

Letty unhitched the horse. Helen stood by, holding their lunch buckets. During the weeks she had been with them, she had lost some of her shyness. Letty had made three dresses with matching bloomers for her and had cut down one of her grandmother's coats to fit her. Grandpa had repaired and polished her shoes and put in new laces. With her clean blond hair parted in the middle, braided, and tied with a blue ribbon to match her dress, she no longer looked like the little girl Doctor Hakes had brought to the farm that cold, blizzardy day. Even Patrick had softened toward her. Today Letty had found them giggling together as she set mouse traps before they left the schoolhouse.

Helen suddenly jerked on Letty's sleeve. "That man who followed us is coming."

Letty's gaze darted toward the lane leading to the barnyard.

"Patrick, you and Helen go in the house."

"Why?"

"Now!"

"Who is he?" Jacob asked after Helen had grabbed Patrick by the hand and pulled him up onto the back porch.

"I don't know, but he looks mean. I'll stay in the barn out of sight until we see what he wants. C'mon, Woodrow. I may have to use you in a surprise attack." The dog followed her into the barn where she led the horse into a stall. "Don't worry, Diamond," she said, stroking the white marking on the horse's face. "I'll feed you as soon as he leaves."

Knowing that Jacob kept a shotgun and shells on the ledge above the stall, Letty climbed up onto the stall rails and reached for two shells which she dropped into her pocket. Then she lifted down the heavy gun. When the gun was loaded, she went to stand just inside the barn door where she had a clear view of her grandfather sitting at the grindstone. The dog looked up at her, his tongue lolling. She patted his head.

Jacob stopped grinding when the rider came into the yard.

"Howdy," the man said. "Are you Jacob Fletcher?"

"Yup. Have been fer sixty years."

"I'd like to speak to you. Do you mind if I get down?"

"Help yore self."

Letty heard the creak of saddle leather, then the unmistakable sound of an angry gander's hissing and honking. She put her hand over her mouth and giggled. The farm protector, seeing that Woodrow was not on the job, was determined to do his.

John Pershing, his long neck stretched, his wings flapping, came from the chicken yard on the run, squawking all the way, and headed straight for the stranger who dared invade his territory. The man stood his ground suffering jabs of the gander's beak on his boots while he held onto the reins of his frightened horse who tried to kick at the feathered beast.

Jacob picked up a cob and threw It.

"Goddammit, John Pershing. Get the hell out a here. If ya wasn't so galdurned old, you'd been in the pot afore now. Ain't too late, ya blasted old fool!"

Having made his point, the gander marched away, his head high, his tail feathers twitching arrogantly.

"State yore business," Jacob said abruptly.

"I'm Mike Dolan, Mr. Fletcher. I'd like to talk to you about Letty Pringle."

The words knocked all the breath out of Letty. She felt as if her heart had jumped into her throat and was ready to explode. She cringed back against the stall rail, stiff with shock.

"What about 'er?"

"I knew her when she lived in Dunlap."

"Zat so?"

"I was hoping that"—Mike drew a deep hurtful breath—"you'd tell me if she was happy while she was here and where she's buried."

"Buried?" Jacob jerked erect, his bushy brows drawn together in a frown.

"Yes, sir. I stopped at the church cemetery, but she wasn't there."

" 'Course she warn't there. She ain't dead yet."

"I'm talking about Letty Pringle," Mike said, his voice raised, "She died here five years ago."

"Christamighty!" Jacob's voice, now, too, was raised. "Somebody should'a told her. She's still walkin' 'round."

With those few words, Jacob managed to knock the breath out of Mike. An icy tingle feathered over his skin. Taking deep, stabilizing breaths, he desperately fought lightheadedness.

"What . . . did you say?"

"Said somebody ort ta a told Letty she was dead."

"Letty's . . . alive?"

"She was when she went in the barn."

"My . . . God! In the . . . barn?"

"It's what I said." Jacob watched as the big man's face seemed to freeze and dark, tortured eyes turned toward the barn door. "Letty!" Jacob bellowed. "Get out here and tell this here feller ya ain't dead."

Coming out of her shock, Letty heard her grandfather's words. All the hurt and humiliation she had endured came flooding back; the years of waiting, giving birth to her baby alone, living the lie that her husband was coming for her, having to say that he had died, and accepting condolences from the neighbors with only Grandpa knowing the truth.

What possible reason could Mike have for coming here now? Patrick! He'd heard about Patrick and wanted to see his son. But how could he know she was pregnant when she left Dunlap? Cora knew! Cora had told him. Letty cringed and squeezed her eyes shut for an instant.

Letty's first thought was to escape out the back of the barn. She feared it would take more courage than she had to face the man who had deserted her. Then, knowing she had no choice, that it was something that had to be done, she lifted her chin to a high, proud angle and stepped out into the sunlight. Her face was set in harsh lines of resentment. Anger burned in her eyes. Although her hands were steady on the gun she held pointed at Mike's chest, her heart was racing like a runaway train.

An expression of disbelief flickered across Mike's hard features. He took an unconscious step toward her, his black eyes fixed on her face, his breathing ragged. He felt himself begin to shake—violently.

"Letty," he said as if strangling.

"Yes, Letty." Her voice was harsh and unusually loud.

"My God! Letty—"

"I'm surprised you remember my name."

"I can't believe it's . . . you—"

"It's me. I want you to leave. Get off our land." She made a jabbing motion with the shotgun.

"I thought . . . I thought, you were dead!"

"Stupid, trusting little fifteen-year-old Letty is not stupid anymore. Now go, or . . . I'll shoot you."

"For Gawdsake, girl. What's got into you?" Jacob came toward her and held out his hand for the gun. Letty side-stepped out of his reach.

"Stay out of it, Grandpa. Mister," she said as if talking to a complete stranger, "if you don't want this dog at your throat and your tail full of buckshot, get on that horse and ride out."

Mike continued to stare at her through a haze of confusion. It was Letty, but oh, such a different Letty than the one he remembered.

"You're different," he managed to say.

"Well, hell, why wouldn't I be?"

"You're older, harder."

"And not the dumb cluck I used to be." Her cold voice sent a chill down his back.

Woodrow, sensing the tension, growled. Short, straight hair stood up on his neck, his tail stood straight out. Mike didn't even notice that the dog was poised to spring at him. His mind, all his senses were fused to the woman he had dreamed of for so long.

"They told me you were dead."

"Ha! Convenient for you to think that," she sneered.

"Your father announced it in church."

"You . . . liar!"

"It's true. They had a memorial service and took up a collection to pay your grandfather for burying you."

"You're a cheap filthy liar!" Letty shouted.

"I'm not lying, dammit!"

"Mama! Mama!" Patrick broke loose from Helen and ran to his mother, "What's the matter? Why'er you yellin'?"

"Go to the house." When Patrick ignored the order, she said harshly, "Do as I tell you."

Helen tried to pull Patrick away. He dug in his heels and glared at Mike.

"You leave my mama alone!"

Mike glanced down at the sturdy little body braced for an attack. The boy's hands were knotted into fists, his expression stubborn. Once more the breath was knocked out of Mike. Letty had a child!

"Your son?" Mike's eyes went from the boy to Letty.

"My son. Patrick *Graham.*"

Mike looked back down at the dark head and scowling face looking up at him. "I wouldn't hurt your mama for anything in the world."

"Then why's she yelling? Why's she mad?"

"Go to the house, Patrick," Letty commanded. "Go, or I'll . . . spank you good!"

Patrick ran at Mike and kicked him on the shin. Then he backed up with his fists held in a fight position.

"Why'er you makin' my mama mean? You're a fart, a . . . poot! You're nasty old do-do!"

"Patrick! Stop it. Go to the house!" Lettys voice quivered. She was on the verge of tears.

Patrick began to cry.

Jacob cursed.

"Ain't right ta take it out on the boy, Letty. He's thinkin' to take up for you. The tad don't understand—"

"That makes two of us, Grandpa. Take Patrick to the house."

"Run on. son. Go with Helen. I'll look after your ma." He waited until the children were on the porch before he spoke. "You'd better get, Dolan. Letty's got her back up. She ain't goin' to settle it down till you're gone."

"When I came home from the logging camp they told me you were dead." Mike ignored Jacob and looked steadily at Letty. "Everyone in Dunlap thought you were dead. Your folks grieved—"

"Shut up. I don't want to hear your lies!"

"A letter edged in black came from your grandmother—"

"No! It came from me telling about Grandma."

"Your mother said—"

"No! They hated me, but they wouldn't do that. For the last time I'm telling you to get on that horse and go. I never want to see your lying face again." Shock and hurt were on her face, anger in her voice.

"Maybe you'll believe 'Sister Cora.' Your *sainted* sister is coming to Boley to con the poor suckers into fillinq the collection plate. Ask her if I'm lying."

Mike took the paper from his hip pocket and held it out to Letty. She refused to take it from his hand. He dropped it on the ground and stared at the woman who had been the sweetheart of his youth, the girl who had lived in his heart for so long. The expression on her face, contempt and hatred, cut him like a knife. It was killing him. He could hardly breathe for the tide of panic that rose in his throat—*he was losing the sweet dream.*

"I'll be back, Letty. I've grieved for you for five years. I'm not giving up because you think I deserted you."

"I'm no longer Letty Pringle. I'm Letty Graham, now. Does that tell you anything?"

His gaze caught hers. "You're married?"

"Of course, and I have a son. Do you think I've been waiting all this time for you?"

"Where's your husband?"

"Working. Working for one of the neighbors." The lie came easily, so easily Letty was proud of it. "You'd better not be here when he gets back. He'll tear you apart."

"I doubt that. Maybe I'll just wait. I'd like to meet him." A burst of anger exploded in Letty's head and her finger tightened on the gun trigger.

"My husband will want nothing to do with you. Stay away from him and stay away from this farm!" She held her head high, her hard brown eyes refusing to look away from his.

Mike mounted his horse and sat looking down at her. *Sweetheart! You're breaking my goddamn heart.*

"I'll be back, so if you're going to shoot, go ahead." He turned the animal toward the lane and kicked him into a gallop.

After Mike left, the starch went out of Letty's backbone and her face crumbled. Tears rolled down her cheeks. She hurried into the barn. Jacob followed, put his hand on her shoulder, and turned her to him.

"There, there, girl—"

"Oh, Grandpa! What'll I do?"

"He's the one ya was waitin' fer, ain't he? He's Patrick's daddy."

"Yes, but he didn't come back for me like he said—"

"Maybe it's like he told ya. Could be yore pa, that righteous son-of-a-bitch, put out the word ya was dead."

"I'll never believe that Mama would let him have a memorial service, take up a collection— No! He's using it as an excuse. Somehow he's heard about Patrick and is curious to see him. Why did he have to come back now? Patrick thinks his father is dead."

"I kinda believe the boy," Jacob said thoughtfully. "Reckon he ain't no *boy* no more. He's a man to be reckoned with, Letty. Been in the war. 'Twas a army coat tied behind his saddle."

"I don't care where he's been. He wasn't here when I needed him. And that's all there is to it. I hate him, Grandpa. I waited and I waited. I almost grieved myself to death over him. Now, I've blocked him out of my heart. Patrick is mine, all mine. I'll not share him with a floater who suddenly remembers me."

"They're as alike as two peas in a pod."

"Oh, lord! Do you think he knows?"

"He was lookin' pretty hard at the little bugger. If he don't know, he's wonderin'. He'll be back, girl. He don't 'pear to be a man what backs off once he's got the bit between his teeth."

"He will this time," Letty said firmly and lifted the hem of her skirt to wipe her eyes. "Me and Patrick are doin' just fine, Grandpa, thanks to you."

"I ain't goin' ta always be here, Letty."

"Don't talk like that! Don't you dare say that!" Letty turned her striken face away. "I hurt Patrick by yelling at him. I've got to go apologize. Tonight I'll make his favorite custard. Then after supper we'll play 'Chopsticks' on the piano. You'll just have to cover your ears, Grandpa."

"Well, now, that's all fine and good, but sooner or later ya got ta let the boy know his daddy ain't dead."

"But . . . oh, lordy, people will know we weren't married. What'll that do to Patrick?"

"There's worser things. He'd have a daddy case somethin' happens ta me 'n' you."

"We don't have to worry about Mama and Papa taking him," Letty said with a bitter twist to her mouth.

"I ain't so sure. The boy'd have a farm."

"Oh, Lordy, mercy me! I hadn't thought of that."

Mike automatically guided the horse back toward the road. A panorama of thoughts swirled in his

116

mind. Shocked and numbed by what had just occurred, he felt a little sick. It was as if he had suddenly stepped through a hole and into another life.
The shock of seeing Letty after thinking her dead
all these years was making him a little crazy. He
wanted to shout, race the horse, throw his hat in
the air.

He wanted to . . . cry.

She had waited and he hadn't come. It was no
wonder that she was bitter. Goddamn that family
of hers! He would never forget the look on her
face when he told her about the memorial service.
She couldn't face the fact her family had cut her
off so completely. My God! What had she done
to make them do such a thing?

She was thinner. He was sure he could encircle
her waist with his hands. Clear white skin was
drawn tightly across the delicate bones of her face.
Dear Lord! The Letty of his dreams was no longer
a girl. She was a woman with a child.

The thought that sprouted in the back of his
mind as he looked at the boy blossomed into full
bloom.

Holy Mother of God! *The boy was his!*

He had a son! The little fellow was the spitting
image of his younger brother at that age. Beneath
the willows beside the creek, he had made Letty
pregnant, and her folks had thrown her out, dis-
owned her. My God! He could see it now. She
had every right to be bitter.

Had she married to give his son a name? The
thought of her belonging to another man was like

a knife in his gut. Letty was his, had always been his. He had a sudden overpowering desire to see the man Letty had married. He turned into the next farm and rode to within a dozen yards of a woman who was taking clothes from a line. She was a large woman with pendulous breasts hanging down over the belt of her apron.

"Howdy, ma'am," Mike called before he urged his horse closer.

"Howdy to you."

I'm looking for Mr. Graham. Is he working here today?"

"Graham?" The woman's round, weather-worn face took on a puzzled frown. "I don't know a Mr. Graham."

"Do you know Letty Graham?"

"Sakes alive. Of course I do. Everyone knows Letty."

"It's her husband I'm looking for."

"Letty lives right down the road, but he ain't there. He died right after Patrick was born."

"Is that right? I'm sorry to hear it."

"He was working in the logging camps in Montana. Letty was staying with the Fletchers until he could come for her. First her grandma died, then her husband. Poor little thing almost grieved herself to death."

"It must have been hard on her." Mike was doing his best to keep his features arranged soberly.

"She took hold and managed. It's hard on a woman now days without a man. Letty Graham's a mighty fine woman. Did you know Mr. Graham?"

"I . . . ah . . . met him in the logging camp."

"Why don't you ride on down and talk to Letty. She's helpin' out at the school, but she ort to be home by now. Folks round here think a heap of her. Hardest workin' little woman you ever did see. Don't know what Jacob would do without her."

"I'll do that, ma'am. Thank you kindly for the information." Mike tipped his hat again, wheeled the horse, and left before his face broke into a smile.

Letty had claimed marriage in order to keep her reputation unsullied and Patrick, his son, from being labeled a bastard.

His sweetheart was alive: she was free. She was the mother of his son.

She would be his again.

He laughed aloud: the sound startled him: he hadn't heard his own laughter for a very long time.

CHAPTER
8

"It's already past your bedtime."

"Aw . . . Ma. Play 'Crawdad Hole' again."

"We've already played it three times. It's Helen's turn to choose."

"I don't know any songs."

"Don't ya even know 'Jesus Loves Me'?" Patrick asked with a disgusted look on his small face.

Helen hung her head.

"Maybe Helen's family didn't like to sing." Letty pulled the child up close to her.

"Her maw couldn't play the piano, that's why." Patrick squeezed up close to Letty's other side.

"She could so," Helen blurted. "But . . . but we didn't have no piano."

"We'll teach Helen a song, Patrick. How about 'Get Along Home, Cindy'? It's easy to learn."

"I wish I was an apple hangin' on a tree,
every time my Cindy passed, she'd take a bite
   of me.
Get along home, Cindy, Cindy, get along home
   I say,
Get along home, Cindy, Cindy, I'll marry you
   someday."

Letty played and sang several verses of the song. Helen stumbled along on the words in a voice so low only Letty could hear, By the time Letty ended with a ripple of extra notes and a few loud chords, the little girl had a huge smile on her face.

"I like it, Mrs. Graham. Can that be my song?"

"I don't see why not." Letty put her arm around Helen and hugged her close.

"I don't want it to be my song. I ain't never goin' to sing it," Patrick grumbled. "It's ugly,"

Helen's smile faded. Letty wanted to shake her son but chose to ignore his remark.

120

"That's all for tonight. Goodness, my fingers are tired." Letty lowered the cover over the keys and straightened the fringed scarf on the piano. "I'll go upstairs and light the lamp for you, Helen. Patrick, start getting ready for bed. Your night-shirt is on the chair in the kitchen."

Since Helen had come to stay, Patrick slept on a cot in Jacob's room and Helen on his cot in Letty's bedroom. When she had time, Letty intended to fix up the room across from hers for Helen. But first she would have to find a place to put the things that had been stored in there for years.

Grandpa was sitting at the kitchen table reading the newspaper Mike had thrown on the ground at Letty's feet.

"Mighty good readin' in this here paper."

"Say good night to Grandpa, Helen. Patrick, I'll be right down." Letty opened the door to the stairway leading to the upper rooms.

"Night, Grandpa."

"He ain't your grandpa," Patrick said belligerently.

"Patrick!" Letty's patience with her son was becoming thin.

"Night, Helen. Come give Grandpa a hug." Jacob held an arm out to the little girl.

Letty stood in shocked silence. It was the first overture he had made to the child. Helen's eyes went to Patrick as Letty gently urged her forward. She went to the old man and shyly kissed him on the cheek. He hugged her just as he hugged Pat-

121

rick each night. When he released her, she scampered up the stairs.

Patrick's lower lip puffed out in a pout and his eyes filled with tears. Letty's heart ached for him. She didn't know what to do to ease his pain. Did he fear he was being pushed out to make room for Helen? *Oh, sweetheart, you are my life. No one could ever be as dear to me as you are.*

"Why doesn't Patrick like me?" Helen asked as Letty settled her into bed.

"It isn't that he doesn't *like* you, honey. I think he's afraid that if Grandpa and I love you, we won't love him."

"Can't you love both of us?"

"Of course. Patrick doesn't understand that yet."

"Mama loved me. She said she d-did."

"I'm sure she did. You're such a sweet little girl."

"I m-miss my m-mama."

"I know how lost and lonely you feel, but you've got your papa, and me, and Doctor Hakes, and Grandpa."

"I wish she hadn't d-died. I wish it'd been Papa!"

"Honey, it's hard to understand why things happen," Letty said when she got over her surprise. This was the first time Helen had mentioned her father.

"Can I stay here, Mrs. Graham?"

"For the time being. I don't know for how long—"

"Will I have to go with Papa when he gets out of jail?"

"Honey, I'm not sure—"

"I don't want to go with him. I want to stay h-here—" Helen sniffed back the tears. "Will Doctor Hakes make me go?"

"We can talk to him about it." Letty saw real fear in Helen's eyes. *The child was afraid of her father!* Letty made a mental note to find out more about Cecil Weaver.

"You don't have a little girl—" Helen said hopefully.

"No, But if I did, I'd want her to be just like you." She kissed Helen's cheek and smoothed her hair. "Don't worry about it now, If you want to stay, I'll do everything I can to keep you here. Go to sleep. I'll be up in a little while."

Letty lingered in the dark outside the bedroom door. The child was scared, she thought, just as she had been when she came here almost six years ago. Memories came flooding back—memories of being cast out by her family, being alone, pregnant, and so hoping she wouldn't be turned away.

For the past few hours Letty had involved herself in a frenzy of activity in order to keep from thinking about the afternoon visitor who had brought back the pain she had tried so hard to put behind her. She dreaded having to go to bed. There would be nothing then to keep thoughts of him at bay.

Letty stopped at the bottom of the stairs, Patrick, in his nightshirt, was curled up in Jacob's lap

"—But she's a girl."

"What's wrong with bein' a girl? Yore mama's one. Think how you'd feel without a mama or a grandpa and your papa was in jail. Poor little girl is plain scared is what she is. She ain't got nobody 'n' yore actin' mean to 'er."

"I ain't mean."

"I reckon ya don't think so, but it comes 'cross that way. Us men have got to take up for the womenfolk. I just betcha Helen'd take up for you, if it come to a fight."

"I ain't needin' no girl to fight for me."

"By golly, if'n a bunch a rowdies jumped on me, I'd take all the help I could get."

"I'll take care of you and Mama, Grandpa. I'd'a whupped that mean man today. I kicked him a good'n."

"Wal, now, I thought ya was a bit hasty on that. Why do ya say he was mean?"

"He made Mama mad."

"She was just surprised to see him. He knew her a long time ago. I kinda liked him."

"Ya did? But he was—"

"Patrick, time for bed," Letty interrupted.

"Night, Grandpa."

"G'night, ya little muttonhead." Jacob dug his fingers into Patrick's ribs and tickled him playfully.

Patrick giggled. When he could get his breath, he gasped, "Stop! Stop! I gotta pee-pee, Grandpa—"

Jacob spread his knees and let Patrick's feet

124

slide to the floor. "Then get off my lap, ya rascal."

"I love you, Grandpa . . . you and Mama—"

Letty's eyes misted over when Patrick threw his arms around Jacob's neck. She had been determined that her son would say the words that she had never heard from her own mother or her father. Grandpa and Grandma Fletcher had said them often to each other. At first Letty had been embarrassed, then later, she cherished the words when Grandma said to her. Unwelcomed memories flooded her mind. Mike had said he loved her, said it many times. How foolish of her to believe him. He had probably whispered those words into the ears of many women during the past five years.

After putting Patrick to bed, Letty came to the kitchen and sank wearily into a chair, her elbows on the table, her chin in her hands. She caught Jacob looking at her, dropped her hands, and sat up straight. He moved the newspaper across the table.

"Cora is comin' to Boley to hold a revival meetin'. Tells all about it here in the paper. She's called *Sister* Cora now. Claims to heal the sick. Hogwash! Anybody that'd be taken in by that shim-sham ain't got nothing but hot air between the ears."

Jacob pushed the newspaper across the table to Letty. With her elbows on the table, her hands cupping her cheeks, she read the article.

"She won't come here, Grandpa. She doesn't

want anything to do with a *fallen* woman. She's always hated me. It was probably the happiest day of her life when . . . when Papa ran me off." Letty sighed deeply. "I try not to think of her and Papa."

Jacob lit his pipe and puffed on it thoughtfully. Letty scanned the newspaper then tossed it aside. It was a treat to have one, and ordinarily she would have read every word, but tonight her mind was in such a turmoil she couldn't concentrate.

"Ya been skitterin' round like a ant on a hot stove. Yore goin' to have to simmer down and face a few facts."

Letty met Jacob's stare head-on. He knew what had been eating at her all evening. Suddenly, she wished that she were Patrick's age so that she could curl up in his lap.

"What am I going to do?"

"What do you want to do?"

"Nothing. I want things to go on as they are. I don't need *him!*"

"Guess that's up to you."

"He deserted me, Grandpa. Lord, I hate to think of what would have happened to me if not for you and Grandma."

"Could be he ain't lyin'. Could be he was hoodwinked into thinkin'—"

"Fiddlesticks! You don't believe that cock-and-bull story about . . . about him thinking I was dead?"

"Well, seems likely he thought that, considerin'—"

"He lied. Pure and simple."

"Harumpt!" Jacob snorted. "I'd not put nothin' past Albert Pringle if'n there was a dollar in it somewhere."

Letty shook her head in vigorous denial.

"Mama was never able to stand up to Papa, but she wouldn't have let him declare me dead, hold a service, and . . . and take up a collection. I know she wouldn't." Letty drew in a long ragged breath and continued to shake her head.

"She let the bastard throw you out, didn't she?"

"Yes, but it all happened so fast. She could have thought about it later and . . . worried about me."

"Face up to it, girl. Yore maw has the brains of a flea. I knew it from the start, but yore grandma wanted to believe different. Right from the start Mable thought the sun rose and set in Pringle 'cause he could get up at church, shoot off his mouth, and get folks stirred up."

"She'd have balked at declaring me dead: I know she would," Letty said stubbornly.

Jacob lifted his shoulders in resignation. In the silence that followed, the clock on the mantel chimed nine times.

"While Mike was at the logging camp, he changed his mind about me," Letty said as if talking to herself. "He didn't want to be tied down. When he went back to Dunlap and found me gone, he . . . he just took off to sow his wild oats. Somewhere he must have met up with Cora. She'd have taken delight in telling him that I was a fallen woman and Papa had run me off."

"Only saw the girl once, She was spiteful even then."

"Mike knew that he was the only boy I'd ever been alone with, and that if I was pregnant the baby had to be his. He got curious to see it." Letty recited the words as if they had been playing over and over in her head.

"He didn't have to tell a tale just to see Patrick. He could'a just rode up and said, 'I want to see the boy.' "

Letty's head jerked up. "If he wanted to claim his son, he did. He'd need an excuse for deserting me. Someday he'd have to explain his absence to Patrick."

"Funny thin'. I didn't read 'im as a man who'd feel he had to explain hisself."

"I know him, Grandpa. He's as proud as a game rooster. The Dolans were poor but proud. He'll try to get Patrick away from m-me." The last word was a sob.

"Bullfoot! What'd he do with him while he's roamin' around sowing his wild oats?"

"Maybe he has a wife somewhere . . . and kids. Catholics have lots of kids. He isn't getting Patrick! If he comes back, I'll fill his hide with buckshot."

"He'll be back."

"I don't want him near my son! If he comes while we're at school, tell him that I don't want to see him ever again. If he's got any decency, he'll not come where he isn't wanted."

Jacob noted the flush on her cheeks. Letty was

the daughter he never had. She and Patrick were his life. He dreaded to think of the two of them here alone after he was gone. Every sidewinder in the county would be after her. She was a handsome woman, and she'd have the farm. She needed a good man. He had given careful scrutiny to every single man in the area, and there wasn't a one that hadn't come up short.

He'd seen Mike Dolan's bleak expression when he asked about Letty's grave. When she came out of the barn, the shock on his face had to be real. When the shock wore off his black eyes shone with pure joy, then confusion, hurt, anger. Jacob would bet the farm Mike Dolan had sincerely believed that Letty was dead.

"Oscar Phillips came by today."

"What did he want?" Letty asked absently.

"Offered to come help with the plantin'. Said he'd like to trade off work with us."

"I hope you told him no. All I need is *him* hanging around. We don't need anyone, Grandpa. We've been doing all right by ourselves."

"He's got his eye on ya."

"He can just get it off me! I'm closing school on Friday. Saturday we can start the field work."

"Been thinkin' about gettin' some sheep and turnin' 'em loose in the clearin' north of the woods," Jacob said after several minutes of silence.

"Sheep? You said that was full of nightshade and it would kill the sheep."

"If'n we had that nightshade cleared out, sheep

129

would clean up the pasture slicker'n a whistle, and we could put cows on it next year. I'm thinkin' I'll find somebody to clear it out."

"Uh-huh."

Jacob arched a quizzical eyebrow. Letty's mind was far from sheep and nightshade. He got to his feet and went to the door. Before he opened it, he glanced back at the girl at the table. Her eyes were focused on the dish towel hanging above the cookstove. Jacob shook his head and headed for the privy. He had some serious thinking to do.

The clock on the mantel downstairs struck three times. In another two and one-half hours she had to start the new day. Letty turned over onto her back and stared at the ceiling. The night had been so long, so black, so quiet. Even with her eyes squeezed tightly shut, she couldn't get the image of the big dark man with the hard face out of her mind. It was difficult to think of him as Mike, the boy she had loved so desperately. *Her* Mike had had a quick smile. This grim-faced Mike was as hard as nails. So much had happened to her because of her love for the sweet and gentle boy he had been. Letty flipped over and covered her ear with her arm in an atrempt to keep her father's harsh, angry voice from booming in her head.

Slut! Whore! You're a bitch in heat is what you are. Get your hot little twat out of my house. Damn you, and damn your bastard!

Her father's words had made ugly the act that had been so beautitul; the act that had given her

Patrick. But at the time she had wrapped Mike's love about her like a cloak and refused to believe that what they had done out of wedlock had been so wrong. For two long, lonely years she had clung to that belief. Finally she'd had to face the truth. With a heart full of love she had given herself to a boy who had taken what she had offered. She had been exactly what her father had said she was—a cheap floozie who had allowed herself to be used to satisfy a boy's lust. Now she had to suffer the humiliation, the hurt of knowing her son was a bastard.

Damn you, Mike Dolan. Why did you come back?

On Thursday, after the children left school, Letty lingered to talk to Oleta Pierce who had come to walk home with her sister.

"We're havin' a singin' Saturday night," Oleta said. "Harry's bringin' his guitar 'n' Papa'll play his fiddle. Can you come?"

"I don't think so. We plan to go into town on Saturday. Monday we start the planting."

"I wish you'd come. Papa says if there's enough folks for a set we can build a fire in the yard and square-dance."

"We'll see. If Grandpa isn't too tired, we may come for awhile."

"Goody. Well, bye. I told Ma I'd hurry back." Oleta went to the door, looked out, then shrank back against the wall. "Oh, shoot! Oscar Phillips is out there."

"What's he doin' here?" Letty peeked out.

Oscar was stepping down from his horse. Helen, Patrick, and Celia Pierce stopped chasing each other around the schoolyard to watch him.

"I don't like that man," Oleta whispered.

"Has he been bothering you?"

"He's always tryin' to talk to me. He cornered me last week when I went to town for the mail and tried to hire me to come take care of his kids. Papa 'bout had a fit."

"I don't blame your papa." Letty put her shawl around her shoulders and picked up the lunch buckets. "Let's go out before he comes in."

"I'm scared he'll follow me home."

"He'll not follow you. I'll see to it," Letty said testily. Then just before they went out the door, "You and Celia scoot on home."

"Now ain't this a treat?" Oscar's voice was loud and overly friendly. "I just never thought I was 'bout to meet up with two of the prettiest women in the county." His eyes roamed over them and his mouth stretched into a wide smile.

"School's out, Mr. Phillips. We're on our way home," Letty said briskly. "Helen, you and Patrick come get your hats so I can lock the door."

"I aim to talk to ya 'bout my Alice comin' to school."

"Alice isn't old enough to come to school. It seems to me I've told you that before."

"She's old as your boy 'n' she's smart."

"I bring Patrick with me while Grandpa is in the field. The school superintendent knows it."

"Well, I ain't meanin' to cause no trouble over

it." He made no attempt to conceal the admiration in his eyes as they roamed down over the front of the white shirtwaist tucked snugly into the band of Letty's dark walking skirt. His gaze lingered on the six inches of exposed leg and on the "common sense" black oxfords she wore before his obvious stare traveled up to the straw hat anchored to her auburn hair with a large hatpin.

In an attempt to look his best, Oscar had parted his hair in the middle and slicked it down on each side with a curl plastered to his temples. His white shirt had been scorched across the front with a too-hot flatiron. He wore a bow tie and new black shoes.

"Bye, Letty." Oleta grabbed her sister's hand and headed for the road.

"See you soon."

"Ya be careful, Oleta. Hear?" Oscar called. "It ain't as safe as it was for a pretty gal to be walkin' the roads."

"Why is that?" Letty asked, to draw his attention from Oleta and Celia who had started to run toward the woods where they would take the path home.

"Hoboes walkin' the tracks lookin' fer a handout. Mrs. Fowler saw a stranger on a big buckskin horse nosin' around. Nobody seems to know who he is, but ever' body knows he's lookin' for somethin'. White lighnin', more'n likely."

"If that's what he's looking for, I hope he finds it. Helen, will you shut the privy door? Someone left it open. We don't need a skunk in there." Letty poked some loose hair up under her hat and took Patrick's hand." Hurry now. We've got to be getting home."

"I'll walk with you, Letty. That stranger was even snoopin' round in the graveyard at the church. No tellin' what kind a feller he is. My girl ain't got to put up with that sort. No-siree—"

"Oh?" Letty turned, her eyes were made brilliant by her anger. *"Your girl?* And who is that, Mr. Phillips?"

"Ah, Letty, hon. You know I've had my eye on ya ever since you came ridin' into Claypool in Doc Whittier's touring car."

"That was almost six years ago. Your *wife* was pregnant with Billy. You're a low-down polecat, Oscar Phillips." Letty glanced toward the woods. In another few minutes Oleta and Celia would be within sight of home.

Oscar laughed. "Hold on, hon. A ball and chain don't keep a man from lookin'."

Letty lifted her straight dark brows and stabbed him with her gaze. "You're . . . despicable!"

"Des . . . what?" His laugh grated on her nerves. "What's that you're callin' me, hon?"

"I'm calling you an ignorant, worthless, sorry excuse for a man with the morals of a tomcat. Now get this straight. Stay away from me and stay away from Oleta Pierce."

"Or . . . what?" He was still smiling. He reached out and grabbed her arm.

"Turn loose my arm!"

"Ya don't mean that. Yore a hotblooded woman.

I heared tell all redheaded women was hot-blooded,"

"If you don't want to find yourself in a peck of trouble, let go of me and leave."

"Who's goin' to make me?" He moved his grinning face closer to hers.

"Me! Let go of my mama!"

Patrick jerked his hand from Letty's and charged like an enraged bantam rooster. With all the force of his sturdy little body, he butted Oscar in the groin with his head. Oscar let out a cry of pain and shoved the child so hard that he fell to the ground. With a cry, Letty dropped the lunch buckets and knelt down beside her son.

Oscar was bent over, holding his privates and cursing.

"I hurt 'im, didn't I, Mama?"

"Yes, honey, you did. Are you all right?"

"I'll hurt him again.'

Loud gasping screams drew Letty around to look at Helen. The little girl was almost hysterical with fear. She stood with her eyes squeezed tightly shut and her hands clasped over her ears.

"Helen! Oh, honey—" Letty hurried to the child and grasped her shoulders. "What in the world?" she exclaimed as Helen continued to scream.

"Shut that kid up!" Oscar yelled.

Helen's screams turned to sobs and Letty turned on him. "See what you've done. You've scared her to death."

"I hate you! You old . . . poot!" Patrick shouted.

"Patrick!" Letty grabbed her son's hand to keep him from running at Oscar again.

"He's nasty. He made Helen cry."

"Goddamned brats!" Oscar cursed and yanked the horse's reins from the bush where he had tied them. He mounted the horse and sat looking down at Patrick with loathing on his face. "You little bastard!" he snarled, kicking the horse cruelly and causing the animal to sidestep before taking off in a run.

Letty's face mirrored her anguish. She felt tears burn her eyes. She turned abruptly away from the children and stared across the field toward home, listening to the clip-clop of Oscar's horse as he went down the lane toward the road.

You little bastard! Three words. They echoed in her brain, brought a pain to her heart, but she couldn't let the children see how they had knocked the wind out of her. She smiled brightly and hugged them to her.

"We showed him, didn't we? Come on. We've got to be getting home. Didn't I promise bread pudding for supper?"

CHAPTER
9

It had taken Mike a full day to get over the shock of finding Letty alive, seeing her, and learning they had a son. It took another couple of days to get his head out of the clouds so that he could

136

make plans. Knowing that she lived filled him with unspeakable joy. They had made a baby beneath the willows and she had given birth to his child. A part of him had been with her all this time. A whole new world had opened to Mike since he had ridden into the Fletcher farmyard.

Letty was angry and hurt that he had not come for her as he had promised. He understood the torment she had endured. But he would never give her up now that he'd found her. Never! He would devote the rest of his life making it up to her. Somehow he would win back her love, and together they would raise Patrick. Partrick, his son. Dear Lord, he had missed out on seeing her body swell with his baby, missed out on five years of his son's life.

But first things first. He had to make his plans known to Jacob Fletcher. He owed the man for taking care of his family. *And they were his.* It was a debt far greater then he would ever be able to repay.

It was almost noon when Mike reached the Fletcher farm. The horse he rode up to the watering tank was his. Everything he owned was either in the canvas bag that hung from the saddlehorn or tied behind the saddle. The shaggy brown dog came out of the shed and ran halfheartedly at him when he stepped down from the horse.

"Hello, boy. Remember me?" Mike held out his hand. Woodrow tilted his head and looked at him, tongue lolling. "Come on. I think we can be friends after we get to know each other." He reached into his pocket for a lemon drop, squatted down, and held it out on the flat of his hand. Woodrow eyed the candy, then inched forward and took it with only his cold nose touching Mike's palm. Mike patted his head. "Good boy."

With loud squawking and hissing, John Pershing suddenly shot out from under the back porch as if propelled by a slingshot. With his long neck stretched out in front of him, he came at Mike on the run.

"Good Lord! You again." Mike looked around for a cob to throw, but it wasn't needed. Woodrow, fearing he would have to share the unexpected treat, snarled and lunged at the gander. Startled by his barnyard companion turning on him, John Pershing flew for a yard or two, then ran a few steps, and flew again until he was a safe distance away. "Thanks, friend." Mike gave the dog another lemon drop and patted his head.

Jacob came out and stood on the porch. "Tie your horse up there by the windmill and come on in," he invited.

Surprised and pleased by the invitation, Mike tied the horse, patted the dog's head again, and went to the house.

"I figured you'd be back," Jacob said.

"I'd have come if I'd had to crawl on my belly through a den of rattlesnakes."

Mike followed Jacob into the kitchen. He stopped just inside the door, his hat in his hand. This was where Letty had been all the time he had thought she was lost to him forever. The flesh on his face tingled. He could feel her presence in the pores of his skin and in the air he drew into his lungs. His dark eyes roamed the room. Her apron and a shawl hung on the peg beside the door. Against the far wall a Sears Roebuck treadle sewing machine was covered with a lace-edged scarf. A stick horse made from a broomstick stood in a corner. Beneath it was a small-size baseball bat, an iron locomotive, and a set of building blocks. A lamp hung over the table which was covered with a flowered oilcloth. In the center was a spoon holder and silver-based cruet set. The checked curtains at the windows were freshly ironed.

A feeling of deep peace settled over him.

Chopping potatoes in a skillet with the open end of a shiny tin can, Jacob watched the big dark man. Mike stood as still as a stone, gazing first at Patrick's toys in the corner, then at Letty's apron on the peg.

"You et yet?"

"No—"

"Hang your hat. There's plenty."

"I don't want to put you to any trouble."

"No trouble. We feed our hired hands."

"You have a hired hand?"

"Not yet. Yore lookin' fer a job, ain't ya?"

"Do you have one?"

"Plantin' time, ain't it? I got a mess of night-shade that needs to be cleared out. Windmill needs greasin' 'n' I'm gettin' too damned old to climb it. Board and five a month. Take it or leave it."

"I'll take it." A wave of elation flooded Mike, causing his heart to pump like a piston.

"Wash up then. Ain't nothin' better than fried taters to my way a thinkin'. Letty boils plenty for supper so I can fry 'em for dinner." Jacob attacked the potatoes in the skillet with the improvised chopper.

Mike hung his hat on the knob of a chair, went to the tin-lined sink, and pumped cold well water into the washbasin.

"Warm it from the teakettle if ya want." Jacob took a bowl from the cupboard and filled it with the potatoes. "We ain't fancy here as some; ain't as righteous either. I got me a batch of apricot brandy workin' in that crock behind the stove. You got anythin' to say about that?"

A smile spread over Mike's face, changing it magically. "Not a word. How long has it been working?"

" 'Bout a week. Another week or two 'on' I'll siphon and bottle it."

"My Pa makes home-brew."

"That right? Have any trouble with the law?"

"Not as long as he makes it for his own use."

"Maybe we can make us up a batch . . . if you're here long enough. Get the coffee." Jacob set a crock of butter and a jar of jam on the table.

"What's Letty going to say about me being here?" Mike poured coffee and set the pot on a trivet within reach.

"Oh, she'll fly off the handle 'on' rave for a spell, but she'll simmer down after a while. Sit and cut me off a hunk of that bread."

Mike looked unflinchingly into Jacob's faded eyes.

"Before I accept your grub, I want you to know that I didn't get Letty pregnant and abandon her."

"I ain't the one ya need to be tellin'."

"It's important to me to square things with you. I'll be forever in your debt for taking her in."

"Letty ain't a taker. She gived as much as she got." Jacob spooned sugar into his coffee cup.

"Her folks put out the word she was dead. It's the truth, so help me God. I'm not sure I'll be able to keep my hands off Pringle if I come face to face with him."

"Be all right with me. I ain't never had no use for the bastard."

"He cheated me out of five years with my wife and child." Mike's knife and fork were gripped in his hands, the ends resting on each side of his plate. He leaned forward. "Letty is my life. I've loved her since I was seventeen. I was eighteen when I went off to earn money so I could marry her."

'I believe ya. Pass the butter."

"The boy is mine. I want to be with her and my son."

"Don't be gettn' any notions about a claim on that boy if she don't want to give it to you."

"When I went back to Dunlap and heard that she was dead, I almost went out of my mind."

"Pringle's a hardhearted flimflammer. Never had no use for him."

"Letty was scared to death of him."

"She grieved somethin' awful when ya didn't come."

"I've been through hell. During the war I didn't give a damn if I lived or died. I told myself that I'd come here and find her grave, that maybe I could let her go, and get on with my life."

"She says she don't want ya. Patrick thinks his daddy is dead."

"I've got to change her mind."

"I'll give ya a chance, but if she don't want ya, ya'll hightail it outta here in front of my shotgun if need be." With his fork poised over his plate, Jacob's wrinkled face took on a look of grim determination. "I think a heap of that girl. I'm a old man. My life is about over. But before I go I aim to see her and the boy settled with a good man to take care of them. Know this now, if ya hurt that girl, I'll put a bullet right between yore eyes."

"Fair enough."

"Know anything about farmin'?"

"Some."

"I can't abide a shiftless farmer. I keep things tidied up."

"I can see that. You better know now that I've not had much farming experience."

"I ain't worryin' none 'bout that. I got plenty."

"All I've got to offer Letty and my boy are

these two hands, a strong back, and a heart full of love."

"Reckon it's more'n what most women get." Jacob said and took a gulp of hot coffee.

"How long do I have to change her mind about me?"

"Middle of summer."

"Fair enough," Mike said again. "First thing I'll do is grease the windmill."

Patrick, kicking clods of dirt with the toes of his shoes, walked a few paces ahead of Letty and Helen. He could hardly wait to get home to tell his grandpa how he had made Mr. Phillips let go of his mother's arm. Grandpa had said that men had to take care of their women and he had. He wished he was bigger. He would have bloodied old Mr. Phillips's nose. A puzzled frown spread over his small freckled face. Mr. Phillips had said, "you bastard." What was that? If he was one he wanted to know what it was. The way Mr. Phillips said it, it couldn't be anything good. Grandpa would know. Grandpa knew everything.

When they reached the farm, Patrick ran ahead. He shouted a greeting to Jacob, who had pulled his grain drill planter out of the shed and was working on it.

"Hey, Grandpa—" Patrick skidded to a halt when he saw the mechanical sowing machine that was a source of wonderment to him. "Whatcha got that out for?"

"Goin' to sow some wheat."

"When?"

"Soon as I get the field dragged." Jacob poked the long neck of the oil can into a working joint on the planter.

"Can I ride on it?"

"Nope."

"Ah, shoot! You said I could when I was bigger, and I'm bigger."

"I said when yore big enough to handle the mules."

"That'll be a long time."

"Not if ya get busy and grow some."

"I'm growin' as fast as I can." Patrick stuck his lip out in a pout. Then he remembered his exciting news. "Guess what, Grandpa? I butted Mr. Phillips like a billy goat. He let go of Mama . . . pushed me down and yelled something awful."

"What's this? What did you say?" Patrick was pleased to see that at least he had his grandfather's full attention.

"Mr. Phillips comed to the school. Mama didn't like what he said. He grabbed her arm and wouldn't let go. She yelled and I butted him with my head . . . and . . . hurt his dinger. He pushed me down and . . . Helen was awful scared. She cried loud, and Mr. Phillips called her a brat and . . . here's Mama . . . she'll tell you." Patrick was so excited his words were running together. "Tell Grandpa what I did, Mama."

Jacob set the oil can on a barrel, wiped his hands on a rag, and waited.

"What's all this?" he asked as Letty and Helen approached. "Did Oscar bother you again?"

"Not much. He got a little excited, but Patrick took care of it." Letty smiled and winked at Jacob. "You'd have been proud of him, Grandpa. He took up for me and Helen."

"I run at him like this," Patrick said, putting action with his words. He lowered his head and charged. "I butted him with my head and hurt him. He pushed me down and yelled at Mama to make Helen shut up. I was goin' to punch him agood'n—"

"Shhh . . . honey," Letty put her hand on Patrick's head. "Here comes Mr. Phillips. Coming to apologize, no doubt," she added drily.

"He was mean. He said to me, 'you bastard.' That's what he said. What's that, Grandpa? Is it somethin' nasty?"

To have her son called that dreadful name was almost more than Letty could bear. Pain knifed through her like a fistful of needles. Suddenly, there was an emptiness inside her so deep that she could almost feel wind blowing through her. She gripped her hands together and blinked back the tears.

Oscar dismounted and came to within a few feet of her, his hat in his hand.

"I'm plumb sorry, Letty girl. I'm jist as sorry as I can be for what I done. I jist don't know what come over me."

Letty stood stiff and silent.

"Get off my place, Phillips. Don't come back." Jacob spoke with quiet authority.

"Ah, Jacob. You don't mean that. We been neighbors for ten years. Letty jist got a little excited and scared the boy. The little feller was right in what he done and—" Oscar's eyes moved past Letty. "What's *he* doin' here?" he snapped rudely.

Letty turned to see a man climbing down from the windmill. His back was to her but there was no mistaking that broad back and blue-black hair. *He* had come back! Her throat froze up solid. He had the grease bucket in his hand. *He had been working on the windmill!* She watched him climb down the ladder, his hair blowing in the wind. Casually, he set the bucket down and strode toward them, his dark eyes never leaving Oscar's face. He walked up to him and, quick as the flick of a whip, his hand, black with grease, shot out and grabbed a fistful of Oscar's white shirt.

"What? W-what? W-who?" Oscar stammered. "You're that feller what come in the store."

"I'm the one that's goin' to stomp you into the ground if you ever touch Mrs. Graham again. And this"—Mike hit him so hard that his feet left the ground before he sprawled spread-eagled on his back—"is for what you did to the boy. Get on that horse and ride out. But first apologize to the lady for what you called her son."

A sudden paralysis kept Letty rooted to the spot where she stood. Helen's arms were around her waist, her face buried between her breasts. The two seemed to be holding each other up.

Patrick gazed open-mouthed at Oscar Phillips lying on the ground, blood gushing from his nose.

Oscar got to his knees, then slowly to his feet and stood on not quite steady legs. His forearm was pressed against his mouth trying to stop the flow of blood from his nose.

"Sorry, Letty," he muttered. It took several attempts before he was mounted on the horse. He looked down at Mike. "You'll be sorry fer this."

"Mr. Fletcher told you to get off his land and not to come back. I'll be here if you do." With his fist on his sides, Mike watched Oscar ride out of the barnyard.

"Jimminy Christmas!" Patrick shouted. "Did ya see the blood, Grandpa? Did ya see old Mr. Phillips fly up before he fell down? Bam! Bam! Boom! Boom!" He danced around flaying the air with his fist in a make-believe fight.

Mike turned around and met Letty's eyes head-on. She was the Letty of his dreams only much more beautiful. Her hair was the same rich auburn, her mouth wide and sweet, her eyes like empty stars. The desolate look on her face cut him to the bone. *Sweetheart, you're tearing the heart right out of me.*

Letty stared at him. Their eyes held in a silent war. She was afraid that if she moved the frustration and anger inside her would explode. Vibrantly aware of the big, dark man towering over her, she finally spoke.

"Grandpa? What's he doing here?"

"Greasin' the windmill."

She broke her gaze with Mike and turned to look at Jacob. "And that's all?" she asked as if she couldn't get enough air into her lungs.

"No. There's a heap a thin's what needs to be done. Dammit, Letty, ya know we been needin' help—"

"I've closed school. Helen can watch Patrick and I can help—"

"There be thin's ya can't do, girl."

"Such as?"

"Greasin' the windmill," Jacob said with exasperation in his voice.

"I've greased the windmill."

"—And scared hell outta me thinkin' ya'd fall."

"I don't want him here. I told you that."

"I know ya did. It'll be fer jist a little while."

"Pay him off, Grandpa, and make him leave."

"No." His face turned stubborn. "I hired him on . . . fer a spell."

"For how long?"

"Middle of summer."

Swallowing her rising panic, she said, "Why are you doing this to me, Grandpa?"

Jacob walked over to the barrel and picked up the oil can. Mike watched the emotions play across the old man's face and saw that he was visibly shaken. This confrontation was hard on him. For a moment Mike feared he would relent and tell him to leave. Then the muscles clamped above his jawline and determination claimed his expression.

"Ain't it time to fix supper, Letty?"

"What just happened is not a good example for Patrick," Letty said with equal determination in a voice not quite even. "I don't want *my* son copying *him.*"

"Phillips got what was comin' to him. If I was younger I'd a done it myself."

"I can handle Oscar Phillips. I've been doing it for years."

"Now you have someone to do it for you," Mike said, wiping the grease from his hands and wishing there were some way he could ease the old man's anguish.

Letty knew that Mike was looking at her, but she didn't move. Shocked and hurt that Jacob would go against her wishes, Letty lowered her burning eyes to the ground. She swallowed the assortment of lumps in her throat and stared so hard at the toes of her shoes that the very effort dried out her eyes. She spoke to Jacob without looking up.

"You'll not change your mind?"

"Dolan'll not bother you none. When the work's done, he'll go."

"All right." She took Helen's hand and started for the house. "C'mon, Patrick." Patrick ignored the summons. He was rubbing the toe of his shoe in the blood on the ground. "Patrick!" she called again. He dropped to his knees to examine the dark, wet spot in the dirt. Stiff-limbed, Letty stalked to the house without him.

Mike watched her until she disappeared into the house.

"Ready to give it up?" Jacob asked.

"Not on your life." Mike hurt. He hadn't realized she hated his presence quite so much, or that her cold treatment would leave him feeling quite so forlorn. "How long's this bird been bothering her?"

"He's been tryin' to court her since his woman died. He brings a cottontail once in a while 'n' offers to get me some white lightnin'. Got hisself all duded up today to come callin'. Haw! Haw! Haw!" Jacob's mirthless laugh was more of a dry cackle. "You shore played hob with that white shirt of his'n."

"Hey, Mister—"

Mike looked down at the boy tugging on his pant leg. An extremely powertul emotion grabbed and shook him. This spirited little black-haired, black-eyed tyke was his son. His and Letty's. He wanted to pick him up and hug him to his chest. He wanted to feel his little arms about his neck. *I'm your daddy, son.* The words pounded in his mind. He couldn't say them. Not yet. It was too soon. The boy didn't know him, he thought with a pang of regret. He squatted down on his haunches.

"Call me Mike."

"Mama won't let me call grown-up people by their first names."

"Well in that case, call me Dolan. That's my last name."

"I know my ABC's."

"You do? Aren't you a mite young to know so much?"

"I'm five." Patrick held up one hand, fingers spread.

"Not yet you ain't," Jacob said. "You won't be five till Sunday."

"You got a birthday Sunday? Well, what'a you know."

"Grandpa says I . . . jump the gun when I say I'm five before my birthday."

"Guess your grandpa's right."

"Grandpa said I shouldn't'a kicked ya and now I wish I hadn't'a."

"I understand how it was. You were protecting your mama. It's what you should have done. No hard feelings on my part."

"She don't like ya no more'n she likes Mr. Phillips."

"We'll have to see what we can do about that."

"You like her?"

"Yes, I do. I knew her a long time ago."

"Before me?"

"Before you. We'll have to work together to make things easier for her. Is it a deal?"

"Yeah."

"Want to shake on it?"

Patrick's small hand was swallowed in Mike's. It was an effort for Mike not to squeeze it too tight. He didn't want to let it go. His heart was pumping like an oil well in his chest. *I'm your daddy, son.* How he longed to say the words. He silently got to his feet before the boy could see that his eyes had misted. His watery gaze passed over Jacob's face. The old man was silently watching Patrick's reaction to him.

"You stayin' for supper, Dolan?" Patrick asked. "You sure did hit old man Phillips a good'n. Boom! Boom! You bloodied his nose. Wait'll I tell Jimmy Watkins. I bet you can beat up on anybody, Dolan."

"Wait a minute, Patrick." Mike put his hand on the boy's shoulder and hunkered down again. "I hit Mr. Phillips because he grabbed your mother and because he pushed you down. I thought he needed a lesson. A man who goes around beating up on people because he's bigger and stronger is a bully."

"Ya didn't hit him because he called me a b-bastard?"

Mike glanced quickly at Jacob. The old man had his head bent over the machine he was working on. He wouldn't get any help from him.

"That was part of the reason I hit him."

"Is that a nasty word like shit and pee?"

"I guess so . . . but in a different way."

"How?"

"How?" Mike scratched his head and searched his mind for a way out of the fix he found himself in. "It'll take some explaining. Tell you what. One of these days we'll get us a fishing pole, go down to the river, and fish. I'll tell you all about it then."

"Go fishin'? Grandpa! Hear that? Me'n Dolan is goin' fishin'."

"Not until the planting's done," Mike said quickly. "A farmer has to get his work done before

152

he can go fishing. And . . . your mother will have to give her permission."

"Mama'll let me. She likes to fish. I'll go tell her."

"Don't bother her now. Who feeds the chickens and gathers the eggs?"

"Mama does. Sometimes Helen helps."

"I'd do it, but that goose makes a run for me every time I go near the chicken house."

Patrick grinned. "He won't if I'm with you."

"I'm glad to hear that. How about showing me what's to be done and you and I will take over the chore."

CHAPTER
10

Letty stood in the middle of the kitchen, seeing nothing and hearing only the drumming of her heart against her ribs. She felt as if the breath had been sucked out of her. Absorbed in her own thoughts, she at first failed to hear Helen calling to her.

"Mrs. Graham? Mrs. Graham, is he . . . is he a bad man?"

Letty jerked her attention to the little girl peering up at her and holding onto her skirt with both hands. An odd, frightened expression darkened her blue eyes.

"What did you say?"

"Is he a bad man?"

"Mr. Phillips?"

"No. That other man."

"He isn't a *bad* man. We don't have to be *afraid* of him."

"But . . . but you were s-scared." You wanted Grandpa to send him away."

"I was angry, not scared. I knew him a long time ago when . . . when he was a boy."

"He won't hit us? Or do bad things?"

"Heavens no! Oh, honey, you don't have to be afraid of every man you meet."

"I don't like Mr. Phillips."

"He wanted me to stay and listen to what he had to say. Patrick just *thought* he was going to hurt me. I wasn't afraid of him."

"I don't like him," Helen repeated softly, her head bowed.

"To tell you the truth, I don't either." Letty lifted Helen's chin to look into the child's face. "Honey, did your daddy hurt you and your mother?" she asked softly.

Helen pulled her chin from Letty's fingers and looked down at the floor. "Sometimes," she whispered.

"Oh, honey." Letty hugged the girl to her and dropped a kiss on the top of her head. "That's over and it's best not to think about it. No one will hit you here. You don't have to be afraid."

"I wish . . . I wish I could stay with you . . . forever."

"So do I, honey. I'll talk to Doctor Hake and

see what we can do." Letty held the girl away from her and smoothed the blond hair out of her face. "Go upstairs and change out of your school dress. We've got the chickens to feed and the milking to do."

Helen left the room and Letty went to the window. Mike was hunkered down talking to Patrick. Oh, Lord! What was he telling him? Patrick began to jump up and down. Mike stood and put his hand on Patrick's shoulder. They went toward the chicken house, Patrick chattering and looking up at the tall man.

Letty moved away from the window and put her hands to her cheeks. Never had she imagined that Mike would come back to claim his son, and never had she dreamed that Grandpa would go against her wishes and allow him the opportunity to win Patrick away from her. She was caught in a trap of circumstances. It was unbearable. Day after day she would be seeing the man who had used her, gotten her with child, and deserted her. The pain of that realization and knowing her beloved grandpa had betrayed her almost sent her to her knees.

"Mrs. Graham?" Helen's voice seemed to come from far away. "What's the matter, Mrs. Graham?"

Letty took her hands from her face. The child had that scared look on her face again. Letty forced a smile.

"Nothing is wrong. I felt a little dizzy for a minute. Must be the excitement. The milk pail

155

is there on the shelf. While you rinse it out, I'll change into my work clothes."

Letty escaped to the room upstairs. She must be careful not to distress Helen. The child had seemed quite happy of late. Patrick was so excited over the attention he was getting from Mike, he wouldn't notice if she dropped dead, she thought with a pang of self-pity. Oh, Lord. She needed to get away so that she could think. They would go to town Saturday. If Grandpa would rather have Mike's help than hers, he could have it. While in town she would see Doctor Hakes and ask him about Helen's father. Now that she thought of it, she would spend the day away from the farm and visit the Pierces and the Watkins' on the way home from town. It would be a way of keeping herself and Patrick out of Mike's company for an entire day.

Determined to show Mike just how little his presence meant to her, Letty slipped into a faded, patched, brown dress. black cotton stockings and her old high-laced shoes, and tied an apron made from a flour sack around her waist. After she had twisted her hair into an unbecoming knot, she fastened it to the back of her head, looked into the mirror, and grimaced at her reflection.

Helen, with the milk pail in her hand, was waiting for her beside the kitchen door. Letty threw a shawl about her shoulders, and they went out onto the back porch. Thank heavens, Mike was not in sight. But neither was Patrick. Jacob was still working on his planter. Letty, with Helen's hand clasped in hers, walked past him and into the cow lot where Betsy usually waited. She was not there. They went on into the barn and found her in her stall chewing contentedly on the feed that had been put in her feedbox.

"Mama! Me 'on' Dolan got the eggs 'on' fed the chickens," Patrick screeched, startling Letty and sending her heart racing. He jumped off a stall rail, fell to his knees, and bounced to his feet. "Me 'ca 'on' Dolan's goin' to fix the chicken house. Dolan said a fox could get in and eat the chickens. We're goin' fishin' when the plantin's done. Dolan said I'd have to ask you if I can go. I told him you like to fish too."

Mike came slowly down the aisle behind Patrick. Letty could feel his eyes on her face. His tall body seemed to fill the space all around her, and there was no way out. She moved to escape out the side door, but Helen blocked the way.

"Patrick and I gathered the eggs and fed the chickens Letty." Mike held out the egg basket with one hand and took the pail from her hand with the other. "I'll milk. I'm sure I haven't forgotten how. Ma made all of us kids take a turn."

Letty snatched the basket from his hand. Without a word or a look in his direction, she pushed Helen ahead of her out the door. For the briefest moment he was the boy she had known so long ago. She wouldn't let herself soften toward him. She wouldn't. Seeking the safety of the house, Letty walked so fast that Helen had to run to keep up with her. When they passed Jacob, she failed to see the concerned look on his lined face when he saw the look of despair on hers.

Letty hung her shawl on the peg beside the door and went to the stove. Patrick's voice rang in her ears. "Me and Dolan. Me and Dolan." Damn you, Mike Dolan. You're not wasting any time. Letty opened the door to the firebox, shoved in several pieces of wood, and closed it with unnecessary force. The loud clang cleared her head momentarily.

"Helen, would you like to practice the scales on the piano while I get supper going?" Letty asked in as pleasant a tone as she could manage.

"Oh, yes. I'll be careful—"

"I know you will. Take off the scarf and fold back the keyboard cover. Keep both hands on the keys, use all your fingers, and play softly. I'll light the lamp in a little while."

Grateful to be out from under the child's watchful eyes, Letty let her shoulders slump and the corners of her mouth sag. Damn! Damn! Damn! How in God's name was she going to endure reliving the agony of a past she had thought was behind her? Being rejected by her parents, fearing her father's wrath, taking the night trip to Huxley to catch the train, facing her grandparents and telling them she was an unwed mother were things she tried not to think about. The man responsible for all that misery was here trying to win her son away from her.

Oh, Grandpa, I thought you loved me as much as I love you.

With her mind in a turmoil, her thoughts racing from one thing to another, Letty put potatoes on to boil, stirred up a batch of baking-powder biscuits, fried side pork, and made pan gravy. When it came time to set the table, she took four plates from the shelf, hesitated, then took another one. She had come to the conclusion that she was not going to lie down and be walked on. This was *her* home. Patrick was *her* son. She'd not step aside and let Mike Dolan waltz in and take over.

The back door opened. Jacob came in and silently went to the washbench. Letty ignored him, bent over the skillet on the stove, and vigorously stirred the gravy. Patrick's loud and excited voice came from the porch seconds before the door opened again.

"I played first base, Dolan. I catch better'n Jimmy. Harry played too. He's Jimmy's big brother. Mama played, but Grandpa didn't. Mama couldn't run fast, but I could, couldn't I, Mama?"

"Yes. Wash up," Letty answered briskly without turning around. "Supper is about ready."

"Is this where you want the milk?" Mike had come up beside her and set the full pail on the work counter.

It took all of Letty's will power not to cringe. He was taller than she remembered and broader. She grunted a reply, turned, and reached into the cupboard for a jar of pickled beets. Her heart was beating so hard that she was sure he could hear it. She wanted to rant and rave and cry at the injustice of having to endure his presence. Instead, she had to put on a good face for the children's sake.

Mike looked down at Letty. Her lips were slightly parted as she breathed through her mouth. The flush on her cheeks and the vein that throbbed in her neck were signs of her agitation. She was smaller than he remembered, or was it that he had grown taller? When he had last held her in his arms, her head had fit nicely on his shoulder. Now if he cradled her against his chest, his chin would rest on the top of her head. So much time had gone by. They had both changed. Only one thing had remained the same. He still loved her with all his heart.

"Dolan, looky," Patrick demanded. "Grandpa made me a box so I can reach the wash dish. It was higher when I was little. He cut it off 'cause I'm growin'. Grandpa said I'd be big 'cause he measured me when I was two 'on' I'd be twice that tall when I was growed up. Will I be tall as Dolan, Grandpa?"

"More'n likely."

Mike watched Letty's jerky movements. She was hurting. She was afraid that he would tell Patrick that he was his daddy. *Oh, sweetheart, someday we'll tell him together.*

"Hear that, Mama. Grandpa said I'll be tall as Dolan."

While pumping water into the washbasin Mike heard the thump of the dish Letty slammed down on the table. He waited until Patrick washed and was drying his hands before he picked up the soap bar and lathered his own. After he washed, he reached into his back pocket for a small comb and ran it through his unruly hair.

"Can I sit by Dolan? Mama, can I?" Patrick persisted when she didn't answer him.

"You'll sit in your regular place," Letty snapped and went to the door to call Helen. "Come to supper, Helen."

Mike stood back and waited. It was an effort to keep his eyes off Letty. Somehow he knew that she had deliberately tried to make herself as unattractive as possible. She set the biscuits on the table, pulled out her chair, and sat down.

"Have a chair, Dolan." Jacob indicated the place between him and Helen before he took his place at the head of the table.

"It ain't fair. She got to sit by Dolan," Patrick said and stuck his tongue out at Helen who sat across from him.

"Another stunt like that, young man, and you'll leave the table," Letty said harshly. "Bow your head while Grandpa says Grace."

Patrick was blissfully unaware of the tension during the meal. It would have been eaten in total silence if not for his continual line of chatter. He was enjoying himself immensely. The grown-ups interrupted only to ask for food to be passed. His mother had said "hush up" one time when he started to tell once again how he had butted Mr. Phillips with his head.

Mike listened to the child with only half an ear.

161

In his thoughts he was talking to Letty. *This is the first time we have sat down to a meal together, sweetheart. The biscuits are as good as I've ever eaten. I wish you would look at me without that tight, angry look on your face.* Mike's eyes swung around to Jacob and saw that the old man was eating with a hearty appetite. This was a tough old bird, Mike thought. He had made up his mind that he was doing the right thing by giving him time with Patrick and Letty.

Milk from Patrick's glass spread across the table.

"For heaven's sake!" Letty exclaimed as she grabbed a dish towel to stop the flow before it ran onto the floor. "That's what happens when you don't pay attention to what you're doing. Now be quiet and eat because you are going to sit there until you clean your plate."

Patrick looked at his mother with tear-filled eyes. He was embarrassed because he had spilled the milk, and embarrassed more at being scolded in front of his new friend. His lips quivered. Letty knew she had been unduly harsh, but to sympathize now would invite more tears. She carried the milk-soaked cloth to the tin sink and refilled the glass.

The meal ended in silence. Jacob went to the big chair and Mike took the rocker. Letty and Helen cleared the table while Patrick sullenly worked at the food on his plate. Letty wanted to hug her son, to tell him she knew he hadn't turned over the milk intentionally. She couldn't bring herself to do it with Mike's watchful eyes on her.

"Smoke?" Jacob asked.

"No. Had to give it up."

"Had to?"

"Doc thought it best after I got a whiff of German gas."

"I heard tell it'd tear up a man's lungs."

"It does that all right. Throat and eyes, too. Some blisters the skin. I was lucky."

"How long were ya there?" Jacob had an inquiring mind and liked to visit.

"From start to finish."

"Harumpt! Influenza got about as many as the war."

"That's what I hear. I lost a little sister while I was away. The epidemic is still going strong in some areas."

Hearing snatches of the conversation, Letty wondered if the little girl who had died was the dark-eyed child whose eyes had shone with mischief that day at the post office when she told her that her goat had eaten Mrs. McGregor's hat.

"Most folks around here lost someone," Jacob said and struck a sulphur match to light his pipe.

"Mama, I cleaned my plate—"

"Bring it here." Letty dried her hands on her apron as Patrick got carefully off the stool and carried his plate and empty milk glass to the sink. Before he could dart away, she hugged him and whispered to the top of his head. "Mama's sorry she was cross. We'll finish *Robinson Crusoe* tonight and maybe even start *Treasure island.*"

"Goody! Can Dolan hear? Grandpa likes to hear the stories."

"I think we should read in the other room and let Grandpa visit."

"Ah . . . Mama," Patrick whined. "I want to sit with Dolan."

"Then sit with him," Letty snapped, unable to hide her irritation. "I'll read to Helen."

In a rage of jealousy but not realizing what it was that was eating at her, Letty finished the cleanup, talking calmly to Helen.

"Careful, honey, the water from the teakettle is hot. I'll take the plates out of the rinse water and stack them here on the counter. It'll be easier for you to reach them. When that towel gets wet, hang it up and get another."

Letty kept her eyes away from the men at the end of the room, but she couldn't turn off her ears. Jacob was telling Mike that Sheriff Ledbetter had stopped by several times this spring looking for whiskey runners.

"Somebody's furnishin' them bootleggers with whiskey from Canada," Jacob added.

"They'll have to legalize alcohol sometimes," Mike said. "The gangsters in Omaha and Chicago are getting rich. The government might as well be getting the tax money.

The conversation moved around to airplanes, and Mike told Jacob about the German flying ace they called the Red Baron, and that he had heard

164

airplanes were carrying mail between New York and Chicago.

"Who's a thought them flyin' things would come to any use?" Jacob shook his head in disbelief. "Things is movin' fast. Some folks in town is thinkin' they got ta have a automobile and a telephone. We ain't got neither 'n' I don't see it's hurtin' us none."

Letty worked until there was nothing else to be done. She dreaded having to turn around, and wished that there were some way she could get to the parlor without having to face Mike and her grandfather. She hung the wet dish towels on the line above the cookstove and removed her wet apron.

She headed for the parlor, and in spite of her resolve not to do so, her eyes flicked to the end of the room and hung there. Patrick was curled up in Mike's lap, his head resting on his shoulder. Shiny black curls tumbled on the foreheads of both father and son. Two pairs of intense black eyes gazed at her from beneath straight dark brows. Realization struck Letty with the force of a kick in the stomach. A poof of air came out of her mouth. *Patrick was the spitting image of Mike.* Anyone with half an eye would see the resemblance.

Mike's dark eyes soberly searched her face. Letty felt a stir of something in the marrow of her bones and in that small corner of her heart that she kept locked away. She knew it for what it was; a hunger for the love she had thought she had, a yearning for someone to share her thoughts, her dreams. A spurt of anger knifed through her. Her eyes widened and the pounding of her heart warmed her face. In a hurry to get out from under Mike's straightforward stare, she walked quickly from the room.

Mike had seen the stricken look on Letty's face. Did she hate him so much that she resented his holding their son? Did she think he was trying to steal the child's affection away from her? He eased Patrick off his lap and stood.

"It's time for me to turn in."

"Where'll ya sleep, Dolan?"

"In the hayloft."

"Grandpa let a bum sleep in the barn once. Why can't you sleep in the house?"

"There's nice soft hay in the loft . . . and I'm not used to sleeping in a house." Mike's hand lingered on the top of Patrick's head as if reluctant to break contact with his son.

Jacob pushed himself up out of his chair. "I'll have Letty get some blankets."

"Don't bother. I have a bedroll. Tell Letty to set out a clean pail and I'll milk in the morning."

"You ain't goin' to go?" Patrick asked.

"No. I'll be here a while. I'm going to help your grandpa put in the crops."

"Can I help?"

Mike chuckled. "We'll see. Good night."

"Night, Dolan," Patrick called.

Letty heard the door close, then her son was there leaning against her knee. Resentment churned inside her. Now that *he* was gone Patrick came to her. Letty hated herself for the thought.

A half-hour later she finished the final chapter of the book and closed it.

"It that all?" Patrick asked.

"It's all for tonight. It's time to get ready for bed."

"Ah . . . you said you'd start *Treasure Island*"

"It's too late to start a new story. You can hardly keep your eyes open. Helen's tired too."

"But you said . . ."

"Stop whining!" Letty snapped, then in a gentler tone. "Go on, Patrick, and be quiet. Grandpa's already gone to bed."

Mike leaned against the door frame of the barn. He was too keyed up to think of sleep. In spite of Letty's attitude, he had never spent a more wonderful evening. His Letty was a lovely woman. He had watched her as she went about her work, and he had held his son on his lap. It was more, much more, than he had expected when he left Piedmont that morning. One thing was sure in his mind; Letty wasn't indifferent to him. His presence had made her cross.

Long ago Mike had ceased to wonder why this woman had remained the all-consuming factor in his life. He had been a mere boy when he gave his heart to her. Since that time, she had been his love, his only joy. The urge to be near her was so strong that, at times, it gave him an odd, uneasy feeling.

There had to be a way of convincing her that what he had told her was true. He hadn't deserted her! Dear God. He would have crawled through a snowstorm on his hands and knees to reach her if he had known she was alive and carried his child. Ideas floated around in his mind. His mother would write and tell Letty the truth if he asked her. The thought roamed around in his mind, then he decided he would bide his time and wait until Cora came to Boley. He would force her to tell Letty what her parents had done or he would choke it out of her.

His thoughts turned to his son. The kid was really something. All boy . . . and smart. Resembled him too. Mike's mouth spread in a grin. He and Letty had a son to carry their blood into the next generation. It was a miracle.

The house had been dark for a long while. Now suddenly there was light in the upstairs room, and his eyes became glued to the small square of light. A restless, twisting feeling churned inside him at the thought of Letty lying in bed remembering, in vivid detail as he did, the time they had spent together. Did she remember the words she'd said as they lay beneath the willows?

"I want to give back to you as much as you've given to me. Oh, Mike, I love you so!"

After what seemed an eternity, Letty passed the window and Mike realized that she hadn't been to bed. Had she been sitting in the darkness thinking of him? As he watched, his breath suspended, she removed the pins from her hair. Thick,

168

auburn tresses fell down over her shoulders to her waist and hung in wide, deep waves.

Thank God she hadn't bobbed it. He had been shocked at hairstyles when he returned from the war. Some "finger-waved" their hair in tight stiff waves and others wore it as short as a man's.

She was undressing. He shouldn't look, but he couldn't force his eyes away. She opened her dress to the waist, wiggled her shoulders and arms out of it, and let it slide down over her hips revealing the white undergarment she wore beneath it. Lifting her arms, she massaged her scalp with her fingertips, turning slowly toward the window. Her head was bowed and her shoulders sagged wearily.

Then, as if she could feel his eyes on her. she lifted her head and seemed to be looking right at him. For a second or two, she froze like a frightened doe sensing danger. Then she stepped out of his sight and the light was gone.

Mike drew in a deep, ragged breath and cursed. His hunger for her was driving him out of his mind.

Letty, sweetheart, I'm so damned lonesome.

CHAPTER
——11——

On Saturday. Letty rose at first light, dressed, and hurried downstairs to prepare breakfast.

"I'm going to town this morning, Grandpa," she said when Jacob came from his room and headed for the wash dish. "I'll leave something in the warming oven for your dinner."

"There'll be two of us," he growled, sloshing water on his face with his two hands. "What ya goin' to town for?" he asked as he jerked the towel from the towel bar.

"Well, for one thing I want to see Doctor Hakes." She set a platter of meat and eggs on the table.

"You sick?"

"No. I want to talk to him about Helen. And I need a few things from the store." She pulled biscuits, hot and golden brown, from the oven and set them on the top of the stove to keep hot while she took butter and jelly from the cupboard.

"Dolan milked." Jacob jerked his head toward the full pail of milk on the work bench as if Letty hadn't noticed it there. "Reckon he's doin' the rest of the chores." When Letty didn't say anything he said, "He's right handy 'bout fixin' thin's. Fixed the windmill up good 'n' proper. It don't hardly squeak atall anymore." He paused while he ran the comb through his hair. "He'll drag the south field this morning and I'll plant." Jacob pulled a dish towel from the line over the stove and used it as a pad when he lifted the hot coffee pot. "It'll be good havin' him here when we harvest the winter wheat."

"Anything you want from town, Grandpa?"

Jacob gave her a cold, exasperated stare. "Yeast," he growled.

Letty's face was set in a blank mask and her

lashes veiled her eyes. She chose to ignore his grumpy tone.

"We have yeast."

"I'm makin' me up a batch of home-brew," Jacob said in a tone that reminded Letty of Patrick when he was sulking.

"Oh. In that case I'll get more yeast. Need anything else?"

"What I need is fer ya to get down off'n yore high horse 'n' act like . . . like . . . act decent-like," he blurted, sloshing coffee in his saucer as he set his cup down with unnecessary force. "Ya know I ain't a likin' it when thin's is in a twister like they is."

Letty's chin went up, her back straightened. She stared straight into her grandfather's eyes.

"It was your doing, Grandpa."

"It ain't no such!"

"I'm going up and get dressed. I want to catch Wallace before he goes out on a call."

"Wallace? Who'n hell's that?"

"For crying out loud. Grandpa. He's been your doctor for years."

"Doc Hakes? Harumpt! Hell! How'd I know his name was . . . Wallace? You gettin' cozy with him?"

"Maybe," Letty threw the word back over her shoulder as she left the room.

Letty drove the buggy into the area behind the general store where two wagons were already parked.

While she was tying the horse to the hitching

rail, Patrick kicked at the dirt with the toe of his shoe, sending dust over Helen's white stockings. Without a word of complaint, Helen backed away and tried to wipe the dirt away with her handkerchief.

"Patrick!" Letty exclaimed, taking him by the shoulder and spinning him around. "There are times when I could shake you until your teeth rattle. I'm tired of your pouting and I'm tired of you being so inconsiderate to Helen. Apologize, right now."

"Sorry," he mumbled and raised dark, resentful eyes to his mother's face. "I didn't get to talk to Dolan."

"That's no excuse for acting like a spoiled brat." Letty had been relieved that Mike was not in sight when they left the house. Jacob had hitched the horse to the buggy as he had done the mornings she drove to school.

"He won't be there when I get back?"

"He'll be there. I've told you that at least three times since we left home." Letty grabbed her son's hand and started for the street. Patrick's steps lagged and she was forced to pull him along. When they reached the walk in front of the stores, she stopped and looked down at him. "You're not going to ruin this day for Helen and me. You can straighten up and stop pouting, or I will spank you right here on the street, then you'll go sit in the buggy and wait for us. The choice is yours."

"I'll . . . go," he answered in a bored voice, but

when they started walking again, he kept pace, knowing his mother would do exactly as she said.

Helen's hand squeezed Letty's tighter and tighter as they approached Doctor Hakes's office. He had recently relocated in a small frame building at the end of the Piedmont's two-block business district.

"Helen'?" Letty questioned gently. "What's wrong. honey?"

"Will he make me stay here?"

"Of course not. What gave you that idea?"

"The sheriff come once and got me."

"Honey, the sheriff wanted you to be where someone could take care of you. He's not going to take you away from me," Letty said firmly, then to herself, *God, help me keep that promise.*

A shiny new automobile was parked in front of Doctor Hakes's office. He was standing beside it, grinning like a schoolboy. It was a side of him Letty had not seen during the five years she had known him.

"How do you like it?"

"You finally bought one," Letty exclaimed. "I didn't think you'd ever put poor Molly out to pasture."

"She's earned a rest."

"Does it have a horn?" Patrick asked.

"Sure does. Right here on the side." Doctor Hakes reached out and pushed down on a plunger atop the shiny brass horn.

"Oooh-gaa! Oooh-gaa!"

The blast was so loud that both Patrick and

Helen jumped back, causing the doctor to laugh.

"I'm going to get an electric horn that works off the battery; then all I'll have to do is press a button."

"The car is beautiful, Wallace, but won't you miss being able to sleep while Molly takes you home?" Letty asked teasingly as she ran her fingertips over the shiny black fender.

"Maybe, but you've got to keep up with the times."

"I've seen cars like this but never one this new."

"It's a Model T. One of the best. It's got electric headlights and curtains I can snap on in case of a heavy downpour. I can even fold the top back in nice weather and, Letty, look at this double windshield. It will tilt out to let the breeze through, or I can close it. When the glass breaks, I can take out the bolts and replace the whole thing."

Letty's smile broadened. "I hope you're not planning on its breaking right away."

"I'm not planning on it, but it could happen. There's even a place on the back for a spare tire, and if I go on a trip, I can get a rack to attach to the running board to store luggage." He rubbed dust from the hood with the sleeve of his coat. "I ordered it a month ago from Mr. Ford's plant down in Kansas City. It came in on the train yesterday."

"Who taught you to drive it?"

"The fellow that opened the gas station. It wasn't hard. I bet you could do it. Want to try?"

"No! Heavens, no! Good grief. I'll never forget the ride I took with Doctor Whittier when I first came out here. I was scared to death. Patrick, get off the running board. Don't—"

"He isn't hurting anything, Letty. Want to go for a ride? I promise not to scare you to death."

"You mean ride in the . . . car?" Patrick's eyes widened at the possibility.

"Why not?" Doctor Hakes opened the back door of the automobile and Patrick scrambled in.

"Keep your feet off the seat, Patrick," Letty cautioned. "Move over and make room for Helen."

Doctor Hakes, looking happier than Letty had ever seen him, put his hand beneath her elbow as she stepped up on the running board and into the car. The seats were springy and covered with something that looked like heavy, dark oil cloth.

Letty watched as Wallace moved a lever beneath the steering wheel and took the crank from behind the driver's seat. The motor fired to life on the first twist and purred softly. Beaming, the doctor got behind the wheel, set the car in motion, and guided it down the street.

Letty turned to find Patrick standing behind her. "For goodness' sake, Patrick. Sit down."

"He's all right, Letty, I'm not going fast."

"It seems fast to me."

"Yesterday I took her out on the road north of town and opened her up to forty miles an hour." He looked at her and grinned like a naughty boy expecting to be chastised. He was not disappointed.

"Wallace Hakes! You'll get yourself killed, is what you'll do," Letty said in her school-teacher voice.

"Would you care, Letty?" The doctor's serious tone wiped the smile from Letty's face. She glanced at him. He was staring straight ahead.

"Of course I would, Wallace," she said seriously. Then with a bit of laughter in her voice, "If I got a good dose of poison ivy, I'd sure hate to go all the way to Boley to see Doc Whittier. He might want to take me for another ride in his touring car."

They circled the town, and when they came back to the office, stopped.

"I'm goin' to have me a car when I grow up," Patrick announced. "I'm goin' fast. Oooh-gaa! Oooh-gaa!" His mimic of the horn was loud in Letty's ear.

"Mercy. There's nothing wrong with that boy's vocal cords," she said as Doctor Hakes helped her out of the car.

"Most boys are fascinated by automobiles."

"Including you." Letty smiled at him. He held her elbow a moment longer than necessary. "I'd like to speak with you for a minute, Wallace," she said softly, seriously.

"You feeling all right, Letty?"

"I'm fine." Helen had taken Letty's hand. She untangled it gently. "Will you keep an eye on Patrick for me, Helen?"

"They can sit in the car."

"No. They might—"

176

"It's all right. They can't hurt a thing." Doctor Hakes opened the office door and followed Letty inside. "Sit down, Letty. What's on your mind?"

"Helen. The child is scared to death her father will come back and she'll have to go with him. Wallace, I think he was mean to her and her mother."

"There's no think about it. I know he was. I saw the marks of a razor strop on Mrs. Weaver and I saw them on Helen."

"I figured as much. She's afraid of him. Is there any way I can keep her with me? I'm willing to keep her permanently."

"You mean adopt her? Not without her father's consent, and I don't see him giving it. He'll be out of jail any day now."

"If he comes for her, do I have to let her go with him?"

"I'm afraid so. He's her father."

"Are you telling me the sheriff will let that . . . that jailbird take her away from a good, decent home and . . . and subject her to . . . I don't know what?"

"Letty, the law is the law. The courts are very reluctant to take a child from its natural parent. The man can be a convicted bank robber or a no-good whiskey runner, but if he is willing to support the child and the child's life is in no danger, there is not much we can do."

"Even if he beats her?"

"He could say it was discipline."

"Wallace! Whose side are you on?"

"I'm on your side and Helen's side. I'm just pointing out what you're up against."

"You're the county health officer, Wallace. Can't you do anything?"

"I'll write to Mrs. Knight. The governor appointed her to handle cases such as this. She may listen to my recommendation, and then again, she may not.

"Helen almost went into hysterics one day when . . . I had a little trouble with Oscar Phillips. He grabbed my arm and Helen screamed and screamed."

"Phillips bothering you?"

"Just that one time. I doubt he'll do it again."

"He's not much good, but he takes care of his kids," the doctor added drily.

"I'm glad to hear that. What about Helen, Wallace? You know she's better off with me—"

"I know that. I'll do what I can." The door opened and Doctor Hakes stood. "Hello, Mrs. Crews."

"Hello, Doctor Hakes. I feel so poorly this morning, I had to come. My back has been killing me of late. If you're busy. I'll just sit and wait till you're through with Mrs. Graham." Mrs. Crews lowered her immense bulk onto a chair. The eyes of the barrel-shaped woman looked like small black buttons in her fat face. They shifted from Letty to the doctor and back again. "I saw you gettin' a joy ride in Doc's new car."

Letty stood. "Yes. It was a treat."

"You still got the Weaver girl?"

178

"She was in the car. Didn't you recognize her?"

"Was that her? Reckon I never seen her so spruced up."

"I'll be going. Goodbye, Mrs. Crews. Thank you, Doctor Hakes, for the ride and the . . . advice."

"Goodbye, Mrs. Graham. Tell Jacob I'll be out soon."

Letty stood on the porch outside the door and called to Patrick and Helen. Mrs. Crews was a gossiping old biddy, and before the day was over, everyone in town who hadn't seen her in the car with Wallace would know about it. Helen came to Letty immediately and took her hand. Patrick, however, had to be pried away from the car.

"How about dinner at the Cattleman Cafe?" Letty had read the menu posted outside when they passed and knew they could get a plate lunch there for fifteen cents.

"I ain't never eat in no cafe." Helen looked up at Letty with a bright smile.

"I have never eaten in a cafe," Letty corrected gently.

"You ain't—" Letty squeezed Patrick's hand hard and glared down at him. He felt his mother's displeasure, swallowed the rest of his disparaging remark, and asked, "After we eat can I get a soda pop?"

"I think so. What do you want, Helen? You can have a soda pop or an ice cream."

"I don't care."

By the middle of the afternoon Patrick was tired

and whining to go home. Helen, ever patient and uncomplaining, trailed along beside Letty as she looked over the dry goods in the stores, selected a piece of dress goods, bought thread and ribbon, and thumbed through the pattern books.

It was an effort for Letty to keep her mind away from the farm. Had she prepared enough food for the noon and night meal? Had Grandpa filled the water jars and taken them to the field? Oh, Lordy! She had never in the world thought she would see Mike Dolan again. He had turned her life completely upside down. He hadn't wanted her five years ago. He didn't want *her* now. It was Patrick he was interested in. Damn him. He was the reason she was here in town trying to kill the day.

Before heading for the general store to buy groceries, Letty and Helen waited on the walk in front of the bank while Patrick went behind the building to the public toilet to relieve himself. When he returned they went up the steps and into the mercantile.

"Hello, Mrs. Graham. How are you and young Patrick? Jacob doin' all right?" Mr. Howard who owned one of the two grocery stores in town was a pleasant but shrewd business man. He always called his customers by name and usually inquired about the health of a family member.

"We're all fine, Mr. Howard. How's Mrs. Howard?"

"Good. Real good. Did I see you go by in Doc Hakes's new Ford car?"

"Yes, he gave us a ride around town. I have a

list." Letty dug into the bag hanging on her arm and brought out a folded paper. "While you're filling it, I'll look around. There may be something I forgot to write down."

"You just go right ahead. Let me see now. Peaches, corn meal, yeast—" Mr. Howard paused and looked at her over the tops of his spectacles, "I'm sellin' lots of yeast lately. Haw! Haw! Haw! Folks must be eatin' nothin' but bread."

Letty removed the wooden lid from the candy jar, took out a handful of peppermint sticks, counted them, and handed one each to Patrick and Helen.

"Add ten candy sticks to the bill, Mr. Howard."

"Sure thing. Got your slips for the sugar? They're sayin' by summer we won't be rationing it no more. Be fine with me. I do hate to turn down a body 'cause they don't have the slips. Hear her pa's gettin' out soon," he said, tilting his head toward the front of the store where Helen and Patrick stood looking out the door.

"Shh . . ." Letty cautioned, shaking her head.

"Well, now—" Mr. Howard's face had reddened.

"I don't want her to know. She's scared to death of her father."

"Well, now," he said again, "I reckon I did hear somethin' 'bout him bein' downright mean to his family. Did the little'un say much about it?"

"Hardly anything, but I could tell."

Mr. Howard waited to see if Letty would say more. When she didn't, he reached behind him and brought down a box from the shelf.

"Here's the large box a starch. The bottle a blu-ing and the sulphur matches is right over here. Mrs. Graham, you got on here a five-gallon can of coal oil. Did you bring the can to exchange?"

"It's in the buggy."

"You can pull right up to the back door, Mrs. Graham, and I'll carry out your order. I got a good price on a hundred pounds of chicken feed," he said hopefully and named a price.

"I'll take it. I don't need it now, but it'll keep. Add a jug of molasses, and four pounds of raisins. How much is this little bank, Mr. Howard?" Letty ran her fingers over the small iron figure of a hunter holding a rifle and a bear standing upright just inches away. When a penny was placed in the right position on the gun barrel and a lever pulled, the rifle would shoot the coin into the bear.

"I'd have to have eighty-five cents for it."

"Put it in a sack so Patrick won't see it. Tomorrow is his birthday."

"He'll be plumb tickled, I know."

When everything was boxed, the bill tallied and signed for, Letty called to the children. They went to where they had parked the buggy. After leading the patient horse to the water tank, Letty drove to the back of the store and Mr. Howard loaded her purchases.

"Come again, Mrs. Graham."

"Thank you, I will."

On the way out of town, Patrick said, "I'm goin' to ride on the drag with Dolan when I get home."

"We're going to see the Pierces first."

"Why? I want to go home—"

"Can I play with Celia?" Helen asked.

"If Celia wants to play."

"They ain't got no little boys at Pierces."

"They don't have any little boys. I'll swear, Patrick, you've tried my patience today. I'm sure you can find something to do while I visit with Oleta and Mrs. Pierce."

"They got puppies," Helen said hesitantly.

"Who said?" Patrick demanded.

"Celia."

"She don't know nothin'. She's a girl," Patrick said sullenly, crossed his arms over his chest, stuck out his lip, and sank down in the seat.

Letty gritted her teeth.

"Stay for the singin', Letty." Oleta begged. "Please stay. The Watkins' and the Tarrs are comin'. Sharon is bringin' her mandolin."

"It'll be too late—"

"Harry will drive you home. Oh, please say you'll stay. We'll have enough for a square dance."

Letty thought about it. She had told Grandpa about the singing. He would know that they were all right and that some of the neighbors would see them home. It would give her a few more hours before she had to face Mike again.

"All right, we'll stay. But I don't want you peeved at me when Harry leaves to drive me home."

"I won't." Oleta leaned toward her and whispered. " 'Cause he'll be back."

The May evening was cool, but not uncomfortably so. The Pierce boys built a bonfire in the yard and hung lanterns on the porch. Just before dark the Watkins family arrived and shortly after that the Tarrs. Mrs. Watkins brought a chocolate cake and Mrs. Tarr a pan of doughnuts. The men disappeared into the barn shortly after the families arrived. When the music began, they were all in a happy mood.

Sharon Tarr Burris, a year or two older than Letty, had married her sweetheart before he went to war. When he was killed, she came back home to live with her parents. Sharon played the mandolin, Stanley Pierce and Harry the guitars. Mr. Pierce, well fortified with homemade spirits, played the fiddle enthusiastically.

Celia and Helen giggled and huddled together at the end of the porch. Patrick pouted for a while because Jimmy Watkins had gone to Claypool to visit his grandparents, and he had no one to play with. Finally, his face caked with sugar from Mrs. Tarr's doughnuts, he fell asleep, his head pillowed on Mrs. Watkins's lap.

After an hour of singing and clapping, the men made another trip to the barn. When Mr. Pierce returned, he picked up his fiddle and began to play a lively square-dance tune. Chairs were pulled back to make room for the dancing.

"Form a square," he yelled when he took the fiddle from beneath his chin.

Sharon and Stanley took their places beside Harry and Oleta on the hard-packed yard. Mr. and Mrs. Tarr joined in. Fifteen-year-old Walter Tarr pulled Letty out to make up the set. Letty had learned to square-dance the summer after Patrick was born. It had taken her a while to loosen up and enjoy herself that evening at the Watkins', but her love of music set her feet to dancing. Later, she had wondered how anything that had been so much fun could be as wicked as her father said it was.

Those wicked Dolans are dancing their way to hell. The words came back to Letty as clearly as if her father were standing beside her. She shook her head to rid her mind of a thought that had lurked there since the day Mike had told her that her parents had declared her dead. In her heart she knew her father and Cora were capable of doing just that—but her mother? Was it possible that her mother would have cut her so completely out of her life? The pain in her heart made her feel as if there were a wide chasm between her and everyone else in the world.

The music started and Letty threw herself into the dance. Mr. Pierce fiddled, stomped his foot, and shouted the calls:

"Ladies to the center, gents all around, Swing that gal right off the ground.
Sing and march—first couple lead. Swing and march and then stampede.
Ladies to the left, gents to the right, meet in

the middle and hug her tight.
Swing that gal, swing her sweet. Swing that gal
right off her feet."

The calls and the fiddle didn't stop until the dancers were breathless. Mr. Pierce placed his fiddle on a chair and wiped the sweat from his forehead with his sleeve.

"Time for the ladies to take a breather and the gents a trip to—"

"—Papa, shh—" Mrs. Pierce said quickly. "There's a man on horseback there by the woodpile. He's been there since the dancing started."

CHAPTER
——————12——————

The singing voices carried far on the night wind. The sound of the party reached Mike about the same time he saw the flicker of the bonfire through the trees. He stopped his horse when he reached the lane leading to the well-lighted farmhouse and listened to the music. The bonfire and lanterns placed on the porch and from tree limbs made light for a dozen or more people sitting on the porch and in the yard. One of the first things Mike noticed about Letty was that she had let her hair down and had tied it at the nape of her neck.

The fiddler suddenly stopped sawing away on his violin.

"Form a square," he yelled.

186

A scramble occurred to get the chairs out of the way and to form the set. Feeling more like an outsider than he could ever remember and hating it, Mike rode slowly up the lane as the dancing started. He stopped the horse outside the circle of light and watched.

Letty was dancing. He had wanted to be the one to teach her after he got her out from under the control of the preacher and her sister. Mike's eyes followed her every movement. She was having a good time. Her feet were light, her head high, and from time to time her laughter rang out as clearly as a bell above the music. Her skirts whirled until her knees showed, her long hair, caught at the nape with a ribbon, flew out behind her as she pranced to the tune of the music. He had never seen her so lighthearted and gay.

She was enjoying herself now, but he feared that would change when she caught sight of him. He stored her laughter in the dark regions of his mind to bring out and enjoy when he was alone and lonely.

The music stopped. As the last note faded, the dancers bowed to each other and sank down on the edge of the porch to catch their breath. The gray-haired fiddler spoke to another man, and then both men came toward Mike. He moved his horse out of the shadow and into the light.

"Howdy," Mike said, with his fingers to the brim of his hat. "Mr. Pierce?"

"I'm Pierce."

"Name's Mike Dolan. I work for Mr. Fletcher.

He was uneasy about his granddaughter and asked me to escort her and the children home when she's ready to go."

"I hadn't heard Jacob had hired a man," Mr. Pierce said and turned to the man beside him. "Had you, Guy?"

"Harry was over there today and met Dolan. He fixed a wheel on our planter. I'm Guy Watkins," he said to Mike. "You met my boy, Harry."

"Step down, Mr. Dolan," Mr. Pierce invited. "We're a bit leery of strangers, times as they are."

"I understand. Glad to know you, Mr. Pierce, Mr. Watkins." Mike shook the hands offered.

"Tie your horse there to the fence and come meet the folks."

"I don't want to interrupt the party. I can wait here."

"You're not interruptin' a thin'. The young folk'll want to be dancin' another square if I'm readin' them right."

Mr. Pierce led the way to the house. Mike walked beside Mr. Watkins, towering over the shorter man. Letty had moved to the far side of the porch in the shadows and all he could see was her white face. So tuned to her emotions, he could almost feel her fear that he would embarrass her. *Letty, sweetheart, don't be scared—*

While Mike was being introduced, Oleta sidled over to Letty.

"Why didn't you tell me about him? Where did he come from? He's downright handsome.

Sharon thinks so too. Her eyes are about to pop out." Oleta nudged Letty with her elbow. "She's man-hunting so she can get away from the farm."

Letty's face burned, her throat so choked with bitterness she couldn't speak.

"Howdy, I remember you now." Mrs. Watkins said, holding out her hand. "You was at our place looking for Letty's man. Said you knew him before."

"Yes, ma'am," Mike said, looking down at his son sleeping in her lap. "Little fellow is all tuckered out, isn't he?"

"He's a corker, he is," Mrs. Watkins said fondly. "I was there when he was born. He come into the world on the move and he's been on the move ever since."

Mike moved on until all the introductions were made.

"The ring you put around the axle worked just fine, Mike." Harry said.

"It'll hold for a while. Jacob's got an anvil. If we could rig up a forge, we could fix a few things without having to go all the way to town to the blacksmith."

"Done some blacksmithin', have ya?" Mr. Tarr asked.

"In Pennsylvania, before the war. Worked in a coal mine and helped a blacksmith on the side. I liked the work. Never got into putting on horseshoes though. Always wanted to try it."

"Sure would be a help if we didn't have to hightail it to town when we have a breakdown," Mr.

189

Pierce said. "Come on out to the barn. I'll show you what I think might work for a forge."

Mike strolled toward the barn with the men. Resentment built in Letty. *He hadn't even looked at her.* And her friends had taken him in as if he were one of them.

"That's not the only reason they're going to the barn." Mrs. Tarr sank down in a chair on the porch. "I keep tellin' that man a mine he'd better stop haulin' that white lightnin' in the wagon or he'll get caught sure as shootin'."

"You won't have to worry about carryin' any home from the looks of them." Mrs. Pierce said.

"How long has Mike been working for your grandpa?" Sharon asked.

"Since yesterday."

"He's handsome as all get out. He doesn't look like he'd need to work as a hired hand."

"Harry said he was at Argonne in France, but not in Robert's division," Mrs. Watkins said in a choked voice. "Harry talked to him a little bit about it today. I'd like to hear about how it was at Argonne and about Flanders' Field where Robert is buried."

"Was Mike Dolan wounded, Letty?" Oleta asked.

"I didn't ask him."

"He might be one of those who'll not talk about the war."

"He talked to Harry about it today," Mrs. Watkins said. "I'll wait until we're better acquainted, then I'll ask him."

190

Letty stood. "I'd better start gathering things up. It's time I was getting on home."

"Pa said we'd have another square," Oleta said. "You've got to stay for that. And we haven't had cake yet."

"Stay, Letty," Sharon added. "I want to dance with Mike. Oh, shoot! What if he doesn't dance?"

"He dances," Letty said drily and sat back down, then added when all eyes turned toward her, "I never saw an Irishman who didn't."

"I wonder what brought him all the way out here from Pennsylvania," Sharon mused. "Did he say, Letty?"

"Who knows?" Letty said, evading the question.

Oleta jumped up when she saw the men coming from the barn and skipped out to meet her father.

"Play another set, Papa, please—Letty thinks she's got to be getting on home."

"Youngun, you'll wear my arm off," he said and gave her an affectionate little swat on the back. "All right, one more. Grab your partners."

Sharon was off the porch like a shot. "You dance, Mr. Dolan?"

"Well, sure, but don't you have a partner?"

"Stanley will dance with Letty. He's kind of got his eye on her," she whispered and winked.

Mike's eyes leaped to young Stanley Pierce. The tall youth was trying to pull Letty up off the porch. His heart had missed a beat before it registered in his brain that the boy was not more than sixteen.

"I'll sit this one out, Stanley."

"Ah . . . come on, Letty. We got to have four couples to make up the set."

Letty had no choice but to get in line with Stanley behind Sharon and Mike. Panic knifed through her. She was sure she wouldn't be able to keep her mind on the calls. What if she got mixed up and threw everyone off? *She'd have to hold his hand. He would whirl her around.*

Through the pounding of blood in her ears she heard Mr. Pierce strike up a tune on the fiddle, then begin the calls:

"All join hands. Circle to the left. Circle to the right.
Now, do si do."

Mike's hand, warm and hard, grasped Letty's and the circle moved. She moved on instinct, her feet feeling as if each weighed a hundred pounds. She moved back to back with Stanley when the caller directed. After being swung by her partner the next call was, "Men to the right, women to the left." Letty found herself weaving in and out, clasping hands with first one male dancer and then another. When the call came to "swing your partner," she was with Mike. He held tightly to her hand, the arm about her waist drew her close against him. He swung her off her feet. Breath left her. His dark eyes were fastened to her face.

She could feel the hardness of his chest and his hot breath on her cheek. Her heart thumped in a strange and disturbing way as she stuggled to get sufficient air into her lungs.

"Letty, sweetheart—" The words were murmured close to her ear.

She swallowed drily, feeling the frantic clamor of her throbbing pulse. When he released her, he held tightly to her hand until he had to give her over to her partner. Letty responded automatically to the remaining instructions from the caller, and wondered if the torment would ever cease.

When the dance ended, she was on the far side of the square. She saw Sharon slip her arm through Mike's, laugh up at him, and pull him out of the circle of light. So much for the grieving widow, Letty thought caustically. Sharon's husband had been dead less than a year and here she was doing her best to latch onto Mike.

"You're a great dancer, Mike. And you like to dance. I can tell." Sharon's voice was low and intimate but plenty loud enough for Letty to hear.

"My folks liked to dance. They taught all of us kids."

"There's a dance in Piedmont every week during the summer—"

"Come on in, Mike," Stanley interrupted. "There's chocolate cake, doughnuts, and coffee."

Sharon's eyes shot daggers at Stanley as Mike gently disengaged his arm from hers. "Chocolate cake? I sure can't miss out on that."

Letty gritted her teeth. He was making himself right at home with *her* friends. She sank down on the edge of the porch. While they were dancing, Mrs. Watkins had taken Patrick inside, and Helen was off somewhere with Celia.

"This night turned out better than I thought." Sharon sat down beside Letty. "I haven't met such an attractive man in a coon's age. And can he dance!" She looked at Letty strangely. "Did your grandpa know him?"

"As far as I know he had never set eyes on him until he rode into the yard."

"Golly-darn! Some people have all the luck. Why couldn't he have ridden into *our* yard?"

"Is Mr. Tarr looking for help?"

"Well no," Sharon admitted. "Not till harvest. I've been helping out some in the field."

Oleta came out onto the porch and gave Sharon and Letty each a plate filled with cake, pie, and doughnuts.

"Goodness gracious, Oleta," Letty exclaimed. "I can't possibly eat all of this."

"Eat what you want and leave the rest. Nothing goes to waste here. The boys'll finish it up. They'd fight the hogs over something sweet," Oleta said over her shoulder.

Letty picked at the food, wishing the time would hurry by. More than anything she wanted to be at home in her room, in her bed, away from everyone. She wanted to relax her stiff face. If she didn't do it soon, she feared it would crack.

Sharon had ceased talking and was watching

Mike. He sat in the yard with the men, forearms resting on his thighs, holding his plate between his spread legs with one hand and forking cake into his mouth with the other. A cup of coffee sat between his booted feet. The one time Letty looked at him, their eyes met. After that she kept her eyes on her plate. When she could sit still no longer and got up to go into the house, Sharon didn't notice, but Mike did. His eyes followed her until she was out of his sight.

"I just can't hold another bite, Mrs. Pierce." Letty set her half-filled plate on the table.

"Don't worry 'bout it. Walter or Stanley'll be in and finish it off. Law me, but them boys has hollow legs when it comes to eatin'."

Glad to be where Mike couldn't see her, Letty chatted with Mrs. Pierce and Mrs. Watkins. She told them about Doctor Hakes's new Ford car and that Mr. Howard had a good price on chicken feed.

"Did you hear about that fancy preacher lady coming to Boley?" Mrs. Tarr asked, coming into the kitchen.

"We heard that. Sister Cora, they call her," Mrs. Pierce said. "Claims to heal the sick. I wonder if she could do anything for Moss Ringland? That poor sot has drank denatured alcohol till his brain is pickled."

"It's plumb pitiful," Mrs Tarr said. "I saw him last week in Claypool. He's got jake-leg now. His feet flop something awful when he tries to walk."

195

"I'd like to hear Sister Cora preach." Mrs. Pierce cut another pie in wedges and sent Oleta out to serve the men. "The Fleetwoods saw her in Denver. They said she comes out on the stage suspended on a wire like an angel floatin' down. Don't ya know that's a sight to behold. She wears a white robe with big sleeves and holds her arms up while she's talkin' so them sleeves look like wings. People just eat it up. Young girls in pink robes and shiny leaves in their hair pass the collection plate. Martha said nobody she saw dropped in nickels or dimes. No sirree. 'Twas all foldin' money."

"Did Martha see her heal anyone?" Mrs. Tarr asked.

"Martha said she placed her hands on a blind man's eyes and afterwards he swore he could see light."

Letty swallowed a groan of disgust and wondered how people could be so stupid that they couldn't see through Cora's theatrics. She prayed to God her friends never found out that Cora was her sister.

"Guy wouldn't go all the way to Boley just to see her. He thinks she's a quack."

Hurrah for Mr. Watkins. He doesn't know how right he is. It wasn't hard for Letty to imagine Cora crowing over the collection plate.

"Law no, he wouldn't," Mrs. Watkins was saying. "It's nigh on forty miles to Boley. I might persuade him to go if we made up a get-together and go for a lark. We'd have to camp out. Us

196

women could go to the church meetin'. The men wouldn't have to go."

"Let's do it," Mrs. Tarr explained. "We're not liable to get another chance to see her. How about you. Letty? We'd be pleased to have you come."

"Count me and Grandpa out." Letty shook her head. "It would be too hard on Grandpa. Which reminds me, I've got to be heading home. Tomorrow is Patrick's birthday and I've got to make an early start if I'm going to get a cake baked and all his favorites for dinner."

"He'll be five, won't he?" Mrs. Watkins exclaimed. "My, how time flies. Seems like it ain't been no time at all. I ain't never goin' to forget that night he come squallin' into the world. He was the prettiest little black-haired bugger I ever did see."

"The buggy is ready when you are."

Letty spun around at the sound of Mike's voice. He stood in the doorway, a strange, haunted expression on his face that quickly faded. She turned away from his probing eyes.

"I'll get Patrick."

"I'll get him. He's getting too big for you to carry."

Without waiting for her to reply, he went to the cot at the end of the kitchen and scooped the sleeping child up in his arms. Patrick's dark head drooped on Mike's shoulder and his arm went about Mike's neck. Mike adjusted the boy carefully and lovingly against him. Unable to look at him holding their child, Letty went into the parlor to get Helen.

When she reached the yard, Mike's horse was tied behind the buggy. He stood beside it, talking to Harry and Mr. Watkins, Patrick asleep on his shoulder.

"Put Patrick on the seat. Helen will hold him," Letty said crisply, helping Helen up into the buggy and climbing in beside her.

"That won't be necessary." Before Letty could take up the reins, Mike placed the sleeping child in her arms. He went around to the other side, stepped into the buggy and settled himself beside Helen. Letty, settling Patrick against her, felt the little girl cringe away from him and snuggle to her side.

"Bye, Letty. Bye, Mike," Oleta called. "Next time we'll come to your house, Letty, so you can play the piano."

"Yes, do that," Letty said automatically. "Thanks for the lovely time."

"Come again," Mrs. Pierce called.

"I'll be over soon, Letty." Sharon spoke with her eyes on Mike.

Finally, the buggy moved down the dark lane to the road. The silence was thick and heavy. Letty felt as if she were in another world. She clung to Patrick. He was a precious weight in her arms, and Helen, snuggled against her side, was a buffer between her and the man whose silent presence screamed at her. Filled with misery and bewilderment, Letty's mind skittered in a thousand directions.

Tired in body and mind and longing to drop

into a deep dreamless sleep, Letty kept her face turned to the side. The voice in her head that had nagged at her persistently for the past week whispered that Mike could be telling the truth about that spring five years ago when he was told that she was dead. Even so, she thought now, too much time has gone by. She had cut herself loose from that old life, built for herself and Patrick a new background and a future here on Grandpa's farm.

She was not the frightened, insecure girl who had trembled in her father's presence. Nor was Mike the delivery boy who plucked the ribbon from the lilac bush and waited for her beneath the willows. She had been rejected and condemned by her family, thrown out into the night, and told not to come back. Instead of crushing her spirit as her father had hoped it would do, it had made her stronger.

Mike was a man now. He had gone to war. Jesus, my God! The thought came to her that perhaps he had suffered an injury that would prevent him from fathering more children. That would explain his interest in Patrick. A small sob escaped her.

Mike glanced at her when he heard the sound. Now was not the time to talk to her. He would wait until they reached the farm. By then, the little girl between them would be asleep.

Woodrow barked a greeting when they drove into the yard. The shaggy dog ran around the buggy, then stopped to thump at fleas with his hind paw as he waited for Mike to notice him.

"You keeping an eye on things?" Mike patted the dog's head and went around to Letty's side of the buggy. "Sit still," he said when she began to shift Patrick in her arms. "I'll help you with him in a minute. Is the little girl asleep?"

Letty nodded and worked at pulling the legs of Patrick's breeches down to cover his knees.

"Letty, look at me. Please—"

Letty turned her face a fraction and looked down at him. He had removed his hat and placed it on the top of the buggy. The moon, dim behind a wayward cloud, shed a pale light on his upturned face. Midnight-black ringlets, always resentful of brush and comb, fell down on his forehead. If she could believe what she saw in his eyes, it was tenderness, it was pleading, it was . . . pain.

Inside she trembled.

"Letty, sweetheart, I want you to know that I'm not here to cause you trouble," he said quietly. "I'll not hurt you and I'd die before I let anyone else hurt you."

"Then why are you here?" she demanded in a shaky voice. "Go away before Patrick gets too fond of you."

"I can't do that, Letty. I've just found you."

"You came here to embarrass me," she accused.

"No, sweetheart—"

"Don't say that! I don't know you. You don't know me."

"I know that I'm not alive without you. I've been half dead since I came home that spring and found out I'd lost you."

200

"I'm Letty Graham now. My friends think I'm a widow. Patrick thinks his daddy is . . . dead."

"Don't ask me to leave. I can't."

"Why did you have to come back now and upset my life and Patrick's? You've put me in the position of having to be decent to you or make a fool of myself."

"I swear to God, Letty, I believed you were dead."

"I waited for you—humiliated and scared. When you didn't come, I had to make up a lie and live with it. Only Grandpa knows the truth."

"As God is my witness, I've told you the truth. That spring when I went back to Dunlap they told me you had died during the epidemic. A service had been held at the church. My mother knew of my love for you, but she didn't go because she knew that she wouldn't be welcome."

"Even if what you say is true, too much time has gone by. We're not the same now."

"My feelings for you are the same. I still . . . love you—"

"No! You want Patrick!" she blurted.

"I want both of you. I never knew I had a son until the day I rode in here. I won't deny that I want Patrick to know that I'm his daddy. I'll love him and work as hard as I can to give him a good start in life, but I'll not tell him anything unless we tell him together."

"I'll not have him thinking of himself as a . . . as a bastard," she hissed the last word.

"When he grows up, he'll think his mother was a . . . was a loose woman."

"Patrick was conceived out of our love for each other," Mike said almost angrily. "If he's half the man I hope he'll be, he'll be proud. Have you forgotten the vows we said beneath the willow, Letty? I've always considered you my wife."

"But I'm not your wife. When Cora told Papa I was pregnant, he threw me out. He said that as far as the family was concerned, I was *dead*. He called me a whore, a slut, a harlot, a spawn of the devil. I was fifteen—" Her voice broke and she swallowed a sob.

An angry rumble came from Mike's throat.

"I had nowhere to go but here. Grandpa and Grandma took me in. They never condemned me. They loved each other and they . . . loved me. Grandpa almost grieved himself to death when Grandma died." Words tumbled out as if a dam had broken. "He gave her such loving tender care. And when Patrick was born, he . . . he was here to do for me when I was too weak to get out of bed. I'll never leave him. Never! Patrick and I are all that he has now. He took care of me when my. . . own mother turned her back on me, and I'm going to take care of him for the rest of his life."

"I'm not going to try to take you and Patrick away from your grandpa. I just want to be a part of your lives too. I explained that to him. He understands."

"It wouldn't work." Letty drew in a sobbing breath. "Do you think I could face the Watkins', the Tarrs and the Pierces if they knew I had made up the story about my *husband* being killed in the logging camp?"

"Dear God! I could kill that son-of-a bitchin' father of yours and that conniving sister for what they've done to you."

"Oh, Lord! I don't want anyone to know I'm related to *her!*" She spit the word out of her mouth as if it were as bitter as gall.

"Don't worry, sweetheart. Please don't worry." Mike's fingers moved over Letty's hand and squeezed before she wiggled it free. "I've heard your voice in my dreams a thousand times saying, 'Mike, I'm scared.' My sweet love, you don't have to be afraid now. You're not alone. As long as I live you'll not be alone." His voice vibrated with tenderness.

"I'm ashamed of Cora. She's a hypocrite! A flimflammer!"

"She'll be found out . . . someday."

"And when she is, it'll bring disgrace down on Grandpa and Patrick. She'll try to bring me down with her . . . tell that I lied when I said I was m-married. Everyone will know that Grandpa lied too. And the disgrace would follow Patrick for the rest of his life."

"What happened is more my fault than yours. I shouldn't have gone away until we were sure you were not . . . in the family way. You're not alone in this," he insisted.

"I have Grandpa—"

"He won't always be here. I think he's worried about that."

"When that time comes I'll . . . do what I have to do." Her words came out on a strangled sob.

They stared at each other for a moment that was so still that it seemed time had ceased. A feeling of emptiness shot through her at the thought of what might have been.

Her wet eyes blurred her vision.

The realization that except for chance he would never have known she lived or that he had a son sent a surge of emotion through Mike that was both tender and fierce. Memories blazed for an instant in his eyes. He longed to pull her into his arms. He loved this woman with a cherishing kind of love that made him only half alive when he was not with her. He wanted to hold her in his arms, plant another child in her warm, fertile body, keep her by his side forever.

"Letty, Letty—" he sighed. "You're my same Letty, yet so different."

"You're different too."

"Can't we try to work this out together . . . for Patrick's sake?"

Before Letty could answer, Helen stirred. "Are we home?"

"Yes, dear. We're home," Letty said gently, her eyes still on Mike's face.

Mike let out a long slow breath. He had not said half of what he had wanted to say, yet he had made progress. He covered her hand with his and squeezed it gently. She didn't pull her hand away and his heart filled with hope.

"Let me have Patrick." He took the child from Letty's arms. "We're home, son," he said when, disturbed, the boy whimpered a protest. "You'll be in your bed soon."

CHAPTER
—————13—————

Morning came and with it a spring storm. Letty let Patrick sleep after Jacob announced they would not be going to church.

"We'd be wet as a couple drowned rats by the time we got there," he grumbled. "God ain't goin' to slam shut the pearly gates 'cause we miss a time or two."

Letty agreed but didn't voice it. She hadn't been inside a church since she walked out of her father's church that Sunday, the day Cora told him and her mother she was pregnant. She had attended the graveside services for her grandmother and for a few friends who had died during the epidemic but steadfastly refused to go to Sunday services with her grandfather and Patrick. She knew it was a source of gossip in the neighborhood, but it didn't bother her.

The storm was still raging at midmorning. Thunder rolled and wind-driven rain lashed the house. Letty checked the doors and windows for leaks. A small puddle of water began to form under the door in the parlor. She placed a rag rug against the door to absorb the water. A stunning crash of thunder seemed to fill the house. It was still echoing when another roared in its wake.

Letty hurried back to the kitchen. Helen, sitting on Jacob's lap, had hid her face in his shoulder.

"There, there, little'un. It ain't nothin' but a old spring storm givin' my wheat field a drink a water. It takes thunder to jar the water outta the clouds."

"Helen's scared of the storm, but I ain't," Patrick announced proudly. He played with the iron bank, shooting the same five pennies into the bear time and again.

"You're *not*," Letty corrected as she stirred the syrup she was making to pour over egg whites to make icing for Patrick's birthday cake.

"I'm glad it rained 'cause me 'n' Grandpa don't have to go to church. But I wished it hadn't'a rained on my birthday 'cause Grandpa said we could fire off the Roman candle."

"You won't fire it until tonight. By then it'll have stopped raining. Then everyone from miles around will see the lights in the sky and know it's your birthday."

"Oh, boy! Can I go tell Dolan we're going to fire the Roman candle tonight?"

"In this rain? I should say not!"

"I didn't get to see him. He went out before I got up. I wanted to tell him it's my birthday." Patrick's chin was tilted defiantly; a stubborn look covered his face.

"I expect he knows," Letty said and dribbled a little of the hot syrup in a cup of cold water. As it immediately formed a solid ball, she removed the pan from the cookstove.

"Why'd you tell him to stay in the barn?" Patrick demanded suddenly.

Letty's head jerked up. Her eyes moved from the stiffly beaten egg whites to where her son sat on the floor. He was looking at her with his head resting on his fist, his eyes slanting up at her, his brows drawn down in a frown. She turned her face away and closed her eyes for an instant as an exquisite pain caused her heart to stumble. She had seen that same expression on his father's face many times.

"I didn't tell him to stay in the barn," Letty said calmly, and automatically moved the wire whisk as she poured a thin stream of the hot syrup into the bowl of egg whites.

"You don't like him. Bang!" Patrick shot the bear with a shiny new penny. "You don't look at him . . . bang . . . or say anything to him. Why don't you like him? Did he pinch you?"

"For crying out loud!" Letty set the pan back on the stove. "Why would you think that?"

"You wouldn't look at the man who came to buy Grandpa's cows after he pinched you on the titty. Remember? You slapped him. Then you didn't set at the table when—"

"Patrick!" Letty gasped. She hadn't been aware that her son had witnessed that disgusting scene in the barn with the cattle buyer.

207

"What? What's this?" Jacob asked. "What's this about Cadwaller?"

"He pinched Mama and said she had—"

"I'll tell it if you don't mind, Patrick. Mr. Cadwaller got a little fresh, and I put him in his place. Nothing to get excited about."

"He said Mama had a pretty ass."

"What?" Jacob shouted, scaring Helen who scrambled off his lap.

"Patrick, I swear." Letty's voice was heavy with exasperation. "You're getting too big for your britches."

"Will I get new ones?"

"Young man, you'll get a spanking if you don't shut up even if it is your birthday." Patrick recognized that there was no threat in his mother's words, but rather a reminder that at times boys were to be seen and not heard.

"Letty—"

"I'll tell you about it later, Grandpa. It was nothing. Let's forget it for now." She glanced at the child on the floor and shook her head. He was as smart as a whip. Everything he saw and heard stuck in his mind. Heavens! The confrontation with the cattle buyer had happened months ago. Thank goodness he had been sound asleep when she and Mike had talked last night, or he would be blurting out every word.

While Letty worked, her thoughts scrambled for position in her mind. One surfaced above the others. Soon Patrick would need a man's strong hand. Was she going to be able to handle him?

Another thought crowded out the first one. Her son had the right to know his father. Even if Mike proved to be an uncaring father, Patrick had the right to know him and judge him for himself. But Patrick was a little boy, an inner voice warned. Oh, Lord. What would he think about the lies his mother had told him about his *dead* father?

Last night before sleep claimed her, she had gone over every word that had passed between her and Mike. There was not the slightest doubt in her mind, now, that he was telling the truth about believing she had died during the epidemic. It hurt. Oh, it hurt to face the fact that her mother had cut her out of her life so completely as to declare her dead. It was her parents' fault her child had come into the world a bastard. She would never forgive them or Cora.

Letty stopped beating the icing and stared at the black stovepipe. It had been five years and eight months almost to the day that she and Mike had parted. So much had happened to her since that time. So much had happened to him. Yet, last night he had seemed almost to be the sweet boy she had known so long ago. This morning, however, he was the quiet dark man again. He had brought in the milk, set the pail on the counter, and taken his place at the table without looking at her. During breakfast he and Jacob talked about the wheat crop and the sheep Jacob wanted to put in the woods as soon as the nightshade was cleared out. When he finished eating, he put on his slicker and went out.

"Mrs. Graham—" Helen tugged on Letty's arm to get her attention. "I want to give Patrick a birthday present," she whispered.

"You don't have to give him anything, honey."

"I want to. You gave him the bank and Grandpa gave him five pennies. Do you think he'd like to have my marble?" Helen stared up at Letty with big sky-blue eyes. Her little face had filled out during the weeks she had been at the farm, but she still had the forlorn look in her eyes.

"Honey, are you sure you want to give up your marble? It's one of your treasures."

"I want Patrick to have it."

"All right. In the top bureau drawer you'll find some white tissue paper. Roll the marble in it and tie each end with a piece of that red yarn I used to make your mittens. Slip it on his plate just before we sit down to dinner."

The rain stopped, but the sky remained dark. Letty lit the lamp over the table and placed the birthday cake beneath it. When Patrick heard Mike's step on the porch, he ran to open the door.

"Today's my birthday," he shouted. "Mama gave me a iron bank and Grandpa gave me five pennies to shoot the bear 'cause I'm five.

Mike's eyes met Letty's as he wiped his feet on the rag rug at the door. She saw the regret in them. Something deep within her stirred. He had missed out on five years of his son's life through no fault of his.

"So you're five years old. You're a good-sized boy for five," he said with wonderment in his voice. "I suppose that's too old to be picked up and . . . hugged." His voice cracked, but Patrick didn't notice.

"No, it ain't. Grandpa hugs me. Mama hugs me, too, but she can't lift me up high. She says I'm too heavy."

"Let's see how heavy you are." Mike grasped Patrick beneath the arms, lifted him, and gently bumped his head against the ceiling. "Son of a gun! You are heavy. You must weigh fifty pounds."

Patrick giggled. "Looky, Mama! Dolan can lift me. He's strong."

When Mike lowered him, Patrick wound his arms about Mike's neck and his legs about his waist. With his eyes closed and such a look of anguish on his face that Letty's heart thumped painfully, Mike hugged his son.

"Happy birthday," he murmured.

"We're goin' to have chocolate cake, Dolan." Patrick giggled again. "Your whiskers scratch—"

"So will yours someday."

"I like you, Dolan." Patrick put lips sticky with cake frosting against Mike's cheek.

"I like you too." Mike's eyes sought Letty's. She was staring at him and Patrick, her cheeks red from the cookstove, her hands buried in her apron pockets. Her eyes looked straight into his as if she could read his innermost thoughts, and he sent a silent message. *We've lost five years that we can never regain, Letty. I love you. I love this child we made together. It kills me to hear him call me Dolan.*

An emotion rose up in Letty as acute as pain

when she saw the loving look on Mike's face as he looked at their child. She turned away lest he see the tears in her eyes. She hadn't counted on her life being disrupted this way. All she'd wished for in life, after she had become reconciled to the fact Mike was not coming back, was to live here with her son and take care of Grandpa. Now the thought of the gentle touch of Mike's lips and the safe haven of his arms sent a violent wave of longing crashing over her.

She had to get hold of herself.

"Dinner is almost ready," she said, forcing lightness in her voice. "We're having all the birthday boy's favorites. Fried chicken, mashed potatoes and gravy, green beans, and spiced peaches."

"I don't like green beans," Patrick said as soon as his feet hit the floor. "I don't like 'em."

"You won't have to eat any today because it's your birthday. Next time you will. They're good for you. Come on, Grandpa. Where's Helen?"

"Here I am." Helen slipped around the table and dropped the package on Patrick's plate.

"Another present. Oh, boy!" Patrick tore the paper and the marble bounced on the floor. He dived under the table after it. "Looky, Dolan. Helen gave me her marble."

"Its a dandy." Mike rolled it around in his fingers. "You can use it as a taw."

"What's a taw?"

"That's what you call your shooting marble."

"I'll use it as a shooter." Patrick put the marble

beside his plate. "I like it, Helen. It's the best marble I got."

Helen's eyes fairly danced with pleasure.

Patrick was too excited to eat a proper meal, but Letty didn't scold him. This was *his* day. He talked continually, taking full advantage of the grown-ups' attention.

Jacob, under the guise of listening to Patrick's chatter, watched his granddaughter and Mike Dolan. Although Letty didn't direct any of her conversation to him, the hostility of the last few days had lessened. Jacob congratulated himself. He had made a good move when he sent Mike to the Pierce farm to ride home with her even though he had known the Watkins' would have seen her safely home. Dolan, Jacob noticed, could hardly keep his eyes off her. When Letty laughed, the man's dark eyes shone with pleasure. He listened intently to every word she said. Yessirree, he had made a good move. Mike Dolan would do just fine. He had taken to farming like a duck to water. Jacob chuckled silently. All he had to do now was to sit back and let nature take its course.

Letty cleared the table and, wanting to make the occasion as festive as possible, made a big to-do about cutting and serving the birthday cake, even using clean plates. As she served clockwise around the table, her fingers were sticky with white icing by the time she reached Mike. His eyes lingered on her fingers before lifting to her face. What she saw there made sparks as alive as those

213

in the fireplace race through her veins. *He looked at her as if he were starving.* It took a breathtaking moment for her to come out of her daze. When she did, she felt as if her heart had been suddenly exposed.

Jacob was the first to leave the table. He packed his pipe with tobacco and settled down in his big chair. When Mike stood, Patrick scooted around the table and took his hand.

"Don't go. I want to show you how to shoot the bear."

"I'm only going to the porch. There's something there with your name on it."

"A present? Golly!"

"A present." Mike glanced at Letty, then back to his son. "Stand over there and shut your eyes. It isn't wrapped." He went to the door. "Don't peek," he cautioned just before he went out.

When the door opened again, Mike had a grin on his face like a boy who had been given a slingshot and a pocket full of stones. His laughing eyes darted first to Letty, then to Patrick who stood in the center of the room with his hands over his eyes.

"All right. Open your eyes."

Patrick's hands fell away, his eyes flew open, and he blinked. "Stilts! Oh, boy! Stilts."

"Have you ever walked on stilts?" Mike asked.

"Jimmy Watkins has some, but they're too high for me."

"These are six-inches high. After you learn how to walk on them, we can move the platforms higher or make a new pair. Hold on," he said when Patrick stuck his foot in one of the stirrups. "Your mama won't want you walking on these in the house."

"It'll be all right if you hold onto him," Letty said and turned to pour water from the teakettle into the dishpan. Her hands shook; her eyes misted.

Lordy, how was she ever going to sort out this mess? Grandpa was sitting over in his chair looking pleased with himself. Didn't he know what a scandal it would cause if the neighbors found out Mike was Patrick's father, there was no Mr. Graham, and she had never been married?

In a room above the Piedmont billiard parlor four men sat at a round table playing cards and drinking whiskey from a glass fruit jar. A grossly fat man was dealing. He paused, leaned sideways to spit in a can beside the chair, then continued passing out the cards.

"I knowed he was trouble the minute I set eyes on him," Arlo said and slapped the last card down on the pile in front of him." We was sittin' in the store the day he got off the train. Unfriendly a cuss as I ever did see. He had a mean look on him and eyes as cold as the bottom of a well. Looked like he could split ya end to end and not bat a eye."

"Maybe so," Oscar Phillips snarled. "But he don't know what trouble is. Us Phillipses don't take kindly to being sneaked up on and laid flat like he done. Hell! One minute I was sayin' my goodbyes to Letty; the next I was on the ground. He ain't gettin' away with it. I aim to stop his clock one way or another."

"He's a close-mouthed bastard. I tried to get a word out a him when he was staying over at the hotel 'cause I thought he might be a U.S. marshal, but he didn't give out nothing." The man who spoke had a red face and jowls that hung down almost to his collar. He also wore a tin star with the word *deputy* printed on it.

"Clerk said he asked where the Fletcher farm was." Oscar said out of the side of his mouth because the other side was still swollen.

"I ain't figured out what a man like him is doin' signin' on as a hired hand," the deputy said. "Old Jacob's gettin' on, but he can hire neighbors to help out at plantin' and harvest time."

"Ya reckon he's lookin' for a place to stash a load a white lighting?" As Arlo talked, tobacco juice gathered in the corner of his mouth.

"If he does, he'll get the shit shot out of him sure as shootin'." The deputy's hard eyes stared into the fat man's. "Ain't nobody hornin' in on *my* operation and drawin' attention to that part of the country."

"I heared a big boss is comin' out from Chicago. Reckon it's him?"

All eyes turned to Cecil Weaver who had arrived in town that morning after serving his time for bootlegging.

"Who told you that?" the deputy demanded.

"Boys in the jailhouse." Cecil reached under the table for the fruit jar and took a long drink. Then he set the jar down on the table.

"Get that off the table," the deputy snapped. "Ain't no tellin' who'll come poppin' in that door."

"Ain't nobody goin' to see it," Cecil grumbled as he set the jar on the floor. "I got to go get my little Helen." Tears of self-pity filled his bloodshot eyes. "Poor little motherless girl—"

"Play cards, if you're goin' to," Arlo said.

Oscar placed a card in the middle of the table and gave Cecil a sly look.

"I'm thinkin' you'll have a time gettin' your little girl away from Mrs. Letty Graham. She's taken a shine to her."

"My poor baby needs her pa," Cecil blubbered. "My woman is gone . . . my babies. All that's left is my little H-Helen."

Deputy Elmer Russell gave a snort of disgust. He was a man eaten up with resentment. Born and raised in the county, he had had a gigantic blow to his ego when he ran for sheriff and lost by an overwhelming majority to a man who had lived here for only a short while. He had reluctantly accepted the deputy job because he loved the authority it gave him, and he was privy to information that was helpful not only to him but to certain others. Not even Arlo and Oscar knew the extent of his connections. Men were getting rich selling illegal whiskey, and he intended to be one of them. If a big dealer was coming in

217

to poach on his territory, he wanted to know about it.

"I asked you who told you the big boys were comin'?" Elmer slapped a couple of cards on the table. "Give me two," he said to Arlo.

"My poor l-little motherless l-lamb—"

"Goddammit! Shut up your pissin' and moanin' or get out."

"Tell him what he wants to know, Cecil," Oscar urged.

" 'Bout the big b-boys? Well . . . it was a feller who'd been in that iron bird-cage jailhouse over in Council Bluffs. You know the place? Hit's the most god-awful place—Round, it is. Iron floors, iron walls. Cells is shaped like a piece a pie. He said there was a big old nigger in there who'd killed a white woman. He beat on the bars all night long. Boom! Boom! Boom! He said that bird cage went 'round and round—"

"Ah . . . shit!" Elmer reached over and grabbed Cecil by the shirt front. "You no-good drunken son-of-a-bitch. If you leave this room before you sober up I'll nail your balls to a stump. Hear?"

"He'll be all right, Elmer," Oscar said. "I'll watch him. He's just all tore up 'bout not seeing his little girl."

"Bullshit!" Elmer snarled.

"I'm not worried Cecil'll spill anythin'. It's that big dark bastard out at Fletcher's that worries me. He ain't there just to help out the old man. He's got somethin' else on his mind."

"Like Letty Graham." Arlo snickered and

watched Oscar's face darken with anger. "She's been puttin' the hard on you for years, ain't she, Oscar? She sure can switch her pretty little ass, but I reckon it'd not hold a candle to the pretty little asses Dolan humped while he was over in France."

"It gets to you, don't it, Arlo?" Oscar said with heavy sarcasm. "All that ass out there and you ain't had none yet. All you know about it is what you read in dirty books or hear the fellers talkin' about."

Arlo's face flamed and his jaws shook. "You don't know nothin' 'bout me. I don't tell you ever'thin' I do."

"I know enough to know you ain't seen that stick between your legs in ten years. Maybe more," Elmer said and laughed.

Arlo pushed back his chair and stood chewing viciously on a quid of tobacco. "Just 'cause you're a *deputy* don't give you no right to say things like that.

"Sit down, Arlo. I'm just a hurrahin' you. Tell you what. If you're hankerin' to get your pecker in somethin' soft, I'll take you down to Boley to see Naked Ann. For two bucks she'll ride you till your eyeballs bug out."

"Naked Ann don't hold a candle to Genny at the Nook in Claypool." Oscar leaned back and scratched his armpit. "And she'll do it for two *bits.* "

Elmer gave Oscar a cold stare. "What makes you an authority on whores? You get what you pay for, Arlo. Remember that. Naked Ann knows every trick in the trade."

"She ort to," Oscar grumbled. "She's been at it long enough."

Arlo sat down. "I seen that Naked Ann once. Ain't she a mite old ta be whorin'?"

Elmer snorted. "It ain't her face ya'll be lookin' at, ya dumb cluck! Play cards or I'm headin' out of here."

They continued the card game playing three-handed. Cecil Weaver lolled in the chair, his eyes glared, his mouth agape. When the game broke up, Elmer stood.

"I'll be going out to Fletchers in a few days to see what I can find out about Mike Dolan. Keep your eye on this bird." He jerked his head toward Cecil. "Jesus! He smells like he's messed his drawers."

CHAPTER
—————14—————

Spring arrived in all its glory. Dandelions sprang up: the buds on the lilac bushes popped; birds were busy building nests, and Letty was busy housecleaning. Jacob and Mike worked long hours in the fields.

After the floors had been scrubbed, the curtains and windows washed, the mattresses aired, and kerosene dribbled in the seams to discourage bed bugs, Letty cleaned out the small storage room across the hall from her room, taking some things to the cellar, others to the barn. She washed the floor and walls, laid down one of her grandma's braided rag rugs, and moved in a dresser and Helen's cot. She found a pair of old curtains for the windows and, after they had been washed, shortened them on the sewing machine.

Helen was delighted with the room and fascinated with the sewing machine. Letty cut pillowcases from the outer part of twin sheets that had become so thin in the middle that they were beyond patching and taught Helen how to stitch them on the machine. By the end of the week. she was so adept that she made herself an apron from the skirt of one of Letty's old dresses.

Once in the morning and again in the afternoon, Patrick carried a Mason jar of fresh water to the men in the field. He spent every possible moment with Mike, and, as hard as she tried to control her feelings, Letty couldn't help but feel a twinge of jealousy. How ironic that the man her son had come to idolize was his father.

Under Jacob's guidance Mike was learning every aspect of farming. The work was strengthening his body; the fresh air was healing his lungs. He was up before daylight and had the chores done by the time dawn streaked the sky. After a full day in the field, he spent an hour or two sharpening the plows, mending the harnesses, repairing the chicken house, or whatever else needed to be done.

Patrick looked forward to this time of day. He followed Mike like a shadow. Mike taught him things as simple as how to pound a nail or as complicated as splicing a rope.

The woodbox beside the cookstove was filled each evening. Mike chopped and carried in the wood, Patrick the kindling. Mike let him help sharpen the ax on the grindstone and cautioned him always to leave the blade sunk in a log so that it didn't rust. Before dark they played a game of catch or Mike showed him the proper way to hold the bat, and pitched him a few balls. Jacob usually watched from the porch and yelled encouragement.

At bedtime, when Patrick had to be separated from his idol, the child threw his arms about his neck. Mike closed his eyes in an agony of bliss as he hugged his son tightly to him. It never failed to bring a lump to Letty's throat. Patrick had missed so much. He deserved to know that this man he had come to adore was his father. But how could she tell him?

Gradually, Letty ceased to feel threatened by Mike's presence although she avoided his eyes and seldom spoke directly to him. On the rare occasions when they were so close that she could smell the tangy odor of his body, she was steeped in sensation. Her heart thumped and goose bumps climbed her arms. At times she could feel his eyes on her, but he never made any attempt to catch her alone.

On Monday morning, a week after Mike had

brought her home from the Pierces, he filled the iron wash pot and built a fire beneath it. Earlier in the week he had tightened the clothes wire that stretched from the corner of the house to the side of the chicken house and had propped a pole in the middle where the long line sagged.

He was stacking more wood beside the iron pot when Letty came out of the house and attempted to drag the heavy washbench from the porch. He hurried to her.

"That's too heavy for you. let me do it."

"I can do it."

"Not while I'm here you can't."

Letty shrugged and returned to the house for the basket of dirty clothes. Mike's eyes followed her, fastening onto the sight of her smooth back and swaying hips. His insides felt warm and melting.

"You'll be gettin' spoiled, sure as shootin'," Jacob said drily as Letty passed him on her way to the house.

"Glory, Grandpa," she retorted. "I didn't ask him to fill my wash pot or carry the bench. I've been doing it for years."

"If ya didn't have yore back up in the air so dad-burn high, you'd admit that you like havin' him do for ya."

"If you're so all-fired smart, Jacob Fletcher, why din't you go to Washington and tell Mr. Wilson how to run the government?" she retorted sassily.

Jacob chuckled. "By God, somebody ort ta do jist that. He's making a hell of a mess of thin's."

He was still chuckling as he hitched the team to the planter. Things were working out fine. He congratulated himself on reading Dolan right. He hadn't lost his ability to judge a man. Mike had taken to farming even faster than he thought he would, and, most important of all, the man had a heap of love for Letty and the boy—it was as plain as the nose on his face. He wasn't a namby-pamby kind of man either. Lord, it had done his heart good when Dolan laid Oscar Phillips out flat with one blow. The bastard had it coming.

A look of contentment came over Jacob's lined face. Yessirree, there'd be a man. A real blood and guts man, to look after Letty and Patrick when he was gone. Now there was only one more thing he had to do to make sure that what he'd worked for all his life wasn't snatched from their hands when he passed on.

On his way to the field, Jacob stopped beside the tub where Letty was rubbing a pair of Patrick's britches on the washboard.

"The least ya could do fer Dolan is wash his clothes." He cracked the whip over the backs of the mules. "Get on there, Samson. You too, Delilah," he yelled and left the yard before she could think of an answer.

Letty stood with her hands on her hips, staring after him. She knew Grandpa. He liked nothing better than to get her riled up. But he was right this time. She should wash Mike's clothes. She looked out toward the field where Mike was walking behind the heavy drag that was preparing the soil for planting. Saturday he had washed a pair of britches and a shirt and had hung them on the line to dry overnight. He was meticulously clean with his person and his clothing. That much hadn't changed since he was a boy.

For a moment she allowed herself to remember the closeness they had once shared. This man, this almost stranger, had been not only her best friend, but her lover, and later the father of her son. *Mike, oh, Mike, if only we could turn back the clock* .

She dropped Patrick's britches back into the soapy water and dried her hands.

Letty had avoided the room at the front of the barn since Mike had fixed up the end of it for his sleeping quarters. Years ago the room had been partitioned off. Saddles, harnesses, and tools were stored there.

Feeling like an intruder, she went there and stood hesitantly in the doorway looking around. At one end was a newly made built-in bunk; a blanket covered the straw mattress and another blanket was folded neatly at the foot. On a shelf beneath a cracked mirror was his shaving mug, razor, and a few other toilet articles. Nearby, his razor strop hung on a nail. She recognized the chipped granite pitcher and washbasin on another newly made shelf as one she had stored away when she bought the blue and white set for her room. His clothes hung on nails above the bunk, and a bundle wrapped in his oilcloth

225

slicker sat on the bottom shelf of a makeshift table that held a coal-oil lamp.

The whinny of a horse caught her attention as she crossed the dirt floor to take Mike's clothes from the nails on the wall. An answering whinny came from Mike's horse in the corral beside the barn. She went to the window and stood on her toes to look out. A big man on a gray horse was riding up the lane toward the house. Deputy Elmer Russell. Now what in the world was he doing here? Unwilling to get caught in the barn by this man who had the reputation of being less than proper with women, she hurried out to meet him.

"Mornin." The deputy tipped his hat and, not waiting for an invitation, stepped down from his horse.

"Good morning."

Woodrow came out from the shed with his teeth bared. A low tumble came from his throat.

"Call off the dog or I'll shoot him." He spoke around the plug of tobacco bulging his jaw.

"It's all right, Woodrow. It's all right." She patted the dog's head and he moved back to the side of the barn and sat down, his tongue hanging out the side of his mouth.

Early this morning John Pershing had led his family of females through the grove to the creek. The arrogant goose wouldn't have been so easily controlled. He would have been determined to get in at least one jab at the deputy's shiny brown boots.

Letty had never liked this red-faced, fleshy man. His eyes were small and closely set. Once she had seen him without his hat and realized why he seldom took it off. The scrap of hair that grew down to within a mere inch of his eyebrow's was long and combed back to cover the top of his bald head. He wore the wide-brimmed hat and the vest of the old-time lawmen, and Letty was sure he fancied himself comparable to one of the famed Texas Rangers.

"Grandpa isn't here. He's in the field."

"I saw him, Dolan's out there too."

"Then why did you stop here?"

"My business is with you." He gazed steadily at her breasts.

"Then state it." Letty felt the flush of anger heat her face.

"What do you know about this fellow Dolan?"

Elmer Russell's beady brown eyes had a way of sliding away from a direct confrontation. But now they moved up. He fixed his hard gaze on Letty's face.

"He's a good worker."

"What else?"

"What else is there to know?"

"You know what I mean. Where's he from? What's he doing here?"

"Why don't you ask him?"

"I'm askin' you."

"He told Grandpa that this time last year he was in France fighting the Kaiser. But then you wouldn't know about that, would you?"

Letty could use her voice unkindly. She did that now. Her tone made it clear what she thought of him.

"Goddamn you!" He made no attempt to hold back his anger. "You're talkin' to the law. Somebody ort to take the strut out of you once and for all. Now you tell me where this man comes from and what he's doin' here, or—"

"—Or you'll arrest me?" Letty looked him in the eye and laughed. "I doubt that Sheriff Ledbetter would allow it."

"Watch your mouth, you little twat." His hand flashed out and caught her forearm. "The sheriff is down at the capitol and I'm in charge here."

"Get your hands off me, you yellow-backed, pompous ass!"

"And if I don't?"

"I'll scream my head off and Grandpa and Mr. Dolan will come." Letty tried not to wince when he squeezed her am, cruelly. She jerked her chin up and glared at him. He looked away from her accusing eyes and threw her arm from him. After tying his horse to the fence, he headed for the house.

"Where are you going'!" Alarmed, Letty followed close behind him. "There's no one in there but my son and Helen Weaver and they're sleeping."

"Oh, yes. The Weaver girl." He whirled around so fast she bumped into him, then sprang back. "Cecil will be out to fetch her in a day or two."

Letty's face went notably pale. "She's in my care. He'll have to get a court order."

"That's easy to do. She's his kid."

"He mistreated her, you stupid dolt!" Letty hissed. "He'll not get her."

"We'll see about that. I'm not here to argue the matter. Where does Dolan sleep? In your bed?" he added caustically.

A red flood of anger washed over Letty. She eyed him with open distaste as if he were something rotten.

"It's not difficult to tell where your mind is, *Deputy* Russell."

He grinned at her and chucked her on the chin with his fist. He laughed when she jerked her head away.

"Right between yore legs, sweetheart. Bet you ain't never had nothin' as big as I got."

"How dare you talk to me like this! I'll tell Sheriff Ledbetter—"

"You do that, honey. It'll be your word against mine. Now where is Dolan's—"

"Mama—" Patrick, in his nightshirt, came out onto the back porch rubbing the sleep out of his eyes. "Can I have my breakfast?"

"Go on back in the house, honey. I'll get it in a minute."

"Hold on there, son. You know who I am?"

Patrick squinted up at the big star on the man's chest. "Yes, sir."

"Go into the house, Patrick," Letty said sternly.

Something in Letty's voice made Patrick obey. He went inside and stood looking out the screen door. Something was wrong. He wished that Dolan were here. As he watched, he saw the deputy go toward the barn. His mother hurried to keep up with him, talking all the while. After they disappeared inside, Patrick slipped out onto the porch to stand with his arm wrapped around the support post. He stood there wondering what the deputy and his mother were doing in the barn. He jumped off the porch to go see. His mother came out and met him in the yard.

"What's, wrong, Mama?"

She didn't answer until they reached the porch. "Put on your shoes and go get Grandpa and Mr. Dolan. Tell them to get back here fast."

"In my nightshirt?"

"Don't take time to change, but put on your shoes because there's cockleburs. Hurry!" she said urgently.

Patrick put his bare feet in his shoes and, not taking time to tie them, dashed from the house. Holding up his nightshirt, he ran across the yard to the gate leading to the field. His mama was scared—he could tell. She needed Grandpa and Dolan and was depending on him to go get them. Why was she scared of the deputy? Deputies were supposed to help people. Weren't they?

Patrick ran as fast as he could over the plowed ground. Suddenly, he stubbed his toe on a clod and sprawled face first in the dirt.

"Shitfire," he muttered as he sprang to his feet.

After he wiped the dirt from his eyes he saw Dolan at the far end of the field coming toward him. "Dolan! Dolan!" he shouted.

Mike had turned the mules and was heading back up the field when he saw someone coming across the plowed ground toward him. At first he thought it was Helen. After a closer look, he saw that it was Patrick in his nightshirt. Good grief, what had possessed the kid to come out before he was dressed?

"Dolan! Ma . . . Ma wants you to come ho . . . ome—"

The frantic urgency in the child's voice reached Mike and sent a chill up his back. He felt cold with sudden dread.

"Dolan! Hur . . . ry!"

Something has happened to Letty! A wave of sickness rolled over him. *Please, God, don't do this to me. I love her so much.* The words caught in his throat but resounded in his heart.

He dropped the reins and ran toward Patrick as fast as he could. It seemed a million miles across that field. Soon his lungs were on fire and his heart was pumping like a steam engine going uphill, but be kept going. He was so afraid, so goddamn afraid.

Patrick had lost one of his shoes by the time Mike reached him and was dancing around on one foot.

"What is it?" Mike demanded. "What's happened?"

"Mama said get you and Grandpa."

"But what *happened?*"

"The deputy's there. Mama's scared. She told me to hurry . . . not to take time to put on my clothes—She said she said tell you to come fast."

"Is she hurt?"

"She didn't act hurt. But she's scared—I can tell—Dolan?"

"Go tell your grandpa," Mike said over his shoulder and took off on a run for the house.

Letty wasn't hurt. Thank God! But why in hell was she scared of a deputy? "Letty my beautiful, wonderful Letty." The words came hissing through his teeth as he ran. "I love you so damn much. Without you I—" He swallowed, shuddered, and dragged air into his tortured lungs.

Mike was still a distance away when he saw a man come out the back door. Letty, with her arms around Helen, followed and stood on the porch. The man mounted his horse, moved up close to the porch, and spoke to Letty. Then he kicked his mount into a gallop and left the farmyard. By the time Mike reached the gate, the horse was headed down the road toward Piedmont.

"Letty, for God's s-sake!" he gasped. "What h-happened?"

"You shouldn't have run across that field. The way your lungs—"

"To hell with my l-lungs. D-did that man hurt you?"

"He didn't hurt me. Sit down."

"Thank God!" Mike sank down on the edge of

the porch, his chest heaving. "Jesus! I thought sure—Oh, Lord—" He hung his dark head between his knees and fought for breath. Finally, when it became easier for him to draw air into his lungs, he lifted his head.

"Are you all right?" Letty asked anxiously. "Just g-give me a minute."

"I'm sorry I panicked and sent Patrick for you. It didn't occur to me that you'd need to run a half mile over that plowed field."

"Oh, God, Letty. You scared the living hell out of me." His whispered voice was rough with emotion. He raised his eyes to her face; they were filled with utter misery. She was standing in front of him. Helen's arms were wrapped about her waist, and the child's face was buried against her breasts.

"'What did Patrick tell you, for Pete's sake?"

"That . . . that you wanted me to come . . . home. And to . . . hurry. I was sure that you'd had an accident, or . . . or something."

"As you can see, nothing like that happened. I thought you should be here. It's probably better that you weren't. There might have been trouble." Then she added slowly. "He's the law."

Mike got to his feet. "What did he do to you?" he asked tightly.

"Nothing to me." Letty pried the child's arms from around her waist, then wiped the tears from her eyes with the end of her apron. "Go get dressed, Helen, while I talk to Mr. Dolan."

"But . . . that man s-s-said—" Helen began to sob.

"He doesn't know what he's talking about. Go get dressed. Patrick and Grandpa will be here in a few minutes. Don't worry. Grandpa will know what to do."

"What did he say to her?" Mike frowned darkly when he saw the anguish on the little girl's face.

"He said her father was coming to get her." Letty's words brought fresh tears to Helen's eyes. "But he'll not take her if she doesn't want to go." Letty hoped fervently she would be able to keep her promise. "That wasn't why the deputy was here though. Go get dressed, Helen. We'll talk about it when Grandpa gets here."

When she heard the screen door slam, Letty looked up into Mike's face. She saw him take a deep quivering breath. It had been days since she had looked directly at him. He held his jaws rigid. The shining pain in his eyes caused her innards to roll and pitch violently. Oh, Lord! It was both agony and elation to remember the sensation of being in his arms, the pressure of his mouth on hers, a part of him inside her body. Inhaling the earthy scent of him, she was almost overcome with an inner trembling. Emotion and pride seesawed for dominance. He kept staring at her face. She began to feel that helplessness his look and nearness brought to her confused and weakened willpower.

Mike lifted his hands, lightly touched her arms, then let them drop to his sides and ball into hard fists. Wordlessly, he stared into her face and was dumbfounded by the perfection of her skin, the

234

glint of sunlight in her auburn hair. Long gold-tipped lashes framed her eyes. Her pink lips were slightly parted, reminding him of an unfurled rose. He longed to press them with his once again. She was more beautiful now than she had been at fifteen. The scent of breakfast cooking, soapsuds, and the pure sweet musky smell of woman wafted to him from her person. It quickened his nostrils, made his flesh ignite. Her breasts rose and fell quickly with each breath. He suddenly realized she was not as calm as she pretended to be. His hopes rose.

"The deputy questioned me about you.

He watched her mouth move. Slowly the words sank into his mind.

"He saw me and Jacob in the field. Why didn't he ride out?"

"I don't think he wanted you here when he . . . when he went through your things."

"That's strange. I have nothing to hide. But I resent him prowling in my belongings."

"Come see what he did. It's why I sent Patrick to get you."

Mike followed her to the barn. She stepped aside when they reached the door to the tack room. He went in.

"Good Godamighty!'

One end of the room had been completely ransacked; Mike's clothes jerked from the wall, the lining of his army overcoat split open, the pad on his bunk ripped, the straw scattered. The personal belongings he had wrapped in his rain slicker had been dumped on the floor: his war medals, letters from his mother, leather money belt, his discharge papers. On the dirt floor, ground beneath the high heel of a boot was a small white envelope. Mike scooped it up. The scrap of faded blue ribbon was still inside. He breathed a sigh of thankfulness, folded the envelope, and put it in his shirt pocket.

"I tried to stop him." Letty stood in the doorway.

"Did he say what he was looking for?"

"He wanted to know where you were from and what you were doing here."

"What did you tell him?"

"That you were working for Grandpa."

"He could see from these letters from my mother where I'm from. Why should he care? There's no warrant for my arrest. Good Lord, I haven't been home long enough to get into any trouble."

"He thinks you're building a still."

"A whiskey still?" Mike gave a snort of disgust. "Where'd he get that idea?"

"From the forge you and the Pierce boys are setting up in the shed."

"The man must be a fool. It doesn't take a forge and an anvil to make a still. All you need is good spring water, barrels, and sheet copper rolled into tube-shaped pipes and soldered."

"He asked me if you'd mentioned Chicago, or Kansas City."

"I get it now. He thinks the big-city mobs are going to move in and take over this territory. Why should they move out of a city of a million or more to a county that probably has less than three thousand people? Our good deputy is not a deep thinker."

"Evidently logic isn't a requirement for being a deputy." Letty backed out the door. "Grandpa's going to be madder than hob when he sees what the deputy did to his apricot brandy. Thank goodness he didn't go down in the cellar and find what Grandpa's got bottled up down there."

Jacob, riding the planter with Patrick perched on his lap, drove into the yard. Mike went to lift Patrick down, then held the team while Jacob climbed from the iron seat, a look of deep concern on his face.

When Jacob saw what the deputy had done to his brandy, he was more than angry. He was red-hot, hopping mad. His apricot brandy had been ready to siphon and bottle. The lawman had pulled the crock from behind the cookstove where the brandy had been working and had dumped in several scoops of ashes from the ash bucket. Not being satisfied with that, he'd added the soapy water from the dishpan Letty had left on the stove. It filled the crock and ran out onto the floor.

"The dirty, low-down, pea-brained chicken-shit!" Jacob's face was suffused with crimson. He opened and closed his mouth as if strangling.

"Grandpa! Watch what you're saying." Letty's concern was more for him than his language. The veins in his temples stood out, his lips trembled, his voice shook. She feared his heart would give out.

"Son of a mangy polecat had no right to come in a man's house—"

"I know. You can make more brandy."

"It ain't the goddamm brandy, dammit to hell!" Jacob shouted. " 'Tis the idey that a puff-up pissant can come into *my* house 'on' do what he done. It ain't no way right."

"I know that, Grandpa. You'll have to talk to Sheriff Ledbetter. He seems to he a reasonable man."

"You can bet yore bottom dollar I'll talk to Ledbetter." Jacob stomped out of the room and onto the porch.

Letty looked after him helplessly, her brows puckered in a worried frown. Patrick, standing quietly in the doorway leading to the parlor, had put his arm around a wide-eyed and trembling Helen.

"Ain't no reason to be scared, Helen. Grandpa ain't mad at us."

Letty had never been more proud of her son.

"Stay where you are for a little bit. I want to mop up this mess first."

"Letty," Mike spoke from beside the door. He took the two steps necessary to reach her and lifted her hand. "Did he do this to you?"

Letty looked down at her forearm and was surprised to see the dark bruise where the deputy had squeezed her arm. She had forgotten about it. Now she could see nothing but his big hand holding her, hear nothing but the frantic beat of her heart. When she was finally able to raise her eyes to his, his brows were drawn together in a frown. She swallowed, drew in a deep breath, and let it out slowly. For a moment her eyes riveted to his lower lip, remembering—

"It's nothing. I got pretty lippy and he got his dander up."

"Is this the only place he touched you?" His voice was strained. Her legs were shaking so badly that she locked her knees tightly together.

"Yes," she whispered, glad now she had said nothing about the deputy's insulting sexual remarks.

White-hot rage had swept his body when he saw the bruise on her arm, all else deserting his mind. Anger flared brightly in his eyes but he didn't say anything. Soon a look so tender and a smile so endearing caused her heart to flop over. He raised her hand slowly, giving her time to draw it away, and kissed the bruise on her arm. Then he released it quickly.

Oh, Mike. Oh, my love. Letty held the back of her hand to her lips and watched him walk out the door.

Mike stood on the edge of the porch, his hands in his back pockets, and took a long deep breath. If he had stayed a minute longer, he would have pulled her into his arms. Once he had touched her lips, he wouldn't have been able to stop kissing her.

"I'll be taking a trip to town, Jacob."

"Thought ya would. Better wait till Ledbetter gets back and I'll go with ya. I've been plannin' to go to Boley soon as the plantin's done. You 'n' me has got us some business to take care of."

Without saying anything more, Jacob went to the planter, climbed up on the seat, and headed for the field, leaving Mike to wonder what he had in mind.

CHAPTER
—————15—————

After the deputy's visit the atmosphere in the house was more relaxed. The relationship between Letty and Mike underwent a change. Although there was frequent laughter and light banter, he made no move to touch her or indicate that he wanted to be alone with her. Letty waited for a sign, but none came.

Mike took a delight in every aspect of farm life. When one of the sows had a litter of piglets, he came to the house, grinning like a schoolboy with a new slingshot, to take Letty and the children out to see the new family. He was equally interested when the chicks Letty ordered arrived and he helped her make a place for them in the chicken house.

The men worked from daylight till dusk in the fields. Some nights they were so tired that they ate their supper in near silence, and Jacob went to bed shortly afterward. Letty was worried about him. He had lost weight and she noticed a trembling in his hands. She spoke to Mike about it one night after Jacob had left the kitchen.

"Grandpa's working too hard. I wish—" She looked directly into his ebony eyes. They had some mystical power to make her forget what she was saying.

"I've been trying to slow him down,"

"Will you be finished by the end of the week?"

"We'll wind up the planting in about three days. At harvest time I'm hoping to persuade him to stay out of the field."

"I seriously doubt you'll be able to do that. I could help if he'd let me." Her hands trembled as she stacked the plates to take them to the dishpan.

"You have plenty to do here."

"Grandpa's not young, you know."

"I know, but he has his pride, Letty. Let him do what he wants to do."

"He seems different since the deputy was here."

"He wants to finish the planting so he can go to town to see the sheriff."

"And you?"

"I'll go with him."

Letty looked up to meet Mike's gaze. For a long while they stared, barely breathing. Each was still except for the wild chaos going on inside them. The lamplight illuminated his tired face, showing the dark cast of a day-old beard. The hungry look in his eyes caused her heart to slam against her rib cage. A hot anxious feeling took root in the pit of her stomach, spread, and bathed her with its warmth. *If you still want me, say something, Mike. Please say something.*

He did, but not to her.

"Patrick, shall we give that old swing a workout while your mama is doing the dishes?"

"Yeah! Oh, boy. Can we fix my stilts too? You said you'd make them higher. I'm gettin' good at walkin' on 'em, ain't I?"

Mike ruffled his son's dark hair with his fingers. "You betcha. We'll fix the stilts tomorrow night. How's that'?"

"Will you learn me to whistle, Dolan?"

"I can't *learn* you, but I may be able to *teach* you."

"Ah . . . Dolan—"

Letty watched father and son leave, Patrick's hand tucked into Mike's, and had to admit that she was jealous of her son. She hated herself for it.

Two and a half weeks had passed since the night they had come home from the Pierces', and Mike had told her he still loved her and would give her time to sort out her feelings for him. It had taken her less than two days to realize that her love for Mike, the boy, would remain eternally in her heart. Both of them had changed since that long-ago time. She had no doubt that now it was Mike, the man, she loved. Oh, but what a tangled web she had woven around herself. To acknowledge him as the father of her son would disgrace not only herself and Patrick, but Grandpa. She couldn't do it. She couldn't.

The next afternoon as Letty carried a bucket of water to her tomato plants, she saw a horse and buggy coming down the road. She pulled the stiff-brimmed sunbonnet forward to shade her eyes and squinted against the sun.

"Horse apples'." she exclaimed when she saw who it was. She darted around the hedge of lilac bushes and into the house by the time Cecil Weaver turned into the farmyard. The sound coming from the parlor told her that Helen was practicing the scales on the piano.

"Helen," she called anxiously. "Come here."

"Did I do something wrong?"

"No, honey. Your father is here."

The child stopped in mid-stride. A look of utter terror came over her face before it crumbled. She ran to Letty and threw her arms about her waist, holding on as if her life depended on it.

"Don't let him . . . don't let him—"

"Oh, honey! I won't let him take you if I can help it." Letty's mind worked frantically while Helen sobbed against her. There was only one way to buy them some time until she could talk to Doctor Hakes again. "Run upstairs and get into the bed. Hurry." Letty pried the child's arms from around her and gave her a push toward the stairs.

Letty yanked off her bonnet and peered out the window. Cecil Weaver had stopped beside the windmill and was letting his horse drink. She went to her sewing basket and searched until she found

243

a ball of darning thread about the size of a walnut, then hurried up the stairs. Helen was in the bed. Her eyes were flooded with tears, but she was choking back the sobs.

"P-please d-don't let him take me away—"

"Helen, you know I've told you and Patrick that it's wrong to tell a lie." Letty knelt down on the floor and kissed the child's wet cheek. "But there are times when it's necessary. I'm going to tell your father that you're sick. I'll say that you've got the mumps. Open your mouth so I can poke this ball of thread in your jaw. I'll try to keep him from coming up here, but if he does, your jaw will look swollen. Stay just like this, on your side, with the covers pulled up to your chin. Don't move. Understand?"

Helen nodded.

"Try not to cry. We want him to think you're too sick to cry." A loud knock on the kitchen door caused Helen to jump. Her fearful eyes sought Letty's face for reassurance. "It's going to be all right, honey. I'll go talk to him."

Letty waited until two more knocks sounded on the door before she stepped out of the parlor and crossed the kitchen to the door.

"Hello, Mr. Weaver," she said in a hushed tone.

"Good day ta ya, ma'am."

"Step inside, but keep your voice down " Letty moved aside to allow him to enter.

While he looked around the tidy kitchen, she looked at him. His ruddy face was bloated, the eyes that refused to meet hers were red and watery. The sickening odor that wafted from his body told her he hadn't had a bath in months, maybe not a full bath for a year.

"Have you had the mumps, Mr. Weaver?"

"Huh?" His eyes moved from the pot of beef stew simmering on the cookstove to Letty's face, then away. "Mumps, ya say? I don't remember."

"I think you'd remember if you'd had them. They're very painful."

"I come for my Helen, but I ain't in no hurry. We can head back to town after supper, that is if we got a invite to stay."

"Helen is sick. She'd got a bad case of mumps."

"What's that you say? My Helen is sick? Oh, my God! My baby—my only baby—" The beseeching tone in his voice was so insincere it made Letty's stomach roll over. "Is she goin' to die? Ma'am, tell me true. Am I goin' to lose my little girl?"

"Not unless she has a setback," Letty said. Cecil was so busy wiping his eyes and blowing his nose on a rag he took from his back pocket that he didn't seem to notice the bite in her voice.

"I got to see my baby. She's all I've got left of my Edith." His voice had dropped to a whine.

"I wouldn't advise it if you're not sure whether or not you've had the mumps. It can be fatal to grown-ups . . . especially men. Besides . . . she may be asleep."

"Jist let me look at her, Mrs. Graham. She'll think her papa don't love her no more."

Letty fixed him with a cold stare and elevated

her chin. "You can stand in the doorway for just a minute. She must not be disturbed."

She led the way up the stairs, thankful that Patrick had gone to the field to take Mike and Grandpa a fresh drink of water. She had to get rid of this poor excuse of a man before her mouthy young son came back and spoiled everything. She peeked around the door and, seeing that Helen lay with her eyes tightly closed, turned to the man following her and held her finger to her lips.

"Shhh . . . she's asleep." Letty positioned her body just inside the room, partly blocking the door, so he couldn't enter. "Her jaws are so swollen she can't talk."

Letty noticed that Cecil's eyes roamed the room before they rested on his daughter. The cunning glint in them abruptly changed to piety. His face puckered as if he would cry. Letty wanted to laugh in his face. He and her father would make a pair. both could turn the tears off and on like a water tap.

"Hello, baby. Your papa's here," he whispered hoarsely. "I'll be back in a few days and we'll go home."

"Let's go." Letty nudged him away from the doorway with her shoulder and closed the door. "I don't want to awaken her." She jerked her head toward the stairway and waited for him to precede her down the stairs. When they reached the kitchen, she snatched his hat from the knob of the chair where he had put it, after he finally remembered some manners.

"Goodbye, Mr. Weaver," she said and held out his hat. "I'll tell Helen you were here."

"I ain't in no hurry. I can wait till she wakes up."

"You shouldn't linger. The mump germs are in the air. If you catch them, you could be laid up for a long time."

"When will Helen be able to come home?"

Their eyes locked. Letty's words were clipped.

"Not for good long time. I'll have to talk to Doctor Hakes about it."

He stared at her for a moment with eyes suddenly cunning. His lips closed down over his buck teeth like a trap. When he spoke, all pretence of civility was gone.

"I ain't no dumb cluck, Mrs. Graham. You're wantin' to keep my Helen 'cause you're likin' that five dollars a month you're gettin' for takin her in, ain't ya?"

Letty was shocked by the sudden attack. She felt the hot blood rise to the surface of her flesh to stain her cheeks.

"Helen came here in rags. I've spent the money on decent clothes."

"All of it?"

"Every damn dime."

"I ain't likin' my Helen being here with a cussin' woman. I'll tell that to the sheriff."

"You do that. I have a few things to tell the sheriff myself. Goodbye, Mr. Weaver."

Anger darkened his face. "Goodbye, Mr. Weaver," he mimicked. "I ain't hearin' no stay fer supper, Mr. Weaver." His lips curled in a sneer. "Just get rid of the girl's papa. It ain't no wonder things around here is slicked up so grand. Ya got ya a hired girl to do your work and five a month to boot."

"Leave, Mr. Weaver. I don't have to listen to your insults."

"I'm goin'. But I'll be back. That girl ort to be home where she belongs, keepin' house for her pa."

"Get out."

Letty opened the door and slammed it shut after him. She was so angry that she ground her teeth and stamped her foot. Only with effort was she able to hold her temper and not run after him and tell him to never set foot on this farm again. Under her breath she called him every foul name she could think of. That low-down, dirty sidewinder wanted a little ten-year-old girl to come back to keep house for him; cook his meals and wash his filthy clothes and suffer his abuse.

Letty had to do something—but what?

It was dark by the time supper was over, the dishes washed and put away. Letty set out what she would need for an early breakfast, then called Patrick and Helen in to get them ready for bed. Patrick fussed as usual, but his eyelids were drooping even as his head hit the pillow.

Letty went up to say good night to Helen. She was in her nightgown and ready for bed. During supper she had kept her head bowed and her eyes on her plate as Letty had described Weaver's visit, leaving out the heated words she had exchanged with him before he left.

"I know you're worried you'll have to go back to your father." Letty kissed the child's cheek. "Just remember you've got me and Grandpa and Patrick and . . . Mr. Dolan. We all love you and want you here with us."

"He'll be b-back."

"But not for a few days. We fooled him good." Helen got into bed. "Would you like for me to leave the lamp on for a while?"

"No, ma'am."

Helen turned her face to the wall, and stuck her thumb in her mouth. She lay staring into space, almost as if she were in a stupor.

A worried frown puckered Letty's brow. She blew out the lamp, groped her way to the door and down the stairs.

Mike came up from the creek where he had hurriedly bathed. The water was too cold for him to linger. He sat down in front of the barn and tilted back on the chair's hind legs, as he did each night, to watch the house until all the lights were out. As he rested his head against the rough barn boards, water from his wet hair trickled down his neck and glistened on his bare chest, matting the dark hair around his nipples.

He had never been happier. He had found his love, he had a son, and he loved the work he was doing. One day soon he'd have Letty back in his arms again. The trips to the creek each night served two purposes: to clean himself and to cool, for a time at least, his feverish body so that he could sleep. He found it more and more difficult to handle his nightly discomfort. Every night he wakened rock-hard and hurting. In France he had visited a few whores. They had eased his aching loins for a time, but he had always come away feeling dissatisfied and guilty.

Oh, God, Letty. I ache for you. I love you so damn much.

Closing his eyes, he relished the night breeze swirling over his shoulders and chest like a caress. The air was fresh and clean as if it had not been used before. He opened his eyes and gazed up at the sky. The stars were not faded as they had been when he lay in the trenches in France not really caring what the next day would bring. Tonight they were brilliant. The moon looked as if someone had hung a huge yellow balloon in the velvety sky. The night lacked only one thing to make it perfect—Letty beside him. He longed for her with all his heart. His whole being was starved for her.

The light in Helen's room went out. While he waited for a light to come from Letty's window, he thought of the fear he saw in the child's eyes when Letty told of her father's visit. In a way she reminded him of Letty at that age—quiet and cowered. Jacob had told him how they came to have Helen. According to the doctor, Jacob said, Weaver had been mean to his family. Was it just the switch or the strop the child feared or something more terrifying to a little girl? Mike had heard of fathers doing unspeakable things to their children. At the thought of the little girl being used in such a manner, his hands knotted into fists.

The squeak of the screen door was unusually loud in the quiet night. In the darkness, he saw Letty come out onto the back porch. Slowly, he let his chair come down on the two front legs. Was she on her way to the outhouse or—? He swallowed hard, his eyes glued to her shadowy form. When she stepped off the porch and came toward the barn, he felt his knees go weak. *She was coming to him.* Oh, Lord, he'd better not make too much of it yet. She might be coming to tell him that she wanted him to leave. No, it couldn't be that. Lately she had been more accepting of his presence.

She came toward him, her skirt swaying gently against her calves. If he opened his arms, would she run to him as she had done when he waited for her beneath the willows? *No, of course not, you fool.* Stop living in the past, he cautioned himself. It seemed forever before she reached the place where he stood. She stopped several yards away.

"It's a nice evening." Damn his heart for beating so fast and making him feel like a callow youth.

"Yes, it is," she said in a whisper of breath. "Were you going to stay out a while longer?"

"Yes, I don't go to bed until the—" Dear Lord, what was the matter with his runaway tongue?

"Until what?"

251

"Until the lights go out in the house," he confessed in a burst of honesty.

"I'll have to remember that." She laughed nervously.

He was bare from the waist up. His head tilted to the side. Letty could feel his eyes on her face. She waited for him to say something. She couldn't move, couldn't speak, could scarcely breathe. She was here, he was here. They were alone. Her thoughts were so muddled that she couldn't remember what she had come to talk to him about.

"Would you like to walk a little?" His words came out slowly and fell into the quiet pool of silence.

She nodded, then, "Aren't you cold?"

"No. I've been to the creek. Now *that's* cold."

"I don't know how you can stand getting in that cold water."

He picked his towel up off the chair and rubbed at the inky black curls that covered his head. As he moved out into the moonlight, she realized his chest was furred with soft black hair.

"I remember—" The words came out before she could bite them back.

"Remember what?" He hung the wet towel on the back of the chair. When she didn't answer, he repeated. "Remember what?"

"Oh . . . nothing. You'll laugh."

"I won't. I promise."

"I was going to say that I remember when you had only two hairs on your chest and—"

"—And you threatened to pull one of them," he added softly.

"I *did* pull one of them." Light, spontaneous laughter burst from her lips. "Because you said . . . you said—"

"I know what I said." He held onto the back of the chair to keep his hands from reaching for her. "I said your breasts were like two fried eggs."

"I remember."

"You almost cried and I hated myself," he said softly.

She turned away, walked out of the shadow of the barn and into the moonlight. Panic rose in his throat. Was she going back to the house? Had what he said been too intimate? A few quick steps brought him up beside her.

"Would you rather sit on the porch?"

"No. I'd rather walk, but shouldn't you put on a shirt?"

"Not unless it makes you uncomfortable—"

She laughed again. "Why should it make me uncomfortable? It's you who'll have goose bumps."

They reached the road and turned toward the Watkins farm before he spoke. "I was afraid that if I went in to get a shirt you'd not be there when I came out."

She made no comment.

As they walked on, Mike reached for her hand, holding it lightly to give her the chance to withdraw it. When she didn't he drew it up into the crook of his arm, holding the back of her hand tightly pressed to his bare side. He wondered if she could feel the wild tattoo of his pulse.

Letty felt the hammering of a pulse, but she didn't know if it was his or hers. His flesh was warm; the palm that covered her fingers in the crook of his arm was callused.

"I wanted to ask your advice about what to do about Helen," she said without looking at him.

"You didn't tell it all at the supper table, did you?"

"No. I don't want Helen to know what her father said to me before he left. He's a good-for-nothing reprobate! And he's determined to take Helen home. I don't know what to do."

"Did he insult you?" Mike asked, his voice laced with quiet fury.

"No. He accused me of keeping her here to work and to get the five dollars a month the state pays for her keep. Mike, I spent every cent of that money on clothes for Helen."

"You don't need to explain, sweetheart. God-damn! I wish I'd been there."

"Doctor Hakes says we must go through legal channels and get custody of Helen. There's a woman down at the Capitol in charge of things such as this. Wallace said she comes down real hard on parents who mistreat their children. I'd go into town and ask him to write to her, but I'm afraid to leave Helen here and I'm afraid to take her with me."

"Go talk to the doctor. It'll be a good excuse

254

for Jacob to stay at the house tomorrow. He's concerned for the girl too."

"I hadn't thought of that."

"Don't get your hopes up, Letty. It's hard to get the law to take a child from its natural parent."

"That's what Wallace said."

"Wallace Hakes, the doctor?" Apprehension washed over him at the familiar way she used the doctor's name.

"Doctor Hakes is a good friend—and has been for a long time."

"Letty." He stopped, turned, and looked down into her upturned face. "I may be wrong, but it seems to me that Helen is unusually terrified of her pa. It could be that she's afraid of something more than a beating."

"Before he went to jail, he made her do all the housework— washing, cooking—"

"That's not what I mean." His hands moved to her shoulders and down over her arms.

"Then what do you mean?"

"Thank God you've been sheltered here on the farm. There's a sordid side of life out there, sweetheart, that you don't know about. Have you ever heard of . . . incest?"

"That means . . . that means—No!"

"I'm not saying it's true. But there's a reason for the blank stare each and every time her pa is mentioned. It's almost as if she puts herself in a trance so that she doesn't have to think about something."

"Oh, Mike! I noticed that too. Tonight she was sucking her thumb."

"Poor little tyke."

"What'll we do?" Letty whispered.

Mike pulled her gently toward him until her forehead rested on his breastbone. "Go to Doctor Hakes and tell him of our suspicion. He can tell if she's been violated."

"I don't know if I could put her through that." She rolled her head back and forth.

"It may be the only way you can keep her from going back to him."

"The . . . monster! I could kill him." The palms against his chest knotted into fists. She leaned back to look into Mike's face.

"Wait a minute, honey. We're not sure."

"I'm almost . . . sure, Mike. Oh, I'm almost sure now that I think about it. I . . . I wondered why she'd never let me button her drawers. And . . . when I tried to measure above her knees to put a band on the new ones I was making, she backed away when I lifted her skirt."

"Don't think about it. As long as she's here with us he can't get to her. We'll think of something, do something—"

They stood silently for a moment. Then with her head bowed, she whispered, "I'm glad you're here."

"So am I. Dear God, I've missed you." He gently pulled her closer until her breasts were pressed to his naked chest. His arms were around her, her palms lay flat against his sides, then slowly moved around to meet in the small of his back. "Letty, Letty," he groaned, his words muffled in her hair. "This is where you belong."

CHAPTER
16

Letty felt as weak as a baby.

Mike held her against his solid naked chest, cuddling her to him, rocking her, stroking her hair, whispering to her.

"I've been so lonely. So damn . . . lonely" His voice broke. "Long ago, sweetheart, you took over my heart, leaving no room for anyone else."

There was a long moment of silence, dominated by the pounding of their hearts. It didn't matter to Letty that he was drawing away her strength, because he had enough for both of them. A thin thread of panic ran through her. She was getting in too deeply, too fast. A tiny moan trembled from her throat.

"My love, my love, let me . . . hold you—"

"We . . . should talk—"

"I've waited so long. Letty? Let me," he whispered with his mouth to her cheek.

His breath was warm on her skin. She felt the elusive caress of his tongue. His arms tightened and his lips moved across her cheek hungrily seeking her mouth. They were warm and soft yet firm and insistent. A stubble of beard scraped her chin as his mouth settled over hers.

He didn't just kiss her; he made love to her mouth, stroking, nibbling, coaxing with light sweet kisses. He backed away slightly to let her take a breath, then he recaptured her mouth again as if it were cool, sweet water and he was a man dying of thirst.

This time the kiss caught her breath and conquered her desire to deny him. They strained together, hearts beating wildly, and kissed as if it were their last moment on earth and their last to be together. His hands roamed from her shoulders to her hips, pressing her to him, seeking closer contact. He trembled and the kiss became deeper. A ribbon of desire unfurled inside Letty. Her body was flooded with the longing that had lapped at her senses for days.

A warm tide of tingling excitement washed over her as she became aware of the rock-hard part of him pressed against her belly. His sex was large, firm, and throbbing: hers ached with need. Her hands found their way up the corded muscles of his back to press him closer. When his tongue flirted with the corner of her mouth, her pleasure was so intense that it robbed her of strength, of sense and the very power of motion, and her mind whirled giddily.

He released her mouth to take a gasping breath. She turned her face away from him and buried it in his bare shoulder, unaware that her hand was stroking his big upper arm.

"We . . . shouldn't—" she gasped.

"Oh, sweetheart. I'll stop if you want me to."

His voice was husky, and rawly disturbed, like his deep, quivering breaths.

"I don't want . . . you to."

His heart was drumming so hard he could hardly breathe; he was too stunned with happiness to utter another word.

Mike knew he must go slowly or he would frighten her away, and he fought to keep his arms gentle and his lips from ravaging hers. With utmost tenderness and caution he held her, reveling in the softness of her breasts, her belly, and her curving hips.

Letty stirred and gently released herself from his hold. For an instant he feared her sweet surrender was all a dream. She looked up at him, her eyes huge and melting.

"We're standing in the middle of the road," she said with a little laugh so soundless that it was no more than an exhalation of breath.

He laughed with pure happiness. "So we are."

"Your head is wet." She forked her fingers through the curls dangling on his forehead, then moved her palm over his shoulder and down his arm to his hand, then up again. "You're cold. You've got goose bumps."

"Right now I could be standing in a block of ice and not feel a thing." He took both her hands. His eyes feasted on her face. Hungrily, they inspected every detail. "I love you," he said simply.

Neither of them spoke for what seemed an eternity. The tears that filled her eyes made them gleam like twin stars.

"Thank you." The words trembled from her quivering lips.

Mike blinked and stared down into her face. "For what?"

"For loving me. Only Grandpa and Patrick—"

"Yes, they love you. But not as I do. I love you as a man loves his mate, the other part of himself. You are my life, my soul. Not for a moment did I forget the vows we made beneath the willows. I thought I'd lose my mind when I heard that you had died."

"It hurts to know Mama cut me so completely out of her life. I could never turn my back on Patrick . . . no matter what he did."

"Nor could I. We'll be married and raise our son together."

"I don't know. I've got to think—"

"Letty! You love me. Say you do." His face was tilted down toward her and she could see the anguish in his eyes.

She swallowed drily, feeling the frantic clamor of her throbbing pulse. She started to move away, but his hands on her shoulders stopped her.

"I was *so* young. You were my whole world . . . back then. Papa threw me out of the house when I was fifteen because I was pregnant. I had Patrick when I was sixteen. Grandma died several weeks before he was born. It's just been me, Grandpa, and Patrick. I cut you out of my heart, Mike . . . or thought I had. Now you're back and I can feel my safe world crumbling about me," she whispered with tears in her voice.

He gathered her to him, urging her with gentle hands. He was trembling. She could feel the tremor in the body pressed to hers.

"Sweetheart, I'll never do anything to hurt you. Don't ask me to leave. I can't. I just . . . can't—"

"I won't ask you to leave as long as Grandpa wants you here. And . . . Patrick loves you—

"And you? You loved me once—" he whispered in her ear.

She was silent. Her face against his neck. Go slowly, he warned his leaping heart. Did he really want to know? Mike felt the tears gathering in a knot in his throat while he waited for her answer.

"I'll always love you." He heard her voice quiver and felt the movement of her cheek against his naked flesh as she raised her face.

His relief was so profound that he thought his whole being would dissolve, that his heart would cease its beating. Too moved to form words, he could only kiss her lips, again and again, realizing that only her physical warmth pressed close to his own quivering body could convince him that this was not just a dream.

Then he laughed, intimately, joyously, and lifted her off her feet, and swung her around. The full moon shone on her laughing face.

"Mike . . . Mike, put me down!"

"Say it again. Sweetheart, say it."

"I love you." The whispered words came soft and sweet against his lips.

Their lips caught and clung, released and smiled, and caught again. Their kisses spoke not of passion, but of newly rekindled love. He laughed and hugged her tighter.

"And I love you, love you, love you . . ." The words trailed as his lips moved down her smooth cheeks to lips that waited, warm and eager.

Finally, she squirmed and rubbed her cheek against his shoulder. Her fingers combed through the mat of hair on his chest; her lips turned into the hollow of his throat.

"I feel like fifteen again," she confessed huskily.

"Me, too. Oh, God, honey, I'm so sorry for all the lost years."

"What'll we do? How can we make it right?"

"We won't think about it now. I just want to look at you and hold you," he whispered and feathered kisses on her forehead.

Standing there in the middle of the road, Mike would have held her all night long. It was Letty who pulled away and started walking back toward the house. He matched his steps to her shorter ones. Her arm encircled his waist, his held her snugly against his side. They stopped often to exchange quick sweet kisses before moving on.

Mike picked a blossom from the lilac bush that grew beside the back porch and tickled her nose with it.

"There's so much we need to talk about. Patrick? Grandpa? I can't let Grandpa be made a laughing stock." Letty was slowly coming out of her daze of happiness and into reality.

"Sweetheart, don't worry about Jacob. He practically invited me to stay. He wants us to be together but only if it's what *you* want. He said if you didn't want me I'd be hightailing it out of here ahead of a shotgun." Mike chuckled. "He'd do it too."

"He knew right away who you were."

"I feel like a king just knowing you still love me. We'll work something out so that you and Patrick will never feel shamed. Dear God! None of it was *your* fault. If only I had gotten your letter. If only I had come here that spring. There are a million ifs. But we've got to look to the future and not back. I love you so much. You've given me . . . the world."

So much tenderness was in the look he gave her and in the timbre of his voice that Letty blinked back the tears and smiled at him. Her fingers stroked his cheeks, feeling the rough drag of his whiskers. She became braver and trailed her fingertips up through his hair and down around his ears. He remained still, his eyes devouring her.

"Oh, Mike, how could I have thought my love for you had died? I love Mike, the man, every bit as much as I adored Mike, the boy." She laughed with pure joy and wonderment. "Just think—Patrick is a part of both of us."

"Yes," he whispered, planting a kiss in one corner of her mouth. "It's a miracle." He lifted his head and looked into her face. His dark eyes were wet and gleamed in the moonlight. If I could sing, I would. If I could fly, I'd snatch you up, fly over the barn and into the woods and love you all night

263

long." His words teased her, his eyes loved her. He pushed the hair back from her temples. "Take out the pins," he whispered.

"Why?"

"I want to see it like it used to be, lying along your shoulders and down your back. You were the prettiest girl in Dunlap. Let me do it." His hands began to carefully search for the pins.

"Mike." she protested. "I'm not a girl. I'm a woman with a five-year-old son."

He combed his fingers through her hair and then trapped her head between his hands, tunneling his fingers into the hair at her temples.

"You're *my* girl." His lips nuzzled her hair, her neck, behind her ears. "And you are beautiful. Just beautiful."

He flattened her hand against his chest and held it there so that she could feel the rhythmic thump of his beating heart. Her fingers curled gently into the soft dark down that covered it and found a small hard nipple to examine curiously. He took a quick breath and kissed her with hunger, taking care not to scrape her soft skin with his rough cheeks.

"I wish I had shaved," he said, his ragged words trapped in her mouth by his plundering kiss.

"I don't care. I don't care." Her fingers continued to move over his chest while her lips opened to his kiss, meeting his tongue impatiently. Passion raged voraciously within them. Had she been able to think clearly she would have realized his desperate struggle to hold back. His body was trembling violently and his hard sex was grinding against the softness of her belly in a desperate need. Finally, he moved his mouth from hers, took great gulps of air, and moved her back away from him.

"It's been so long and I love you so much. I need another dip in the creek," he added in a hoarse whisper.

"No, don't. It's too cold. I must go in. Tomorrow I'll go to town to see Doctor Hakes, and I want to get an early start."

He wrapped her in his arms again. "I wish I could sleep with you in my arms all night long," he whispered after numerous tender kisses.

"Mike, what will we do? If we could go away from here it wouldn't matter. But I can't leave Grandpa, and how can we tell Patrick without everyone knowing?"

"We'll think of a way. Don't worry. Sweet, sweet, Letty." He followed her up onto the porch, holding tightly to her hand.

"I'm too happy to worry about anything tonight."

He hooked his hand around the back of her neck and kissed her reverently on the forehead, then on the lips, long and hard. "You're my life. Every minute I'm away from you seems like an hour, but I know it must be this way for a while. Good night, sweetheart," he whispered before he opened the screen door and gently pushed her inside.

At the edge of town in the long, narrow three-room house that Oscar Phillips called home, Cecil Weaver sat at the kitchen table drinking from a quart fruit jar.

"Where'd ya say yore kids was at?" He watched Oscar hang a blanket over the window.

"I didn't say, but they're at their grandma's. The old lady takes them once in a while. You better lay off that white lightning till after Elmer goes."

"Him bein' a deputy don't cut no ice with me."

"It'd better. He ain't to be fooled with."

"He'd better walk careful 'round me, is all I got to say."

"And you'd better not be throwin' out no threats. I'm tellin' ya straight."

Cecil grinned and took another drink from the fruit jar. "I know what I'm doin'."

"What's the matter with ya? Where can ya make easier money than takin' that hooch over to Henderson?"

"He ain't the only cog in the wheel."

"Goddammit, Cecil. You dad-blasted clabberhead! Talk like that'll get ya killed. If'n ya screw this up ya'll be in shit up to your eyeballs."

"I ain't goin' to knuckle under to no fat-ass deputy if'n he don't treat me right."

"I done told Elmer you're a man to depend on." Oscar jerked the jar out of Cecil's hand, poured himself a liberal drink in a water glass, and set the jar back in the middle of the table.

"You ain't got no reason to be hot. I got a reason. My kid was put with a prissy-ass woman what

266

looks down her nose at me. I'm bent on makin' me a pile of money, gettin' my kid back, and goin' to someplace big like Omaha or Kansas City."

Oscar leaned across the table, his narrowed eyes so intently on Cecil's face that the man squirmed uncomfortably.

"Why're ya so determined to get that girl back? What you goin' to do with her? Leave her in that pigsty ya call a house while ya hit the road for Elmer? The kid's better off where she is . . . and yore rid a her."

"Just you never mind. She's my kid. She belongs to me. Hear?"

Oscar eyed Cecil's flushed face for a long while. Then a knowing look came over his face and his lips twisted in a sneer.

"Why?" Oscar asked softly.

"Why? Wouldn't ya like to know."

"Ya low-down trash! The girl's buddin' out pretty good, ain't she? Tall for her age."

"Watch what yore sayin'!" Cecil shoved back his chair and stood. "I don't have ta take no shit off'n you. That kid owes me!"

"Owes you what? Have you been ugly to that girl? I saw her at the schoolhouse and she's wound up tighter'n a drum."

"What I do with my kid is my business. Ya ain't so lily pure, y'know."

"I ain't no saint, but I ain't had no hankerin' to diddle with no little girl! You . . . you filthy shithead!"

267

"You got no right to call me names. Before ya was hot on that war-widder, ya was wantin' that Pierce girl."

"She wasn't no little girl that hadn't bled yet! She was sixteen—"

The back door opened. Elmer Russell stepped in and closed the door. He moved quietly and swiftly for a big man. His eyes scanned the room, the covered windows, and the men glaring at each other over the table, before he moved away from the door.

"You fellers havin' a set-to?"

"Naw." Cecil sat down and reached for the fruit jar.

"Arlo ain't here yet?"

"Ain't comin'." Oscar took a drink and wiped his mouth with the back of his hand. "Since ya took him down to Boley to see Naked Ann he's gone around with a smile on his face like the wave on a slop bucket."

"Jesus!" Elmer hooked his booted foot around the leg of a chair, pulled it away from the table, and sat down. "Well?" he said to Cecil. "What did you learn out at Fletchers?"

"Nothin'. My kid's got the mumps. I hinted to stay for supper, but got no invite."

"Your kid's got the mumps?"

"It's what I said," Cecil growled and took several deep swallows from the jar.

"That's funny. She was running round chasing the dog a couple hours ago."

"She's sick abed. I saw her."

268

"I say she ain't."

Cecil's bloodshot eyes looked defiantly into the deputy's. "How do you know?"

"I saw her in the spyglass is how I know."

"That gawddamn slut!" In his rage Cecil raised up out of his chair. "I'm going out thar 'n' stomp the shit outta that woman."

"You'll do no such damn thing. Sit down."

"Don't ya be tellin' me what to do 'bout my own kid."

"Lay off the booze, Weaver. I'll not have no drunks workin' for me.

"I ain't workin' for ya tonight. I'll be sober when I take the load to Henderson."

"You gawddamn better be."

"Or what?"

"Or I'll tear up your ass."

"Just don't be forgettin', *Mister* Deputy, you ain't the only one that can tear up ass."

"What do you mean by that?"

"What'a ya think it means? A hint here or there 'n' yore name'd be mud in this county."

"Are you threatening me, Weaver?" The deputy's face had taken on the expression of a wolf about to attack.

"No, he ain't," Oscar said quickly. "He gets mouthy when he drinks."

"Shut up, Oscar. I can do my own talkin'."

The deputy didn't speak for a long moment. When he did, his voice was flat and wicked, taut with restrained anger.

"Go home, Weaver. Be at the tracks Thursday

269

night at midnight. We'll load the wagon and top it with a load of coal."

Cecil opened his mouth as if to say something, then closed it and got to his feet. He screwed the zinc lid onto the jar, cradled it in his arm, and with a cocky salute to the men at the table, went out the door.

The moment the door closed behind Cecil, the deputy's fist hit the table.

"I knew it! I knew it was a mistake to take in that no-good son-of-a-bitch."

"I'm thinkin' yore right. The bastard's got a hard-on for his own kid or my name ain't Oscar Phillips."

"Nooo?" Elmer's lips drew back in a snarl of disgust. "That's as low as a man can get! You sure?"

"Sure as shootin'. Ya think he'd be glad to be free of her, but he's wantin' her back. Said the kid owed him"

"A bastard that'd do that ain't fit to live."

The words sent a chill over Oscar. There was blazing anger in Elmer's eyes as they shifted from door to window and back. But when he spoke his voice was calm—too calm.

"He ain't goin' to mess me up. This is my chance to make me some money and ain't nobody goin' to mess me up."

"Find out any more 'bout that Dolan feller?"

"Some. According to old man Hartley, he had a wad of bills that'd choke a horse when he paid for that buckskin."

"Three one-dollar bills rolled together would be a wad to that old coot," Oscar snorted.

"Don't figure it was soldier's pay. I tore his nestin' place all to hell. Didn't find nothin'. He's smart. Have to be if he's tied in with Chicago or Kansas City."

"What makes you think he is?"

"Why's he workin' for old Jacob? He ain't no dirt farmer. Ya can see that with half a eye."

"You seen him? Talked to him?"

"Yeah, I've seen him. Ain't talked to him since he was at the hotel. He's settin' up to do blacksmithin' in Fletcher's shed. Good cover if he's planning on building a good-size still. Another thing, a load was took right out from under our nose down at Claypool, and the feller I had haulin' to Blatsberg got his legs broke with a warnin' to get outta the business. None of this happened till Dolan come."

"Did ya tell Weaver 'bout the man's legs?"

"Hell no. I ain't no fool."

"That Dolan's a mean son-of-a-bitch. I wouldn't put nothin' past him."

"There's ways a handling fellers like him and keepin' your nose clean. Plenty a ways." Elmer stood. "Be down at the tracks to help with the load. Tell Arlo to be there too. I reckon we'll have no more than fifteen minutes to unload that boxcar."

"Elmer, you figurin' on comin' down hard on Cecil?"

"Hard as need be. I'll tell you one thing, I ain't

sittin' by and lettin' no shithead tear down my playhouse."

"Don't blame ya none atall. He's queered hisself with me. I got no use for a man who'd be ugly to a kid."

Elmer let out a grunt of disgust and went out.

Oscar sat at the table and stared at the door. He'd done things he wasn't exactly proud of doing, but he'd not killed anyone and he'd not forced himself on a woman, much less a kid.

Yup, whatever Cecil got he'd have coming.

CHAPTER
——17——

"Mornin'."

Letty turned from the stove and met Mike's eyes. They shone with pure happiness. He looked years younger than he had the day before. Her pulse leaped, bringing color to her face, and her flushed cheeks made her soft brown eyes seem all the warmer.

He put the pail of milk on the floor beside the workbench and covered it with a cloth. Without hesitation, he came to her, put his arms around her, and kissed her lips again and again. His mouth was warm and loving. She could smell the shaving soap on his face as her nose pressed into his cheek.

"Mornin'," he whispered against her lips.

"Morning to you." Her voice was scratchy. It

272

was hard to get enough air into her lungs. This smiling, gentle, black-haired giant of a man who watched her with such tenderness in his eyes was the Mike she remembered, not the cold-eyed man who had lashed out so viciously at Oscar Phillips. She was going to spend the rest of her life with him just as she had planned so many years ago. She moved her arms up to encircle his neck. His seeking lips found her ear and loved it.

"Tell me what you told me last night so I'll know it wasn't a dream. Say it, sweetheart.

"I love you." Her whispered words came haltingly.

He laughed aloud and hugged her tighter, lifting her off her feet.

"Shhh . . . you'll wake up Grandpa—"

"Sooner or later he's going to have to get used to seeing me kiss you."

"Wait until I tell him."

"I can't wait. I don't care if the whole world sees me."

She giggled softly and framed his face with her palms.

"Then what are you waiting for, silly man?"

"For Christ's sake kiss her," Jacob said from the doorway. "Then maybe I can have my breakfast."

Letty pushed herself away from Mike, her face flaming. Jacob watched with a grin and twinkling eyes. She glanced at Mike. The smile he gave her spread a warm light into his dark eyes. He was beaming with pleasure, not in the least uncomfortable.

"I ain't no dumbbell y'know." Jacob pulled the red suspenders attached to his britches up over his shoulders, went to the washbasin, and splashed water onto his face. He looked at them from beneath his bushy brows as he dried himself. "I knowed you'd get a itch from him sooner or later." He chuckled. "What'er ya so red-faced for, girl?"

"Grandpa!" Letty held her palms to her hot cheeks. "You just jump right in with both feet, don't you?"

"Ain't no other way as I see it."

"This doesn't mean that—Well, it doesn't mean that Patrick and I will . . . go away with him."

"I be knowin' that too. I want three eggs this mornin'. I'm hungry as a bear."

"Don't change the subject, Grandpa." Letty went to him and put her arms about his waist. "I love you, Grandpa. I'll not leave you . . . ever!"

"Now, now." He patted her shoulder. "What's all this talk about leavin'. You got a hankerin' for the city?"

"You know I don't," Letty said crossly to hide the tears in her voice, "I love it here. This is my *home.*"

"I hope ta hell it is!"

"Letty, sweetheart—" Mike put his hand on her shoulder and turned her toward him. "Don't fret about leaving your grandpa. Jacob and I have already talked about it. We decided that if you still loved me and wanted me to stay that I'd put what money I have in fences and sheep and a good brood mare or two. Remember how we talked of having a farm and raising horses? Jacob is giving me that chance, I'm learning by working with him."

"Hell, there's plans in the wind, girl." Jacob paused and cleared his throat because his voice cracked. "Me 'n' Mike's goin' to be partners. We'll do us some fixin' up round here. Hell, girl, we'll do our own blacksmithin' and a dab for the neighbors. This farm goin' to be top-notch by the time Patrick takes it over. Gol-damn, I wish I'd be here to see it."

Letty looked from one man to the other. Both were looking at her. Grandpa's hand was on Mike's shoulder. *They were really fond of each other!* How could she have been so lucky? She blinked at the big tears that came to her eyes.

"You know what will happen when . . . when people find out that there was no Mr. Graham and that Patrick was born out of wedlock."

"I don't care doodle-d-squat what people think," Jacob snorted.

"Well, I do! I won't have people calling my son names."

"I've been thinking about that, Letty." Mike cupped her cheeks in his hands and turned her face up to his. "We'll go to another county or another state and be married. We'll tell everyone that we spoke our vows long ago—and we did. Remember? Beneath the willows. We can say we had a misunderstanding, and you came here and took another name so I couldn't find you."

275

"Do you think it will work?" Tears rolled down her cheeks and Mike wiped them away with his thumbs.

"Hell yes, it'll work! Mike 'n' me talked 'bout it. Don't start blubberin'," Jacob said gruffly. "I don't want nose droppin's on my eggs. I want 'em top side up with grease splattered on 'em. Hear?"

"I hear. You and Mike have been figuring out a lot of things behind my back."

"We'd a told ya if ya hadn't had yore back up so high. Get hoppin', girl. Times wastin'. We got plantin' to do."

"We want to talk to you about that, Jacob. Sit down and I'll tell you what Letty and I discussed last night."

"Oh, ya had time to talk, did ya? I'm surprised about that."

"Don't be smug, Grandpa," Letty snapped, with a tilt to her chin as she took a spoonful of lard from the crock and dropped it into the iron skillet. She glanced at Mike. He was watching her, his eyes adoring, his face younger and rid of care. She smiled at him, her lips not quite steady. "Grandpa can be aggravating as heck sometimes. I don't dare let him get the upper hand or he'd run me ragged."

Mike chuckled. "I can see you two get along like a cat and a dog."

The mare trotted down the dusty road. The newly greased buggy wheels scarcely making a sound. Letty's hat sat on the seat beside her. The sunny breeze played across her face, moving the hair at her temples, fluttering the collar of her shirtwaist. The air was fresh and scented with blossoms of flowering trees and shrubs. It was a glorious summer day: the world was beautiful.

Letty had had a brief moment alone with Mike before he helped her into the buggy.

"I don't like for you to go into town alone," he had said. "Why don't you stop by and take one of the Watkins girls with you?"

"I've been going to town alone for years. The girls will want to shop and talk and make a day of it. I want to get there, talk to Wallace Hakes, and get back,"

"Will you be back by noon?"

"It will probably be shortly after. I must go before Patrick and Helen wake up. I don't dare take Patrick. He might spill the beans about Helen not having the mumps."

"Be careful of that Phillips. Don't let him catch you alone,"

"I can handle Oscar."

"—And the deputy. I've got a score to settle with him."

"Don't worry. I'll be all right."

"I'll worry. I don't want you out of my sight!" He groaned. "Now kiss me. It'll have to last a while." His mouth moved over hers with warm urgency, kissing her until she was breathless. When he lifted his head, his eyes were dark pools of pure happiness. He lowered his mouth to her ear and whispered, "If I can meet you tonight, I'll tie a ribbon to the lilac bush."

"You remember!" She pressed her palms to his cheeks her fingers tugged at his ears.

"You'd be surprised at what I remember." The intimate tone of his voice brought a blush to her cheeks.

Now, in the buggy on her way to town, Letty thought about the look in Mike's eyes and the gentle way his lips had bushed hers. She waved a big horsefly away from her face and slapped the reins against the mare's back. Even now, thinking about the intimacy she had shared with Mike, she felt warm and tingling.

Letty drove down the main street of Piedmont. It was rutted, and an attempt had been made to smooth it with a drag; but the dust boiled up around the mare's legs. Several automobiles were parked in front of the bank and two more in front of the hotel. A large number of people were on the boardwalk and standing in groups on the street corners. Letty wondered what had brought so many of them to town in the middle of the week. She waved to those she knew and continued on to the doctor's office.

Wallace Hakes looked up from the papers on his desk when she opened the door.

"Letty." He stood. "What brings you to town in the middle of the week? Is Jacob all right?"

"Grandpa's fine. I need to talk to you about Helen. Her father is out of jail. He came out to get her. I told him she had the mumps."

278

"Does she have the mumps?"

"No."

"Come sit down and tell me whatever made you tell him that."

Letty sat across the desk from Wallace Hakes and told him how Helen had progressed from the silent, withdrawn little girl to the one who now joined in the conversation at the dinner table and who was learning to play the piano. She told him how frightened the child was of her father and how she had panicked when he drove into the yard.

"The only thing I could think of to keep him from taking her was to tell him she was sick. I promised her that she'd not have to go back to him. She has an unnatural fear of him, Wallace. Mike and I talked about it and he suggested that maybe her father was . . . molesting her."

"Who is Mike?" Wallace asked quietly and watched color tinge her cheeks.

"He's working for Grandpa. But that's another story."

"You trust this fellow?"

"Oh, absolutely! Wallace, don't make me tell you about that now. I'm so worried that Cecil Weaver will come and force Helen to go with him. Mike says that you can tell if he's been . . . ah . . . you know . . . by examining Helen."

"It's possible that I could, but think of the traumatic experience it would be for the child. I'd consent to do that only as a last resort."

"He's a mean man. He put on a nice face at first. then he turned nasty and accused me of keeping Helen for the five dollars a month the county pays for her keep and for the work the child does. He said Helen *owed* him! Can you believe that? Wallace, if I adopted Helen the county would no longer have to pay for her keep."

"There's not much chance of that, Letty."

"Why not?"

"Because you're single and not blood kin."

"I'll . . . be getting married."

"Oh." He stared at her quietly for a long moment, then removed his eyeglasses and wiped them carefully on the handkerchief he pulled from his pocket. "To this . . . Mike?"

"I've known him a long time, Wallace." Letty reached across the desk and placed her hand over his. "He's . . . he's Patrick's father. No one knows but Grandpa and now you."

"It's safe with me, Letty. Where does Mr. Graham fit in?"

"There is no Mr. Graham. Graham was Grandma's maiden name. You have been my dear friend all these years. I want to tell you about it."

Letty told Wallace how she had been brought up in a fanatically religious home and that she had not been allowed to associate with Mike because he was a Catholic. She explained that Mike had gone away to earn money so they could be married and in the meanwhile she learned she was pregnant.

"My father threw me out. I was only fifteen. Grandpa and Grandma took me in. They decided to give me the name Graham so my father wouldn't know I was here. My parents cut me out of their lives so completely that they declared me dead. Mike returned and believing that, he went off to war. I'm not surprised that my father and sister would do such a thing, but it's hard for me to believe it of my mother."

"How did he find out you were here?"

"He came back to find my grave. He still loves me, Wallace."

The doctor heaved a heavy sigh. "I hope your Mike knows how lucky he is."

"He does. He's suffered too. He's missed out on five years of his son's life."

The door opened and Mrs. Crews's short, stout body filled the doorway.

"I thought that was your buggy, Mrs. Graham. News does spread fast. You got here just in time. She'll be comin' out of the hotel most any time now. My, my! It's excitin'. Just imagine a real star right here in Piedmont." The woman stopped long enough to take a gasping breath, then gushed on. "I was comin' to the store and got a glimpse of her coming up from the depot in a touring car. I hurried back to tell Marthy, Henny, Myrtle, and Bernice to get uptown. I didn't want Doctor Hakes to miss out on seeing her. Just shut down the office, Doctor, and come up to the mercantile. There's a good view of the hotel—"

Wallace took the stout woman by the elbow. "Slow down Mrs. Crews. Who are you talking about?"

"Why . . . why . . . Sister Cora. She's a angel

281

of mercy is what she is. You could almost see the Lord hovering over her. She's on a tour to heal the sick and raise money to build a temple. Doctor, wouldn't it be grand if she built it right here in Piedmont?"

Doctor Hakes let out an indistinguishable word.

"I tell you, Doctor, we're living in the last days."

Letty got to her feet in stunned silence while Mrs. Crews sank down in a chair and wiped her damp forehead with the sleeve of her dress.

"I've got to be going." Letty felt as if her legs had been knocked out from under her. Not knowing how she got there, she was at the door.

"Letty." Doctor Hakes followed her out to her buggy. "What's the matter? Surely *you* don't believe in that faker. She's nothing but a . . . Charlatan."

"No. I've got to go. Please—"

"Then what's wrong? And don't tell me it's nothing because you're white as a sheet,"

"I'm ashamed to say that that . . . charlatan, swindler, two-faced actress who preys on the misery of others and offers them the hope of healing, is . . . my s-sister." Letty forced the words from her tight throat.

"Oh, God!"

"I've got to go. I don't want to see her or have anything to do with her. How can I get to the alley from here, Wallace?"

"Turn here and go back behind my building. You can take the alley all the way out of town."

Wallace handed her the reins, "I'll write to Mrs. Knight, Maybe I can get her up here. Meanwhile, you can use the mumps to hold Weaver off for about ten days."

"Thank you, Wallace."

Letty turned the corner and then headed up the alley toward the back of the building that fronted Main Street. More than anything she wished she could keep on going until she reached the farm and the safety of Mike's arms but she had to stop at the store. Grandpa was almost out of tobacco. In a couple of days they would be out of coffee, Lord! Why had Cora stopped in this little town? She must have had a reason. Cora never did anything without a reason that would benefit Cora.

The back door of the store was open. Letty tied the mare to a rail, went up the steps and into the back room. She paused to allow her eyes to adjust from the bright sunlight to the darkened interior before weaving her way between barrels and crates to the door, A dozen people stood in excited groups looking out the door and the windows. No one was at the counter so Letty went over to Mr. Howard who was leaning on the wheel of the coffee grinder craning his neck to see out the window.

"I'm in rather a hurry, Mr. Howard—"

"Howdy, Mrs, Graham. I didn't see you come in."

"I need a two-pound can of Prince Albert tobacco and five pounds of coffee beans."

"You want that I grind those beans?"

"No. I'll grind them a few at a time."

"Lots of excitement here today. Great for the town, just great."

"What do you mean?"

"Ain't you heard? Sister Cora's in town. She'll be holdin' a meetin' right out here in the street tonight."

"—And she'll pass the collection plate no doubt." Letty couldn't keep the sarcasm out of her voice. Mr. Howard was too excited to notice.

"It's bound to bring a crowd to town. She's raisin' money to build God's temple." He lifted the scoop from the scale and poured the beans into a sack.

"And fill her own pockets," Letty murmured, then said aloud to Mr. Howard. "Ten sticks of peppermint candy, please, and two scoops of lemon drops."

"Well, if it ain't the uppity Mrs. Graham."

Letty turned to look into the bloodshot eyes of Cecil Weaver. His face was red and bloated. A stubble of beard covered his cheeks.

"Mr. Weaver." She nodded a dismissal and turned back to the clerk. "I need two spools of number fifty white thread."

"My girl still in bed with the *mumps,* Mrs. Graham?"

"Mumps last for ten days." Letty scooped up her purchases. "Put this on a bill, Mr. Howard. I don't have enough money with me and I don't have time to go to the bank."

"Sure, Mrs. Graham."

Letty went through the door and into the store-room. She didn't realize that Cecil had followed her until she reached the back door and he jerked the sack of coffee beans from her arms.

"Let me help ya, Mrs. Graham."

"I don't need or want your help."

"Course ya do. I owe ya fer takin' such good care of my girl, her havin' the *mumps* and all."

Letty felt his hand on the back of her neck. She shook free of it and hurried down the steps to the buggy. After putting the sacks on the floor she went to release the horse.

Cecil tossed the bag of coffee beans onto the buggy seat, then put his hand over hers to prevent her from untying the reins.

"Not so fast, ya uppity slut." Quick as a flash he grabbed the front of her shirtwaist and jerked her up close to him. "I got me a notion ta beat the shit outta, ya. Ya played me fer a fool. My kid ain't got no mumps.

"Get your hands off me, you . . . filthy hog!" Her head was erect and she looked him in the eye. She was determined not to cower before this swine or let him know how frightened she was.

"Get yore hands off me," he mimicked. "You dried-up bitch. I've had me younger women than you."

"I'm sure you have! You're rotten through and through. I wouldn't walk on you if you were dirt!"

"Think yore better'n me, huh? Huh?" Furious he jerked at her shirtwaist with both hands, pop-ping the buttons and opening it to the band of

285

her skirt. A thin undervest was all that covered her breasts.

"Ohhh—!" She beat at him with her fists.

"Hit me, will ya?"

He slapped her with his open hand so hard that she would have fallen to the ground if not for the hand he had fastened in her hair. Pain from her scalp and face exploded in her head. Tears filled in her eyes, and she fought to control the frantic sobs that came from her throat.

"Ya fiesty little split-tail. I'll teach ya yore place." The words were breathed in her face from a putrid mouth.

After that the blows came on first one side of her face and then the other. Wild with fear, she fought with all her strength while her mind screamed. *Somebody help me! Please! Help me!* In full panic she lashed out with her foot and connected with his shin.

"Ye . . . oow!" he howled with pain.

The next blow split her lip and sent her stumbling backward to fall on her back so hard the wind was knocked from her lungs. Stunned, she tried to focus her eyes on the man looming over her. Her jaw felt like it was broken and her ears rang. She saw the kick coming and rolled to the side. The heavy boot struck her hip. Excruciating pain shot through her, forcing a scream from her lips.

From far away she heard a shout.

"Gawddamn you, Cecil! Get away from her!"

Seconds later a body came flying over her and

wrestled Cecil to the ground. Letty rolled, her only thought was to get away.

"Letty! Are you hurt? What in the world was he doing that for?"

Dazed, Letty looked up at Sharon Tar. The girl put her arm under Letty's shoulders and helped her to sit up. Letty looked fearfully past Sharon to see Oscar Phillips holding Cecil on the ground.

"You bastard! Ya son of mangy polecat. I ought to beat ya within an inch of your worthless life."

"Get off me," Cecil growled. "She had it comin'."

Oscar's rock-hard fist smashed into Cecil's face.

"What'd ya do that for?" Cecil said, and spit blood.

"You had *that* comin'," Oscar snarled.

"What's goin' on here?" Mr. Howard came barreling down the back steps. "My Gawd," he exclaimed when he saw Sharon helping Letty up off the ground. Letty was holding the front of her shirtwaist together. Her hair hung in strings around her face and blood from her lip trickled down her chin.

"Oscar and I were coming up the ally," Sharon said, drawing Letty's shirt together and fastening it with a pin she took from her own dress. "We heard Letty cry out. He was beating her with his fists and kicking her. It was terrible, just terrible. He ought to be horsewhipped."

"My God, Weaver. Have you lost your mind?"

"She stole my kid—"

"Ya stupid . . . mule's ass! She did no such. Shut

287

your filthy mouth, or I'll shut it for you," Oscar said angrily. "There ain't never no excuse for what you done."

"I want to go home." Letty brushed her hair back from her eyes and stumbled to the hitching rail. Mr. Howard was there and took the reins from her hand.

"Mrs. Graham, I'm just plumb sorry this took place in back of my store, Now, you ain't in no shape to go off alone. Let me get someone to drive you."

"No! I'll be all right. I've got to go. Just keep him here until I get home." A few curious on-lookers stood around. Letty ignored them and looked directly at Cecil Weaver. "Stay away from the farm. Stay away from Helen."

"You ain't got no right to keep my little girl. I'll have the sheriff on you."

"I've got a *duty* to protect that child from a beast like you. Get the sheriff and I'll tell him why you're so eager to get her back. The decent men in this town will hang you from the nearest tree." Letty climbed painfully into the buggy and looked down at him. "When Mike sees what you've done to me, he'll come looking for you. You're big and brave when it comes to beating up a woman or a *child*. Lets see how you stand up against a man. I hope he *kills* you!"

"Do you want me to ride home with you, Letty?" Sharon asked.

"No, I'll be all right. Thank you for helping me. Oscar, I appreciate what you d-did. Th-thanks."

She slapped the reins against the mare's back and the crowd moved aside. With her teeth clamped tightly together, her chin up and her back straight, she drove away. She'd be damned if she'd let the gawkers see how shaken and embarrassed she was. Her pride kept her emotions in check until she reached the edge of town. Then reaction set in. She could no more hold back the sobs that shook her shoulders or the tears that poured down her cheeks than she could hold back a tidal wave. She had never been so mortified, so miserable, or hurt in so many places in all her life.

Letty whipped the horse into a run. The buggy bounced over the rutted road leaving a cloud of dust in its wake. She had to get home to Mike. Thank God, she wasn't alone. She'd tell him what Cecil Weaver had done. Oh, Lord. Her mind wasn't clear. He would *see* what Cecil had done. She needed Mike's strength, his love. He would help her get herself together. She couldn't let Patrick and Helen see her in this condition.

Cora. She had to tell Mike about Cora. Cora was here because she wanted something. What if she had come to expose her sister as a loose woman with an illegitimate child. Cora would love to play on the fact that she was an angel and her sister a slut. The congregation would be sympathetic and put money in the collection plate so *Sister* Cora could save women like her from the eternal fires of hell.

Letty's head throbbed as though a hammer was pounding on it. The pain in her hip where Cecil had kicked her with his heavy boot ached as if it had a life of its own.

The worst part of her pain was the humiliation of being completely vulnerable and helpless against a man's superior strength. Dear God! This was what little Helen had endured. This and more! Much more. The agonizing thought screamed ceaselessly through Letty's mind.

She began to cry again, tears making her blind to her surroundings. She wept silently. Automatically holding the reins, she urged the mare down the road toward home—and Mike.

CHAPTER
——18——

The sky was bluer than he had ever seen it, the air fresher. Mike looked toward the sun. In another hour it would be noon, and soon after that Letty would be home. Letty. His wonderful, sweet Letty loved him. They would be married, find a way to tell Patrick that he was his father, and together they would live here on this land until the end of their days. Mike's heart was fairly singing.

Before he came out to the field he had tied the scrap of blue ribbon to the lilac bush that grew beside the porch. Letty would see it and know that he had carried it with him all the years they were apart.

He laughed aloud.

The thought of all the unnecessary chances he

had taken while he was in France wiped the smile from his face. What his comrades had thought was bravery and actually been a reckless disregard for his own life. Dear God! If one of the bullets that had sailed over his head as he zigzagged across open ground between trenches had been inches lower he'd never have known this happiness.

It was difficult to keep his mind on what he was doing as he walked behind the one-horse corn drill. He set the plate to drop the seeds fifteen inches apart as Jacob had instructed. He was making a great effort to keep the rows straight and exactly three feet apart so that the field could be cultivated a couple of times before the corn got high and had to be weeded by hand. Thank God, Jacob had a riding cultivator to make the work go faster. In another year they would also have a riding two-row planter.

His thoughts switched back to Letty and plans for the future. He was going to buy her a washing machine with a gasoline motor and a wringer as soon as he could afford it. Scrubbing overalls on a washboard was backbreaking work. He knew a lot about motors. He had been assigned to the motor pool until he had gotten into a fight with the sergeant in charge and was transferred to the artillery. He was counting on blacksmithing to bring in a little extra cash money. Another thing he wanted to get was an automobile and to teach Letty to drive it. He laughed aloud at his galloping ambitions. Maybe the car would have to wait until they were better set.

At the end of the field he refilled the seed hopper, turned the horse, and started back down the field. He was almost at the other end when he saw Letty's buggy coming down the lane that ran alongside the wheat field. To get to the lane she'd had to turn off the road before she reached the Watkins farm and cut through a grove that was overgrown with brush. Why would she do that and chance breaking a wheel?

"Christ!" he exclaimed when he realized that she was driving much too fast and must have been for some time. The mare was lathered. A knot of fear formed in the pit of Mike's stomach. Something had happened or she wouldn't be coming toward him at such speed. He stopped the horse, tied the reins to the plow handle, and hurried down the row toward the end of the field.

At the edge of the plowed ground Letty pulled up on the reins. Mike grabbed the cheek strap on the harness to help stop the blowing animal. As soon as the horse calmed enough to be released, Mike hurried to the side of the buggy, threw his hat on the ground, and reached for Letty. Dear God! There was blood on her mouth and chin, Her hair hung in strings her dress was torn and dirty. *Her face!* Her dear sweet face was swollen and bloody and wet with tears.

Letty burst into loud sobs and threw herself into his arms. The force of her weight staggered him. His breath left him in a grunting rush, but he held her tightly against him while he regained his balance. She wrapped her arms around him and hid her face against the curve of his neck.

"Ah, my sweet girl . . . he crooned to her and lifted her face with gentle fingers beneath her chin. "What happened? Did you fall? Are you badly hurt?" He kissed her cheeks, her forehead, her eyes. "Shhh . . . don't cry, love. Let me look at you." He held her tenderly and murmured comforting words.

"Mike . . . Mike . . . I love you—" she gasped between sobs.

"I know. honey! And I love you too. Ah . . . don't carry on so. You're scaring me to death. What happened, sweet-heart?"

"C-Cecil Weaver. He caught me . . . behind the s-store and hit me—"

"He caught you? He . . . did this?"

"He . . . h-hit me and kept on h-hitting me. He knows that . . . Helen doesn't have the m-mumps . . . said I played him for a f-fool. I was so ashamed. P-people gathered around and . . . gawked."

"He"—his voice broke—"hit you?" She nodded and a curse burst from his lips. "I'll kill him! I'll kill that bastard!" His voice was cold and hard, but strangely soft.

"He . . . just went crazy! He knocked me down and k-kicked me. Then Oscar came and . . . fought him. Oh. Mike. I was so scared—I just wanted to get home to . . . you."

The phrase cut into Mike's heart. These were the same words she had said when she was fifteen.

He was so consumed with rage at the man who had hurt his precious woman that it took all his control to master his fury and tend to Letty. Tenderly, sipped at the tears on her cheeks and whispered endearments.

"Darling . . . sweetheart, don't cry. He'll get what's coming to him. I promise you."

"There's more. Just hold me for a while. What'll I do? I can't let Patrick and Helen see me like this."

"Of course you can't." Mike moved toward the shade of a tree, sank down on the grass, and pulled her down onto his lap. She curled up in his arms like a little lost rabbit. "I've got a jug of water at the end of the field. I'll get it in a little while." He cuddled her to him, smoothing her hair back from her face. "It tears me up to see you like this." He took a handkerchief from his pocket and dabbed gently at the blood on her chin.

She lifted her lids and looked into his eyes. "I look ugly."

"Not to me. Never to me. Ah, sweet Letty. Sweet soft woman of mine," He whispered, his voice thick and full of wonder.

"It was so awful—"

"The man who did this to you will wish he was dead before I get through with him."

Her hand cupped his cheek. "When I was ten years old, you tackled a bully who was trying to push me out of a swing. You were so handsome with your black curly hair and your daredevil smile—too wonderful for this world. Later when you noticed me and we became friends, then sweethearts, I knew that I was the luckiest girl on earth."

"And now?"

"I still think so." She wedged her nose beneath his chin and kissed his neck.

"Letty . . . my love," he whispered, his face aglow with love and desire. He kissed her. His mouth was tender on hers, almost reverent, giving, yet taking. "I love you so much it purely scares the hell out of me. I'm afraid I'll wake up and discover that finding you was all a dream."

"For me too. I didn't realize how lonely I was."

"We're together now. Letty and Mike. Mike and Letty and—Patrick," His hand traveled possessively over her back, soothing, caressing.

"All I could think of was getting back here to you." She exalted in the freedom she had to move her hands over his face and neck, and feel the rough drag of his whiskers against her palm. It was heaven to be held close in his arms, feel his strength, share his kisses.

Mike lifted his head and gazed at her upturned face. Her eyes were teary bright and full of love for him. His arms tightened and he slowly lowered his head to hers and kissed her puffed and cut mouth, her wet cheeks. The yielding sweetness of her mouth, the softness of her woman's body and the warmth of her skin made him tighten with desire but he held himself in check. She needed his comfort now, not his passion. This woman was his life. It was as simple as that. He loved her with every breath and would give his all to keep her safe and happy. He sat holding her, arms wrapped around her. She fit so perfectly in the nest made of his arms and thighs.

"Cora is in Piedmont," Letty said as if just remembering. "She's going to hold a street meeting tonight."

"That's strange. Why would she waste her time in a town the size of Piedmont?"

"She's got a reason. She'd not be there otherwise."

"Maybe it has nothing to do with you, sweetheart."

"Oh, Mike. You know better than that. It's got everything to do with me or Grandpa or this farm."

"I don't think it's the farm. If it were sold for cash money, it would be only a drop in a bucket to Cora."

"She would take it to keep me from getting it."

"Jacob would have something to say about that. Let's not worry about Cora now. She can't do anything to hurt us."

"She'll try. I know she will."

"Let her try. If she comes here, we'll face her together."

"I hope she doesn't come, but I'm afraid she will."

They were silent for awhile. The world fell away. and for a moment there was only the two of them. Mike's fingers worried the hair over-Letty's ears and then gently stroked her cheeks. He could feel

her all through him and wanted to hold her forever, but they had to get on with the day.

"It's almost noon, honey. I'll be expected back
at the house. Why don't you get in the buggy?
I'll lead the horse around the edge of the field and
into the barn from the back way. You can wash
and fix yourself in the tack room."

Letty rolled off his lap and stood. Her body
ached in a hundred places. She tried not to flinch
but failed to hide her discomfort from Mike's
sharp eyes.

"Honey? Are you all right?"

"Just stiff. I'll lead the horse around the field.
I should walk and work out some of the stiffness.
By the time I get to the barn, you'll have finished
planting your row.

"Goddamn that son-of-a-bitch!" he swore
when he turned her face to the sun and saw the
bruises. His dark eyes glittered angrily and muscle
jumped in his tightly clinched jaw. "That no-
good bastard hit you with his fist!"

"It's nothing compared to what Helen has suffered." Letty put her hands on Mike's chest. "We
can't let her go back to him. Doctor Hakes is going
to write to the woman in Lincoln. In the meanwhile we've got to keep Helen hidden away."

"If he sets foot on this farm—"

"—He won't. He'll send the deputy. We've got
to get to Sheriff Ledbetter. Grandpa says he's a
good and decent man."

"Letty, darlin'," he whispered, and put his
hands on her neck, his thumbs gently caressing

the bruised line of her jaw. "No one will ever get the chance to hurt you like this again. I swear it."

She covered his hands with hers. "Don't worry. He caught me by surprise—or I'd have taken the buggy whip to him."

"We've got to slip you into the house some way or the other. Go on, honey. I've some thinking to do. Wait for me behind the barn."

It was easier than Letty had thought it would be to get into the house and up to her room without the children seeing her. She waited in the tack room while Mike talked to Jacob. The two men took Patrick and Helen out to the grove to see a nest of young robins that had been hatched that morning. After that, the sack of candy on the porch caught their eyes. Jacob immediately took charge with a promise to divide it after the noon meal.

Patrick was too excited over the candy to notice his mother's swollen lip and bruised face, but Helen kept looking at her in such a way that Letty launched into an explanation without actually lying.

"There are so many speeding automobiles on the roads now throwing up stones that it's dangerous to have one pass you. A person's eye could be put out. Not that the driver would care, mind you. He'd already be miles ahead before he gave it a thought. Helen, Grandpa said you were a big help. He said you peeled the potatoes and that it was your idea to add an onion. My, but they're good."

"My mama always put in an onion when she

fried potatoes. Sometimes, when we had eggs, we . . . baked cookies."

"Cookies?" Mike groaned. "I haven't had cookies since before the war."

"I'll make you some," Helen said, her eyes on her plate.

"What kind?"

"Molasses," she said, hardly above a whisper.

"My favorite kind. My sister used to make molasses cookies. When her back was turned, my brothers and I would grab a handful and run out the door."

"Did she chase you?" Helen looked up and giggled, her eyes dancing.

"Sometimes. But we'd run up into the hayloft and pull up the ladder."

"What did your mama say?"

"Now you boys stop teasing Katy." Mike's imitation of a woman's high voice brought giggles from both Helen and Patrick.

"You can make cookies this afternoon, Helen," Letty said. "We'll have them for supper, that is if there's any left after Mike grabs a handful." Her eyes sought Mike's sending a silent message of love.

It wasn't until after Mike and Jacob went back to the field that Letty went out onto the porch and saw the ribbon tied to the lilac bush. She didn't know whether to laugh or to cry. In the end she did both. With fingers not quite steady, her breath coming fast, her heart thudding irregularly, she carefully untied the ribbon and blinked rapidly to clear her eyes so that she could see it.

It couldn't be the same scrap of blue ribbon she had cut from her petticoat and tied to the bush so long ago—but it was. The thin white stripe went down one side. The blue had faded; the ends and sides were frayed. He had kept it all these years.

Mike. Oh, Mike. Of course I'll meet you. It's been so long.

Letty carefully folded the ribbon and tucked it inside her camisole next to her heart.

The evening light was fading when Mike rode into Piedmont. A crowd was gathering on the street for Cora's street meeting. The hotel balcony was draped with light-blue bunting to form a back-drop for the white pulpit that bore a dramatic gold cross. Workmen scurried about putting up strings of lights. A long banner proclaiming: JESUS IS COMING SOON—GET READY was stretched across the front of the hotel. Another banner, PREPARE TO MEET YOUR MAKER hung from beneath the balcony.

A piano stood on the hotel porch. The musicians, wearing identical gray suits, white shirts and white ties, stood lined up like little tin soldiers with their instruments under their arms. One held a trombone, one a saxophone, and the other, a trumpet. The trumpet player stepped to the edge of the porch and began to play a rousing spiritual— "When the Saints Go Marching

In." People on the boardwalks ceased talking and hurried toward the hotel.

Mike tied his horse in the alley behind the bank and made his way through the crowd to the general store. The double doors were blocked by a group of loafers, They reluctantly moved aside when Mike gave them a cold stare.

Mr. Howard, turning the crank on the giant red and orange coffee grinder, stopped the wheel when Mike walked in. All conversation stopped, and an uncomfortable silence filled the store. A dozen pair of eyes turned on the tall dark-eyed man who stood with feet slightly spread, his thumbs hooked in the side pockets of his trousers, Mike's head moved in the briefest of nods to the man behind the counter before he turned to address the men staring at him.

"I'd be obliged if one of you would point out a man named Cecil Weaver."

Silence.

Mike searched each face in the store carefully, pinpoints of light glittering in his black eyes. He waited a full moment. When no one spoke, he turned to Mr. Howard, anger beating through him,

"Is Cecil Weaver in town?"

"I wouldn't know,"

Mike pulled a coin from his pocket, tossed it in the air and caught it, "A silver dollar to the man who points him out."

"Whatta ya want him for?" The question came from one of the loafers at the door.

"That's my business."

"I betcha I know,"

"Then why did you ask?"

The store owner moved from behind the counter, his hands twisting nervously in his apron.

"You're Mike Dolan, aren't you?"

"You know that I am."

"It was a sorry thing Cecil did to Mrs, Graham, but—"

"—But what?" Mike said coldly.

"Let the law handle it."

"Has the law handled it?"

"Well . . . not that I know of. But I'm telling you this for your own good. The deputy will come down hard on you if you start something."

"That deputy has been acting outside the law and will get his wings clipped. Is Sheriff Ledbetter in town?"

"No, He comes up about once a week, His headquarters are in Boley. Now if you'll take my advice—"

"—I didn't come in here for advice." Mike dropped the dollar back into his pocket and headed for the door.

"Mister." A man in overalls holding the hand of a small boy stepped into the clearing in front of the door. "If Weaver was in town I'd point him out. He needs to have his clock cleaned. I don't hold with the way he treated his family and I don't hold with what he done to Mrs. Graham. She's a good woman, doin' what she can for a motherless youngun."

"He's not in town?"

"I saw him hightailin' it out a couple hours ago."

"Which way was he headed?"

"Looked like he was headin' for Claypool."

"I'm obliged to you, Mister." Mike tipped his hat and stepped out onto the board porch.

Oscar Phillips with Sharon Tarr clinging to his arm were coming down the walk toward him. Theirs were the only familiar faces he'd seen other than that of the store clerk who had sold him the lemon drops the day he came to town. Mike waited. Oscar looked up and saw him. His steps slowed then stopped.

"Hello, Mr. Dolan," Sharon called, pulling her reluctant escort along.

"Evening." Mike tipped his hat.

"Did you come in to hear Sister Cora?"

"Hardly," Mike grunted. "I'm looking for Weaver."

"He took off for Claypool. He sure cooked his goose in this town. Folks are up in arms over what he did to Letty. If me and Oscar hadn't come along, no tellin' what he'd a done."

Mike's dark eyes beamed down on Oscar. "I owe you one, Phillips." He held out his hand. "I appreciate what you did for my wife."

Oscar shook his hand, his mouth hanging open.

"You and Letty . . . are married?" Sharon asked.

"Letty and I said our vows more than six years ago. We had a misunderstanding and she came here to her grandpa. Later, I was told that she was dead. I went to war not knowing that I had a son."

"My . . . goodness gracious me!" Sharon exclaimed. "How exciting. I knew there was something going on between the two of you the night you came to the Pierces' to take her home. I just knew it. Well . . . can you beat that?"

Oscar found his tongue. "—But her name's Graham."

"Family name. She didn't want me to find her."

"Well it ain't no wonder she gave all the fellows a cold eye round here," Sharon exclaimed, her own eyes warm on Mike's face. "Reckon if you've had the cream you don't want the whey."

Mike grinned down at her. "I'll take that as a compliment, Mrs. Tarr."

"Aren't you going to hear Sister Cora?" Sharon was holding onto Oscar's arm with both hands. "It's about time for her to appear."

"No. If I want to see a circus, I go to a circus not to a church. If Weaver's not in town I'll be heading on home. I'll run into him sooner or later and settle my score." He tipped his hat and turned away.

"Tell Letty I'll be over one day soon," Sharon called.

"I'll do that. Come any time. You too, Phillips."

Sharon and Oscar stood on the board porch and watched Mike walk away. Not many men on the street were as tall; none walked with more assurance.

"Gawd. I'd hate to be in Cecil's shoes when that bird gets a hold of him," Oscar said.

"Cecil Weaver is as sorry as they come," Sharon said angrily." I hope Mike stomps his guts out. He made life hell on earth for his wife and his kids. Everyone knows he beat them with his fists and a strop."

Oscar cursed under his breath, remembering the lustful look on Cecil's face when he talked about his ten-year-old daughter.

"How'd you know who Dolan was?" They were walking slowly down the street.

"You've got to admit that once you've seen him you won't forget him." Sharon laughed and hugged Oscar's arm. "Are you jealous? I danced with him when he came to the Pierces' to get Letty. Even then I knew he had eyes only for her."

"It's strange that Letty let everybody think she was a widow woman." They came to the corner and Oscar pulled her into the shadows.

"Folks would've looked down their noses at her if they knew she was married and separated from her man. You know how folks are. They'd a been sure it was her fault."

"Yeah, I know how folks are. Sharon, I've got myself in a hell of a to-do. I need to talk to you about it."

"Well, talk away."

"Not here. So you really want to hear that woman tell us the world is coming to an end?"

"Not really, but let's wait and see what she looks like." The singing was over. A dark-haired man in a white linen suit stood on the hotel balcony with both arms raised. The crowd quieted except for the muffled sound of a baby crying.

"Brothers and sisters in the Lord," he shouted in a booming voice. "This is a joyous occasion. I must confess that when Sister Cora informed me that the Lord had told her to stop in this small hamlet and hold a service, I urged her to continue on to Boley where a pavilion is being prepared to hold the huge crowds that gather when she speaks. Tired as she was from months of carrying the message across this great land, she insisted on stopping *here* because she wants *you* to know *Him*.

"This work cannot be carried on without the help of each and every one of you. Dig deep in your pockets, my friends, when the collection plate is passed. You and Sister Cora will save countless souls from the fires of hell before it's too late. If there be any sick among you, come forward after the service. Sister Cora will pray for you."

The string of lights across the stage went out. A murmur of disappointment rose from the crowd that hushed when the lights came on again. Against the blue backdrop a woman in a long white robe stood with her face lifted to the sky. arms extended toward the crowd. Below, on the porch of the hotel, voices began to chant, "Sister Cora, Sister Cora, Sister Cora—" As if mesmerized, the people in the street took up the chant and it went on and on. The woman on the balcony brought her palms together. lowered her head until her chin rested on her fingertips, and waited for the crowd to stop chanting. After a full moment of tense silence, she walked to the pulpit.

Oscar nudged Sharon. "Let's go."

"Just a minute. I want to hear what she's got to say.

"*He* will come! *He* will come!" Cora's musical voice rang out over the crowd. "We know not the day or the hour. Could you, my dear friends, rise to meet Him in the sky?"

"What the hell is she talkin' about?" Oscar asked.

"Shhh . . ."

"Jesus loves you. *He* weeps that some of you will burn in everlasting hell. *He* cares that your heart aches. *He* cares that you are sick in body and in mind. *He* grieves when you're fallen. *He* waits to forgive you of your sins. You are not lost from *His* sight. When the trumpet of the Lord shall sound and time shall be no more. Will you be ready? Will you meet your loved ones on the bright and blissful shore, or will you be cast into the fiery furnace?"

"Let's go, Sharon. She gives me the jitters."

"She knows how to work up the crowd. They're swallowing every word she says, hook, line, and sinker."

"And will shell out when the hat is passed. Let's walk down to the creamery. Nobody'll be around this time of night."

In a high, clear voice Sister Cora was singing, "Will you meet me over yonder? I'll be there—" Her voice faded as they walked down the dark street toward the creamery.

Oscar lifted Sharon up to sit on the end of an old milk wagon and told her of his involvement with Elmer Russell and the bootlegging operation.

"I started out just bootleggin' a little whiskey now and then to make some extra money. Now I'm in a trap and can't get out. Elmer's bringin' in a half a boxcar load at a time and supplyin' three counties."

"Golly, Oscar. I didn't know you were mixed up in anything like that. Where's Elmer getting the whiskey?"

"Out of Chicago. He thinks Dolan is here to cut into his territory."

"What gave him that idea?"

"He can't believe he's a dirt farmer. He's just sure Dolan's from the mob back East."

"That's crazy."

"I'm 'fraid to tell Elmer I want out. He's meaner than a hornet when he's crossed."

"Golly-darn, Oscar. There's nothin' more dangerous than a crooked lawman. I never did like that pig-eyed polecat."

"What'll I do, Sharon? I've got my kids to think of. Elmer'd put all this on me in a minute if he thought he'd be caught. He could arrest me, and it would be my word against his."

"What's Cecil Weaver got to do with this?"

"He delivers for him the same as me, Arlo Thompson, and Doug Hardesty. We have to be at the siding tomorrow night to load two wagons. One'll be covered with hay, the other with chicken coops. Arlo will take one, Cecil the other, if he's sober. Next week it'll be my turn."

"Don't do it, Oscar. It's too dangerous. What would happen to your kids if you got shot or sent to jail? Their granny couldn't keep them. They'd go to the orphans' home."

"I think about that. I've been a no-good son-of-a-bitch at times and done plenty that I ort not done, but I've took care of my kids. I wasn't but sixteen when I got Clara pregnant and married her. Our first two younguns died, then we had three more. It put Clara in a early grave her bein' so young and all."

"Don't take all the blame," Sharon said soothingly. "Clara had a part in it too."

"Guess it's taken me all this time to grow up. Now that I've met you, Sharon, I just want to get myself a good steady job and make a home for you and the kids if you'll have me."

"I'll have to be sure it's me you want and not just someone to look after your kids."

"It's you, Sharon. You make me feel like I'm worth something." He put his arms around her. She tilted her head to look up at him.

"You are worth something. I often wondered why you wanted folks to think you a skirt chaser."

"I won't lie to you. I've been to the speak-easies and whored around, especially since Clara died."

"I'll not hold that against you. You got tied down so young you didn't have time to sow your wild oats." She slipped her arms about his waist and pressed herself against him.

"Oh, Jesus! Oh, God," Oscar breathed in her hair. "Why didn't I meet you sooner?"

Sharon pulled away. "We've got to get you out of this mess before we can make any plans."

"Elmer'll kill me if I spill anything to Sheriff Ledbetter."

"We've got a week to think about what to do."

Oscar wrapped his arms about her. They sat for a long while in comfortable silence watching the fireflies.

CHAPTER
—————19—————

"He went to town."

Jacob, in his big chair, lifted one foot up and rested it on his knee so that he could untie his shoe.

"You knew he was going." Letty said accusingly. She pulled a chair back from the table and sank down.

" 'Course I did. Any man with a backbone wouldn't rest till he settled the score with the man who mistreated his woman."

"He didn't say anything. He just got up from the table and left. I thought he'd gone to the creek to take a bath."

"'He'll be back." Jacob's boot dropped to the floor with a thump.

"If he's able." Letty replied worriedly. "Cecil

could be waiting for him, with a bunch of thugs to beat him up."

"Mike can take care a hisself," Jacob said confidently, stretched and groaned. "I m gettin' so gol-durn old I ain't fit fer nothin' but to eat and sleep."

"—And wake up Patrick by throwing your shoe on the floor." she replied irritably.

"My, ain't you cross. Ya remind me of a cow with her teat caught in a fence."

"I'm worried, that's what!"

"Ain't no reason to be. Tanglin' with Mike'd be like tanglin' with a buzz saw." He stretched again. "Lordy mercy, my old bones are creakin' tonight."

"You're not walking that plowed ground anymore." Letty' said firmly noticing how slowly he moved and the fatigue lines in his face. "Mike says you're not going to the field during harvest either."

"You two got yore heads together and decided to put me on the shelf, did ya?"

"We decided that since you didn't have enough sense to take care of yourself we'd do it for you. You may be able to bully me, but you won't bully Mike."

"Hogwash" he snorted. "I ain't never been able to bully ya into anythin'. It'd be easier to swing a mule by the tail than to budge you when you get yore mind set. It's good thin' yore man come back to whip ya in line."

Letty looked into his twinkling eyes and burst into soft laughter.

"Grandpa, you're enough to make a preacher cuss."

"That ain't nothin'. Plenty of 'em do it on the sly."

After a long pause. Letty said. "I hope Cora doesn't come here."

"Why would she? Ain't nothin' for her here. Stop yore worryin'. She can't hurt ya none."

"Oh, yes, she can. If she spreads it around that I had a child out of wedlock, they'll never let me keep Helen."

"Yore borrowin' trouble." Jacob got up yawning. "I'm goin' to bed." He passed behind her chair, turned, and sniffed. "You plannin' on doin' some sparkin' when Mike gets back? Smells like that there Christmas perfume me 'n' Patrick got fer ya from Sears Roebuck." He chuckled when he saw her bristle.

"You got it for me to use, didn't you?"

"Now that ya mention it, reckon we did."

"Then why are you complaining?" The foot of her crossed leg began to move back and forth in a rhythmic movement that reflected her restlessness.

Jacob chuckled again. "Mike'd better get back here pretty soon or he'll think he's got hold of a sour pickle 'stead of a sweet, pretty woman."

"Night GrandPa."

"Night, Letty girl." Jacob's gnarled hand came out and swept the hair back from her cheek.

Letty was surprised and touched by the gentle gesture. Tears sprang in her eyes. She knew that his affection for her ran deep but that he was unable to voice it. She took his hand in hers and held it to her cheek.

"You're the most irritating, yet the sweetest grandpa in the whole wide world!"

"Horsefeathers!" he snorted, pulled his hand free, and headed for the bedroom.

Letty sat with her elbows on the table. As the clock began to strike the hour, she counted the strokes although she had just checked and knew that it was nine o'clock. There was still some light in the room. This was one of the longest days in the year. Soon the days would begin to shorten and by fall it would be dark by five o'clock. She remembered the long winter nights when she lay in her lonely bed and wondered why fate had been so unkind to her.

She reached into the neck of her dress and pulled out the scrap of blue ribbon she had taken from the lilac bush. It was warm and scented from being next to her skin. Mike had kept it with him all the time they had been apart! While she was alone and hurting he had been alone and hurting, too.

Sliding the ribbon between her thumb and forefinger she went out onto the porch. The night was warm and quiet except for a few martins that sat squawking on the windmill blades while others, looking for a nightly feast, soared with open mouths through a swarm of flying insects. Woodrow came from his nest of grass beside the barn and stood looking at her.

"Are you waiting for him too?" Letty asked softly as she tucked the ribbon back inio the neck of her dress.

The bushy tail made a half-swing, then the dog turned and walked slowly back to his nesting place.

Letty leaned against a porch post and stared off down the road. *Come back, Mike. Please come back soon.* Presently she realized that she was pacing back and forth across the porch. She stopped and a shiver racked her slender frame. *What if he didn't come back!* No! God wouldn't be so cruel to her again!

When she heard the sound of a gate slam shut and Woodrow's whine of welcome, relief made her weak. She hugged the porch post and strained her eyes for a sight of Mike. He came from around the barn, bareheaded and shirtless.

"Mike! Mike!" She jumped off the porch, ran to him, and threw herself into his arms. He lifted her off her feet and swung her around.

"Sweetheart . . ."

"I found the ribbon tied to the lilac bush." she said breathlessly. "Oh, Mike, you kept it all this time."

"It's what kept me going, kept me sane," he murmured against her cheek. "In the dark of the night. I would hold the ribbon and see your hair blowing in the wind, see your laughing eyes, smiling lips, and feel what it was like to lose myself inside you. Dear God, I missed you!"

"I missed you too. You were my life, my heartbeat."

"I dreamed of kissing you with your arms about my neck, of feeling your breasts against me, and holding your hips in my hands."

"So did I. We don't have to *dream* of it anymore, my love."

His lips moved hotly in search of hers, found them, and molded them to his in a devastating kiss. Letty's senses responded with a deep, churning hunger for his touch. She clung to him and parted her lips to glide the tip of her tongue over the edge of his teeth. Caught in a spinning whirlwind of desire, Letty was still aware that his pulse was racing as wildly as hers. As he pressed his body against hers she could feel that he was as ready for passion as she was.

Her breath came in small gasps when the kiss broke. She lifted her hands and framed his face with her palms before her fingers forked into his hair. "It's wet."

"I bathed in the creek before I came to you."

"I was so worried. Are you all right?" Her hands moved down over his shoulders and arms.

"Weaver left town but I'll find him."

"Oh Mike no. Let it go."

"Never. Let's don't talk about it now. Hummm . . . you smell good. Good enough to eat." His tongue lapped at the skin beneath her ear. It felt so good she pressed against it. "Did I hurt your lip when I kissed you?"

"I was enjoying it too much to notice. Maybe you'd better kiss me again."

Their mouths met. They kissed deeply, hungrily. His hand found her breast, cupped and lifted it. The evidence of his need was captured between them. Letty gave herself up to the abandonment of moving against it. He moved his lips a fraction. Their breaths mingled.

"Sweetheart" he whispered with a catch in his voice. "Stay with me tonight."

"Is your bunk big enough for both of us?"

"God, yes! I could sleep with you on top a rail fence." His broad hand moved down her spine, found her taut buttocks, and pressed her hard against him. "I want you so much . . . I'm about to burst."

"I can't let *that* happen."

She felt a lightness, a sweetness, a rightness and ran her palms over his body from the hollow beneath his armpits to the top of his britches, around and over his back. He stood still, his head tilted down toward hers. She watched his face, as anticipation of what was to come whirled and flitted through her mind and joyous tremors fluttered inside her.

"Take me to bed, my love . . . my only love." She whispered.

A choking sound came from his throat as he scooped her up in his arms. In the tack room he set her on her feet and lit the lamp turning the wick low until it glowed faintly. He looked at her then, and lifted his hands to remove the pins from her hair.

"Shall we leave the lamp on?"

She nodded, leaning her forehead against his collarbone.

"Sweetheart, if you'd rather, we can wait until we're legally wed."

"Do you want to?"

"It would about kill me, but I can do it if it's what you want. I pledged myself to you long ago when we first joined our bodies in love. A few words read over us by a stranger won't make you more my wife than you are at this moment."

Her arms moved up to encircle his neck. "Then love me—"

He groaned her name, then covered her lips with his and left them there while he whispered "I will. I will—"

Without a shred of embarrassment, she unbuttoned her dress and let it fall to the floor at her feet. Then in her petticoat. she sat on the bunk while he knelt at her feet, unlaced her shoes, and pulled off her stockings. She saw his nostrils flare with a quick intake of breath when she slowly pulled the ribbon from its nesting place against her breast and held it out to him. He took it with all the care something so precious deserved and placed it on the table beside the lamp. Then slowly his hands went to his belt buckle.

While he removed his trousers, she slipped off her undergarments and held her arms out to him. Mike sank down on the bunk and gathered her to him, holding her naked length against his.

"You feel so good. Before . . . we had our clothes

317

on." She clutched him tightly, her hands biting into the warm, solid flesh of his back.

The feel of his body, the stroking of his hands, the warm moistness of his breath, the love filling and spilling from her heart brought her mindless pleasure. They were feverish in their desire for one another. Blindly, passionately, he kissed her breasts drawing sweetly on the nipple he took into his mouth. With her fingers tangled in his black curls, she held his head to her, never wanting him to stop that glorious torment.

Gentle seeking fingers moved down over her stomach and toyed with the soft curls before seeking the warm wet entrance to her womanhood. Her breath hissed when his callused fingers stroked and slipped inside. The rough, seeking touch set delicious tremors cascading through her melting flesh. She caught her lower lip between her teeth, but there was no stopping the whimpering cries when a series of small explosions went off in her body. She arched against him, her hand seeking, and finding and caressing his elongated, rigid flesh.

"Letty, Letty, Letty—" He said her name in a sobbing breath over and over. "It's been so long . . . much too long—" She felt him shudder, listened to his outcry, and caressed him as he trembled.

Slowly and carefully, on still-quivering arms, he raised his body, lowered himself between her thighs and entered her, reverently guiding her to accept the gentle invasion. Her hands clung feverishly to him, holding him tightly while she rained kisses on his neck, his shoulders. This joining with him was unlike the coupling they had experienced before, fully clothed, beneath the willow. This time their bodies melted together into a flame of sensation.

There was no room in her mind for anything but the flesh inside hers. She was part of him. He was part of her. He was the universe, vibrating with all the love in the world, and he was lifting her to undreamed sensual heights. At almost the same instant she knew the outburst of his gigantic release, her own flesh shuddered and splintered with an exquisite explosion, sending her into a void where fireworks brightened a blackened sky.

Returning from that infinite space. She was aware that her open mouth pressed against his shoulder. His damp skin tasted salty against her tongue. For long moments there were no words between them, only the sounds of labored breathine and moaning kisses.

Mike turned onto his back, bringing her with him. He pressed her head to his shoulder; she burrowed into the hollow of his arm, tasting the moisture that dewed his chest, her whole body palpitating still. She stroked the damp, crisp hairs and ran her hand over his hard-tendoned belly. He trembled and buried his lips in her hair.

Letty rubbed her cheek against the smooth flesh of his shoulder and whispered. "This was even better than what I remembered."

His arm tightened and his hand moved down

to pull her thigh up over his. He turned his head to look down at her, his expression relaxed and gentle.

"We were children then, sweetheart."

His words fired her with new tenderness. She tilted her head up until she could reach his mouth and kissed it again and again.

"You gave me the only happiness I knew during the first fifteen years of my life."

He groaned. "And misery for the next six years. I should never have given in to my desire for you—"

"Shhhh . . ." She placed her fingers over his lips. "It gave us Patrick. Never, never, have I regretted it. It brought me here to Grandpa and Grandma where I learned what it was to live in a home filled with love and respect. Grandpa never ruled like a tyrant over Grandma the way my father ruled his family."

"I'm not very forgiving honey. I'll never forgive them for what they did to us."

"They hurt themselves more. They'll not have the joy of knowing their grandchildren."

"Someday I'd like for my mother to see Patrick. He resembles Katy. Mama grieved so when she lost her."

"Did your mother want you to marry a Catholic girl?"

"She might have, but she knew how much I loved you."

"Do you want our children to go to the Catholic church?."

"Would you mind?"

"No. But I don't want them to be religious fanatics like my father and Cora."

"They can go to the Lutheran church with Jacob and to the Catholic church with me. When they're older they can choose."

"Don't expect me to go with you. Grandpa doesn't."

"I don't expect you to do anything you're not comfortable doing."

"Mike . . ." His name melted on her lips and when she tried to speak, her words kept fading swept away by his kisses. "Mike—"

"Shhh . . . don't say anything." His lips covered hers before she could speak, and she forgot what she was going to say. His voice was a whisper when finally they broke the kiss.

"I was going to ask . . . I think I was going to ask what happened in town tonight. Did you see the deputy?"

"No, but I saw Oscar Phillips. He was with Sharon Tarr."

"I'm glad they've discovered each other. I never thought Oscar was a *bad* man, only irresponsible and foolish. Maybe with Sharon he'll settle down. One thing in his favor is how good he is to his kids."

"I thanked him for helping my wife."

"Your . . . wife?"

"I thought it a good time to get the story circulating. I told them we spoke our vows years ago. And we did, you know. As soon as I can arrange it, we'll slip away and be legally married."

She sighed. "Everything would be perfect if not for Cora being here."

"Forget Cora. I want all your thoughts to be of me tonight." His hand moved over her breast and down to her hips. He pulled her over until her soft stomach was pressed to his hard one, his sex nestled in the silky down that covered her mound. "I wish I could have seen you when you were pregnant."

"My breasts were like melons. My stomach was as big as a barrel. My back hurt and I waddled like a duck," She felt him laugh,

"I would have rubbed your back." he murmured against her mouth, holding her so close their hearts pounded against each other.

Her lips sought his and open over his mouth with drugged sweetness. Closing her eyes, she reveled in his strong fingers stroking the quivering small of her back. The low, aching fire in her blazed up again. His hands slipped upward. kneading her shoulder blades, memorizing the slender curve of her upper arms while his body ground into hers. Her womanhood throbbed, aching for fulfillment. She rocked from side to side on his hardness in an agony of longing.

"Sweet, sweet, love. I've got to be inside you."

He moved his hands under the softness of her upper thighs, spread her legs, and lifted her. He inserted himself, velvety, hard, and pulsing with life, into her yielding warmth. Minutes later they were interlocked and breathlessly surrendering to their hunger for each other. His face twisted with the intensity of their coupling and the almost painful anticipation of the ultimate pleasure as she met his thrusts.

When he felt the tremors in the silken sheath that surrounded him, he released the hold he had on his passion and filled her with his life-giving fluid.

Letty's arms curved about him possessively, This big, self-assured man had quivered in her arms as she had in his. Slowly his breathing steadied. He reached for the lamp and turned the wick down until the room was plunged into darkness. Then he turned on his side, his arm holding her to him, his hand bringing her thigh up to rest on his. He pulled a blanket up from the foot of the bunk, tucked it around them, and cuddled her warm body against his. Almost instantly she was asleep.

Feeling wonderfully loved and happily relaxed. Mike closed his eyes on the most wonderful night of his life and drifted into a dreamlike state halfway between sleep and awareness, his mouth uplifted in a tired but happy smile.

Letty came out of a deep sleep aware of the teasing fingers between her thighs and strong lips fastened firmly to her nipple. Drowsily, she realized she was lying on her back and Mike's head lay on her breast.

"I love you," she whispered into his dark curls.

His laugh was low and tender. He sucked hard at her nipple then moved swiftly to pull her legs about him. He embedded himself in her moistness and thrust deeply. Incredibly, her body responded to his. His lips moved over her chin to her mouth. The tip of his tongue traced her lips before slipping inside. His fingers pulled gently on her wet nipples, then he tugged, almost roughly. The pressure thrilled her in her belly and deep, deep inside her. She moaned incoherent words of love and tightened her arms about him.

He laughed deep in his throat.

"Are your eyes open love? I wish I could see them. You're so incredibly sweet. I never want to make this trip alone. I want you to always be with me, feel this with me."

"Does it feel as good to you as it does to me?" she murmured against his nibbling lips and arched against him.

"It's heaven! It's . . . pure heaven—"

Her body felt boneless as he fitted every inch of it against his. This was Mike, her mate, her lover. She felt herself being swept away on a cloud climbing, climbing into the sky until that sunlit moment of glorious shared completion.

Letty had never felt so totally a woman. Mike pressed his head into the hollow of her shoulder. Her arms wound about him tenderly. *She loved him so much!* A small spurt of fear knifed through her. What if something happened to him? She had not said a prayer since her preacher father had put her out of his house. She said one now.

"Dear lord, keep him safe. I couldn't bear to lose him . . . again."

The deepness of Mike's breathing told her he was sleeping soundly. Letty gave a little sigh and closed her eyes in sweet exhaustion.

CHAPTER
—————20—————

Letty was thoughtful as she looped a wet sheet over the line.

That morning, when Helen had failed to come downstairs, Letty had gone up to her room to find the child hunkered down at the end of the bed, her face swollen from crying.

"I'm . . . sorry—" she sobbed.

"Sorry? Oh . . . Letty saw the huge wet spot in the middle of the bed and realized what had happened. "You wet the bed? Honey, that's not so terrible, Patrick does it once in a while."

"But . . . I'm ten—"

"You were sleeping so soundly that you failed to wake up and get on the pot," Letty put her arms about the child and hugged her, "Shhh . . . don't cry. We'll wash the sheets. It's a nice sunny day"

"Patrick and . . . everyone will know—"

"No one will know but you and me. We'll wash all the sheets. We'll say we're getting a head start on Monday's washing. With the two of us working we can get it done in no time at all. Hurry now

and get dressed. Patrick went out to the field with Mike and Grandpa. They'll be finished with the planting in an hour or two."

The child's arms went about Letty's neck. "I wish . . . I wish you was my mama."

"I wish it too. We're going to do everything we can to make it happen."

Now, while dumping the rinse water on the ferns growing on the north side of the house, Letty tried not to think of the consequences if the deputy came to get Helen. Thank God, Mike was here. He would know what to do. *Mike.* Her love. Her future. She and Mike would take care of their family; Patrick and Helen and Grandpa.

She hung the tub on the nail on the porch. Her apron was wet and her hair hung about her face in strings. She would start the noon meal and tidy herself before he came in for dinner.

This morning when she had awakened to find him up and doing the chores she had lain in his bunk, smelling the scent of their lovemaking, her heart quivery. The fluttering in her stomach had persisted during breakfast when Mike took advantage of her nearness to give her loving caresses whenever she brushed by him. Jacob's teasing eyes had observed and approved. Now, at mid-morning she was filled with boundless happiness, and it reflected in her face, her bright eyes, and in her bouncy step.

Helen was practicing on the piano and Letty was singing softly to herself which perhaps was the reason she didn't hear the purr of the automobile engine. Suddenly, there was a loud thumping on the door, and Helen screeched and ran for the kitchen.

"Letty! Letty!"

"What is it, honey?"

"Somebody—"

Letty wiped her hands on her wet apron and pushed Helen down in a chair. "Stay here."

A man in a dark suit stood on the front porch. He removed his hat when Letty appeared in the doorway.

"Is this the Fletcher farm?"

"Yes."

"You're Mrs. Graham?" Letty nodded. "Excuse me for a moment. I have someone who wishes to see you."

He stepped off the porch and hurried to the large shiny black automobile parked beside the yard gate. White pennants were attached to the front fenders. A sign on the side painted in large white letters said: JESUS IS COMING.

Cora. An icy coldness swept over Letty, leaving her as stiff as a frozen pond.

Oh, Lordy. She was not ready for this confrontation with her sister, but there wasn't much she could do about it now. With not quite steady fingers Letty stroked the hair back from her face and poked it into the knot at the back of her neck. The smoothing of her hair was not due to any wish to improve her appearance, but to nervousness. She wished that Mike and Grandpa were here. In the next breath she was thankful they were not. This meeting with her sister was bound to happen. It was just something she had to endure. She told herself that there was nothing Cora could do to hurt her, but she knew it wasn't true. So she stood there waiting, a slender auburn-haired woman in a faded blue dress and an apron wet with wash water. The woman being escorted up the path to the house was taller, bigger-boned than Letty, and dressed all in white. Her hair was much lighter than Letty remembered and swept up under a large-brimmed hat. Her dress, made of layer upon layer of gauzelike material, flowed around her like a cloud when she walked. A loosely woven net veil covered a face so pale it looked as if it had never seen the light of day.

Cora came to the edge of the porch and with a look dismissed the man in the black suit. He turned and went back to the automobile.

"Hello, Letty."

"Hello, Cora." Letty stood in the doorway with her arms crossed.

"Are you going to ask me in?"

"Why?"

"Because I'm your sister and I've come to visit. I'm in need of a cold drink. It was a long, dusty ride out here." Without an invitation, Cora pulled open the screen door and stepped into the parlor. The fragrance of lily of the valley perfume came with her. Her eyes swept the room. A look of disgust settled over her features. Her nose twitched as if she smelled something unpleasant Letty remembered the practiced gesture designed to in-

328

timidate and stared into her sister's hard blue eyes when they swung back to her. "This is about what I expected. It hasn't changed but you have."

Letty shrugged. "So have you."

"I should hope so. I've come a long way from that one-horse church in Dunlap"

"Bully for you."

"Humm . . . smart mouthed, aren't you. I see you've still got Mama's piano. I want to hear you play."

"You didn't come all the way out here to hear me play the piano. What do you want?" Letty had promised herself she wouldn't lose her temper, but she was tempted. Cora' eyes were moving over her, assessing her, as if she were a horse Cora was interested in buying.

"Oh, but I do. The piano was the only thing you excelled in, beside the . . . er pleasures of the flesh. I suspect that now you play better than Mama did in her prime. She's lost the touch, you know. Barely beats out a tune. Claims it's rheumatism."

"Then why don't you *pray* for her? Use your magical healing power."

Letty was surprised to hear Cora laugh. She had forgotten that Cora's mouth was so small and thin-lipped and that her features were so sharp.

"Papa needs her. And besides, they're not in my class anymore."

"Neither am I, thank God. I want you to go."

"If I dressed you up, you'd look pretty decent." Cora said, ignoring Letty's order to leave. "I'm here to take you out of this"—she waved a gloved hand—"pigsty."

Letty choked back her anger. "Well thank you very much for your generosity, *Sister* Cora. This pigsty suits me just fine."

Cora's mouth opened, then snapped shut. "Sit down," she ordered. "Sit down and play. I need someone who can tickle the keys, rouse the crowds and put some life into the music. I've been told you can make that piano talk. I want to hear it."

"No, damn you! I'll not play. I want you to leave."

"Still the simple-minded fool. You can make as much as fifty dollars a week, travel, stay in the best places, meet . . . interesting men."

"You have a nerve coming here." Letty's voice trembled with anger. "Get out!"

"I've come here to give you a chance to redeem yourself. Now hush up, and listen." Cora spoke in a sharp commanding voice that was trained to give orders.

"Don't tell me to hush up, you . . . damned hypocrite! The only thing you can say that will interest me in the least is that you're leaving and I'll never have to see your face again."

"That's where you're wrong, Letty. I have plenty to say that *should* interest you. Unless you want everyone in Nebraska to know that you were a bitch in heat and that you were serviced by a wild, black-Irish Catholic, you'll keep a civil tongue in your head."

Cora's attack was sudden and vicious. The words hit Letty with the force of a slap in the face.

"You're evil, Cora. Evil and mean."

"Did you keep your bastard, sister dear?"

"There is *no* bastard! Mike and I were married *before* he left that winter." The lie came easily to Letty. No way was this creature going to call the child born of her love and Mikes a bastard!

"Mike Dolan married you?" Cora's mouth puckered as if she hadn't thought of the possibility. Then she asked, "Why are you using the name Graham?"

"So Papa and Mike couldn't find me. I was angry at Mike for leaving me to face Papa alone. You know as well as I that Papa thinks marrying a Catholic is a sin equal to murder." When Cora didn't speak, Letty continued, hoping to change the subject. "I don't know how anyone as evil, greedy, and grasping as you and Papa can fool the decent, hard-working folk like you do."

"Because they want to be fooled and because I'm so good at fooling them, dear sister. I've come a long way during the past six years. My name is known in every town west of the Mississippi. Crowds gather at every whistle-stop to hear me speak. I live very well. People jump when I issue an order. I have two beautiful homes, my own railway car, money in the bank, and millionaires clamoring to marry me. What do you have? You live on a broken-down farm that will someday be Mama's. Do you think Papa will let you stay here? He'll throw you out like so much trash."

Anger was a heaviness in Letty's chest that threatened to strangle her. Only Cora's insults about her son shook her. Her threats that her parents would take over the farm did not. Mike would never let it happen. Letty was determined not to give Cora the satisfaction of knowing how much her cruel words hurt. The smug look on her sister's face reminded her of the way she looked the day at the dinner table when she told their father about her pregnancy.

"I'm supposed to be dead Remember?"

"Of course, I remember." Cora's smile had a hint of secrecy to it. "Papa got enough donations at the memorial service to get us out of town. Brilliant idea. Mine, as a matter of fact."

"And Mama? She went along with it?"

"You know how Mama is." Cora shrugged. "She rather enjoyed her grief; being fussed over and all. Mama is dumb as a doorknob and perfect for Papa. She obeys him without question. He still rules the roost. Thank God, I got out from under his thumb or I'd still be preaching under a brush arbor."

"You're hard, Cora. They doted on you."

"Yes, they did, didn't they?" She preened. "But I'm not here to discuss them. You should be grateful that I'm willing to take *you* out of this pigsty."

Anger burst forth in Letty like a red tide. "You call my home a pigsty one more time and I swear to God, I'll smear your nose all over your lily-white face,"

For an endless moment Cora stared at Letty.

"Now. Now. Let's be civilized. I know it will be difficult for you, but try, will you?" She raised her brows in question. "I heard about the little set-to yesterday. Did you lose your temper? Did your lover make you angry?" Cora lifted her white-gloved hands and folded her face veil back over her hat. "I suppose it gives you a thrill to have men fight over you"

"You don't miss a thing, do you?"

"It would have been difficult to miss. Men fighting over a whore is news in any town."

"At least a whore gives something in return for the money she takes! You give nothing but false hope after you scare the life out of folks with your 'end of the world' tales. Get out! You're not welcome here." Letty balled her fists. She never wanted to hit anyone so badly in all her life.

"You're being tiresome." Cora sighed heavily. "I don't have much more time to waste here, I want to get this settled before I go. I've not found a pianist that can fire up a crowd like you and Mama. I want to hear you play. If you still have the touch, I'll take you with me."

"You're just like Papa," Letty shouted, her temper flaring anew. "You haven't heard a thing I've said. Can't you get it through your stupid head that I don't want anything to do with you. Long before Papa threw me out, I was ashamed of him, ashamed of you, ashamed of the plans you devised, your schemes to get what you wanted from some poor soul who had hardly enough to feed his own family. There's nothing you can do to me that will hurt me half as much as having my friends known that I'm related to you."

"Have you finished?"

"With you, yes. Get out of my house."

"You must keep in mind, dear sister, that I always have an alternate plan to back up each of my . . . ah . . . er . . . proposals. I understand a girl by the name of Helen Weaver is staying here with you. Her father wants her back with him. He grieves for his little girl, the last of a family taken by the epidemic. The young doctor in town is trying to make arrangements for you to adopt the child. I doubt, Letty, that the Child Welfare Department of this state or any other would place a child in the care of a woman who is living apart from her husband under a fictitious name. Think about that."

Letty shook with disbelief. "Helen has nothing to do with this. Why would you want to hurt that . . . little girl?"

"I don't want to hurt her but I'll use whatever means I can to get what I want. When I go into a town, I make it my business to know as much as I can about the people who live there. You'd be surprised at the things I hear and . . . how I can use that information. Right now, down in Boley, I have people—"

"Digging up dirt for you to use against them, huh Cora?" Mike's voice came from behind Letty. She turned. He was there; big, solid, self-assured and wonderful. She hadn't heard him come into the house. He was looking at Cora and she at him.

334

Letty was aware that behind his calm mask was lethal hatred.

"As I live and br . . . breathe." Cora's voice faltered. "Mike Dolan. Well . . . well—" A half-smile curved her lips.

"In the flesh," Mike snarled. "Ah . . . So your ferrets failed to report that I was here."

"I knew it was you. I told Papa you were the one that got into our little Letty's bloomers."

"You cooked up that scheme to keep us apart. You never thought I'd find out that Letty was alive, did you?" Mike's voice was as hard as nails.

"I never thought about it one way or the other."

"You're a liar and always have been. I've been there in the kitchen listening to you shoot off your mouth. You're the same old sneaking, conniving Cora, working both ends against the middle to get your way."

"Eavesdropping," Cora said haughtily. "I'm not surprised considering your background."

"Get out before I forget you're a woman and throw you out." Mike came to Letty and put his arm across her shoulders,

"That won't be necessary." Cora lowered the veil back over her face, "I'll leave, but you'll be hearing from me." She walked to the door and turned. "Tell me, Mike. What did you see in a mousy thing like her?"

"Things you wouldn't understand. She's beautiful inside as well as outside. Honest, loyal, and compassionate. She's got more integrity in the tip of her little finger than you have in your whole body. I knew when I was seventeen that she was the one woman in the whole world I wanted to have my babies and share my life. She's my wife, my friend, my lover. I love her with all my heart and soul."

Cora laughed nastily. "That's quite a testimonial. It must be nice to be so perfect."

"Stay out of our lives, Cora. Interfere and you'll be sorry." Mike spoke softly, but there was suppressed rage in every word.

"Are you threatening me? I'd be careful if I were you, Mike. I'm a well-known, very popular person. If I complain of harassment, you'll be arrested immediately."

"If that should happen, I have a few tales the newspapers would like to print. Tales of swindle and fraud."

Cora smiled as if enjoying the game of sparring with Mike.

"Then I suggest we call it a standoff . . . for the time being. By the way, Letty. I forgot to mention that I sent Papa a wire telling him that Grandpa Fletcher is ailing and that he'd better get up here and see about Mama's inheritance."

"Grandpa's not ailing—" Letty protested and stopped when Mike squeezed her shoulder.

"You'll get your folks up here for nothing. There's nothing here for your mother to inherit. Jacob sold the farm to me. The deed is recorded at the courthouse."

On hearing Mike's words, Letty did her best

not to look surprised. Cora was studying them with eyes both intense and probing.

"You think you have things tied up here nice and neat. We'll see. I usually get what I go after; one way or the other."

"Not always. You didn't get me, did you, Cora?" Mike's voice was cold and wicked. Surprised again by his words, Letty looked up to see his features set in a rock-hard expression, his cold, black eyes boring into Cora's. "When you discovered I was interested in Letty, you tried every scheme in the book to get me to like you. I'll tell you now as I told you then, the sight of you lying there by the stream, your bloomers off and your legs spread, sickened me. I couldn't stand the sight of you then and I can't stand the sight of you now."

Cora stood perfectly still, her eyes locked with Mike's. Then color came up to flood her face, Her hand fumbled blindly for the screen door. She was so shaken that she stumbled over the threshold when she went out. Mike and Letty followed her to the porch. After she went down the steps to the yard she turned and looked back at Mike, pure hatred hardening her features.

"You poor fool. I've got more money than you ever dreamed of having. You'll never be anything but dirt-poor Irish-Catholic trash."

"And proud of it," he replied. "In comparison with you and your kind, me and my kind smell like roses. Stay away from my wife, my son, and this farm or you'll answer to me."

"I've discovered that there's more than one way to skin a cat. I never let an insult go unrevenged. You'll soon see who has the most influence with Mrs. Knight of the Child Welfare Department, me or your Doctor Hakes." Cora took the arm of the man who came from the car. "You really should come to a meeting and be saved, Letty. The Lord works in mysterious ways his wonders to perform. Our Jesus loves even a lowly whore. Who knows, *He* may let you keep the girl if you ask forgiveness for your sins,"

Mike and Letty stood on the porch and watched her being helped into the automobile. The driver went around to the other side, climbed in, and pressed an automatic starter. The engine sputtered to life and purred like a tamed tiger. The car made a sharp turn and headed back toward Piedmont.

Letty buried her face in Mike's chest and wrapped her arms about his waist.

"What will we do? How did you know I needed you?"

"The car. You can see the flags on the fenders and the sign on the side of it half a mile away. I cut across the field got here shortly after she did, and sent Helen out to stay with Jacob and Patrick."

"Do you think she believed me when I said we were married before you left that winter?"

"Even if she didn't, it will take her some time to run down all the places we could have been married. We've got to figure out a way to be married so it'll appear to have happened six years ago."

"Poor little Helen. Just for spite Cora will do everything she can to get her away from us and turned over to that . . . that animal."

"She'll try, but we have a few cards to play too." Mike lifted her face with a gentle finger beneath her chin. "Don't give up, sweetheart. You were doing a good job of holding your own with Cora. I kept hoping you'd 'smear her nose all over her lily-white face.' " He grinned proudly.

"You heard . . . that?"

"I heard that. Now kiss me. We've got plans to make."

His mouth shaped itself to hers. Letty parted her lips against his and slowly traced the bottom curve of his inner lip with the tip of her tongue before he pressed his mouth to hers in a long, hard kiss. There was a delightful familiarity in the feel of his body, his arms, his mouth, and in the flood of pleasure that washed over her.

Her eyes were cloudy and her mouth half-parted when he moved his head back to look into her face.

"Kiss me again," he whispered.

She pressed her mouth to his again and kissed him softly, sweetly.

"How many hours until dark?" he asked, his dark eyes twinkling.

"Too many," she whispered, letting her breath out in a shaky laugh. "Mike . . . I didn't know you'd bought the farm from Grandpa"

"I haven't . . . yet. Jacob thinks your pa will move heaven and earth to get it after he's gone, claiming your mother the legal heir. He came up with the idea that I buy it for whatever I have and the deed be transferred to my name and yours. That way there'll be no will to contest. We'll still use the money to buy the mares and the sheep. The only thing is, we haven't had time to get the deed recorded."

"Grandpa wants to do this?"

"He insists on it. He's been worried about the farm for a long time. I think that's one of the reasons he decided to take a chance on me. I'm going to ride over to the Watkins place and see if I can get Guy to witness the signatures on the deed and if I can get Harry to take it to the courthouse in Boley. I'd go myself, but I don't want to leave you here alone." He bent his head and placed another soft, tender kiss on her lips.

"Mama!" The screen door flew open. "Mama, did you . . . what'er ya doin' to Mama, Dolan?"

"Kissing her."

"Why?"

"Because I want to. Do you mind if I kiss your mama?"

"Well . . . ah . . . not if she wants ya to."

Letty moved out of Mike's arms "I want him to, Patrick. Mike and I have known each other for a long, long time."

"Before you knew me?"

"Before I knew you. He's going to live here with us. We'll be a family. You, me, Grandpa, Helen, and Mike."

"He'll be my daddy like Mr. Watkins is Jimmy's daddy?"

"Yes, son. Is . . . that all right with you?" Mike asked with a slight tremor in his voice.

"Yeah! Yeah!" The small face split in a snaggletoothed grin. "I'd rather have you for my daddy than anyone in the whole wide world. I'd rather have you than Mr. Watkins."

"Then it's all right with you?"

"Golly! You'll be my *daddy!* Golly-bum! I gotta tell Grandpa and Helen. Whoopee!"

The screen door slammed behind their son. Letty turned her head sharply and looked at Mike, She saw a wet shine to his eyes.

"Did you think Patrick would be unhappy?"

"I was afraid he might resent me. He's had you to himself for so long." Mike's voice was shaky. "Someday I want him to know that I'm his *real* daddy, but we'll wait and pick the proper time to tell him." His hand came up to cradle her head, and he gently touched his lips to hers.

"He's a smart little boy. I'm glad he didn't see Cora . . . or her automobile" Letty laughed. "He's fascinated with cars."

"Maybe he'll be the next Henry Ford."

"I'm glad you'll be here to guide him," Letty wrapped her arms about Mike's waist. "I was going to get cleaned up before you came in for dinner," she murmured against his chest.

Mike leaned down and nipped her earlobe. "You already look good enough to eat."

341

Letty laughed, lifted her arms to encircle his neck, and scattered kisses over his grinning face.

"Tell me that twenty years from now when my hair is gray and I'm fat from having six of your babies—"

"—Only six?"

They were lost in each other's eyes when Jacob's gruff voice boomed from the other side of the screen door.

"Get on in here 'n' tell me what's goin' on. Beats all how ya can lollygag around out there a huggin' and a kissin' and a carryin' on when I'm waitin' to know what that chit was up to," he growled. " 'Side's that, there ain't no dinner on the stove."

Letty burst out laughing. "When Grandpa's stomach's empty, he's cross as a bear!"

CHAPTER
———21———

It was to be a day Letty would never forget.

After the noon meal Mike hitched up the wagon and they all went to the Watkins' farm. While the children played in the yard, the grown-ups sat at the kitchen table listening to Letty tell them the story of her life before she came to the farm, and explain the reason for her being known as Letty Graham. She felt she owned an explanation to her longest and dearest friends before asking them to witness her grandfather's signature on a document turning the farm over to her and Mike.

"Law, Letty, we knew somethin' of the sort had happened to you," Mrs. Watkins said, reaching to cover Letty's hand where it lay on the table. "Jacob and Leona were happy as larks to have you. 'Twasn't our place to judge ya. That night at the Pierces' I just thought if Dolan ain't Patrick's pa he's his twin brother. They're like two peas in a pod."

Mike's dark gaze caught Letty's and glinted with pride and love so warm that she nearly drowned in it. The grin that widened across his face stole away what little concentration she had left.

"It was impossible for me to marry Letty in Dunlap. I'm a Catholic and her pa is a holiness preacher," Mike said, his eyes holding Letty's as if they were alone. "But we were married in our hearts, weren't we, sweetheart?"

"We were married in our hearts," Letty repeated softly. The words, so sweet, so sincere, were mirrored in her eyes, echoed in her heart.

"Well, land sakes," Mrs. Watkins exclaimed after a silent moment. "There ain't no reason why ya can't wed and let folks think ya was wed all the time."

"That's what we want more than anything. We don't want Patrick to suffer because he was born out of wedlock." Mike held Letty's hand in both of his, his dark eyes on her face again were brimming with love.

"Ya ain't got to fear. Not one word you said will leave this room. Ain't that right, Guy? Lordy, what's neighbors for if not to stick to ya when times is bad? Us and the Fletchers has been through tough times together. Fletchers is almost family to us."

"I thank ya, Mrs. Watkins. And you too, Guy." Jacob spoke in a humble tone. "I've thought on this long and hard. Guess ya know me and Leona adopted Mable, Letty's ma. What I'm doin' is fixin' things so Albert Pringle can't come in 'n' take over when I'm gone. I hatched up this plan to sell to Mike. We'll be partners, sort of. We're goin' to get us some sheep and a couple of good brood mares." He grinned around the pipe stem he held in his teeth. "I ain't plannin' or givin' up the ghost yet, mind ya. I'm aimin' to live long enough to raise some fine horses, maybe even take some sheep to the county fair."

Letty looked at her grandpa's wrinkled, weathered face and wanted to cry. Her mind flashed back to the time she had stood in the yard, a scared fifteen-year-old, and he'd said, "Well, come on in girl." He had been her mainstay throughout the lonely years without Mike. Then when Mike came to find her, he had sized him up immediately and had found him to his liking. Oh, she was glad that in Jacob's wise old heart he had known that she needed time to come to terms with what her parents had done and to fall in love with Mike all over again.

"I can't get over you being Sister Cora's sister." Harry said.

"I'm not proud of it, Harry." Letty blinked the

tears from her eyes. "No one knows her as Mike and I do. She's a sham. I learned just today that long ago she wanted Mike. He spurned her. That could be why she hates him. I've never been able to figure out why she hates me, and it no longer matters."

"Well, now, I've said it before, but it's worth sayin' again—ya can't choose yore kin no more'n ya can choose the size of yore feet." Mrs. Watkins got up from the table. "You'd best eat something, Harry, before ya set out for Boley."

On the way back to the farm, Jacob drove the team. The children, sitting on the seat beside him, chattered like magpies. Mike and Letty, hands clasped, sat on the tailgate.

"Mike, our secret will be safe with the Watkins'."

"They deserved to know the truth. They witnessed a lifelong friend signing his farm over to us."

"Grandpa seems relieved that the farm matter is settled. Did you notice? I think he was actually worried that Mama and Papa would try to get the farm."

"It's been on his mind for some time."

"It wasn't his idea to adopt Mama. Doctor Whittier brought her out from Boley because Grandma wanted a child and couldn't have one. Grandpa would have done anything in the world for Grandma. It's too bad that Mama turned out to be such a disappointment."

"Not entirely, sweetheart. Through her they got you. Jacob would be alone now if not for you."

"He's so dear to me, Mike. I hope he lives for a long, long time. I hope he lives to know Patrick as a man."

"That'll only be another fifteen years, honey. Time goes fast."

They had just finished eating the evening meal of warmed-up beans and fresh cornbread when Woodrow began a frenzy of barking. John Pershing, honking with indignation, shot out from under the porch to see what all the fuss was about and then scrambled out of the way as an automobile came up the lane and turned into the yard between the barn and the house. Patrick was the first to jump up from the table and run to the back porch.

"It's Doctor Hakes," he shouted as soon as the motor sputtered and died. " 'Lo, Doctor Hakes. Can I sit in your car?"

Following her son to the porch, Letty waited with a worried frown on her face. Something must have happened to bring Wallace out at this time of day. Mike stood beside her, his hand on her shoulder. They watched the doctor get out of his car.

"Sure, you can sit in the car. Just don't drive her too fast," he said with a grin and ruffled Patrick's dark curls when he helped him climb up onto the seat.

"Be careful, Patrick," Letty called. "Don't track mud into the car."

"He can't hurt a thing, Letty." Wallace Hakes came to the porch, stopped, and stood looking at her. "Are you all right? I heard what happened behind the store."

"I'm all right. No damage, except to my pride."

"I never thought he'd go that far." The doctor's thin hair looked as if it had been stirred by an eggbeater. His eyeglasses were dusty and had slid down on his nose. He pushed them up with a long bony finger and looked steadily at Mike. "Mike Dolan," he said as if to himself.

While the men studied each other, Letty studied them.

"Wallace, I want you to meet Mike Dolan. And Mike, this is Doctor Hakes. He has been my doctor and friend since I came here. He was here when Grandma died and while Grandpa was terribly sick. And he delivered Patrick."

Mike held out his hand. "I'm glad to meet you, Doctor."

Wallace stepped up onto the porch and gripped Mike's hand, still assessing the big dark man who loomed behind Letty.

"And I'm glad to meet you." Wallace looked at Mike and then back to where Patrick sat behind the steering wheel of his car, turning it back and forth. He nodded his head in acknowledgment of the resemblance of the son to the father.

"Weaver may think he's getting off scot-free for what he did to Letty, but I intend to settle the score." The tone of Mike's voice was tight and angry.

Letty put her hand on his arm. "I wish you'd let it go." Mike made no reply. She sighed and turned to the doctor. "Come in. We've just finished eating, but there's beans left and a slice or two of cornbread."

"Thank you, Letty, but I'm not hungry. I need to talk to you folks. Where's Helen?"

"In the house, clearing the table."

"Could she look after Patrick for a bit? We don't want him to run off with the car."

Helen was not in the kitchen. Letty looked at Jacob and he jerked his head toward the parlor. She found Helen leaning against the wall, her face hidden in the crook of her arm.

"Helen, Doctor Hakes is here." When there was no answer, she said, "Helen—? Honey, what's wrong?"

"Has he come to get me?" Letty had to bend close to hear the child's muffled voice.

"No! He hasn't come to get you. He came to visit."

"Really?" Helen looked up, showing a tear-stained face.

"Really. Patrick is in his car. You know how adventuresome he is. I need you to keep an eye on him." Letty wiped the child's face with the end of her apron and then hugged her. "Honey, I wish you wouldn't worry so. Run on out and watch Patrick for me, but speak to Doctor Hakes first."

Wallace and Jacob were sitting at the table, Mike was pouring coffee for them.

" 'Lo, Doctor Hakes." Helen said as she ran past the table and out the door.

" 'Lo, Helen," Wallace called, but his voice was lost in the slamming of the screen door.

"She was afraid you'd come to get her to take her back to her father. Damn that Cecil Weaver," Letty sputtered. "I suppose he's drunk and raising cane."

"He's drunk all right, but he's not our immediate problem."

"Coffee, honey?" Mike asked.

"No, thanks." Letty sank down in a chair.

"It's *Sister Cora!*" Wallace said bitterly. "Goddamn that woman! She gets under my skin."

Letty had never heard Wallace swear before. "What's she done now?" she asked, wishing she didn't have to know.

"I sent a wire to Mrs. Knight asking her to meet me in Boley. Ned, at the office, told me Cora Pringle had sent a wire to Mrs. Knight at the Capitol telling her she had some information about the welfare of a child. She asked Mrs. Knight to meet *her* in Boley."

Letty reached for Mike's hand. "I was afraid of that. Grandpa, Wallace knows Cora is my sister."

"I don't see how two humans from the same sire could be so different. It ain't the way with cows or horses." Jacob's comment was punctuated with a snort of disgust.

"And, Mike, while I was in town yesterday, I told Wallace about us."

"I'd have known if you hadn't told me," Wallace said. "One look at him and at Patrick is all it takes."

Mike grinned. "Sometimes I have to pinch myself to be sure I'm not dreaming, that I'm really here with Letty and my boy."

"Speaking of dreaming. That *Sister* Cora is dreaming if she thinks I'm going to sit still for her coming here and working her flimflammery on my patients."

Letty was seeing a new side of the mild-mannered doctor. He was passionately angry.

"I'm thinking she has overplayed her hand this time," Wallace said. "I've been wanting to get something on her since a woman over at Forest Grove refused to let me treat her little boy because *Sister Cora* had come through town on one of her whistle-stop tours and had healed him. Boy died a week later of typhoid." Wallace clenched the fist that lay on the table. "Damn her, I've got something now. If things work out right, I can prove she's a sham."

"Cora and my father have been claiming for a long while that their prayers heal the sick. If there really was goodness in their hearts, I might be able to believe *some* of it, but I know for a fact that their motivation is purely greed."

Wallace looked at Letty and shook his head. "It's so hard to believe she's your sister."

Letty smiled. "That's the second time I've heard that today. What have you uncovered, Wallace?"

"I went to the meeting last night. I wanted to watch her praying over the sick. It makes me sick to the stomach to see people crowd around so that she can place her hands on them. 'I've got the he . . . al . . . ing power,' she'd say." The doctor mimicked Cora's voice. "Then at just the right moment—I'm sure it was timed perfectly—two men came forward carrying a man on a stretcher. They pleaded with her to pray for their brother. Cora knelt down beside the stretcher and ran her hands along the man's legs. Then she prayed. She prayed loud and long for the poor soul who had been unable to walk since he was crippled in an accident ten years ago. Then very dramatically, she stood, held out her hand, and told him to get up and walk. Of course, he did, to the cheers of the crowd. He walked unassisted up the steps to the hotel porch."

Wallace got up from the table and paced back and forth. "That's when I got a good look at him. He was no more a cripple than I am. He's from the town of Briskin about ninety miles west of here. I spent a few days with Doc Perkins over there, and we visited an old woman whose lazy, drunken son lay on a cot on the porch. The house was a run-down shack a couple of miles out of town. Doc Perkins kicked the drunk awake and made him go fetch a fresh bucket of water for the old lady. Man's name is Fellon. I'm going over there and get that son-of-a-bitch and bring him back by the scruff of the neck if I have to."

"Will you need any help?" Mike asked.

Wallace looked from Mike to Letty. "I was hoping you'd ask."

"What do you plan to do with him, Wallace?" Letty asked.

"Take him to her service in Boley and confront her. Doc Perkins will attest to the fact the man has never been a cripple."

"Do you think that will influence Mrs. Knight to disregard what Cora says?"

"Maybe. I think we can get around Mrs. Knight, but only if you two are legally married and have been for some time. She'll want to interview Helen. She's a compassionate woman where children are concerned. What we're concerned with is that she give Helen to you and not to someone else." He held up his hand when Letty opened her mouth to speak. "There's a justice of the peace at Weatherford about ten miles south of Briskin who owes me a favor. With a little arm-twisting, he'll date the marriage paper with any day you want and pretend that it was lost and he had just found it when he takes it to be recorded. The town, by the way, is just over the line in Wyoming."

"But . . . isn't that illegal?"

"In a way. But isn't it better than having Patrick branded a bastard for the rest of his life and better than giving Helen back to Cecil Weaver?" the doctor asked in a hard, flat tone.

"He's right, Letty," Jacob spoke for the first time. "Hell, it ain't nobody's business when ya

352

was wed. It don't make ya any less wedded 'cause the right date ain't on the paper."

"What do you think, Mike?"

"The doctor is giving us a chance to secure a respectable future for our son and to present a united front to this Mrs. Knight. It's what we planned to do, honey: go somewhere and be wed quietly, letting people assume we'd been married all along."

"We hadn't planned to falsify the date. But if it's what we have to do, we'll do it."

"As soon as we get custody of Helen, Weaver is going to get the beating he deserves." A deep frown puckered Mike's brow. "I guess it's a good thing I didn't find him last night. I was mad enough to kill him."

"Good God!" Wallace said. "Stay away from him for a while. We need the sheriff on our side. I want to charge Cora Pringle with fraud."

"How do you know Fellon went back to Briskin?"

"Cora will want him out of town, and he'll want to show off the money to his cronies."

Mike stood. "Go get ready, honey."

"What if Cecil comes while we're gone?"

"Jacob can handle him."

"He won't come tonight. I heard he was already so drunk he could hardly walk," Wallace said and then to Mike, "do you drive?"

"Sure do. I was in a motor pool and drove everything from trucks to tanks to the general's car."

"Good. We'll take turns driving. I figure it's two

hundred miles there and back. If we leave now, we'll not be back until morning. Jacob, do you have a can I can fill with water and take along for the radiator?"

Letty marveled at how the car engine continued to run, carrying them down the dirt road made bright by the two beams of light. Tired from the long ride and the emotional stress, she sat inside the curve of Mike's arm, her shoulder tucked into his armpit, her hip and thigh in contact with his. Few words were spoken, but Letty and Mike communicated silently. He hugged her closer to him and occasionally dropped a kiss on the side of her head. She squeezed his hand.

She was now legally Mrs. Mike Dolan. The justice of the peace, after a brief private conversation with Wallace, seemed to be glad to accommodate them. He got his wife and mother up out of bed to serve as witnesses. Wallace explained to Letty and Mike that he couldn't sign as a witness because he wasn't in the area six years ago. The ceremony that made Letty and Mike husband and wife lasted only slightly longer than the kiss Mike gave her afterward. The signing of the papers took more time.

"Sweetheart," Mike whispered while they stood next to the car, waiting for Wallace to finish his business with the man who had married them. "Will you regret not having a wedding you can tell our grandchildren about?"

"What makes you think I won't tell them about

it? I'll just fail to mention that we already had a five-year-old son. They'll think it exciting."

Letty giggled and glanced in the back seat of the car. Fellon lay where Mike had tossed him. On the way to Weatherford they had stopped in Briskin for gasoline and when Wallace inquired, he had been told where to find the man he was looking for—in a shack beside the tracks. He and Mike had gone inside while Letty waited nervously in the car. Minutes later, Mike had come out carrying the man on his shoulder.

"Is this kidnapping?" Letty had asked worriedly.

"Kidnapping?" Wallace snorted. "Who's going to charge a doctor with kidnapping a patient who needs treatment?"

"Wallace Hakes, you're taking advantage of your profession," Letty teased.

"Yeah, maybe. The no-good slob has been drinking distilled alcohol used for car radiators."

"I'd think it would kill him."

"It will sooner or later. But right now he doesn't care. He'd sell his mother's eyeballs for enough to buy a gallon of white lightning. Tie the bastard up, Mike. We don't want him sobering up and jumping out."

They had left Weatherford with Wallace hunched over the wheel, one of his hands leaving it occasionally to push his eyeglasses up on his nose. They passed farms and drove through small towns where not a single light was visible. When they needed gasoline, they stopped at a station that was closed for the night. Wallace pounded on the door of the adjoining house, shouting that he was a doctor and needed gas. The response was immediate, and soon they were on their way again with Mike at the wheel.

Letty was proud of the way Mike handled the car. He was a much better driver than the doctor; stayed in the middle of the road and didn't swerve toward the ditch. He didn't drive as fast, but the speed was consistent.

The spunky little Ford ate up the miles. It was daylight when the car stopped in the yard between the house and the barn. Mike was at the wheel with Letty sitting close beside him. The doctor, fast asleep, snored on the other side of her and their trussed-up prisoner moaned in the back seat.

It had also been an eventful night for Oscar Phillips—one he would never forget. The dreaded Thursday night had arrived, when the shipment of whiskey was be unloaded from the boxcar on the siding, loaded into the wagons, and delivered.

Already apprehensive, Oscar had a severe attack of jitters when he discovered that Cecil Weaver was drunk as a skunk! Elmer Russell would be furious when he saw the condition of his delivery man.

Oscar realized that he had better keep out of Elmer's way or he'd have to take Cecil's load into Blatsberg. Wishing Sharon were with him, Oscar sat in the dark peering out the window. When a heavy pounding sounded on his back door, he silently slid under the bed lest whoever was out there should decide to come in. It would probably be Arlo, Cecil, or the deputy, and he didn't want to see any one of them.

A long while after the pounding ceased, Oscar went from window to window and peered out. After he had made absolutely sure no one was lurking about outside, he slipped out of the house, crossed a field, and moved into the woods.

The desire to know what Elmer would do to Cecil drew him to the railroad yard. He approached the siding cautiously and found a place behind a pile of ties and scrap iron where he could see the boxcar. The back of a wagon had been drawn up to the gaping doors. Arlo and the deputy were carrying cartons from the boxcar and stacking them in the wagon. As soon as the wagon was full, they began to break open bales of hay to scatter over the boxes. When the load was covered to the deputy's satisfaction, Arlo crawled up onto the seat. The men talked for a moment. Oscar wished he were close enough to hear what Elmer was saying. Judging from the tone of Elmer's voice, Oscar had no doubt that he was angry.

The wagon made a creaking noise when the mules, straining in the harnesses, pulled it away from the siding. It was a dark night and in seconds the wagon was out of sight, but Oscar could still hear the ring of the iron horseshoes striking stones.

Elmer paced back and forth beside the open

door of the boxcar. Oscar saw him take out his pocket watch, look at it, then put it away. Minutes passed. Then he heard the sound of a wagon approaching and a drunken voice raised in song:

"I ain't got me no use fer the wom-en;
   A true one can't never be found.
They use a man ter his mon-ey;
   When it's gone they turn him down.
They be all alike at the bottom—"

"Hush your mouth!" Elmer stepped out quickly, grabbed the harness, and stopped the team. "Damn you! Want everyone in town to rush down here?"

"Howdy-do, Mister Deputy." The slurted voice was exceedingly loud and carefree.

"Gawddamn! You're drunk! Shut yore mouth up or I'll break your blasted neck!"

"Ya won't do no such." Cecil's voice was loud and full of bravado. "Ya'll treat me with re . . . spect."

"Get down and start loading that wagon."

"Not till I have me a drink. Not till ya ask me . . . nice." Cecil snickered, climbed off the wagon, reeled drunkenly, and fell on his hands and knees in the cinders. "Hell, Elmer, ya pushed me."

"Gawd! I ought to beat the drizzlin' shits outta ya!" In a red rage, Elmer grabbed Cecil by the shirt front and hauled him to his feet, shaking him so hard that his head whipped back and forth.

"Ye . . . ow! I'll have the law on ya, ya big-bellied bast—" A slap across the face cut off his words.

Elmer pushed him up against the side of the wagon box. "Bastard! Worthless piece of trash! You're in no shape to drive a team."

"Ya hit me!"

"I'll do it again if you open your trap—"

"Ya do and . . . I . . . I . . . I'll—"

"You'll what?" Cecil didn't answer and Elmer said again, "You'll do what, flap-jaw?"

"Tell . . . S-S-Sheriff Ledbetter what yore up to."

"Don't you threaten me, shithead! You work for me. Understand?"

"I quit! I ain't workin' for the likes a you no m-more. Gimme two bottles a whis . . . key," Cecil demanded belligerently. "It's what ya promised. Two bottles and . . . and my pay right now, or . . . I'll tell the s-sheriff."

"You . . . son-of-a-bitch! You . . . you—" Elmer croaked. He was so angry that he choked on his words. "You breathe one word. Just one word and . . . I'll rip out your guts and use 'em for shoelaces."

"Ya ain't scarin' me none." Cecil made an attempt to stand straight but swayed back against the wagon. "Ya need me 'n' Oscar 'n' Arlo ta do yore dirty work. Ya think yore a big muckety-muck with yore b-badge 'n' folks jumpin' when ya holler." Too drunk to realize he was pushing the deputy into an uncontrollable rage, he rambled on. "Ya'll not be so high 'n'

359

mighty when ya get yore ass throwed in a jail cell. Ain't nobody goin' to treat Cecil Weaver like ya done."

Oscar heard every word. Fear that something terrible was about to happen sent chills up and down his spine. The drunken fool was going to get himself killed as sure as shooting. Lifting his head for a better view, Oscar saw Elmer standing on spread legs, fists clenched, and his head jutted forward.

In a last act of defiance, Cecil shook his fist in Elmer's face and reeled down the track toward town.

The deputy bent over and picked up a thick stake as Oscar watched in horrified fascination. His head throbbed viciously with the realization of what was about to happen. He screamed a silent warning as Elmer took several running steps after the unsuspecting man. The club smashed into the back of Cecil's head with such a force that it propelled him forward before he dropped face down in the cinders.

Oh, my God! Oh, my God! Oh, my God! Oscar was sure he was going to faint.

Elmer stood over the fallen man, the club raised to strike again. Finally, he dropped the club, nudged Cecil with his foot, then grabbed his hair so he could look into his face.

"Ya had it comin', ya son-of-a-bitch! World's better off without ya."

He stood for several minutes as if thinking about what to do, then he lifted the inert body as if it were a bag of grain and dumped it over the side rails into the wagon bed.

Eyes wide with shock, Oscar stood stone-still. The thump of the body hitting the boards made an empty hollow sound. It brought him to his senses. He dropped to the ground and hugged the earth, his heart slamming against his chest, his ears ringing. He had been sure Elmer had a streak of meanness in him, but this was murder!

Oscar had no idea how long he lay hidden behind the discarded railroad ties, but it seemed an hour. Then he heard the boxcar door slam shut and Elmer speak gruffly to the mules. The squeak of the wagon wheels told him it was leaving the rail yard.

All was quiet.

When the soft music of the cicadas and crickets mingled with the sound of a nocturnal animal scurrying through the dry leaves, Oscar got to his feet. His stomach roiled. Vomit gushed from his mouth. After he had emptied his stomach he wiped his mouth on his sleeve. He could still hear the sound of the club connecting with Cecil's head. It was the same sound he had delighted in when, as a kid, he used to squash rotten melons with a baseball bat.

Lordy mercy! He couldn't go home. Elmer might come looking for him. The only person besides Arlo who knew about his connection with Elmer and the bootlegging operation was Sharon. He had to go to her. She would know what to do.

CHAPTER
———22———

Can I have one? Please—"

Patrick was on his knees in a chair watching Helen place hot molasses cookies on a cloth she had spread on the table.

"Say please, pretty please with sugar on it." Helen adjusted the rag she was using to hold onto the pan she had just taken from the oven.

"Oh, all right. Please, please with sugar on it. Now can I have one?"

"Just one or you'll ruin your supper."

"Goody! Can I take one to Dol . . . to my daddy?"

"No! And don't you tell him. They're a surprise."

"Well . . . gol-darn—"

"Patrick Graham! Stop swearing. It ain't nice."

"Mama said my name is Patrick Dolan now."

"Well, whatever your name is, stop swearing."

"I want another cookie—"

"Darn you, Patrick! Put that back! I'll get you and . . . and knock your block off."

The children's voices drifted up the stairwell to the room upstairs where Letty had just finished hanging Mike's clothes in the wardrobe alongside hers. She heard the screen door slam shut and recalled Mike telling about grabbing cookies from his sister's fresh batch. From the sound of things Patrick was bedeviling Helen in the same way. Letty looked out the window to see him racing for the shed where Mike and Jacob worked on the hay rake. She would have to tell Mike to be careful about relating his childhood escapades to his son.

Patrick was copying him in every way he could. Just this morning she caught him trying to tie a bandanna around his neck because Mike had tied one around his. At noon, when they came in to dinner, Mike's handkerchief was sticking out of his back pocket and so was Patrick's.

Letty smoothed the cover on the bed and plumped up the extra pillow she had brought up from downstairs. Tonight she and Mike would share this bed as man and wife. They were finally married. Even though it was a ceremony performed by a justice of the peace in the middle of the night, they were as legally married as if they had stood in front of a preacher with a church full of witnesses.

Her eyes fell on the scrap of blue ribbon lying on the dresser. Someday she would put it in a small frame along with the valentine Mike had given her so long ago, but for now she wanted it where she could see it. She fastened it to the wooden frame of the mirror with a straight pin and stood back to look at it. That little scrap of ribbon had been all the way to France and back with Mike. Suddenly, she felt a stab of sympathy for her sister, for any woman, who would never know the joy of being Mike's love, Mike's wife.

Wallace had stayed only long enough to eat a bite of breakfast. He left the farm with Fellon still asleep in the car. Mike had volunteered to go with him, but the doctor had refused the offer.

"Weaver might show up here today. You'd better stay here just in case. Fellon won't be in any shape to give me trouble. When I get to Boley, I'll have him put in a jail cell." Even though his eyes had been bloodshot from lack of sleep and he had needed a shave, the doctor's face had broken into a grin, and his blue eyes had lit up. "I'll claim he attacked me, or . . . something—"

"I'll declare! Wallace, you're the limit here lately. You've got all kinds of deviltry hidden under your mild manner. You're usually so nice," Letty had teased.

"I like to think that I am . . . most of the time. But nothing gets my dander up like the sham that preacher woman is pulling off on my patients. The sheriff will hold Fellon. I'll telephone Doc Perkins. If he can't come to Boley and testify, he'll send a wire stating that Fellon had been walking right up to the day *Sister Cora* healed him."

"That oughta put a crimp in her meetin'," Jacob had chortled gleefully.

Letty looked about the room once again to make sure it was neat and orderly, but her thoughts were elsewhere. When Wallace exposed Cora's sham, she would probably leave the state. Now if only this ugly business about Helen could be straightened out . . . Wallace was reasonably sure that he could persuade Mrs. Knight to leave Helen here, but there was a good chance that even if she didn't send her back to her father—and Letty shuddered at the thought—she would be taken to an orphanage or to another family. If Helen were allowed to stay here, would that mean they would have to contend with Cecil Weaver from now on? With Mike beside her, Letty felt sure she could handle that.

When Letty came into the kitchen, Helen was taking another pan of cookies out of the stove. Her face was flushed and damp from the heat. Her hair stuck to her damp cheeks. With the pancake turner she carefully lifted the hot cookies from the pan and placed them on the table to cool.

"My, they smell good!"

"Patrick snatched some and ran." Helen's grin wrinkled her nose. "I didn't care, but I let him think I did."

"Small boys have a way of getting in the cook's hair."

"He did it 'cause his . . . his daddy said he did that when he was little. He wants to be like his daddy." Helen turned her face away but not before Letty saw the look of utter longing on the child's face.

"Helen, honey—" Letty put her arms around her and with a gentle hand brought her head to her breast. "You are such a wonderful little girl. Honey, things are going to work out. Doctor Hakes is helping us."

"I'm . . . afraid—"

"I know. But you've got me and Mike and Grandpa and Doctor Hakes. We want you here. Mike and I want you to be our little girl. We'd be so proud."

"He'll . . . come. I know he will."

"If he does, he'll have Mike and Grandpa to contend with. You and I will hide upstairs under the bed," Letty said lightly.

Helen's lips trembled and tears wet her lashes. "Really?"

"Really. I hid from Patrick one day and he never did find me." Letty's fingers wiped the tears from the child's cheeks. "It's almost suppertime. We'd better get something ready for our men. Shall we have a picnic on the porch? I'll make potato salad if you'll put on some eggs to boil. When Mike sees your cookies he'll not want anything else."

During supper Mike teased Helen and the child's face was radiant.

"Is this *all* the cookies?" His complaint brought a proud smile to the child's face.

"Patrick got some . . . and run."

"What? That rascal stole my cookies? I'll hang him up by his heels."

Both children giggled happily.

Letty had eyes only for the smiling curly haired giant of a man who watched her with such tenderness. She was going to spend the rest of her life with him right here on this farm. A wonderful, warm feeling of permanency wrapped around her as happiness filled her heart and shone in her eyes.

"Tomorrow," Mike was saying, "we'll go fishing in the creek if Patrick will dig us some worms."

"Gol . . . ly! I'll dig a whole can of 'em."

"Can I go, too?" Helen asked breathlessly.

"Of course. I wouldn't think of going fishing without my cookie-maker."

Letty realized with a gigantic surge of pride that Mike clearly understood that Helen needed attention badly. The loving look in the eyes he turned on the child brought a flush to her cheeks and a smile to her lips.

Letty's eyes kept straying to him. His head and shirt collar were wet from the dipper of water he had poured over his head before he came to eat. He was so handsome with his unruly black hair and dark face. His eyes caught hers and held. He smiled and winked. In spite of the fact he hadn't slept the night before, he looked younger now that his face was free of the sober expression it had worn when he first came to the farm.

Evening shadows softened the outline of the huge trees that surrounded the homestead. It was the gloaming time of day that poets wrote about. Before now it had been the lonesome time of day for Letty, reminding her of the stolen moments spent alone with Mike when they were young. Tonight she welcomed the golden time of the evening. Soon she would take Mike's hand and lead him to the room upstairs.

With Helen's help she washed the supper

dishes. Mike played a game of catch with Patrick. Jacob smoked his pipe and watched from his chair on the porch. The sounds were familiar: the clatter of the dishes, Patrick's laughter. Mike's deep voice, the chirping of birds settling in the treetops for the night.

The sound of a motor car turning into the lane beside the house sent Helen scurrying to grab Letty's skirt and look at her with fear in her eyes.

"Who is it?"

"I don't know, honey. Stay inside until I find out."

Letty pushed open the screen door and went out onto the porch just as a big touring car jerked to a stop not a dozen feet from where Mike stood in the yard. The door flew open and Deputy Russell leaped out, a shotgun in his hand.

"Hold it right there, Dolan, unless you want this shotgun to go off."

"What in the tarnation—" The front legs of Jacob's chair hit the floor and he stood.

Letty leaped off the porch and ran to Mike, only vaguely aware that another man was getting out of the car.

"Get away from him," the deputy ordered and gestured Letty back with the barrel of the gun.

Sheriff Ledbetter strode to Mike, jerked his hands behind him, and fastened them with a pair of handcuffs.

"What the hell is going on?" Mike demanded.

"You're Mike Dolan?" Sheriff Ledbetter asked.

"Yes, but what have I done?" Mike turned to

the deputy. "You're the one who went through my things a few days ago? Why?"

"Looking for evidence. Perfectly legal."

"That's a matter of opinion."

"It ain't legal to come in a man's house and destroy his property. Do you know what he done?" Jacob demanded then answered his own question. "He tore this man's place apart, then went into the house and ruined my crock of brandy. That's what he done."

"I'm sorry about that, Jacob," Sheriff Ledbetter said. "But that's a trifling affair compared to what we're arresting Dolan for."

"Arresting?" Letty croaked. "What for?"

"Murder," Elmer spat. "Pure-dee old cold-bloodied murder."

"Who am I supposed to have killed?" Mike asked quietly.

"You know who, you bast—"

"Watch it, Elmer," Ledbetter cautioned. "Dolan, we're arresting you for the murder of Cecil Weaver. We have plenty of witnesses who will swear you threatened to kill him for what he did to Mrs. Graham."

"But I didn't! I haven't seen him—"

"Do you deny you went looking for him?"

"No, I don't deny I went to town looking for him. I didn't find him. That was night before last."

"You offered a silver dollar to the man who would point him out."

"Yes, I did that."

"When?" Letty found her voice. "When did it happen?"

"Sometime last night. His body was found in the back of his wagon with his head bashed in. The mules wandered about three miles west of town. A farmer found the wagon in a fresh-planted field about daylight this morning."

Letty laughed in relief. "It couldn't have been Mike. He was with Doctor Hakes last night. We went to Weatherford to—"

"—No, Letty," Mike said quickly.

"But . . ."

"Stay out of this, Letty," Mike said sharply. "Don't say another word." He shook his head.

"I won't"

"You will! This can be cleared up tomorrow."

When Mike made a move to go to her, Elmer poked him in the stomach with the barrel of the gun.

"Stand still or I'll blow ya into Kingdom Come."

"Grandpa! Tell them Mike was with Doctor Hakes," Letty cried.

"Now look here, Ledbetter," Jacob said. "You got no cause to be takin'—"

"Who said we ain't got no cause?" Elmer jabbed at Mike with the barrel of the shotgun again.

Suddenly a small body flung itself against the deputy's legs causing him to stumble backward. Patrick's fist pounded on a fleshy belly.

"Leave my daddy alone, you . . . you old fat . . . stinky poot!"

"Get this brat off me!" Elmer yelled, holding Patrick off with one hand and trying to balance the shotgun with the other.

"I'll beat ya up! I'll beat ya up!"

"Patrick!" Letty charged in and grabbed her son by the arm. "Stop it!"

"He's mean 'n' ugly. I hate him!" Patrick shouted.

"Calm down, son," Mike said firmly. "Mind your mother. These men are doing what they think is their duty. We'll straighten it out."

"Sheriff," Letty took a deep gulping breath. All you need to do to clear this up is talk to Doctor Hakes. If you don't believe me, surely you'll believe him."

"Dolan will get a chance to clear himself."

"But . . . you can't take him!"

"Who says we can't?" Elmer said belligerently and shoved Mike toward the car. "Hold the gun, Sheriff, while I put on the leg irons."

"Leg irons? Have you gone daft, Ledbetter?" Jacob demanded.

"Just a precaution, Jacob. We shackle all suspected murderers until we get them to the county jail in Boley."

"Why won't you listen?" Letty wailed." Sheriff, find Doctor Hakes when you get to Boley. He'll tell you Mike was with him. They went to Briskin to get a man the doctor wanted. They got home this morning and Wallace went on to Boley. Didn't you see him?" she, asked desperately.

"No. I was in Piedmont all day."

"Sounds to me like they already set up an alibi with the doc," Elmer said and slammed the car door.

"Let me go with you, Sheriff. Please—" Letty begged.

"I can't do that, ma'am."

"Letty, sweetheart, don't. They've made up their minds. It'll be cleared up tomorrow."

"Back off, woman." Elmer shoved Letty aside when she approached the car.

"Keep your hands off her!" Mike snarled.

"You ain't in no position to be givin' orders." Elmer cradled the gun in his arms and got into the front seat of the car.

"Don't shove her again." Mike's voice was icy cold.

"I'll get in touch with Wallace." Letty climbed up on the running board, reached in, and kissed Mike's lips. "Don't give that hotheaded deputy an excuse to hurt you," she whispered. "He's mean."

"For Patrick's sake don't mention our going to Weatherford to be married," he whispered.

"I hadn't thought of that. I don't want you to go."

"I'll be all right. You'll have to tell Helen about her pa."

"I will. I love you."

"I love you too, sweetheart. Don't worry. Be a good boy, Patrick," he called. "Take care of your mother and Helen. I'll be back and we'll go fishing."

The car motor started and Letty had to back away. "I'll be down to Boley as soon as I can get there."

The car made a wide loop and headed down the lane to the road. Letty stood with her arm around Patrick as tears slipped from her eyes and ran down her cheeks. She had been so happy, looking forward to spending the night in Mike's arms. Why had God let this happen? Had she been so wicked that she deserved such punishment?

Letty held her son while he sobbed and tried to reassure him that this was all a ghastly mistake and that his father would be home soon. She had no time to feel sorry for herself. Helen had come out of the house and stood silently waiting. She had to tell the child her father was dead.

When the children were in bed, Letty sat at the table with Jacob. She looked at his lined face. Deep crinkly grooves marked the corners of his eyes. There were other lines there too that experience, fatigue, age, and harsh weather had made. His eyes, however, were clear and sharp.

"Grandpa, did you ever dream that something like this could happen?"

"Don't rightly think I have. The sheriff's doin' his job, misguided though he be."

"I'll go to Piedmont and find someone to take me to Boley. The train comes through around two o'clock, but I can't wait until then."

"When you get to Boley, go straight to

Doc Whittier. He'll know where to find Doc Hakes."

"Wallace will stay in Boley until Cora's meeting. What if they don't believe Wallace? Mike will have to stay in jail until the justice of the peace comes up from Weatherford."

"Don't borrow trouble. They'll believe Doc Hakes."

"Oh, glory, I hope so."

"Somethin' botherin' me about Elmer Russell. I do believe he'd a shot Mike given half a chance."

"Mike said he had never met the deputy, yet the deputy seems to hate him. I wonder why."

"That sucker's got a chip on his shoulder a yard wide 'cause he wasn't elected sheriff. I don't trust him none at all. Didn't even before he ruined my brandy and tore up Mike's sleepin' place."

"I'm worried. Do you think Mike'll be all right?"

"As long as he's with Ledbetter. Ledbetter's as straight as a string. When he gets the proof, Mike'll be set free."

"This is a nightmare, isn't it, Grandpa?" Letty thought she had cried all the tears she could cry, but thinking of Mike in the back of that car, his hands handcuffed behind him, his legs in irons, brought a fresh batch of tears to her eyes.

"It'll pass, youngun," Jacob said gruffly and puffed on his pipe.

"I know, but it's so unfair."

"Mike didn't want ya draggin' out that marriage

paper. Folks would know that you warn't wed when Patrick was born."

"I want Mike to come home and I don't give a damn what folks think."

"Mike does. He ain't wantin' his boy carryin' the label of bastard. You heed what he says. Hear?"

They sat in taut silence. Letty slowly removed her hairpins, placed them on the table, and begin to plait her hair. Jacob knocked the ashes from his pipe.

"The youngun didn't seem to be tore up 'bout her pa being killed."

"Grandpa, it's sad, but when I told her, she seemed relieved. All she said was 'now he can't come get me.' She put her arms around me and asked if she could stay here forever and ever."

"It'd be a pity to lose her." Jacob got up from the table. "Better get to bed, Letty girl. Ya got a big day tomorrow."

CHAPTER
—— 23 ——

Letty got up early and dressed in her good light-blue skirt and white middy blouse. She attached a floppy brimmed straw hat firmly to the auburn curls piled on top of her head. Before she left her room, she took the scrap of blue ribbon from the mirror frame and pinned it securely to her chemise. The feel of it against her bare breast somehow made her feel closer to Mike. After a critical look at herself in the mirror, wishing she had something more stylish to wear, she stuffed a pair of stockings, a nightgown, and a hairbrush in a small straw bag, and went down to the kitchen.

Jacob had hitched the mare to the buggy and started breakfast.

It was just daylight when Letty left the farm and headed for town. As she neared the Watkins' farm, she could see a light in the kitchen and guided the mare up the lane to the house. She found Mrs. Watkins in the barn milking the cows.

"My land, Letty. What's happed to bring you out so early?"

After Letty related the story, she said, "I wanted you to know that Grandpa and the kids are alone over there. I don't know when I'll be back, but when I do, Mike will be with me."

"Well, land sakes! What in the world would make Sheriff Ledbetter think Mike would do such a thing anyhow'?"

"He doesn't know Mike. And Mike was in town looking for Cecil. I should never have told him that Cecil Weaver hit me."

"Well . . . if ya can't tell yore man, who can ya tell? My menfolk would'a done the same."

"As soon as Doctor Hakes verifies that Mike was with him, the sheriff will let him go."

"It makes a body creepy to know a killer's on the loose. Even a no-good drunk like Cecil Weaver don't deserve to have his head bashed in. It's the times, I tell you. There's more meanness goin' on than ya can shake a stick at."

"I'll be going. I want to get to Boley as soon as I can."

"Is there nothin' we can do, Letty? Do ya want Guy to go with ya?"

"That isn't necessary, but thanks just the same. I'd appreciate it if Guy would look in on Grandpa. So many strange things have happened lately, I don't know who'll show up at the farm next."

"Don't ya worry none about that. I'll send Irene and Jimmy over this mornin' and Guy'll wander over this afternoon. Don't worry about a thin' here. Just go on now and get Doc Hakes. He'll put things right."

Out on the road, Letty whipped the mare into a trot. For the first time she wished for an automobile and the know-how to drive it. Her mind raced ahead to what she would do when she reached Piedmont. She would leave the buggy and the mare with Mr. Hartley who ran a sort of a livery stable on the edge of town, then she'd go to the garage and see if she could find someone who would take her to Boley no matter the cost. In her pocketbook was the total sum of her cash money—thirty-five dollars.

A crowd had gathered in front of the store when Letty reached it after leaving the horse and buggy with Mr. Hartley. As she approached, the murmur of voices died and all eyes turned to her. The men tipped their hats and the women nodded.

"Good morning."

"Mornin', Mrs. Graham."

"I suppose you've heard about Cecil Weaver being murdered," Letty said, knowing full well that was the reason for the early-morning gathering.

"Yes, ma'am."

"Yes, ma'am, we have. Ain't it a shame?"

"It is. It's a shame when anyone is killed. It's also a shame when an innocent man is accused of the killing." Letty looked each man in the eye. Some looked back; some turned away. "The sheriff has arrested Mike Dolan and has taken him to the county jail."

"Yes, ma'am. We heard."

"He was the likely one." The man who spoke was a farmer who had bought hogs from Jacob and attended his church. "He was here in the store makin' threats and all. I heard him myself."

"I know he did that, Mr. Miller, but he didn't kill Mr. Weaver. He was with Doctor Hakes when Cecil was killed. He went to Briskin to get the man Sister Cora was supposed to have healed the night before." Letty's eyes went from face to face. She knew these people, liked them, and thought they liked her. Well, almost all of them liked her. "So you see Mike couldn't have done it. That means a killer is loose in Piedmont."

"Bullfoot! I ain't takin' your word," Mrs. Crews snorted. "I'll believe that big dark devil innocent when Doc Hakes says so and not a minute sooner. What's this about Sister Cora not healin' that poor man? I was there and saw it with my own eyes."

Such fierce anger swept over Letty that she trembled from the force of it.

"It's what I would expect from you, Mrs. Crews. I trust you'll also believe Doctor Hakes when he tells you that *Sister Cora* is a shake-down artist and her healing a trick to pry money out of people. Excuse me. I need to find someone with an automobile who'll take me to Boley."

"Well! I never!"

"No, and you never will, Mrs. Crews. You're too narrow-minded to see beyond your own double chin."

After her outburst, Letty's stomach churned, her heart pounded, and her eyes watered. She had never spoken to anyone in such a manner before. Her nerves, she realized, were at a breaking point.

"There's a salesman at the hotel." Mr. Howard had come to the porch during her set-to with Mrs. Crews. "He'll give you a ride. But he usually spends a couple of hours in Claypool before going on to Boley."

"I'd better find someone else. I want to get to Boley by noon."

"Inquire at the garage, ma'am."

"Thank you. I will."

Letty's heels clicked on the boardwalk that fronted the stores. Most of them were just now opening their doors. Letty had no doubt that the town would come to life soon and be buzzing with news. A cooling breeze fanned her face and her nerves calmed a bit. She had given them something else to talk about. Of course there would be some, like Mrs. Crews, who wouldn't believe Sister Cora would do any wrong even after Wallace proved it.

"P-s-s-t! P-s-s-t! Letty—"

Letty stopped when she heard the hissing sound. In the new space between the hat shop and the outside stairway that went up the side of the bank building, she saw Sharon Tarr. When Sharon beckoned, Letty looked around, slipped into the opening, and followed her to the shadows beneath the stairs where Oscar Phillips squatted on his heels. He got slowly to his feet as they approached.

"What are you doing back here?" Letty asked with a puzzled frown.

"Hiding," Sharon blurted. "Hiding in case Elmer Russell comes back to town,"

"What on earth for?"

"We saw you in front of the store and sneaked back here in hopes of talking to you alone. We know Mike didn't kill Cecil Weaver."

"I know that. He was with Doctor Hakes. I'm trying to find someone to take me to Boley to find the doctor. He'll clear Mike."

"We know who did it! Oscar saw it happen!"

"Good Lord!"

Letty's startled gaze fastened on Oscar's haggard face. His eyes were bloodshot, he needed a shave, and a look of deep worry had replaced his usual leering expression. He was holding tightly to Sharon's hand as if he were a child and she his mother.

"We had about decided not to tell," Sharon said. "Then we heard that Mike had been arrested because he was in town looking for Cecil after he slapped you around. We saw him on the street that night and he was mad enough to break Cecil in half. We can't let Mike be blamed for something he didn't do."

"Of course not!" Letty looked at Sharon with a new awareness that there was something more to her than what she had first believed.

Oscar fidgeted and looked at the ground.

"Honey," Sharon said gently. "We've gone over and over this. You've got to tell Letty what you saw that night down by the tracks. We'll go with you to the sheriff."

"Gawd! You don't know him like I do, Sherry. He'll kill me!"

"Not if he's in jail."

"He might not go to jail."

"Oscar, you're either going to stand up and be a man, or you're not," she said firmly. "Personally, I've not got much use for a weak-kneed sister who'd let a nice guy like Mike Dolan rot in jail and a mean son-of-a-bitch go free." Sharon was unmerciful in her attempt to make him shoulder his responsibility. When he didn't speak she tried to jerk her hand from his but he held on. "I'll not live with a man who won't stand up for what's right."

"Elmer Russell killed Cecil," Oscar said in a desperate whisper.

Instinctively, Letty stepped back. "The deputy? You saw him?"

"I saw it all," Oscar said sorrowfully. "I hope to God I never see such a thing again."

Sharon hugged Oscar's arm. "I'm proud of you, honey. I know this is rough on you, but tell her about it." She reached out and drew Letty beneath the stairway.

Letty listened with rapt attention while Oscar told about the deputy's bootlegging operation and how he thought Mike was from one of the big-city mobs and trying to cut in on his territory.

"Why would he think that?"

"He was suspicious of every man that came to town. He didn't think Mike came here to do farm work."

"He didn't. He came looking for me. But go on, Oscar."

Oscar told about the whiskey shipped in the boxcar and the deliveries made weekly to the nearby towns. He said he had become more and more afraid of being caught with a wagon-load of whiskey. He worried what would happen to his kids if he went to jail. He met Sharon and had promised her he would break away from Elmer as soon as he could. After he explained how he came to be hiding behind the railroad ties at the siding, he told Letty of what he had seen happen.

"It was . . . awful. It didn't seem to bother Elmer at all. He dumped Cecil in that wagon like . . . like he was nothin'."

"Oh, Lord." Letty took a deep breath and let it out slowly. "We've got to go to the sheriff."

"What if . . . what if he takes Elmer's word against mine?"

"Why would he do that when you take him to the siding where the whiskey was unloaded? You've got Arlo to back you up." Sharon said. "We'll make him tell about the bootlegging."

"Elmer could pin this whole thing on me!"

"You had no reason to kill Cecil," Sharon argued.

"Who do you know that will take us to Boley, Oscar?" Letty was impatient to be on the way.

"Keith Rowe over at the garage. Offer him five dollars. He'll ask for more, but he'll jump at doin' it for five if you hold out."

"I'll go make the arrangements. Wait in the alley behind the bank. We'll pick you up."

Letty turned away, then turned back and kissed Oscar on the cheek. "I always knew that underneath you were a good, decent man. You just needed someone to curb your wild ways. I'm glad you and Sharon have found each other."

They reached Boley at noon. Signs announcing Sister Cora's revival meeting in the pavilion at the fairgrounds littered the town. Letty scarcely noticed them. She directed the driver to take them to the Hewitt Hotel where she had spent the night more than five years ago: a frightened, pregnant, fifteen-year old. She walked into the hotel, confidently this time, and signed the register.

The clerk looked at the signature, swallowed, and looked again.

"Mrs. Mike . . . Dolan? Is that . . . is that the man the sheriff—?"

"Mike Dolan is my husband. We'll be spending the night here. Did you say Room 209?" She pulled the key from his still fingers wondering how long he was going to leave his mouth hanging open.

"Yes, ma'am. We'll bring up your luggage."

"I don't think so. I don't have any."

Letty motioned to Sharon and Oscar and they went up the broad carpeted stairs and down a narrow hallway to the room. Inside, Letty shut the door, put the key in the lock, and turned it. Oscar and Sharon stood in the middle of the room looking around. Letty went to the window. All she could see was the sky and the roof of the building next door.

"This will be a good place for you to stay out of sight. I'll find Doctor Hakes and bring him here before we go to the sheriff."

On the street the noonday sun was hot on Letty's back. Sweat trickled down between her breasts. Her wide-brimmed hat offered some shade, but not enough to keep the moisture from plastering her hair to her temples. She caught sight of herself in the reflection of a store window she passed and thought how outdated her hat and clothes were. It really didn't matter. Nothing mattered at all but finding Wallace and getting Mike released from jail.

She climbed the stairs and opened the door to Doctor Whittier's office, and there sat Wallace across the desk from the older man. They stared at each other for several seconds. Then Wallace jumped to his feet.

"Letty! What in the world are you doing here?"

"Thank goodness. I never dreamed I would find you so soon. The sheriff has arrested Mike for the murder of Cecil Weaver," she blurted breathlessly. "Oh, hello, Doctor Whittier. Do you remember me? I'm Jacob Fletcher's granddaughter"

" 'Course I remember you."

"Wallace, Mike was with us when Cecil was murdered. I tried to tell the sheriff he was with you. He wouldn't believe me, but he'll believe you—"

"I went out on a call with Doc Whittier. We got back to town about an hour ago and heard that Mike had been brought in, but I didn't hear when Weaver was killed."

"The body was found at dawn, about the time we got back from Briskin. They came after Mike because he had been to town the night before looking for Cecil after Cecil . . . after he hit me, But, Wallace"—she grabbed his arm—"Oscar Phillips saw who killed him. He and Sharon Tarr are over at the hotel."

"Did he tell you who did it?"

"The deputy, Elmer Russell. Oscar is scared to death. He's afraid the sheriff will take the deputy's word against his. Let's get Mike out and take the sheriff to talk to Oscar."

"Wait a minute. Let me think. Mike is all right where he is for a few hours. Let's leave him there while Ledbetter talks to Oscar."

"Oh, but—"

"He's right," Doc Whittier said. "Ledbetter is a good man. I never did have any use for that hotheaded deputy. Your man will be better off in a safe cell until Russell's locked up. You two go on back to the hotel. I'll get Ledbetter and bring him over."

"Good idea." Wallace ushered Letty to the door.

"Room 209," Letty said over her shoulder. "And . . . please hurry."

Oscar told his story to Doctor Hakes and thirty minutes later repeated it for Doctor Whittier and Sheriff Ledbetter. Letty listened anxiously, watching the sheriff's face for his reaction. He fingered his chin, bored his ear with a forefinger, and scratched his head. When Oscar had finished, he got up and looked out the window. As there was no way for Letty to know what he was thinking, her anxiety grew.

"Charging a law enforcement officer with bootlegging is one thing, but charging him with murder is a serious matter. I've got to have more than your say-so, Phillips. Not that I don't believe you. But rock-hard evidence is needed."

"Take him to the siding, hon," Sharon said. "You said Elmer threw the club in the bushes."

"Well now, that would be evidence,"

"Oh, Gawd!" Oscar moaned. "I sure as hell don't want to go back there but I will if it'll help."

"Take me along, sheriff," Doctor Whittier said.

I've been reading up on forensic medicine. Fascinating stuff. Where's Weaver's body?"

"At the undertaker in Piedmont."

"If you find the club I might be able to match it to the blow on Weaver's head."

"Good idea, Doc. Glad to have all the help I can get."

"Elmer will kill me when he finds out what I've told you," Oscar said.

"No, he won't," Sheriff Ledbetter assured him. "I've got a fellow headed for the state pen. I'll put him and Elmer on the three o'clock train, then we'll head up to Piedmont." When the sheriff went to the door, Letty jumped up off her perch on the end of the bed.

"What about Mike? You know he's innocent. You can't just go off and leave him in jail while you chase around looking for . . . for clubs and things."

"I'll release him after three o'clock, Mrs. Dolan. It's just another forty-five minutes. I want Elmer to think we have a cut-and-dried case until I have the evidence to arrest him."

"I guess I can wait. But it seems to me you'd have the decency to apologize for putting us through this." Letty's chin lifted defiantly.

"I'll not apologize, ma'am. Dolan was a logical suspect because he sought revenge against Weaver. If I hadn't arrested him, Phillips might not have come forward and Elmer would have gotten off scot-free."

"I realize you were doing your duty, but . . .

oh, well, I'm sorry, Sheriff. I've just been so upset." Letty sank back down on the bed.

The sheriff took out his watch and flipped open the lid. When he spoke, it was to Wallace.

"Bring her over to the jail when you hear the train leave. I'll be there shortly. You'll have to sign a paper that Dolan was with you from six in the evening until you left the farm at eight in the morning. After that he'll be free to go."

The minute the door closed behind the doctor and the sheriff, Sharon drew Oscar over beside the window and talked to him in low tones. He listened attentively. Letty couldn't help but think that Sharon was going to have her hands full raising Oscar's children—and Oscar! Perhaps he was just what Sharon needed—someone to need her.

"Have you had anything to eat?" Wallace asked, bringing Letty's attention to him.

"Not since morning, but I'm not hungry. Did you have any trouble with Fellon? Did he sober up?"

"No trouble to speak of. And he's sober and suffering. Tonight I'm taking him to Sister Cora's meeting. Then he can go to the devil for all I care."

"What do you think will happen?"

"I'm not sure. But I have to try to expose her for the crook she is."

"I'm sorry—"

"Don't be sorry, Letty. It has nothing to do with you."

"You're right, yet . . . I'm still sorry."

At times it was hard for Letty to believe she had

ever been a member of the Pringle family; singing duets with Cora, passing the collection plates, handing out religious pamphlets, never being free to run and play and shout like the other children. And there was always Cora—watching to tattle to their father if she did anything *wicked* or *unladylike*.

Letty had almost completely blocked those miserable details of her unhappy childhood from her mind. Now, when she thought of her life in Dunlap, her thoughts were always of the times she spent with Mike. He had been her best friend. Now he was her lover, her husband, her life's companion. They had made their own family.

The stone courthouse in the middle of the town square was surrounded by trees and flowering bushes. It was the pride of Tillman County. The clock set in the high arch over the doorway was always on time, the windows shiny clean, the lawn mowed and raked, the walks swept. Each day from one of the four towers, a blast from a whistle announced twelve o'clock noon at which time shops closed and business people went home for dinner.

Sheriff Ledbetter's office and the county jail were located in the basement of the courthouse. Letty sat in a barrel chair in a room separated from the office by a frosted glass partition. Her eyes were fastened to the door that had closed behind Wallace and the sheriff. Her hat was on a chair beside her. With forked fingers she loosened the damp hair at her temples, then tried to smooth the wrinkles from her skirt.

The courthouse clock struck half-past three. The only other sounds to reach her were muffled voices, footsteps, and the occasional clang of an iron door being closed.

It seemed to her she had been sitting there forever when, without warning, the door opened and Mike came into the room. He looked tired. A stubble of dark beard shadowed his cheeks. The dark eyes that fastened to her face were full of concern. A sob caught in her throat. She couldn't say anything. Emotion made her eyes fill with tears and her voice break.

"Mike! Oh, M-Mike—"

He crossed the room in quick strides, arms reaching for her. Letty found herself crushed against his hard chest while he covered her face with fierce kisses and murmured words of concern and love.

"Are you all right, sweetheart? Love . . . are you all right?"

"Now I am!" She sobbed with relief. "I was afraid. Hold me tight, Mike, darling. Hold me tight—"

"I will, I will!" He clasped her to him. "Letty, my sweet Letty . . . honey, don't cry. It's over. We can go home." He held her away from him so that he could look with adoring eyes into her tear-streaked face.

"Did they hurt you?" She ran her hands over the strong line of his back and shoulders, then up to clasp around his neck. "You look so tired."

He grinned. "I need a shave and . . . a bath."

"We have a room at the hotel, but Oscar and Sharon are in it right now."

"Doctor Hakes filled me in on all that's happened."

"Did he tell you that Elmer Russell killed Cecil Weaver and Oscar saw him do it?"

"He told me. You were so right about Russell. I swear he'd have found an excuse to shoot me if the sheriff hadn't been along. It's over, honey, it's over," he said when he saw the worried frown on her face. "And now Helen won't have to worry about going back to a father like Weaver."

Letty framed his face with her fingers, touching the tired lines written there. Her eyes, soft and loving, carefully scanned each feature.

"I was so worried about you," she whispered and kissed his lips again. "Every day for the rest of my life I'm going to tell you how much I love you. You are my love, my life, my stength, my . . . happiness. I love you with every beat of my heart." She buried her lips in the smooth skin of his throat. He responded to her words with muffled love words of his own, his arms straining her to him.

"Darling wife." His voice trembled with emotion. "I'd walk through hell to hear you say that."

She fitted her mouth to his. The kiss was long and sweet. She wasn't even aware when it ended because his lips were still on her face.

"My whiskers are scratching your face," he murmured. "I'll try to be careful."

"I . . . don't care!" She laughed happily. "Oh.

Mike, we can be alone tonight, really alone. The sheriff is going to take Oscar and Sharon back to Piedmont."

"I don't have a cent with me, love."

"I have thirty dollars." She delved into her pocket and shoved the small leather purse in his hands. "I had to pay five dollars to the man who brought us down from Piedmont. Let's stay here tonight and tomorrow and go home the next day. We'll have a honeymoon."

"I don't have clean clothes—"

"We'll buy you a shirt. We'll eat in a restaurant and . . . and just be alone together."

"And we'll make love in a bed." His lips rubbed hers in sensuous assault.

"Oh, yes, yes—" She laughed softly, gayly. "We'll find a barber shop. You can get a shave so you won't have to be careful of scratching my face."

"I need a bath—"

"—There's one in the hotel."

Because they were absorbed in one another, they were unaware that Doctor Hakes had come into the room until he cleared his throat.

"Wallace!" Letty exclaimed. "Thank you."

"Thanks, Doc." Mike held out his hand, one arm still around Letty.

Wallace clasped Mike's hand and shrugged. "Do you plan to stay here tonight? I'll be going back tomorrow. Be glad to give you a ride."

Mike smiled down into Letty's glowing face. "We were just talking about staying over tomorrow and going home the next day."

"Well, the offer's open if you change your mind."

"Are you still planning to take Fellon to Cora's meeting tonight?"

"It's what I came here to do."

"I'd like to go with you, Doctor." Mike's expression turned serious. "You'd have a little trouble handling Fellon by yourself. He's rip-roaring mad right now and bragging about what all he's going to do when he gets out of that jail cell."

A grin brightened the doctor's face. "I was hoping you'd say that. God didn't give me all that much physical strength."

"I can handle Fellon if you can handle the other."

"Sounds good to me. I'll meet you here at the jail at eight o'clock. Do you want to come along, Letty?"

"I'd not miss it. I know just when you should present your faker, but I must warn you that you may not be believed."

"Why not?" Wallace frowned. "I'll read Doctor Perkins's telegram and make Fellon tell of being paid to impersonate a cripple."

"By the time Cora gets to the healing part of the service, she'll have the people believing that she's an extension of God. I've seen crowds so riled up they would believe that black was white if my father told them."

"Surely people will believe what they see with their own eyes."

"You're a good man, Wallace Hakes. I hope

they'll believe that you're trying to help them." The worried frown left Letty's face when she looked up at her husband. "I want to get out of this place and into the sunshine."

Wallace watched them leave with their arms entwined. A feeling of loneliness settled over him and a look of wistfulness blanketed his face. Lately, he had come to realize how much he had missed by devoting all his time to medicine. He wondered if Mike Dolan realized just how lucky he was.

Mike and Letty climbed the stairs to the main floor of the courthouse, then hand-in-hand they strolled down the steps to the walk that led to the street. Out in the bright sunshine Letty couldn't stop smiling.

"Isn't this wonderful? We've never even walked down a street together."

He smiled down at her with a lazy grin that caused a heavenly torment to erupt in her belly.

"Yes, love. It's wonderful. I want the whole world to know that you belong to me—you and Patrick."

"Has anyone ever been this happy before?"

"I doubt it, sweetheart." His eyes were shining with love and pride. He pulled her arm up under his and laced their fingers together. "How far to the hotel? I don't think I can wait to kiss you. I'm starved! Just starved!"

Laughter bubbled from her lips. Happiness sang in her heart.

The white-haired man in the black serge suit placed his hat on the counter and waited impatiently while the hotel clerk registered another guest. He drummed his fingers on the polished wood. The clerk ignored him and kept up his polite chatter to the other guest.

"We hope you and Mrs. Williamson will enjoy your stay with us here at the Hewitt," he said with a practiced smile that faded from his face the instant the key left his fingers. "Now, sir, what can I do for you?"

"A room. Why else would I be standing here while you waste time in idle chitchat?" The booming voice was heard in every corner of the lobby. The clerk's face reddened from his stiff high collar to his slicked-down hair.

"You're in luck, sir. We have one room left. It's on the top floor. You see, Sister Cora is in town and rooms have been booked ahead."

"I'm Sister Cora's father. I'll not accept a room on the top floor of this hotel or any other."

The clerk swallowed repeatedly.

"You're . . . you're . . . her father? Oh, my goodness. What'a you know. Sister Cora's father right here in our hotel. Mrs. Hewitt will be pleased. Well, sir, you shall have a room right down the hall here on the first floor. It's one of our better rooms we save for just such an occasion as this. We're mighty proud to have you with us." The clerk dipped the pen in the inkwell. "Sign the register, sir, and I'll have the porter take care of your luggage."

The impatient man snatched the pen from the clerk's hand. He wrote with a flourish, *Reverend Albert Pringle and wife.*

"I want a pitcher of ice water brought to the room immediately." He plucked the key from the desk clerk's hand. "Is there a fan in the room?"

"Oh, yes, sir, We have ceiling fans in all our better rooms. If there is anything we can do, anything at all to make your stay pleasant, just let us know."

The Reverend grunted a reply and turned to look at the woman who waited beside two suitcases. She wore a long-sleeved dark dress with a small white collar. The straight-brimmed black hat sat squarely on her head. Her eyes never left The Reverend and when he indicated she was to follow she hurried after him.

"Pompous ass," the clerk muttered.

"What's that you say, Mr. Beryl?" The porter picked up the suitcases,

"I said Room 102. Take the luggage then get the old boy a pitcher of ice water."

CHAPTER
—————24—————

Mike threw the packages on the bed and pulled Letty into his arms the minute the door closed behind them. He looked at her for a long moment, then tilted his face down and kissed her mouth. It was a soft, lingering kiss. When he lifted his lips his face was so close to hers they were breathing the same air, so close she couldn't look into his eyes.

"I was afraid Oscar and Sharon would still be here," he said with his nose touching hers.

"If they're riding to Piedmont with Doctor Whittier, they're in for a wild ride." Letty giggled happily and rubbed her nose against his smooth cheek. "You smell good. What did the barber put on your face?"

"Something that stung like the devil. What did you buy while I was getting a shave?"

"I bought a shirt for you and something for me. Want to see it?"

"Hummm . . . I kind of like what we're doing now." Magnificent dark eyes, filled with love and tenderness, gazed into hers.

"So do I. You can keep on doing it, if you want to."

"I don't have anything else to do at the moment, so I might as well—"

"Hush."

Unembarrassed and uninhibited, she eased her mouth around to his. Her lips parted softly as they touched his. The hands at her waist moved down to press her hips against the part of him that was fast becoming hard. His mouth opened over hers and she sensed his growing hunger. Her tongue darted between his lips to taste him. He gathered her to him, desperate in his desire to become one with her. The need for air forced her to tear her mouth from his. She pressed her lips and nose against his cheek. The heart of her femininity had heated, liquefied, and now throbbed.

"My love, my love—" The words came from the center of her being.

"My love, my love," he repeated in a voice rough with desire. "We'd better stop. I want to make love to my wife, but I need a bath."

With a deep breath, she hid her face against his neck. "Do we have to wait until tonight?"

His laugh was deep, soft. "No, darling. Twenty minutes at the most. I can't come to you with that jailhouse smell on my body." He put her from him and her arms slid from around his neck.

"The bathroom is at the end of the hall. Don't you dare go into the one that says W-O-M-E-N." Sudden unexpected laughter burst from her lips. Her hands moved up to his cheeks and into the thick black curls over his ears and pulled.

"Ouch! What was that for?" His dark eyes were luminous.

"That was just in case you don't . . . hurry back!" She moved away from him, pulled a towel from the wall rack beside a small china lavatory, and pushed it into his hands. "I'll be waiting—"

"You'd better be," he said threateningly and dropped a kiss on the end of her nose.

After he left, Letty stood in a daze of happiness before she pulled the rolled shades down over the windows to darken the room. She quickly took off her shoes and stockings, then removed her skirt and middy blouse. In the small washbasin, she washed the dust from her face, arms, and neck, and opened one of the packages Mike had tossed on the bed.

On impulse she had bought the nightdress of fine white lawn material, with a narrow ruffle edged with fine torchon lace around the low round neck. A blue satin ribbon hung from the neckline to the wide flounce at the bottom of the gown. Letty removed the satin ribbon and replaced it with the small scrap of faded ribbon she had pinned to her chemise. She slipped out of the rest of her clothes and into the new gown.

She could hear her heartbeat as she removed the pins from her hair and placed them on the bureau. The heavy mass of auburn hair dropped down her back to her waist. Should she turn down the bed? Would he think she was too eager? While she was trying to decide, the key turned in the lock and the door opened.

Mike stood shirtless and barefoot with his back to the door, the wet towel slung around his neck. Her eyes clung to his. The expression on his dark face was easy to read. Letty saw hunger, lust, possession, and something more, much more. She saw love, adoration. It stopped her breath.

"Sweetheart . . . ! Are you real or are you a dream?"

She held out her hand. "Come find out."

He went to her, leaving the towel, his shoes, and shirt on the floor beside the door.

"You are so . . . pretty!"

Their arms reached for each other. He crushed

her to him, flattening her breasts against his chest. Hungry mouths searched, found each other, and held with fierce joy. His skin was smooth and hard. Her hands couldn't stop sliding up and down his back and finally into the waistband of his britches.

He broke away gasping.

"Letty . . . my Letty of a thousand dreams," he whispered hoarsely as he swung her up into his arms and placed her on the bed. "Take off the gown, honey. Please—"

Without thought she pulled the gown over her head and lay back. Her eyes clung to him. She could see the pulse throbbing in the side of his neck as his eyes moved over her. She waited for what seemed like an eternity for him to unbutton and slip out of his britches. Finally, his naked body covered hers and he rained fervent kisses on her face.

She welcomed the weight of his hard-muscled body and wrapped her arms about him, loving the feel of his skin against hers, his chest hair against her breasts.

"I love you. I love everything about you . . . your pride, your independence, your honesty, your beautiful smile." he whispered urgently and settled his mouth on hers for a long, tender kiss.

He lifted his head so that he could see her face. "I was on the brink of destruction, love. Right on the brink when I found you. I thank God that Jacob gave me the chance to be with you and Patrick. Oh, I would have stayed around had he given me the boot. I hate to think what would have happened if I had found you married to another man.

"Don't think about what might have been. Love me. Please love me." Her arms encircled him and her hands caressed the smooth skin of his back.

A deep longing compelled her to meet his passion equally. She was wildly, burningly alive, and the driving force of her feeling was taking her beyond herself into a mindless void where there were only Mike's lips, Mike's hands, Mike's hard demanding body.

His beloved weight pressed her gently but securely to the bed. She could feel the pounding of his heart against her breast. Without hesitation their bodies joined in mutual, frantic need. She welcomed the hard insistent pressure, welcomed him into her body with eyes wide, looking into the dark depths of his.

Almost unbelievable pleasure swept through her as he entered and filled her. She was aware of nothing but the broad shoulders she clung to, heard nothing but the low murmur of love words that poured from his mouth before it covered hers. Then she was beyond seeing, beyond hearing, as she teetered on the edge of the world.

After a long moment, still deep inside her, Mike supported himself on his elbows and gazed into her face, then he brushed back her hair with gentle fingers.

"I didn't want it to be over so soon. I was so hungry for you I couldn't help myself."

She captured his face between her palms, her thumbs caressed his lips. "Me too. Oh, Mike, darling. We can do it any time we want. Unless"— her eyes teased him—"you're afraid you'll wear it out."

Their happy laughter filled every corner of the room. Letty felt him deep inside her where he still nestled against her womb. His hands, holding her buttocks to him, squeezed.

"With you around there's a real danger of doing just that. Just looking at you puts me in a loving mood."

"You're looking at me now."

"Yes . . . yes . . ."

Suddenly, he was quivering with the tension of trying to love her gently and slowly, but tenderness was not what she needed. She ached again for a surging rhythm, and her hips began to move. He thrust with urgency again and again, until he arched his back with an inarticulate cry and they slipped into uncharted but beautiful oblivion.

Awed into silence by the glorious thing that had happened between them for the second time, Mike slid to her side and gathered her gently to him, cradling her head on his chest. He ran his rough palm over her breast, teasing her nipple. She captured his hand and held it there. He moved his other hand down her side and patted her bare bottom affectionately.

More content, happier than she could remember ever being, Letty lay molded to his side, her arm across his hard, flat stomach, his hand caressing her breast.

"I brought our ribbon. I pinned it to my new nightgown."

"I didn't even notice, love. All I could see was you.

"How much time do we have?" she asked.

He stirred, his lips touching her forehead. "While I was in the bath, I heard the courthouse clock strike five-thirty. Then I lost all track of time."

They fell into a warm, languid silence. Mike's hands continued to stroke her body gently, his breathing slower, his heart quieter beneath her palm.

"Do you think I'm a wanton hussy for . . . liking to do . . . what we just did?"

His laugh rang out. He rolled, pulling her on top of him, their arms and legs tangled in the bedclothes.

"You silly, crazy, loveable little innocent! Every man dreams of having a wife who likes to do what we just did."

"They do? Goodness, I've got a lot to learn, haven't I?" After a thoughtful silence, her hands moved from his shoulders down to his ribs, "There's one thing I won't have to learn, I haven't forgotten how ticklish you are." Her fingers were merciless, and they went up and down the skin over his ribs.

"Stop it! Don't tickle me! I c-can't stand it!"

"Can't . . . huh? What'll you do?"

"I'll . . . I'll dump you on the floor!"

She locked one of his legs between hers. "Go ahead. You'll go with me."

"You . . . little devil . . . you!" He grabbed her wrists and pulled them away from him. "Do you know what you're doing? You're making me horny again, and we don't have time—"

"Horny? What's that?"

"Oh, Lord!" He flipped her on her back and bent over her. She was giggling uncontrollably.

"You don't have to tell me. I can feel it. You're getting as hard as a horn."

"My God! I'm married to a little redheaded imp!" He rolled his eyes to the ceiling before dropping his head and kissing her laughing mouth. "I'm so happy," he confessed when he could speak again. "I am so *damn* happy."

The tablecloth was as white as snow and there wasn't a wrinkle in it. The knife and spoon sat on the right of the plate and above that a long-stemmed goblet. On the left were two forks and a folded linen napkin.

Letty leaned over the plate. "I've never eaten in such a fancy place," she whispered. "I hope I don't spill something."

In his new white shirt and the tie they had bought on the way to the restaurant, Mike was the handsomest man in the room, also the only one without a coat, which didn't seem to bother him at all. He had eyes only for the woman across from him. She had coiled her hair and pinned it to the back of her head. Her eyes sparkled, her face glowed, and her lips curled in a satisfied smile. She was even more beautiful than she had been at fifteen and he loved her a million times more.

"You won't spill anything, honey. Don't worry about it."

The waitress came and Mike ordered roast beef dinners with cherry pie for desert. They enjoyed the meal, floating along on a cloud of happiness. Their conversation was light, bantering, never serious. As far as they were concerned they were the only people in the dining room. Mike touched her at every opportunity, his dark eyes caressed her.

The love between them was obvious even to the waitress who picked up their empty plates and returned with the cherry pie.

"Are you on your honeymoon?" she asked.

"Sort of," Mike said smiling. "We left our five-year-old son at home with his grandpa."

"Oh." She gave them a curious look and walked away leaving Letty with the problem of controlling her giggles.

Out on the street, she clung to Mike's arm. The town was crowded, much to the delight of the merchants. Letty and Mike crossed the street to the courthouse square and strolled along on the walk until they completed the round.

The clock struck half-past seven, Carloads of people were going by on their way to the fairgrounds. Mike and Letty continued to walk, looking for an empty bench so that they could sit down and watch the people go by.

"Mike," Letty pulled on his arm. "Here comes Doctor Hakes."

Letty had expected to see the doctor as had been arranged, but she was surprised to see a pleasant-faced, nicely dressed woman beside him. Her dress was a soft flowered material with a scooped neckline and short sleeves. Her shoes were white and she carried a straw hat. Letty felt shabby in comparison.

Doctor Hakes's face was wreathed with smiles. "What luck. We were just talking about you two." The two couples moved off the sidewalk and onto the grass to let the strolling people pass. "Roberta, this is the Mr. and Mrs. Dolan I was telling you about. Folks this is Mrs. Knight, Roberta Knight."

"Hel . . . lo," Letty stammered. *This was the woman who could take Helen away from her.*

"I'm very glad to meet you, Mr. and Mrs. Dolan." The lady offered her hand to Letty and then to Mike.

"And we're glad to meet you, ma'am."

Letty was thankful for Mike's composure. This woman in no way resembled what she had pictured Mrs. Knight to be. She wasn't old enough to have such a responsible position; she appeared to be in her early thirties.

"I have corresponded with Doctor Hakes for several years, but this is our first face-to-face meeting. When he wired that he was going to be in Boley, I decided to come."

She came to meet Cora, Letty thought.

"During dinner I explained Helen's situation." Wallace said, and Letty's worried eyes turned to him. Her heart began to flutter painfully.

"Dear," Mrs. Knight's hand touched Letty's arm, bringing her attention back to her. "Don't look so worried. The state of Nebraska wants its orphan children to be safe and happy. Wallace assures me that Helen is well and happy with you. He has also told me that you believe her relationship with her father was an unnatural one and that you are dealing well with it,"

"You mean that . . . we can keep her?" Letty's tear-filled eyes sought Mike's before she looked at Mrs. Knight.

"For the time being. Should you decide to adopt her—"

"We've already decided, ma'am," Mike said. "We want Helen to be a part of our family, carry our name. We're very fond of the child and she's fond of us. She feels safe with us."

"You'll have to petition the court."

"Oh, but—"

"Roberta doesn't think there'll be much if any objection to the adoption," Wallace said quickly when he saw the stricken look on Letty's face.

"Mr. Knight, my late husband, was a judge, Mrs. Dolan. The courts are fair. They want to place orphan children with people who want them and will give them a proper home."

The courthouse clock struck eight while she was speaking.

"Roberta is going with us to the meeting, Mike. We'll take the ladies to the automobile. They can wait for us there while we fetch Fellon."

407

"You won't change your mind after you talk to Cora?" Letty felt compelled to ask when she was alone with Mrs. Knight.

"No. There is nothing that woman could say that would change my mind. Her brand of religion is not mine."

"Oh, I'm so glad. Thank you. We'll take good care of Helen. We love her and she loves us."

"I know. I wish I were as sure of every family who takes in an orphan child."

CHAPTER
——25——

As they approached the fairgrounds Letty felt caged and longed to be back at the farm. She had been gone less than twenty-four hours but she missed Grandpa and Helen and Patrick's impish little face. She thought of how much her life had changed in the last six weeks. Last year she had been lonely even with Grandpa and Patrick for company. At times she had been so lonely for a companion her own age that she cried. Now that she and Mike had found each other, she had hoped never to feel that loneliness again. Letty clasped her hands involuntarily as if to hold onto her happiness. Tonight, for some reason, visions of her life back in Dunlap kept coming to her mind's eye.

She saw Cora staring at her from across the dinner table, her color high, a smirk on her face, chanting in her shrill voice, *Letty has a bastard growing in her belly. Letty has a bastard! Did you catch Hadley Wells between fits, or was it one of those wild Dolan boys? Dolan boys. Dolan boys—*

Letty closed her eyes hoping to blot out the image of her sister's hateful face and accusing voice only to have it replaced by another—her father's. Hatred blazed in his eyes. *Bitch! Slut! Whore! Damn you to hell and damn your bastard. From this day on you are dead! You are dead, you are dead—*

What on earth was the matter with her? She thought she had blocked that terrible day from her mind. Why now? Why did she have to see her father's face and hear his hateful words? *You are possessed of the devil—*

Once again feeling the fear, the hurt, the despair. Letty wanted desperately to climb over the seat of Doctor Hakes's car to nestle in Mike's lap, and feel the security of his arms.

Was it one of those damn Catholics? Damn Catholics, damn Catholics, damn Catholics—

Letty sat up straighter in the seat, her arms crossed under her breasts, her hands gripping her elbows.

On the night breeze, floating over the treetops. Letty could hear the sound of several hundred voices raised in song:

"I am bound for the promised land,
  I am bound for the promised land.

409

O who will come and go with me—
    I am bound for the promised land."

The music and words were etched in her memory. It was the song the congregation had been singing the night she passed the church on her way out of Dunlap to catch the train in Huxley. It seemed a lifetime ago.

Her eyes were drawn to Mike who sat in the back seat of the automobile. Fellon sat between him and Doctor Hakes. Roberta Knight was driving the car. It was the first time Letty had ridden in an automobile with a woman driver. Had she not been so nervous about the confrontation ahead, she would have been impressed by the way Roberta handled the machine.

What she was hearing now was the rousing spiritual. "When the Saints Go Marching In." Letty knew the routine well. The service was well-planned to stimulate the audience.

The next song had a rapid beat that made the people clap their hands and lift their voices

"Give me that old time religion
    give me that old time religion—
It's good enough for me!"

The congregation was being primed for Cora's appearance. If the song leader and the musicians worked hard enough, they would have the people shouting and speaking in tongues by the time Cora came on the stage.

The car stopped alongside the road near the entrance to the parking area, well back from the pavilion. Letty got out and waited while Mike pulled the reluctant Fellon out and backed him up against the side of the car.

"Listen good, Mister. You do what Doc tells you to do. Give him any trouble and you'll be saying goodbye to your teeth."

"I want a drink. Doc, you promised—"

"I said I'd give you five dollars to get back to Briskin. If you want to drink it up and walk home that's up to you.

One of Mike's hands was clamped to Fellon's arm, the other reached for Letty. "Honey, are you all right?"

She didn't speak for a minute, pressed herself against him, drinking in the closeness of his body, feeling his comforting strength, grateful, oh, so grateful, that he was with her.

"I'm fine."

"If we should get separated, go back to the hotel," Wallace said.

"And miss out on the fun?" Roberta looped her purse over her arm. "If we get separated, head for the car. I'll have the motor running."

They walked up the road to the crowded pavilion. The large shutters on the sides and back of the building had been pulled up and fastened giving an open-air effect. The ground inside the structure was covered with sawdust. A string of lightbulbs lighted the area. Row after row of benches, placed in two sections, were filled with people. Those not lucky enough to find a seat stood along the back and the sides.

Letty led the party to stand at the end of the center aisle. On the stage a man in a white suit stood with arms lifted.

"Hallelujah!" he shouted. "Stand up, folks. Stand up for the Lord. Don't hold back. Stand and praise Him!" The crowd surged to its feet. "All together now—hallelujah!"

"Hallelujah!"

"Praise the Lord!"

"Praise the Lord!" the crowd echoed.

"Jesus loves me!"

"Jesus loves me!"

The chant went on for several minutes, the response from the congregation getting louder each time. Finally, the crowd was told to be seated. Some of the more fervent had moved out into the aisles and were jigging up and down as if in a trance and clicking their tongues. Others continued to shout, "Amen. Glory hallelujah."

The man on the platform ignored the people still standing, and spread his arms wide.

"O God, we thank Thee for our Sister Cora who has been on her knees this entire day praying to Thee for the forgiveness of our sins. She is weak in body, O Lord, but strong in spirit. We ask You to hold her in Your hand, keep her safe from harm. We need her, O God."

Letty's hand tightened on Mike's. The hypocrisy was making her sick to her stomach. Cora weak in body? She was as strong as a mule and as poisonous as a viper!

Some of the people covered their faces with their hands, others moaned and sobbed. The speaker's voice rose above the murmur of voices.

"Brethren, hear me! You will remember this night for as long as you live. You will tell your children about it. They will tell their children because tonight, here in Boley, Nebraska, you will look upon the face of an angel."

"For crying out loud—" Letty turned her face to Mike's arm.

He grinned down at her. "Sickening, isn't it?"

"Worse than that!"

"Here she is! Sister Cora! Sister Cora! Sister Cora!"

The overhead lights suddenly went off, plunging the pavilion in darkness. A few tense seconds passed. Then a spotlight shone on the white curtains at the back of the stage.

The crowd was on its feet. Necks were stretched and all eyes were on the curtain. They took up the chant. "Sister Cora, Sister Cora, Sister Cora—"

Awe was visible on the faces of the people when a vision in a long white robe came floating down. Her arms were outstretched, her head bowed. Around her neck a large gold cross hung from a heavy gold chain. She was lowered gently to the floor where she dropped to her knees. Her associate went to her and lifted her to her feet.

"He's taking off the harness," Mike whispered.

"This is so awful! Look at the people staring at her as if she were something . . . holy."

When Cora began to speak, an awed silence fell over the crowd.

"I thank Thee, Lord, for this opportunity to bring the word to the good brothers and sisters in Boley county. I pray that Thee will bless each and every one of them and Thee will show me the way to lead them to the arms of their Heavenly Father. Amen."

Her voice was rich and full as she began her sermon.

"The last days are upon us, my dear, dear friends. The book of Revelation tells us of the terrible things that will come to pass during these last days. You only have to look around you to see that these predictions are taking place in every corner of the world. There are wars and rumors of wars. Sickness and starvation are spreading over the land like a plague. Brothers are slaying brothers. Women are leaving their children to peddle their flesh on the streets. Husbands and fathers are deserting their families. Hearts are hardened against aging parents and they are left to fend for themselves, no longer having the strong arm of son or daughter to lean on—

"Soon our Lord will descend from the heavens and only the pure will follow Him back to His heavenly home. The rest of you will be cast in the fiery furnace, doomed to torment for all eternity."

"Can you believe that charlatan has the nerve

414

to stand up there looking so pious?" Wallace said in a voice that carried. A man turned to glare at him threateningly.

When Cora sank down on her knees in a position for prayer, the man in the white suit spoke of the need for funds to carry on Sister Cora's work. He called on everyone to "dig deep," for with each dollar given a soul could be saved.

Young town girls, chosen for their light hair color and dressed in long pink robes, passed collection plates. During this time soft music was played on the piano and Cora stayed on her knees.

"Do you reckon she's praying for a full collection plate?" Mike whispered.

"Probably. Oh, Mike, I'm embarrassed."

"Sweetheart! You needn't be. In another thirty minutes we'll be out of here and you'll never have to see or think of her again."

When the sermon resumed, Cora's voice never ceased its entreating pleas.

"Jesus is calling. O sinner come home. Come and be saved. Kneel at the altar of God. He will forgive your sin. All things are possible if only you believe."

Well-trained men and women moved into the crowd, stopping to talk with a member of the congregation who appeared to be tempted to go be "saved." People began to move into the aisle and go forward to fall on their knees in front of the long platform. Cora went among them, placed her hand on each head, and prayed.

Suddenly, she lifted her arms and began to chant in an unknown tongue. The crowd shifted uneasily as if they expected disaster. Was she being given a message from God about the end of the world? The thought ran through the minds of those who watched.

"If there be any among you who are sick, come to me," she called in her pleading voice. "God is merciful. The power comes from Him. I am only the messenger. Come . . . come—"

"Go, Doctor Hakes," Letty said. "Go before one of the fakers can get up there."

"I ain't goin'—" Fellon tried to break free of Mike's grasp.

"Yes, you are. Get moving, or I'll break both your legs and ask Sister Cora to heal them."

Wallace Hakes led the way down the aisle. Mike, pushing Fellon ahead of him, followed. They reached the front and stepped up onto the stage.

"Attention! Attention!" Wallace shouted.

"What's this? What's this? You can't get up here." The man in the white suit tried to push Wallace off the stage.

Mike's free hand lashed out and fastened in the front of the man's coat.

"Back off, Bud, or you'll find yourself on your butt. The doc will have his say."

"Ladies and gentlemen, I'm Doctor Hakes from Piedmont. A week ago at a service in Piedmont, Sister Cora claimed to have healed this man. She said he hadn't walked for years. The truth is—"

416

"Forgive them, Father!" Cora shouted. "Forgive them for they know not what they do!"

"The truth is," Wallace yelled, "is that he has never been a cripple. I'll read you a telegram from Doctor Perkins of Briskin where this man lives—"

"O mighty God, the devil has sent thee men to try to undo our good work. Don't let him have his way, God! We are here to save souls—" Cora knew how to throw her voice so that it reached into each corner of the pavilion. She did that now.

Shouting at the top of his lungs, Wallace read the telegram.

"Now, tell them you were paid, Fellon. Tell them who paid you to put on that little act down at Piedmont."

"Well . . . I—"

"Tell them, damn you," Mike hissed.

"Uh . . . she did. Uh . . . her man there—"

"My dear, dear friends, the devil is here. I can feel his evil presence. Can't you feel it? We must cast him out. Help me, O Lord—" Cora began to sob, holding out her arms as if to embrace the crowd. "This is just one more tribulation," she entreated in a sobbing, trembling voice. "God is testing me, but I'll be strong. I will not bow to the devil."

Suddenly, a group of men rushed the stage. Mike let go of Fellon to dive in and help Wallace as he struggled with two burly farmers in overalls. Fellon broke free and ran.

417

"Heathens!"

"Unbelievers!"

"Sinners!"

People surged toward the platform shouting, "Sister Cora, Sister Cora—"

At the back of the pavilion, Letty stood as if transfixed, then she galvanized into action and started shoving her way down the aisle.

"Letty! No!" Roberta grabbed her arm.

"I've got to help Mike!"

"No! We'll get the car started. They'll break away and that's where they'll head. Come on."

Once out of the pavilion, Roberta held up her skirt and ran. Letty had a hard time keeping up with her because she kept looking over her shoulder for Mike.

They reached the car. Roberta started the engine, turned on the headlights, and drove to a spot where she could turn around. She was as cool as if fighting her way out of a mob was an everyday affair.

Letty was a bundle of nerves. She felt a wave of sickness rise in her throat and struggled to swallow it. What if one of Cora's men struck Mike down? Oh, Lord, what if he never came back? She couldn't lose him again. Her chin trembled. Thoughts swirled around and around in her brain. Would she have to tell Patrick his daddy wasn't coming home? Would she lose Mike so soon after finding him?

"Buck up, girl," Roberta said firmly. "That man of yours can take care of himself."

"Wallace can't . . ."

"That little man may surprise you. I'm thinking he has plenty of grit. Holy Moses! Here they come—" Roberta honked the horn, then shouted, "Here! Wallace, here!"

Mike and Wallace had no more than stepped on the running boards when the car shot off down the road leaving a dozen men standing in the road shaking their fists. As soon as they were away from the fairgrounds, Roberta slowed the car and Mike and Wallace climbed inside.

"Whee!" Wallace said when he could catch his breath. "Roberta, you're a regular Barney Oldfield."

In the back seat of the car, Mike gathered Letty in his arms. Her control broke and she began to cry.

"Honey . . . sweetheart, what's the matter?" His arms tightened.

"I w-was afraid-d—"

"Afraid of what, love?"

She pressed herself against him and put her arm around him.

"I was afraid-d you'd not come b-back."

"That was a strain on you being there and seeing Cora put on her act. You've worried yourself into a state of nerves."

She looked up, eyes sparkling with tears. "I'm silly."

"Ah . . . darlin" ' His mouth closed over hers. The kiss was long and sweet and conveyed a

419

meaning far too poignant for mere words. "I'll always come back, darlin'. Always."

"I couldn't bear it if . . . if you didn't."

Roberta stopped in front of the hotel. Mike and Letty got out. Letty reached in and touched the doctor's arm.

"Wallace, I'm sorry they wouldn't believe you. I was afraid they wouldn't. Cora has been at this many years and she has a knack for swaying the audience."

"I tried. At least my conscience is clear."

"Goodbye." Letty held out her hand and clasped Roberta's warmly. "Will we see you again?"

"You certainly will if I have anything to say about it." Wallace spoke quickly, then looked as if he had surprised himself.

"Of course we'll see each other again," Roberta spoke to Letty, but her eyes were on Wallace and his on her. "Good-bye."

Letty held tightly to Mike's arm as they entered the hotel.

"Wasn't Mrs. Knight nice? She wasn't at all what I expected. Bless Wallace's heart. He paved the way for us to keep Helen. Mike!" she stopped walking. "I think he *likes* her."

Mike chuckled as they started up the steps to their room.

"I noticed. She likes him too. That's fine with me. I was afraid he had eyes for my wife."

"Oh, Pooh! Wouldn't it be nice if they got together?"

420

"Matchmaking, Mrs. Dolan?"

"I'm so happy, I want everybody to be happy too." In the hotel room, Mike raised the window and turned on the ceiling fan. He sat down on the bed, pulled Letty into his arms, and settled her on his lap. He lifted her arms to encircle his neck and cuddled her against him.

"Tell me what brought on that crying spell? Has it been a long night?"

"The longest of my life. I've been thinking about that day, that Sunday after church when Cora told Papa I'd missed two months of having my monthly and . . . and I had a bastard growing in my belly."

"Damn her to hell," Mike gritted.

"That's what Papa said. He said, 'Damn you to hell and damn your bastard.' " Letty burrowed deeper into Mike's arms. "I knew my baby wasn't a bastard. He was conceived in love."

"Yes, he was, sweetheart. Oh, God, what a fool I was to leave you to face that alone."

"No. You had no way of knowing. You were doing what you thought was—" She leaned back to look at him and forgot what she was saying. A cut on his cheekbone was filled with dried blood. "Oh! Oh." Now she saw that his shirt was torn and bloody. Her fingers moved around to his cheek.

"A little scuffle is all," he said before she could question.

"Mike Dolan, don't treat me like a child. You had to fight, didn't you?"

421

She jumped off his lap, went to the lavatory for a wet cloth and returned to stand between his spread legs and dab at his face. He held her buttocks in his hands.

"Just a good handful," he murmured.

"Don't change the subject. It was more than a scuffle. Your new shirt is torn, but I can fix it. I'll have to soak it in cold water to get out the bloodstain. Start at the beginning and tell me everything that happened. Roberta wouldn't let me go to the front. She thought we should get the car started."

"She was right. Get into bed." He gently moved her aside and stood. "I'll wash the blood off my knuckles. Two or three of Cora's followers are nursing broken noses tonight." He grinned. "I'm glad I went with Doc. He may know doctoring, but he knows nothing about fighting. That's my specialty. I've not been in such a good brawl since the days I worked in the coal mines. Those Pennsylvania miners really know how to fight."

"Well, for goodness' sake! Tell me—"

"You'll not need a nightdress, honey," he said when she pulled it out of her bag.

Mike took off his shirt and hung it over the back of a chair. From a spigot water trickled into the tiny lavatory. Using the sliver of soap provided by the hotel, he washed his hands, then sloshed water on his face.

Mike turned out the light, removed his clothes, and stretched out beside her.

"Come here. I want to hold you. Hmmm, you feel so good."

422

"You don't have anything on!"

"And neither will you in a little while. Hush so I can kiss you."

They lay face to face, legs entwined as intimately as their arms, lips touching, sharing the same pillow, the same breath. He was content just holding her. She was filled with indescribable peace and contentment. Finally he turned on his back, cuddling her against his side, and raised her knee to nestle against the most intimate part of him.

"Doc was disappointed," he said at last. "He thought sure everyone would get up and walk out after he read the statement from Doctor Perkins and we put Fellon on display. I doubt if six people left the pavilion."

"They didn't believe Wallace and he's a doctor."

"Honey, they didn't want to believe him. I was counting on you getting out of there when the action started. It's a good thing Mrs. Knight knows how to drive. Some of those men were mad as hornets and hot on our tail."

"Wallace said she was a regular Barney Oldfield. Who's that?"

"A race-car driver. Honey, I've something else to tell you." He turned to face her and held her tightly against him. "Your mother and father were at the meeting. They were sitting within six feet of where I was holding Fellon."

Letty was quiet for a moment. "Did he call you a damn Catholic?"

"If he did I didn't hear him."

Letty was quiet for a time. Then all she said was, "I want to go home."

"If you want to see them, I'll arrange for a private place and I'll not cause you any embarrassment, although I swore I'd break him in half for what he did to us. I realize now that nothing I could do to him would make up for the five years we lost."

"No! I don't want to see them. I'm dead to them. They're dead to me. Let's go home."

"All right, honey. I just thought—"

"No!" She locked her arms about his neck. "That's all in the past. Love me, Mike."

He found her lips and kissed her with what felt like all the pent-up longing of years. She returned the force of his kiss, holding nothing back. His hand moved up under her gown and covered her breast, his fingers stroking her nipple until it was hard. He bowed his head and nuzzled the ribbon, *their* ribbon, pinned between her breasts, then slipped the gown over her head and pressed her naked body to his.

She felt an urgency building in her and savored the sweet ecstasy his mouth created with its warm exploration of hers. She returned the pressure, the nibbling, giving as much as she was receiving. She ran her fingers down his sides from his armpits to as far as she could reach along his lean thighs. His hand searched her smooth flesh and finally moved downward until he found what he sought.

They loved each other frantically, their bodies

coming alive and singing for them as they did years before when they lay together in their private place behind the schoolhouse.

Letty and Mike checked out of the hotel early. She stood beside the door while he paid the bill. He was so handsome, so capable. She would never be afraid of anything as long as he was with her. His dark eyes strayed to her while he waited. Her heart swelled with pride. They walked down the street to a small whitewashed diner, sat on stools at the counter, ate sausage and eggs and drank strong black coffee. After breakfast they walked along the street looking into the store windows, killing time until Wallace came to take them back to Piedmont.

Mike brought her to a stop in front of the jewelry store, pulled out the little purse she had given him, and counted the money.

"There's enough left to buy a wedding ring. I'll pay back the money when we get home."

"You don't have to pay it back."

"I do. I'm not having my wife buy her own wedding ring. Come on."

When they left the store a half-hour later, Letty wore a gold band on her finger.

"Someday I'll have it inscribed," Mike said, holding up her hand so that he could see the ring."

"What will you say?"

"Then, now, and always." He brought her hand to his lips and kissed it while she held her breath at the wonder of it.

"I'm anxious to get home," she said, smiling up at her husband, her eyes bright with happiness.

"So am I."

At first he didn't recognize the couple walking toward them. When he did, he looked down at Letty and saw that she was no longer smiling. Her face was set and her eye never wavered. When they were no more than six feet apart, Letty stopped on the narrow walk, forcing her father and mother to face her.

"Hello, Mama." Her mother looked away, ignoring her.

"Move aside," Reverend Pringle's voice rang with authority.

Letty ignored him. "Why, Mama? Why did you let him tell everyone I was dead?"

"She does not hear you. She does not see you," Reverend Pringle said harshly.

"She would see me, she would hear me, if not for you," Letty said calmly, still looking at her mother. "I' ll never understand how you could collect money to pay for my burial expense when you knew perfectly well I was alive. You ruined five years of my life. Don't you care?" Letty exchanged a look with Mike, then shrugged. "I can see that you don't."

Reverend Pringle tried to pull his wife off the walk and into the street so that they could pass. Mike blocked his way.

"Stand still, damn you. She'll have her say if I have to throw you down and sit on you."

Mable's head turned slowly and she looked

at Letty. Her eyes were vacant pools, her face bloodless. Her thin lips barely opened.

"You . . . slut!" she hissed.

Letty's only response was to draw in a deep breath. "Your insults no longer hurt me. I feel sorry for you," Letty said softly.

"You disgraced us with this . . . Catholic."

"You disgraced yourself. I thank God every day for this Catholic. Without him I might have become like Cora."

"You're behind it," Mable's voice rose to a shriek. "You're trying to ruin Cora! You and this Catholic trash!"

Letty ignored the accusation. "You've missed out on so much, Mama, by allowing this . . . this fanatic hypocrite to dominate you until you no longer have a mind or a will of your own. I want you to know that I have never regretted, not even for a second, that Mike made me pregnant. I found Grandpa and Grandma and learned what real love and sharing is about. What I do regret, however, is that your blood and his runs in my veins." She jerked her head toward her father, but did not look at him. "If there was any way to drain it out and replace it, I would."

"You're evil, rotten, a throwback—" Mable gasped.

"Thank God, I'm a throwback." Letty paused, looked at her mother's resentful face, and said firmly, "Goodbye."

With his arm under hers and his hand attached to her wrist, Mike guided her off the walk and around her parents. Letty walked beside him, her head high, her eyes tearless. At the corner she turned to look back.

A large touring car had pulled up beside her parents. Cora got out and lifted the gauze that covered her face up onto the brim of her hat. Letty saw her mother reached to put her hand on Cora's arm and saw Cora move away. Reverend Pringle was talking and Cora was shaking her head. When Cora moved to get back into the car, Mable began to cry. Without a backward glance, Cora waved for the driver to move on. Letty's parents stood on the walk. Her mother dabbed at her eyes with a handkerchief, her father stared after the car.

"She snubbed them!" Letty said with disbelief. "Mama's crying." She took a step toward them. Mike put his hand on her arm.

"They'd not appreciate your sympathy, honey. They would just hurt you more."

"I know. How could Cora treat them like that?"

"She learned her behavior from them. Come on, honey." He turned her and they walked on down the street. "Are you all right?"

There was so much concern and love in his eyes that Letty lifted her fingers to his cheek as she gazed into his beloved face.

"Don't worry, love. I'm not sad. I'm glad we met them. The tie is cut completely now. I'm ready to go home." She laughed softly. "Do we have time to buy a present for Patrick and Helen?"

"Sure, Mrs. Dolan. I may have to kiss you first."

"Right here in public?" Her voice was stern, but there was adoration in her eyes. When he hesitated, she said, "Well, get on with it."

He swung her around until his back was to the street and kissed her quick and hard.

"Is that all I get?" she complained. "When I get home I'm going to tie the ribbon to the lilac bush and meet my sweetheart down by the creek. His kisses much better than that."

His chuckle was warm and deep. "He might ravish you," he warned.

"Ravish. Is that bad?"

They strolled toward the mercantile, arms entwined.

"I think Patrick would like a pocket knife." Mike smiled down at his wife.

"Helen would like a brush and comb all her own."

Mike was so proud of her he could scarcely keep his eyes off her face. She had weathered the meeting with her parents and had come through the ordeal with Cora unscathed and serene. This proud level-headed woman was his wife, the sweetheart of his youth.

Holding her close to his side, he bent his head so that he could place his mouth close to her ear.

"I love you," he whispered. "I loved you then, I love you now, I'll love you always."

EPILOGUE

Mike Dolan stood on the station platform, his back to the cold north wind, thinking about his arrival in this town twenty-five years ago when he had come to search for the grave of his lost love. He had thanked God many times for giving him the urge to come here. His arms tightened about the small woman who stood in front of him, his big body shielding her from the wind. His Letty was still the love of his life.

They had shared with their children the wild ride they took to Weatherford in Doctor Hakes's open Ford to be married, and how the sheriff and his deputy had come and arrested Mike for the murder of Cecil Weaver. They told of how Deputy Elmer Russell was convicted of the murder of Weaver, Helen's father, and was sentenced to life in prison without possibility of parole. The trial and the sentencing had taken place in the Boley courthouse the same week Mike and Letty signed the adoption papers making Helen their daughter. Jacob, Doctor Whittier, Doctor Hakes, and Roberta Knight helped them celebrate with a dinner at a fancy restaurant.

Letty seldom mentioned her parents and her sister, but it was a well-known fact that, although Doctor Hakes failed in his attempt to discredit *Sister Cora,* she never obtained the status she sought. Another evangelist, Aimee Semple Mc-Pherson, came on the scene. Known as *Sister Aimee,* she was attractive, had a dynamic personality, and retained the loyalty of her followers. She raised $ 1.5 million and built the Angelus Temple in Los Angeles.

Cora Pringle's popularity declined rapidly after her revival in Boley. A few years later she was shot and killed by the distraught mother of a child she had claimed to have healed. The child had been bitten by a rabid dog. Believing in *Sister Cora,* the mother had refused medical attention for the child and the baby had died a horrible death.

Reverend and Mrs. Pringle lived out their lives in a small town in Oklahoma and died with only a tiny, poor congregation to mourn their passing.

Mike and Letty had two girls two years apart Katy and Leona. Helen, later married to one of the Pierce boys, was delighted with her baby sisters. Patrick tolerated them during their younger years as brothers are wont to do. In later years he adored them.

The Dolans weathered the depression years far better than some of their neighbors. The farm had provided them with a good living and they had sent their son to agricultural college. It would have paid for their daughters' continued education had they wanted to go.

On this cold November day, Mike and Letty were waiting for the train that was bringing Patrick home. Another war was over. Their son was coming home after serving three years in the United States Navy.

"Are you cold, honey," Mike bent to murmur in Letty's ear. Her back was pressed tightly to his chest, his arms wrapped around her.

"No." Her head was covered with a wool scarf, hiding her auburn hair only slightly sprinkled with gray. She tilted her head to look up at him. "Are you?"

"I'd be warmer if I opened my coat and snuggled your tight little butt up against me."

"Shame on you," she said with mock indignation. "I know what's on your mind—and at your age it's indecent."

"I'm not over the hill yet, for Christ's sake. I'm only forty-seven."

"Forty-eight," she corrected. "You're two and a half years older than I am. I keep track of such things. I'll be going through the change soon."

"Honey, are you going to be one of those women who kick their husbands out of their beds and get the sweats all the time?"

"I don't know. I might." She tilted her head up and impishly grinned at him.

His warm mouth brushed over her cold nose. "It would take a team of mules to pull me out of your bed, lady, sweats or no sweats."

Mike wore a mustache now—black as his hair and eyes except for a few threads of silver. This husband of hers was still the handsomest man Letty had ever seen, and she loved him as fervently as she had thirty years ago.

"Isn't Grandpa the limit, Mike? He wasn't about to stay at home and wait with the girls. I'm surprised we got him to stay in the car."

Mike chuckled. "He may be near ninety, honey, but there's no pushing Jacob Fletcher into doing something he doesn't want to do. You should know that by now. Patrick is his boy. It was hard for him seeing his favorite go off to war."

"Oh, Mike. We're so lucky. Jimmy Watkins isn't coming home. Neither is Sharon and Oscar Phillips's boy."

"Yes, sweetheart, we're lucky. Here comes the train. Now, don't cry. Ahh . . . honey, you promised you wouldn't cry—"

The employees of G.K. HALL hope you have enjoyed this Large Print book. All our Large Print titles are designed for easy reading, and all our books are made to last. Other G.K. Hall Large Print books are available at your library, through selected bookstores, or directly from us. For more information about current and upcoming titles, please call or mail your name and address to:

G.K. HALL
PO Box 159
Thorndike, Maine 04986
800/223-6121
207/948-2962